Robert Edric was born in 1956. H[...]
Garden (1985 James Tait Black Priz[...]
(1986 runner-up for the *Guardia[...]
Eclipse, *The Earth Made of Glass*, *Elysium*, *In Desolate
Heaven*, *The Sword Cabinet*, *The Book of the Heathen*
(shortlisted for the 2001 WH Smith Literary Award),
Peacetime (longlisted for the Booker Prize 2002) and *Cradle
Song*, the first book in the Song Cycle Trilogy. *Siren Song* is
the second book in the trilogy, the final book, *Swan Song*,
is now available from Doubleday.

www.booksattransworld.co.uk

OCT 2005

Cradle Song

'Deeply intelligent novel . . . it is refreshingly anchored to recognizable realities and is infinitely the more powerful for that. The vertiginously devious plot twists all close like a fist around the throat of the reader.

In prose as dry as a bone left to bleach in the tropical sun, Edric delineates a relentlessly dark world where human motives and desires are unreadably murky, all truths are provisional and compromised, and human complicity casts a long shadow over our best intentions. Robert Edric makes it impossible for the crime novel to be considered the country cousin of serious literature any longer.'   *The Times*

'Skilfully written . . . both disturbing and sensitive'
Sunday Telegraph

'Edric shows he has the potential to be a formidable crime writer'   *Sunday Times*

'Edric creates an intricate plot in which every theory is cleverly chewed over'   *Mail on Sunday*

'Edric brings a brand of Spartan prose to the party that makes the tiniest occurrence momentous'   *Arena*

'*Cradle Song* is a superbly paced book . . . This is classic crime noir . . . Edric can also produce beautiful prose and arresting images as well as incisive social satire . . . Magnificently achieved'   Giles Foden

'Highly accomplished . . . Fans can look forward to his usual sharp realized characters operating in a tense, pressured environment'   *Independent*

'His novel is something substantial and distinctive . . . Edric has a clear, almost rain-washed style, eminently suitable for his Hull setting . . . *Cradle Song* is a strong and serious novel, soberly entertaining and well worth your while'
Literary Review

'A rewarding experience . . . This is murder at its most foul, crime at the deep end'   *Spectator*

'Impressive in its narrative, drive and in its glimpses of the nastier end of provincial working-class life, where its realism recalls Gordon Burn'   *The Times Literary Supplement*

Peacetime

'There aren't many novelists whose new book I would read without question (Banville, Marias, Proulx) but I would read a new novel by the Yorkshireman, Robert Edric, even if its blurb told me that it was about a monk calculating how many angels could dance on a pinhead . . . If other novels deserve this year's Booker Prize more than *Peacetime*, then they must be very remarkable indeed'
John de Falbe, *Spectator*

'*Peacetime* has a seriousness and a psychological edge that nine out of ten novelists would give their eye teeth to possess . . . it will be mystifying if, 50 years hence, Edric isn't taught in schools'   D. J. Taylor, *Sunday Times*

'A marvel of psychological insight and subtly observed relations . . . Why Edric has not yet been shortlisted for the Booker Prize is a mystery'   Ian Thomson, *Guardian*

'Edric is one of those immensely skilled novelists who seems fated to be discovered insultingly late in a productive career when caught in the arbitrary spotlight of Booker nomination or television adaptation. Booksellers take note: this is a writer to put into the hands of people looking for "someone new"'   Patrick Gale, *Independent*

'This is a novel of ambition and skill, at once a historical meditation, an evocation of a disintegrating society and, perhaps most strikingly, a family melodrama . . . *Peacetime* deserves the recognition that Rachel Seiffert's Booker-nominated début received in 2001'
Francis Gilbert, *New Statesman*

'A gripping read, full of meaningful conversations and bleak introspection'   *Sunday Herald*

'Edric's evocation of far horizons, tumultuous seas and drifting sands is masterly ... There are many memorable things in this novel ... Edric has cleverly created a microcosm to represent a world still haunted by its terrible past and uncertain of its future'
Francis King, *Literary Review*

The Book of the Heathen

'The best historical fiction has something to say about the present as well as the past. Edric has demonstrated this in his previous novels and does so again, with accomplishment, in his latest work ... Edric, prolific and critically acclaimed since his prize-winning debut in 1985, has struck an especially rich vein of form of late ... the writing is as clear and intelligent as ever, without being showy, and achieves the vital unities of theme and story, past and present, personal and political. Europe's colonial grip may have relaxed since Victorian times, but Edric offers a characteristically subtle counterpoint to the relationship between men, and between the strong and the weak in today's global economy'
Martyn Bedford, *Good Book Guide*

'Stunning ... evocatively brings to life the stifling humidity and constant rainfall of the Congo'   John Cooper, *The Times*

'Edric is a prolific and highly talented writer whose books give historical fiction a good name. They are distinguished not only by their formal skill and wide-ranging subject matters, but by their hairless, unshowy prose. In *The Book of the Heathen*, he uses suspense and thriller techniques to telling effect. His linguistic minimalism can also be effective – his low-key description of a hanging is quite the most harrowing I've ever read'
Sukhdev Sandhu, *Guardian*

'A very gripping story . . . the reader is drawn in inexorably to discover what horror lies at the heart of it . . . an apocalyptic fable for today'   John Spurling, *TLS*

Also by Robert Edric

SIREN SONG

Robert Edric

BLACK SWAN

SIREN SONG
A BLACK SWAN BOOK : 0 552 77143 0

Originally published in Great Britain by Doubleday,
a division of Transworld Publishers

PRINTING HISTORY
Doubleday edition published 2004
Black Swan edition published 2005

1 3 5 7 9 10 8 6 4 2

Set in 11/13pt Melior by
Falcon Oast Graphic Art Ltd.

Black Swan Books are published by Transworld Publishers,
61–63 Uxbridge Road, London W5 5SA,
a division of The Random House Group Ltd,
in Australia by Random House Australia (Pty) Ltd,
20 Alfred Street, Milsons Point, Sydney, NSW 2061, Australia,
in New Zealand by Random House New Zealand Ltd,
18 Poland Road, Glenfield, Auckland 10, New Zealand
and in South Africa by Random House (Pty) Ltd,
Endulini, 5a Jubilee Road, Parktown 2193, South Africa.

Printed and bound in Great Britain by
Cox & Wyman Ltd, Reading, Berkshire.

Papers used by Transworld Publishers are natural, recyclable
products made from wood grown in sustainable forests. The
manufacturing processes conform to the environmental
regulations of the country of origin

for Jayne Hoole

1

The phone rang just as I was about to leave the office. It was after nine on a late July evening. There had been no rain for almost a month and the weathermen were already talking about the coming drought as though it had been long foretold. It had been the warmest July for eighteen years, they said, as though that, too, meant anything; as though their own unremarkable predictions of what lay ahead were already assured and unassailable.

In the warehouse beneath me, men were unloading a late consignment of fruit after doing little all afternoon other than wait for it to arrive. They often worked through the night in the summer, preparing for the early-morning markets and deliveries. The smell of crushed and trodden peaches filled the air.

I waited for the answering machine to come on. My cards said I was available twenty-four hours a day. Yvonne told me I should have new ones printed with

'24/7' on them. Everyone knew what it meant. Everyone used it. I pretended to be persuaded by her and then showed her the 980 cards that remained of my original order. She tore one of these up in front of me. First impressions, she said. The right image. I told her I had 980 arguments against her one.

My recorded voice asked whoever was calling to leave a message.

Someone coughed before speaking, and before anything was said, I knew that the caller was John Maxwell, my old partner.

I went back to my desk and picked up the phone as he started speaking to the machine.

I asked him how he was.

'You probably know exactly how I am,' he said. 'How are you?'

'Same as you, but twenty-five years younger and with all my dreams, hopes and ambitions still intact,' I said.

'They're not worth much,' he said, and asked me why I was working so late.

'So I could be here when you called.' It had been almost four months since we'd last spoken.

His own lingering dreams, hopes and ambitions had died with his wife of thirty-seven years after a cruel and painful illness, through which he had nursed her, never fully understanding what was killing her or the true nature and extent of her suffering.

Both of my high windows were open and I closed them in an attempt to shut out the noise from below. He guessed what I was doing and waited before going on.

'Have you seen today's *Mail*?' he said.

He still had the Hull daily paper delivered to his County Durham home every day. Hull was where he had grown up, worked and lived with his family, and where he felt he could no longer go on living without his wife. During the final phase of her illness he'd told me that she was 75 per cent of them as a couple. At the time, I'd considered this an uncharacteristically melodramatic remark for him to make. At her funeral he'd raised the figure to 80 per cent. By then I'd seen what had happened to him and so I said nothing to deny the remark.

The paper lay unopened on my desk.

'Which part?' I said, opening and scanning the pages. Grief, misery, joy and elation, and all of it belonging to someone else.

'Page nine,' he said, waiting for me to turn.

On page nine was a photograph of a woman who, the headline announced, had recently been found dead at her Willerby home. Beside her was a photograph of her son in a graduation gown and cap, clutching a rolled and ribbon-bound degree certificate. I read the brief article. Woman found dead, possible suicide, less than a month after the graduation of her only son.

The second paragraph said something about a double tragedy for the family. Perhaps something had happened to the son, too, and in the absence of a recent photo of him they had resorted to using his graduation picture. I'd seen seventeen-year-old girls displayed as smiling twelve-year-olds, and forty-year-old men clutching their own rolled-up promises of the future.

'She's calling herself Annette Bellingham,' John

Maxwell said. 'Perhaps it was her maiden name. When we knew her, she was Simpson.'

I recognized the name, but remained uncertain how I knew it.

He reminded me about the case. It concerned a man we had investigated for fraud and embezzlement, who had killed himself in his exhaust-filled car a month before he was due to stand trial. I remembered his wife and young son. And I remembered that the man had killed himself at a beauty spot overlooking the Humber. His wife said it was one of their favourite places and that they had gone there often as a family. I remembered how she had almost choked every time she cried.

With the windows closed it had grown warmer in the office. It was almost ten o'clock, but even in the falling dark the room held its warmth. The sound of the men and the lorries below was muted, but could still be heard, and added to this now was the music from the sports club opposite, where young boxing hopefuls danced around their portable CD players. The smell of the liquefying peaches persisted. There were thin gaps between the boards of my floor, and light and dust rose through these along with the smell of the fruit. In winter there was only the light.

I wondered if the news of the dead woman and her blighted history had been John Maxwell's only reason for calling me. Talking openly on the phone did not come easily to him. Even when talking face to face with someone, he seldom said more than he needed to say. When we had first worked together, I imagined this had something to do with him having been a police officer, but I saw later that it was simply the kind of man he was.

He had taught me most of what I knew about private investigation during our partnership, and for a year after his departure I often found myself wondering how *he* would respond to a given situation instead of working things out for myself. But that time had passed and I'd been working things out for myself for long enough to know that his call now was not simply some cold indulgence of the past, no airing of distant remorse or regret.

A few minutes later, the bells of Holy Trinity struck ten. He heard this and identified the drawn-out tolling. It was a rare sound, but everything carried on that still night.

'You should go home,' he said eventually, timing his words to the last toll of the bells.

He hung up after that, and I imagined him sitting alone in the same airless dark, the picture of the woman and her son in his lap and a photograph of his own dead wife somewhere close by, watching him through another of the countless empty nights of his life.

I opened the windows and let in the noise. I watched a line of men unload crates of oranges from a lorry into a store, throwing the boxes from man to man, perfectly synchronized, the fruit vivid beneath the glare of the lights, and moving as smoothly as though it were on a conveyor belt.

2

The call was still on my mind the following morning when, at eleven, shortly after my own arrival, there was a knock at my door and I saw a woman's face and hand come close to the frosted glass. I seldom saw anyone without an appointment, and then I preferred to visit them rather than have them come to me.

The woman's forehead touched the glass and she immediately withdrew. The tips of her fingers remained where they touched.

I waited for her to knock again, and when she didn't, I went to the door and opened it.

She stepped back from me, avoiding my eyes.

'Mr Rivers?' she said. Her fingers remained splayed between us, as though she were reaching out to me. She looked at them, drew them together and held out her hand to me. 'You undertake private investigations?'

'I undertake investigations which I endeavour to keep private,' I said.

She remained nervous, reluctant. She looked into the room behind me, and then back to the glass of the door, as though the writing there might confirm the little I'd said.

'There's a crack,' she said. She withdrew her hand and pointed to the flaw running across the top left-hand corner of the pane.

'It's probably been there since the war,' I said, which was probably true.

She smiled briefly, an obligation fulfilled.

I stood aside and gestured into the room.

She came in, caught her reflection in the giant mirror on the back wall and smiled.

'I thought so,' she said. She went to the mirror and ran her hand around that part of its frame she could reach.

'Have you been here before?' I asked her.

'It must be forty years,' she said. 'Perhaps longer.'

I guessed her to be in her late fifties, perhaps sixty. She was a foot shorter than me, slender, well-dressed, but with a drawn face and a darkness under her eyes which her make-up did little to conceal. Despite the heat, she wore a thin yellow scarf bunched at her neck.

'I was a florist,' she said. 'When I started out there was a wholesaler across the road where we used to come to buy our flowers. This room was used as a store for all the cardboard boxes.'

'It's still there,' I said, indicating the building opposite, where the few remaining letters of the words Fresh Cut Flowers, once vividly scarlet and gold, were now peeling and fading against the wood upon which they'd been painted.

She put her hand to her mouth at seeing the words. 'It's changed a lot,' she said.

I told her I'd only been there three years.

'Long enough,' she said, as though places like this might crumble to dust in less.

Her recognition of the room and memory of the flower store relaxed her and we returned to the desk.

She took a bottle of mineral water from her bag and stood it between us.

'Are you still a florist?' I prompted her.

'I retired,' she said. 'A few years ago. By the time I finished I had eight shops.' She stopped abruptly, as though I had diverted her from her prepared path. 'I didn't even know if all this would still be standing or not. I thought it might all have been converted into flats and bars like everywhere else along the water.'

It was what most of the owners and landlords still hoped for, but it was a dream that had faded faster than the flower store lettering. There had once been a plan for refurbishment and renewal, and then another plan for destruction and redevelopment. The city council had never properly decided which of the two should happen, and their indecision – along with all its hope-raising and hope-quashing variants – had lasted twenty-five years. There had been rumours of work about to start upon my arrival, but nothing had happened. I leased the office on a six-month tenancy. There had been no improvements to it during my time there.

'I think everyone concerned just wants the street to fall down,' I said. Since the opening of the aquarium across the river, the dereliction of the street and of the lanes and alleyways adjoining it had been brought into

18

sharper focus. The aquarium was a template for renewal, the heart around which a new and healthy body would soon start to grow.

'How many of the traders are left?' she asked me.

I guessed at twenty. After the activity of the previous evening and earlier that morning, the street was empty and quiet. Quiet enough to hear a phone ringing in one of the buildings opposite.

She turned from the window to face me. 'My name is Alison Brooks,' she said. 'No "e".'

'Tell me what you want me to do for you,' I said.

She took her bag from the table, drank from the bottle and closed her eyes for a moment before speaking. 'You'll have heard of a man called Simon Fowler,' she said, her voice low, but her intent clear.

'I know as much as anyone else,' I told her, which was a lie. 'And anything I need to learn in conjunction with whatever you want from me, I can find out.' All I could bring to mind was that Fowler was involved in some of those redevelopment schemes sponsored by the council, and that he endlessly promoted himself in the local press. He was a young man, perhaps in his early thirties, and his acquirements and speculations had made him wealthy. It was enough of an understanding to cover my lie.

'Simon Fowler killed my daughter,' she said, watching closely for my response. 'Her name was Helen, and she drowned a little over a year ago.' Her voice dried and she held a hand to her scarf.

'You believe Fowler drowned her?'

'She drowned, and I believe Simon Fowler was directly responsible for her death. There was an inquest. You may remember.'

19

I was starting to. I remembered an accident on the river in which two people had drowned, and whose bodies had never been recovered. I remembered that one of these people had been a young woman, and that despite the inquest's findings, her family had continued to insist that there was more to her death than had been revealed.

'You mean you hold Simon Fowler responsible for your daughter's death?' I said.

'Helen. No – I mean that he killed her. I do understand the distinction you're trying to make.'

'Without the bodies having been recovered, the inquest would have had little choice but to bring in an open verdict with the strong possibility of accidental death or death by misadventure,' I said.

'It did.'

'And you can't accept that?'

'I did everything I could at the time to get the people concerned to look again at all the details. I wrote to everyone I could think of.'

'And you were treated as a distraught mother who couldn't come to terms with what had happened?' I had a vague recollection of a news report of a woman gathering signatures for a petition to re-open the inquest.

'Something like that,' she said, her voice still faltering.

'When did Helen die?' I asked her.

'Last April. Fifteen months ago.'

I started making notes. Names, dates. I remembered something else.

'They said she was Simon Fowler's girlfriend,' I said.

She looked away for an instant, back to the window. 'I know.'

'And was she?'

'My daughter was what people called "wilful". She and I rarely saw eye to eye.'

Meaning she was Fowler's girlfriend. And meaning the two women had possibly become estranged because of this.

'I take it that wasn't something you were happy with,' I said.

'Not particularly. She was a bright girl, intelligent. She was only twenty when she met Fowler. She was at university, here, working hard.'

'And you believe Fowler put an end to all that?'

She studied me. 'You think I'm what they all said I was, don't you – a bitter old woman with nothing better to do than cling to the past and to something which was probably never worth having in the first place.'

I was uncertain exactly what she meant by the remark, but I let it pass.

'No. But I doubt if there's anything I can do this long after the inquest to make them reconsider their findings and verdict,' I said.

'They only said what they said because the bodies were never found,' she said.

'It's been a long time. They haven't turned up since, and—'

'If you're going to tell me to be realistic, Mr Rivers, then save your breath; I've heard it all before.' Her voice had become little more than a hoarse whisper. 'And, please, no little lectures on hope. I know all about hope and hopelessness.' She took a large brown envelope of press cuttings from her bag. 'It was only ever local news,' she said. 'A thirty-second mention one night on the nationals, and then nothing. It went on for longer in the local papers and bulletins, but even there it soon stopped being interesting.'

I remembered something else. 'Simon Fowler threatened to sue you for defamation, and the papers for libel, for repeating what you said about him to them,' I said.

'It put an end to it all. One word from his lawyers and they all stopped wanting to know.'

'What did you do?'

'What little I still could, which wasn't very much. They said I was conducting a vendetta against him. He said he was heartbroken – that was the word he used – at the death of Helen, that he loved her, that they had plans for the future together, and they believed him. But it was all lies. She would never have done that, not with a man like him. He never knew her, not properly. The only person who *really* knew her—'

I resisted the urge to say, "Was you?".

She began to cough and held a hand to her mouth, and the effort of this caused her pain, which she tried unsuccessfully to disguise. I waited until she was composed.

When she next looked at me, there was a wariness in her eyes.

The envelope still lay on the desk between us.

'Why now?' I asked her.

She wiped a finger across her lips and straightened her already straight collar.

'Because I'm ill,' she said. 'And because I'm unlikely to recover from this illness. And because I want to at least make one last effort to sort this out before I die.' There was neither pleading nor self-pity in her voice, and she held my gaze as she spoke.

'What is it?'

'Three years ago, the year before Helen started university, I was diagnosed with lung cancer. I was treated; it went away; I was in remission. Two years ago, I had a small, supposedly benign tumour removed from just here.' She turned her head and lifted the hair behind her ear. There was nothing to see. 'Once again, I was cured.'

'And now?'

'And now they've found other tumours in my throat, my oesophagus. Nothing much to actually see, as yet – no unbearable pain to speak of – but the doctor who found the tumours and who told me what they were seemed less than wholly convinced that this time they were benign. We've already started to plan a course of treatment. The prognosis at this stage is not good. I may lose the power of speech. I may have to have liquid food fed directly into my stomach when I can no longer swallow. I may lose my tongue and the tumours may spread to invade my face. It's a lot of "mays", Mr Rivers.'

I considered all this. 'Will you do nothing at all?'

'I'll do whatever he recommends to keep the worst of whatever pain I *may* yet have to endure at bay. But I've decided not to start anything that will become unstoppable or irreversible. I've been there before, only then I had a good reason for doing it.'

'Your daughter?'

'Daughters. I have – had – two. Helen and Louise. I was married and widowed twice, and had a child by each husband. My first husband – Louise's father –

was a trawlerman and he was lost at sea.' She paused for a moment to let the full significance of this become clear to me. 'We'd only been married three years. Louise was two when he died. I didn't meet my second husband until fourteen years later. Helen was born a couple of years into the marriage. I was thirty-seven when I became pregnant. My second husband died when Helen was fourteen. It's been just me and the girls for the past seven years. And for all those years before that, it was just me and Louise.' Her words were again drying in her mouth. 'That's it,' she said. 'I don't want or need your sympathy, Mr Rivers. And I certainly don't want all this to be part of your reckoning if you do choose to help me. I just want you to know why I'm doing this, and why I'm doing it now.' By then even her whispering was painful for her.

'How long does the doctor think you have if you refuse all treatment?'

She shrugged. 'I haven't told him that it's what I'm going to do yet.' She looked at her watch. 'I'm seeing him in two hours.'

'And what you tell him then may depend on what I decide now?'

She half-smiled. 'I know – good old honest emotional blackmail. No – I've already made up my mind what I'm going to tell him. I wouldn't do that to you.'

I turned the envelope, still without opening it.

'The reason I don't want your sympathy, Mr Rivers, is precisely because I need someone who isn't emotionally involved in all of this, someone detached, apart, to go back over everything instead of me doing it again. I *know* you're not going to make the coroner reconsider his verdict; I know Helen is lost for good – as lost as

24

Louise's father was and is – but I need this for *me*, for my own peace of mind.'

'Why did you continue to insist that Simon Fowler had killed Helen and not simply that he perhaps knew more about her death than he ever let on?'

She was ready with her answer. 'Because it's all only words,' she said. 'And those words, the way things were said and phrased – it all became evasions, excuses and concessions. You make one concession and then another and another. Everything gets made convenient, everything gets explained away. And for people on the outside, looking in at every-thing, that's probably the best way for everything to be. But for those of us caught on the inside, those of us still looking for something believable, still looking for the truth of the matter, things are very different.'

'Like the journalists and broadcasters were on the outside?'

She nodded. 'I accused Simon Fowler of killing Helen because it was the only way I could keep any-one interested in trying to discover what had truly happened to her. If you want to know what everybody else thought had happened to her, it's all in there. "Local Girl Drowns In Tragic Circumstances". Or if not "Tragic" then "Mysterious". "Unforeseen Circum-stances", "Unpredictable Tides and Dangerous Currents". You can only read the same few tired words and phrases so many times before they become mean-ingless. And once they mean nothing, then they hide and obscure and confuse considerably more than they were ever likely to reveal.'

'You've said all this before,' I said.

She laughed. 'Probably no more than a thousand times.'

'To the journalists?'

'*They* stopped listening when they considered I was becoming too ungrateful and critical of them.'

By then I was having difficulty in hearing what she said.

She rose and went back to the window, looking across to where the faded lettering called back to her from forty years ago. If everything she had told me was true, then the remnants of the carefully painted words would outlive her.

She pointed to the corner of the room in which my dry sink stood. Men had washed and laundered clothes there when the whole building had been a ship-chandler's.

'We used to flick water into the boxes to keep the flowers moist,' she said.

I slid the envelope across the desk towards me, and though knowing what I was doing, she remained looking away from me.

'I'm very grateful,' she said. But by then her words were little more than air.

3

The clippings Alison Brooks had left me told me nothing she hadn't told me herself. They were new copies, carefully cut to size, and some were only those parts of longer articles which dealt with the death of her daughter. She had written in the margins of most of the pieces to identify their source. I knew that there would have been considerably more written at the time of the drowning. I knew, too, that Alison Brooks would have known that what she had given me would not have satisfied my curiosity, and that, as my investigation progressed, I would have uncovered everything else that had been reported anyway.

The one thing that most of the reports agreed upon was that the deaths of Helen Brooks and her unknown companion had been tragic accidents, that the pair of them had been ill-prepared for the river upon which they had sailed.

I sorted the clippings by date, knowing that many of

the later ones – they spanned only twelve days – would do little more than repeat what had already been reported. I noted each time the word 'Tragic' was used, just as Alison Brooks had done.

On the night of the twelfth of April, last year, a man called Peter Nicholson, a resident of Paull Holme, on the Humber, had been walking between Cherry Cobb Sands and his home when he had seen a small yacht beached a hundred metres from the shore on the Foulholme Sands. The Humber here was more mud, silt and shifting, shallow channels than running water, and at the time of the sighting the river proper was at least a further hundred metres beyond the stranded vessel.

Peter Nicholson was not carrying a phone, and said that at first he was undecided about what to do. His attention had been attracted to the yacht by someone standing at its prow waving and shouting to him. He wasn't certain if they were calling to him – to anyone – for help, but judging by the vessel's position and its angle in the exposed mud, this had been his assumption.

Peter Nicholson had lived at Paull Holme all his life and he knew the river well. He'd worked as a Humber pilot, guiding tankers in and out of Immingham and Hull docks, until he was fired by Associated British Ports upon their employing all the previously self-employed pilots anew under less profitable contracts.

Peter Nicholson was an eye-witness and an expert. There was no doubt in his mind, he said, that there would not be sufficient water to refloat the beached yacht for at least a further six hours, during which time it and its occupants would be stranded on the mud.

Foulholme Sands, apparently, was notorious for the wrecks and beachings it had caused. It surprised Peter Nicholson to see that a vessel had come so close, even one so small and with a shallow draught, and especially on a falling tide. It was his opinion that whoever was sailing the yacht was a stranger to the river.

In addition to the waving, shouting figure – which Peter Nicholson did not at first identify as either a man or a woman, but whom he afterwards believed to have been a woman – he said there was one other figure on board. The second figure sat towards the stern of the vessel and made no attempt to join in his or her companion's efforts to attract attention.

It was eight o'clock, and already growing dark on the river. There had been rain earlier in the week, adding to the outflows running into the Humber and the Sands – but the night was dry and clear. Peter Nicholson clearly remembered other, much larger vessels at anchor and towards the far shore, sitting out the night in their deeper berths.

As he watched, the figure at the prow of the vessel appeared to start climbing overboard, and then to fall. Peter Nicholson cupped his hands and shouted for whoever it was to stay where they were, that the liquid mud was uncrossable, and that with the tide still draining through it, it would support no weight. It wasn't clear from the article whether this is what he had shouted to the person on the yacht, or if it was what he had told the reporters afterwards. I guessed at the latter.

Peter Nicholson's name was mentioned in several other articles. Peter Nicholson, I guessed, was a man with a grievance, and a man who liked the sound of his own voice.

Having climbed or fallen overboard, the figure then disappeared from view. Whoever it was can have been little more than a vague outline at that distance. When asked if either of the yacht's occupants had been wearing life-jackets, Nicholson could not remember. It was something he took for granted, he said. Later he said that he could not remember seeing jackets through the falling darkness, and that if whoever had climbed down from the yacht had been wearing one, then he would have seen it against the darkness of the water and the mud.

Peter Nicholson waited where he stood, shouting occasionally, to see if the figure on the mud reappeared. It didn't. He then directed his shouting to the person still sitting at the stern, but received no response. He wondered if an attempt was being made to repair a failed engine or to somehow work the vessel free and back out into the deeper water. Whatever was being attempted, Nicholson was convinced that it would be unsuccessful.

He was two miles from his home, and so instead of returning there to raise the alarm, he turned inland, towards the lights of a farm on the track between Little Humber and Thorney Crofts, where he arrived breathless and told the occupant – a woman well-known to him – what he had seen. She immediately called the Spurn coastguard, handing the phone to Nicholson as the man began asking questions.

Nicholson repeated everything and the lifeboat was launched, crossing the twelve miles of the estuary mouth in under twenty minutes.

Afterwards, the story was taken from the hands of Nicholson and was couched in the language of the rescue services. The police were contacted, and four men were sent from Hull and another two from Hedon to help co-ordinate a rescue from the shore.

The lifeboat was an inflatable, and it was hoped that it might be able to get close enough to the stranded yacht to carry out an evacuation from the river. It was almost nine o'clock before this arrived and its search-lights began playing back and forth over the water.

It was considerably darker by then, and it was difficult for the men on the river to see anything clearly, or to locate either of the two figures Peter Nicholson had seen. Contrary to their expectations, the lifeboatmen were unable to approach closer than fifty metres to the yacht. A spokesman said afterwards that their plan had been to attach a line to the vessel – not to help pull it free; one of their larger, more powerful rescue boats would be needed for that – but to attempt to pull themselves closer to it and to at least take off the people still on board.

The police ashore continued searching for the person Nicholson had seen climb overboard, but they found nothing.

Peter Nicholson left the farm and returned to where he had first spotted the yacht to tell these newcomers what he had seen. He showed them where the firmest land lay, where old groynes and long-abandoned wooden jetties were still revealed amid the mud. If anyone was attempting to save themselves, then these were the routes by which they would most likely find their way to the solid ground.

More lights were rigged on the shore, scanning each

of these features in the hope of finding someone clinging to one of them. But there was nothing.

The larger lifeboat arrived. The inflatable withdrew
and began moving back and forth over the river in the
hope of finding someone floating there. Peter
Nicholson was asked how certain he was that there
had been a second figure on the yacht, because
there was certainly no one aboard now.

The controller at Spurn had tried to contact the
vessel by its radio, but this had been switched off. No
flares had been fired, no other signals of distress given.

A helicopter arrived from RAF Leconfield and began
passing in a zigzag overhead, its own searchlights
adding to the illuminations below.

I imagined all this frantic activity as I read the
reports. They were familiar enough images and
routines to anyone living on the Humber. It was a big
river. People drowned there every year. Some were
recovered immediately; some were found days and
months later. And some were lost for ever. There were
few variations on the theme.

With a falling tide, the water, cold and silt-laden,
would be moving in excess of twenty miles an hour.
The hour between eight and nine that night might
have seen anyone adrift in the water beyond the
estuary mouth and out into the expanse of the North
Sea. Swimming in those conditions was never an
option.

Police divers were called for, but their work would
not begin until the following morning. Anyone free of
the clinging mud and out in the water would be taken
away from the shore and the crumbling jetties and into
the middle of the channel.

Peter Nicholson was asked again if he was certain there had been a second person present on the stranded vessel when he had first spotted it. I could imagine his indignation at being doubted. He told a reporter that he was certain this second figure had been present. He pointed to the size of the yacht — forty feet — and said that it was unlikely that anyone would attempt to sail it alone. And especially not at that time of night. And even more especially not in the direction of Foulholme Sands with the tide running as it was. I could hear the grievance in his voice at the questioning of his own lost authority.

Most of what had happened that night was speculated on at length over the following three days. Additional background material was slowly added.

The yacht had belonged to Simon Fowler and had been taken earlier in the afternoon from its mooring at Hull marina, with his blessing, by his girlfriend — some reports said 'partner', some said 'close acquaintance' — Helen Brooks. She had tried to persuade him to accompany her, he said, but he had been too busy.

It had been raining for several days previously, and April the twelfth had been the first clear, warm day of spring.

They had eaten lunch together at a restaurant on Scale Lane, and afterwards they had parted. The yacht had been recently serviced and overhauled and was in good running order. It had a full tank of fuel, a full complement of sails, and the radio, distress beacons and location-finders were all in perfect working order. The navigational lights were all operational; there was a locker containing several dozen distress flares, and at least six life-jackets on board. Charts detailing the waters for a hundred miles in every direction lay in the chart drawer.

Simon Fowler said he was devastated at the loss. He had agreed to Helen taking the yacht only if she could find someone capable of sailing it to accompany her. And then only if she contacted him at regular intervals while she was on the river. He had a record of his calls and text messages from her. He had made her promise to return to the marina before darkness fell. At lunch, he said, they had arranged to meet again for dinner to make up for his absence during the afternoon. A reservation was made and then left uncancelled as the events of the day unfolded.

Asked if he had grown concerned when the yacht had failed to return as anticipated, Fowler said he had been completely unaware of the fact. He had been in an important meeting until seven that evening. It was this meeting, he said, that had made it impossible for him to accompany Helen that afternoon.

He was asked about Helen Brooks's experience on the water and he described her as 'competent', adding that he imagined whoever she had found to accompany her would have had more experience of sailing. Helen had not told him of her intended route. When asked if he had tried to contact her, he said he hadn't, that he had been unable to. Her own messages had reached him at his meeting, the last being recorded at six-twenty. He had last seen her at two in the afternoon; he was expecting to see her again at eight that same night. When the beached yacht was finally identified, Simon Fowler had been traced to his apartment home in Robinson Court. Twenty men confirmed that he had been among them all afternoon.

Fowler himself had last been on the yacht the previous September. He and Helen and several others had sailed to Spurn Point, anchored in the Trinity Channel, and had then sailed back to Hull as it grew dark. He said it had been a happy occasion for the pair of them. When asked why he used the yacht so infrequently, Fowler said he had bought it from a friend – a hint of a favour, of helping someone out – and that he had never had a passion for the water. He had owned it for two years and had sailed it on fewer than a dozen occasions, and always accompanied by someone more accomplished than himself.

He continued to insist that he had no idea who had been with Helen on that 'fatal day'. She had even made a point of refusing to tell him who had gone with her, he said. Perhaps she wanted to make him jealous following her accusations that he was working too hard and neglecting her. He repeated how much he had loved her, and when he was asked about their future together, he had been unable to answer.

Helen Brooks's death joined a long list of drownings. It was a river. It was what happened there. It was what happened to people who went out on it with no real idea of what they were doing. Experienced sailors who had sailed on every ocean in the world drowned there. Small boats survived the fiercest storms; tankers collided with others, visible from twenty miles away, on the calmest of seas.

The sea was a different world, and different laws and procedures operated. What might be considered straightforward and simple on land became complicated and eventful on the sea. There was a sense of the commonplace in these reversals; a sense, based on that unquestioned inevitability, of acceptance. People drowned because they were out of their element or their depth.

It was this simple understanding that Alison Brooks was unable to accept. Perhaps the sea was too *big* a thing to blame for her daughter's death.

The clippings ended only a few days after the incident. If I wanted to know what had happened after that then I would have to visit Sunny at the news agency. It was something I had hoped to avoid, but which I now realized had been inevitable from the start with a case already so rooted in the past and in the manner of its revelation.

I called Alison Brooks and told her I'd finished reading. She was already at the hospital and waiting to see the doctor. I wished her luck, and she asked me immediately if I was prepared to help her. I repeated what I'd told her earlier – that there was little possibility of changing the verdict of the inquest – and that if this was what she secretly hoped, then it was pointless for me to even begin.

I heard a nearby loudspeaker announcement, the noise of people around her. She remained silent for a few seconds before saying that she'd appreciate anything more that I might be able to discover for her.

'Do you believe everything Peter Nicholson told the reporters?' I said.

'No,' she said. 'And before you say it, yes, fifteen months is a long time to go on banging your head against a brick wall.'

I heard another voice close by.

'I have to go,' she said.

I waited until the line was dead before saying 'Good luck'.

I returned the clippings to their envelope, folded it and put it in my pocket.

4

I walked to Spring Bank, where Sunny and Yvonne ran their news agency. I'd seen Yvonne several times recently, but had not spoken to Sunny for almost two months, and then we'd met by chance, in a city-centre bar, surrounded by others. We were awkward with each other, and we both regretted that, but the bar was no place to talk properly. We'd agreed to contact each other, but the weeks had passed and neither of us had made the effort.

Six months earlier I'd accused him of using one of my clients and my own investigation as a means of acquiring valuable copy concerning the appeal and subsequent murder of a convicted murderer. In truth, we'd been using each other, but my own accusation had been the first and the most forcibly made and I had given him no opportunity to counter it.

I knew from Yvonne that he regretted this rift between us as much as I did.

Traffic queued along Ferensway and at the Beverley Road junction, making the already hazy air even hazier with its fumes.

Arriving at the doorway leading to the fire-escape which led to the agency, I retraced my steps into the nearby off-licence and bought a bottle of malt whisky.

I went back through the doorway, along the alley-way and up the stairs. The intercom at the door was broken. It was impossible to climb the stairs silently. Half way up, the door opened above me and Yvonne came out onto the metal platform there.

She watched me without speaking for a moment. Beside me, the handrail was hot to the touch.

I heard Sunny behind her, asking her who it was.

'Not sure,' she said. 'It's either Mohammed or the mountain.' She flicked the cigarette she held into the debris of the yard beneath us and held out her arms to me. I went up the stairs and put my own round her, holding the bottle into the small of her back.

'You're either *really* pleased to see me,' she said. 'Or you've brought a bottle of expensive whisky as a pathetic and, frankly, unnecessary peace offering for that ungrateful, deceitful, lying and manipulative bastard in there.' She shouted this last part so that Sunny would miss none of it.

In my ear, she whispered, 'He's off again tomorrow and not taking me with him after he'd promised.'

'Where?' I said.

'Scunthorpe,' she said. The name always sounded like an admission of defeat of some sort. 'Advertorial for a motel chain.'

' "Advertorial"?'

39

'Try and keep up,' she told me, her arms still around me.

'If *I* were free, I'd take you away somewhere even more exciting,' I said.

' "Free" as in . . . ?' She released me and held me by the shoulders. 'Anywhere would be exciting with you,' she said.

'You're just guessing.'

'It's what I'm good at. Guessing what other people are doing and thinking and then having to do everything *they* should be doing, but aren't, because they're off doing something they shouldn't be doing.' She was shouting again.

Sunny appeared on the fire-escape behind her. He wore an orange shirt, and shorts. There were parrots and Hawaiian dancers on the shirt. They appeared to be holding small guitars. Flowers covered their nipples.

Yvonne stood to one side. 'Well, if it isn't the lying, cheating, deceitful bastard himself. We were just talking about you.'

'You missed out manipulative,' he said. He looked past her to me.

I knew the conference in Scunthorpe was something he could not afford to ignore. The agency also acted as a broker for advertising firms, and advertisers and their customers always appreciated appreciative copy and news items.

'Scunthorpe?' I said to him.

'It's the summer,' he said. 'You want any real news in this neck of the woods you're probably looking at Doncaster or Goole.'

'Things bad?' I said.

' "Slow" is probably a better word,' he said. He held out his hand to me and I clasped it for a moment. He let go of me and I gave him the whisky.

'Careful with these shows of affection, boys,' Yvonne said. 'You don't want people getting the wrong idea.'

'Yvonne was all candles, crystals and aromatic oils twenty-five years before everyone else was all candles and crystals and aromatic oils,' Sunny said. 'The world catches up with her and she doesn't like it.'

'Let me guess,' I said. 'You were having an argument before I arrived.'

'You can leave that here when you go,' Yvonne told him, pointing to the bottle. She put her hand to the side of my face. 'It's good to see you,' she said. She put her arm through mine and led me into the agency.

The room looked as confusing and as cluttered as always. Computers, fax machines and photocopiers were arranged in no apparent order, and between these were mounds of newspapers and magazines, some still standing, some already toppled. Half a dozen telephones sat where they had last been used. Small fans stood on each of the two desks.

The blind had been lowered at the front of the room, but this had been prevented from falling its full length by the clutter of directories, dead plants and padded envelopes on the sill. A television sat playing but muted in the corner of the room, a stack of cellophane-wrapped cassettes piled on it.

Sunny took three plastic cups from his desk and poured us each a drink.

I tried to remember what of any consequence had happened recently, and which he might be selling on, in all its guises, to the regionals and nationals – all of them as voracious as ever for news even when nothing was happening.

'Shark gets ill in aquarium,' he said, holding up a sheet on his desk.

'And I'm still "Twenty Ways With A Pineapple",' Yvonne said, giving me a chair and sitting beside me. 'Don't ask.' She cast a cold and pointed look at Sunny.

'Motel owners own catering companies who import pineapples,' Sunny said. 'Sometimes they import too many pineapples, or they're full of giant spiders or monkey piss, and they need for people to go out and buy more of them. How many pineapples does a mother of four and living on state benefits buy in a year?' He dropped the sheet and drained his cup.

'What do you know about Simon Fowler?' I asked him, and the instant I finished speaking he held up the flat of his hand and then looked over it at me with an expression on his face intended to suggest that he could not believe what I'd just said.

'Stop right there,' he said eventually.

'Oh, nice one,' Yvonne said behind me.

'What?' I asked her.

'You wait six months, arrive unannounced, and then the first thing you ask us is if we know anything about Simon Fowler.'

'Meaning you do?'

'Oh, please,' she said. She took the bottle from the desk and poured more into her cup.

I looked back to Sunny, who slowly turned his hand and put it over his mouth, blowing out his cheeks. Silver hairs protruded from the top of his shirt. His eyes never left mine.

'You're serious, aren't you?' he said.

'I don't even know what you're suggesting,' I told him.

He waited until he was convinced of this before going on.

'Simon Fowler,' he said, adding a cold emphasis to each syllable, 'is a jumped-up fucking developer buying up everything he can get his hands on in and around the Old Town and either developing it or hanging onto it until the city council makes its mind up what to do. Either way, he becomes a part of their considerations and makes another fortune for himself in the process.'

I expected Yvonne to add something to this, but she said nothing. When I looked at her, she simply nodded.

'Simon Fowler either sends out threatening letters or takes out injunctions against anyone who so much as breathes a whisper of a hint that anything he might be doing is not entirely above board and done solely for the long-awaited and lasting benefit of this city and its grateful citizens,' Sunny said.

'Meaning he's done it to you.'

'Five times.'

'And each time you've laughed in his face and fought against him and his wealth, power and influence to claim freedom of speech.'

'Something like that. We sent him an apology saying it wouldn't happen again.'

'Until next time?'

'To begin with he didn't seem too concerned. The man's a crook. All he's interested in is empire-building and money and he doesn't much care how he gets either.'

'Bringers of piazzas, mocha-latte bars and patio heaters to areas of inner-city blight aren't all necessarily crooks,' I said.

'He's a crook,' he repeated flatly. There was something solid and unavoidable about the way he said it. 'Believe me, he's a nasty piece of work, and if you're involved with him – either working for him, which, God forbid, I hope is not the case – or investigating something which involves him, then I honestly think you ought to look long and hard at whatever it is you're doing before going too much further with it. I take it you haven't encountered him personally yet, otherwise you wouldn't be here asking me these stupid questions.'

'It's true,' Yvonne said beside me, her voice low, and all the confirmation I needed.

I told them about Alison Brooks's visit.

Sunny knew who she was before I mentioned the death of her daughter.

'And that's the Simon Fowler connection?'

'So far,' I said.

'We covered the drowning. The nationals were only interested for a day or so, but it ran locally for over a week. There was a bit of Additional Reportage for a few articles.'

'Did you speak to Fowler?'

'Once or twice. I doubt he'll remember me. He was too busy playing the distressed and grieving boyfriend at the time.'

'You don't think Helen Brooks meant as much to him as he wanted people to think?'

'Not nearly as much as he meant to her, probably.' He rubbed his thumb and forefinger together.

'You think he only said what he said because she died?'

'Because she died on his yacht.'

'Even though it was an accident?'

'That's not what her mother believes,' he said.

I drained my own cup.

'I spoke to her mother a few times,' he said. 'I know true grief when I see it, and I know which of the two of them – her and Fowler – was suffering from it.'

'Difficult for him, though, considering the yacht.'

'Or awkward. I bet nobody asked him how many other *girl*friends he'd got. All he ever did was cover his own back, like he always does.'

'And the mother?'

'She called us a few times, wanting to tell us things.'

'Things we couldn't put into the reports,' Yvonne said. 'I spoke to her myself as well. She told me things her daughter had allegedly told her.'

'Things about Fowler?'

'Among others. Things the daughter seemed excited to be a part of. When I suggested to the mother that she was making unfounded accusations, she became angry and told me I was just like all the rest.'

'The truth is,' Sunny said, 'the daughter was in over her head and probably knew next to nothing about Fowler, his deals and all his little friends.'

'Was no one able to confront him with any of Alison Brooks's allegations?' I said.

'Why should they?' Yvonne said. 'In all probability they had nothing whatsoever to do with the circumstances of the girl's death. That's all anyone was ever interested in then.'

I turned back to Sunny. 'So you think Helen Brooks's

death and her involvement with Fowler were entirely coincidental?'

He nodded. 'However much I'd like to believe otherwise.'

I told them about Alison Brooks's cancer.

'I think she was still recovering from a previous course of treatment at the time,' Yvonne said uncertainly. 'She always seemed exhausted, easily worn out. I think I just assumed it was because of what had happened.'

I told them everything she'd told me, and nothing I told them surprised them.

'She's just repeating the same old accusations,' Sunny said when I'd finished. 'But now, perhaps, there's another ending in sight.'

The remark was not intended to sound uncaring, merely another explanation of why the woman was unable to relax her grip on those past events.

'There was another daughter, much older,' Yvonne said. 'I met her once or twice, with her mother at the inquest.'

'Did she share her mother's conviction concerning Fowler?' I said.

'I don't remember. I expect she did, or at least in her mother's company she did. They used to sit together in front of the cameras. She always had her arm around her mother.'

'Did you ever see them *with* Simon Fowler, at the same press conferences, for instance, or at the inquest together?'

She thought about it. 'I honestly can't remember. I doubt they'd want anything to do with him.'

'What I do remember,' Sunny said, 'is how all of

Fowler's evidence of the day in question, all his little recordings and meetings, all his acquaintances and people waiting to see him – how all of them seemed to take him from minute to minute through the day once he'd seen the girl for the last time.'

It was something that had also occurred to me reading Alison Brooks's file.

'A perfect alibi?'

'A host of perfect alibis, and all of them seemingly coincidental, each overlapping and confirming the other. But that's never what they were, of course – alibis. It was all a terrible accident. No one was ever looking to lay any blame or responsibility at Fowler's door.'

'Except Helen's mother.'

'A woman crazed by grief and anger,' he said.

'And the second death? The figure on the boat who was never identified and who might even never have existed.'

'There was no record whatsoever of the girl telling Fowler who she was taking with her.'

'And only his word that he tried to find out.'

Sunny clicked his tongue. 'Perhaps he really didn't care.'

'Or perhaps he already knew.'

'I imagine all these things were given the proper consideration at the time,' he said.

'Before Fowler started sending out his injunctions?'

He shook his head in disbelief at the remark. '*They'd* been happening for years, ever since his arrival in Hull. He's a London man and he likes everyone to know it. I don't remember any warnings to us personally over anything we wrote concerning the death of the girl. They tended to be connected to all the stuff we published and sold regarding his developments, acquisitions and plans for rebuilding. He's not a stupid man, and he's careful. I imagine public sympathy and some acknowledgement of his own grief and loss were enough to shield him from Alison Brooks.'

We sat together for a further hour. The bright sun moved from one side of the blind towards its centre, from one dead stalk in a pot to another. I had seen Yvonne's own small garden and the abundance it contained.

When I rose to leave, the heat and the whisky had taken effect, and I stood for a moment to catch my balance.

'I can let you have a look through our file,' Sunny offered.

'A disk would be good.'

'I can let you have a look through our file on the drowning and the inquest,' he repeated. He went to one of the cabinets, searched it, and drew out a file considerably thinner than I had anticipated after all they had just told me. 'I'm away until Monday. You can have it until then.'

'Why would you need it back?' I asked him.

He laughed. 'Well done,' he said. 'You're right. You go stirring through the bucket of shit that is Simon Fowler and I might need the file for background when a third body finally turns up.' He pushed the folder under my arm.

'In which case,' I said, 'I don't suppose I could borrow your file on everything else connected to Fowler for the same time.'

'Fowler and his lawyers were adamant about no records relating to his business activities being kept or used without his explicit and written permission.'

'Meaning you don't have a file on him?'

'Meaning I'm having to think a little harder about this one before handing it over to someone like you.'

'I won't mention your name if he finds out and tortures me,' I said.

'Hm, big joke. And of course, once he knows *you* exist and what you're up to, he'll never make the connection back to here.' He looked at Yvonne, waiting for her to decide whether or not I was to be trusted with the second file.

'We're waiting on the word of "Miss Pineapple"?' I said.

'The funny bit finished,' Sunny said, his eyes still on hers. 'This is Simon Fowler we're talking about.' He trusted her with his life, and she trusted him with hers, and anywhere else these would have sounded like portentous and unbelievable claims.

'Fowler will make the connection anyhow,' Yvonne said eventually.

Sunny went to another cabinet, unlocked the bottom drawer and took out a considerably thicker folder.

Yvonne rose beside me. She, too, was surprised by the effects of the drink.

Sunny gave me the folder.

'Have a good time in Scunthorpe,' I told him.

'I'll try,' he said. At the door, he took my hand again. 'I'm glad you came,' he said.

I nodded.

Beside me, Yvonne put her arms round both our shoulders and said, 'Group hug, anyone?'

She alone came with me beyond the cool air of the fans back out onto the heat of the fire-escape, where she stood and watched me go, just as she had stood and watched me arrive. She raised her hand to me as I turned the corner, and I waved back.

5

The file on Helen Brooks's death told me little that I hadn't already learned from her mother's own carefully chosen clippings. Again I read the subtext over and over – that death by drowning was both something that should not surprise us, and that it was, in most instances – always that qualifier – something that was avoidable. We were an island flowing with rivers, seas that came and went; and some of those rivers and seas remained unfathomed even today; and others changed their configuration with every tide.

And of all these dangerous rivers and unfathomable depths, the Humber ranked high on everybody's list of dangerous waters to sail on.

I noted the names of the local reporters, and saw that Sunny himself had written several of the articles, that he had interviewed Peter Nicholson at length the morning after the drowning.

I turned to the file on Simon Fowler. Its contents

proved even more disappointing. Listening to Sunny, and watching him as he had retrieved the file for me, I'd imagined it to be stuffed with details of Fowler's property dealings and development plans. Instead, there were only several dozen clippings, most of which showed Fowler receiving an award for his building work or revealed him at some function surrounded by the better-known faces of the city councillors and other civic dignitaries. By and large, the two groups were interchangeable.

Fowler was referred to as a major property-holder and developer. He owned letting agencies. Local contractors and tradesmen had nothing but good to say about him. He had been invited onto the boards of several regeneration committees. Hull was in a state of perpetual regeneration. Jerusalem was always waiting to be builded here.

Several of these reports referred to the recent tragedy in Fowler's life, and repeated his comments that he was now working even harder than before to help get himself through a difficult time.

In two of the later articles, he was pictured with a woman on his arm, in a revealing dress, a few inches taller than him, and with long, vividly blonde hair. He introduced her as Nikki and said she was a great comfort to him. Those were his words, and after what Sunny had told me, I imagined all the pieces had been seen and vetted by Fowler before being published.

And somewhere between these two folders, Helen Brooks and all the concerns of her mother had disappeared.

At the bottom of the file were several whole newspapers, folded tight and laid together. I took these out, hoping for a more detailed profile of Fowler, or even something to substantiate what both Sunny and Yvonne had suggested concerning his alleged criminal activities upon which much of this bright and shining enterprise was supposedly founded. The papers were nationals, complete, and all dated within the last month. I searched the first of them, but found nothing. I went through it again, scrutinizing the articles where Fowler might conceivably have been mentioned in connection with someone or somewhere else, but again there was nothing.

Whatever Sunny's reasons for including the papers, I would have to wait until his return to the city to find out. I knew from my previous forays into his files that, in contrast to the apparently haphazard manner in which he lived and worked, his records were meticulously kept, indexed and cross-referenced. Nothing of any value was ever lost to him, and it occurred to me that the material relating to Fowler might have been filed elsewhere by Yvonne, and that Sunny had given me the wrong file.

I called the agency, spoke to the answering machine, and waited. It wasn't late. Sunny might already have left for Scunthorpe, but Yvonne was usually there until at least seven each evening. I told her I could hear her typing and to pick up the phone, but there was still nothing.

6

Three days later, Monday morning, as I crossed Dock Street alongside the marina, I saw a woman sitting on one of the benches overlooking the moored yachts there. At first I thought it was Alison Brooks who had returned to see me, and who had come to wait by the water upon finding my office empty.

I approached closer and saw that it was not Alison Brooks, but a woman twenty years younger – in her late thirties – but who resembled her so closely that she could only have been her surviving older daughter.

As I neared her, she turned to watch me. She knew I had seen and recognized her. She carried a small bag and a newspaper, which remained folded in her lap.

I crossed the cobbles to her. I had Sunny's files with me, but there was nothing marked on the folders to indicate their contents.

'I thought for a moment you were your mother,' I told her.

'She described you,' she said, 'but I wasn't sure.' She put down her bag and held out her hand. 'Louise Brooks.'

She made no effort to leave the seat and its view over the yachts.

'This was where he kept it,' she said.

'Does your mother know you've come to see me?' I sat beside her.

'I told her I wanted to, but she tried to dissuade me.'

'Meaning she knows you're here.'

She nodded once.

'Are you here to tell me you think she's wasting her time and her money?' I asked her.

'I don't know. But that's it, isn't it – time. Whatever she thinks she's doing, whatever she hopes to achieve, I don't want her to tie herself up in all of this Fowler business again when she could be doing something more worthwhile.'

'She didn't strike me as the kind of woman who might take herself off on a world cruise,' I said.

'She isn't.'

'I haven't actually done anything yet,' I said. 'I told her I'd call her and let her know what course of action I considered best.'

'She's convinced you'll do it. I was with her at the hospital when you called her. If you aren't going to do what she wants, then tell her immediately, Mr Rivers.'

'She seemed determined. She'd find someone else.'

'I know.'

'*Are* you here to persuade me to tell her to forget about it?'

'Hardly. She stopped listening to whatever I had to say on the matter a long time ago.' She turned to face me. 'What you have to understand, Mr Rivers, is that my mother and I have never shared the same understanding of this whole Helen thing from even long before she drowned.'

It seemed a clumsy and evasive way of expressing herself.

'Do you think your sister's death – whatever the circumstances – was an accident?'

'And that it should all be left behind us? Perhaps. Especially now.'

'What did the doctor tell your mother?'

'It was more a question of what she told him.'

'That she wasn't going to submit herself to his treatment? Were you with her when she told him?'

'I work at the hospital. I'm on a year's contract. Site Practitioner. Human resources. My predecessor's on maternity leave. Most days it's just a juggling act, begging, pleading, pushing and cajoling. From surgeons to cleaners.'

'Where were you before?'

'Birmingham. Three years. And before that, Nottingham. I've been here for ten months.'

Meaning she'd probably come back to Hull to be with her mother at the time of the inquest twelve weeks after the drowning.

'And afterwards?'

'I'm waiting to see what happens,' she said, meaning her mother.

'What do *you* want to happen?' I asked her.

She smiled at the suggestion, as though even that degree of choice had never before been offered to her.

56

'I wish my mother would concentrate on herself and on her own needs.'

'I think this *is* a need,' I said. 'The two things seem bound together for her.'

'I know. And I sometimes wonder that if she hadn't had the worry and stress of all this—' She stopped abruptly.

'What? That the cancer wouldn't have returned?'

She nodded and then shook her head. 'I know it's not that straightforward or simple, but I know things would have been a lot easier for her if she'd been able to accept the verdict of the inquest and let everything go.'

'I don't doubt it, but the—'

'But what – the return of the cancer's brought everything back into sharper focus for both of us?'

'I was going to say the distinction between the two things seemed clear enough to her.'

She laughed.

'Also on the plus side,' I said, 'I didn't make any remark about you being called Louise Brooks.'

'Not many people know who she was.' Her dark hair was cut in a severe line along her jaw. She wore no eye make-up, only a faint lipgloss. 'It was deliberate. My mother thought she was the most beautiful woman in the world. Sophisticated, intelligent, powerful.'

'And so that's what *you* became?'

'I had the haircut as a girl to please her.'

'It suits you.'

'You don't know me.'

'No. But I know you're here to sound me out and to decide whether or not I'm the man for the job, or if you should persuade your mother to go elsewhere.'

She acceded to this in silence. 'She used to tell us that true choice only ever existed in the province of the rich,' she said. 'One of her sayings. She had a hard life with my father. It was a lot easier for her with her second husband, Helen's father, and after she'd started making something of herself.'

'She told me about her floristry.'

'She owned eight shops and a delivery business. She employed almost thirty people before she sold up.'

'Did either you or your sister work with her?'

'Did she expect one of us to take over from her, you mean? It was the last thing she wanted. She wanted us to make our own ways in the world. When Helen started at university—' Again, she stopped abruptly.

I didn't press her.

'Lulu in Hollywood,' I said.

She understood me. 'That's what Helen used to call me when she was small – Lulu. She'd started doing it again in the few years before she died.'

'Were you close?'

'I'm – I *was* – eighteen years older than her. We were always more like three generations instead of two. And in answer to your question – no, we were never particularly close. Like I said – life with my own father was never easy. They struggled.'

'Whereas the second marriage—'

'Was considerably more comfortable for everyone concerned. I don't know if Helen was planned, or even wanted, but it was a completely different world by then. By then we'd left the flat on Orchard Park and moved to *Brian*'s house in leafy Cottingham. He'd been married before, but there were no children. Helen was only three when I went away to university. London. I saw her often enough, but I was never a proper sister to her, more like an aunt.'

'And you resented the fact that your mother, Helen and Brian appeared to have made a completely new family in your absence, and one which didn't include you?'

'Something like that. He was a good man. He took care of her, of us all.'

'But everything you and your mother had had beforehand was lost?'

She considered this. 'I went away, grew up, and when I came back, it was all gone. She brought me up alone. Most mornings she was up at four or five, and she took me with her most places she went while she was getting her shops up and running. I can still walk into any florist's and name every single flower. I can give you wholesale and retail, blooms and accessories, all across the range. I can make you up a wedding bouquet or a buttonhole. I can probably even spell out your name in tight red roses for your coffin.'

'You sound as though you miss it.'

'Not really. Once, it was all I lived for – I was determined that it was what I was going to do – but, like I said, everything changed. I worked in London for eight years. By the time I moved to Nottingham, Helen was already a teenager and I was just another distant adult to her.'

'Is that one of the reasons why you can't share your mother's conviction now?'

'Probably.'

'Were you jealous of her?'

'Of course I was. And I'd be lying to you if I said

a small part of me didn't still resent my mother's obsession with all this now.'

'She would have done the same for you.'

'I know. But *I* never asked it of her.'

'Meaning there were other things where Helen was concerned?'

'Some.'

'Things you knew about and also resented?'

'Let's just say that certain allowances were always made for Helen which were never made for me. And I doubt if "resentment" is the right word. I think Helen wrapped Brian and my mother round her little finger. With my father gone, it was just me and my mother. But with Brian eager to play the doting daddy there was always another card to play.'

'You think she manipulated them?'

'I know she did. It was never how *they* saw it, of course. Or if my mother did see it, then she made allowances or excuses.'

'And you, meanwhile, continued to feel excluded.'

'I excluded myself. I had a life of my own – first in London, then wherever.'

'Would you have come back here if Helen hadn't drowned?'

'And if my mother hadn't become terminally ill?'

She rose, walked the short distance to the railings and leaned out over the water. Her bag and paper lay on the bench beside me. The sun flashed where it was reflected off the aluminium hulls. She turned to face me, resting on the rail.

'Were you telling the truth when you said you hadn't started looking into Helen's death?' she said.

I patted the folders. 'Mostly.'

'And you haven't done anything yet to alert Simon Fowler that the whole thing's about to be stirred up again?'

'Not as far as I know. Why?'

She turned back to look out over the yachts. On the far side of the marina, a crane was lifting one of the vessels on to a waiting lorry. She watched the slow progress of this before answering me.

'I don't necessarily share my mother's conviction that Fowler was wholly responsible for Helen's death. If you'd known her those last few months of her life, you'd understand a little better about what she was and wasn't capable of doing all by herself. I'm not saying Fowler *wasn't* somehow involved, just that his part in it all might not be what my mother wants it to be, that's all.'

It was a lot to take in. The remark about her sister had seemed unnecessarily harsh, and her comment on Fowler obscured more than it revealed. I sensed there was little to be gained by confronting her directly on either of these points.

'But, like your mother, you believe Fowler – what? – led her astray?'

'Nice word. But, yes, I do.'

'Did her studies suffer?'

'Her studies were practically non-existent by then. In fact, she'd already had one written warning that her non-attendance at lectures was causing concern.'

'What was she studying?'

'Media Studies. She thought she wanted to be a photographer.'

'And you think it would have been difficult for her?'

'She liked the *idea* of it, Mr Rivers. She liked

anything that was easy. She was beautiful. She used to do some modelling for the other students. She had a lot going for her, but she lacked commitment. Always the line of least resistance with Helen.'

'And so when Fowler came along . . .'

'When that evil little creep got his hooks into her, everything else just went for nothing. If you knew how much money my mother had handed over to her . . . She had cameras and equipment costing thousands.'

She came back to me, pushed the files to one side of the bench and sat close beside me.

'You said "hooks",' I said. 'Drugs?'

'I don't imagine it was an entirely new development wholly dependent upon the appearance of Fowler,' she said.

'But he did nothing to dissuade her.'

'Far from it. He probably had more of anything than any other man she'd ever met. She certainly thought he had what she wanted, and that whatever that was, it could be hers for the asking or the taking.'

'*Was* she his girlfriend?' I asked her, remembering Yvonne's remark upon hearing the word.

She considered this, and because she was unable to respond immediately, I needed no other answer from her.

'I think *she'd* convinced herself that there was something special between them,' she said eventually.

'But something of which no one else was necessarily convinced?'

'Least of all Fowler.'

'Have you told your mother all this?'

'That her daughter was only one of a dozen women,

and all of them used by Fowler depending on whatever it was he wanted from them?'

I waited a moment before making my next remark. 'You seem to know a lot about him for someone who was living away while all this was happening.'

'Do I?' she said. 'Do I really?'

I said nothing.

'Fair enough,' she said. 'I'll tell you. I would have told you at some point. And let's face it, whatever *I* don't tell you, he'll be telling you himself soon enough, and all of it thickly coated with his Mr Benefactor, Man Of The People gloss.'

'What is it?'

'Four years ago, when my mother decided to retire – Brian had died three years earlier – she put her shops on the market and one of the big florist chains made her a good offer. She accepted. She even asked them to keep on as many of her old staff as possible, and they agreed. They were buying the shops as going concerns; it was what they wanted. And the business and the expertise were what they wanted most.'

'But?'

'A week after they made their offer, two of the shops were attacked in the night and had their windows smashed and their stock destroyed. A week after that, another of them was gutted in a fire. Some of the staff were intimidated and threatened. Florists. Who threatens florists?'

'And you're going to tell me that Fowler was involved in all of this?'

She closed her eyes briefly against my disbelief.

'A few days after the fire, the chain withdrew its offer. Some of the staff were too scared to go on working.'

'And then someone else offered to buy the shops?'

'Not for almost a year. During which time, others were broken into and vandalized.'

'What did the police think?'

She laughed. 'That some underworld mastermind was conducting a vendetta against one of Hull's oldest established flower-sellers, what else?'

'There was no evidence? Was no one ever caught?'

She shook her head. 'And it went on happening.'

'Until?'

'Until three of the eight shops were finally closed for good and she decided to sell the lot of them, but not as going concerns.'

'By which time, presumably, she'd had another offer.'

'Which the police also refused to believe was part of what was happening. A development company contacted her. They gave her half of what she'd originally asked.'

'Because she had no choice.'

'It was the only offer in a year.'

'And Fowler owned the company.'

'Of course he didn't. He owned the company which had a sister company which had shares in the development agency which owned the company which bought the shops.'

'It's probably not that uncommon,' I said. 'And it certainly doesn't prove any kind of criminal or malicious intent on the part of Fowler.'

'You sound like the police,' she said.

'Perhaps. But what I also sound like is a man who might now have to confront Fowler knowing he's endured a whole history of these confrontations and accusations since the death of your sister. And if the police think your mother *is* carrying out a private, grief-blinded campaign against him, then I'm not going to get much help or understanding from them, either – especially if they view me as an extension of that campaign.'

'You would have found all this out anyway.'

'So you said.'

'I just didn't want you to learn it all from Fowler and then imagine that he was justified in his claims of persecution.'

'Your mother didn't see fit to tell me any of this.'

'I don't – she – she's got other things to worry about.'

It was an excuse, and both of us knew it.

'Meaning that she's probably not as convinced as you are about Fowler's involvement.'

'The attacks scared her. She'd known some of the women who worked with her from the very beginning. She felt responsible for what happened to them.' She put her hand on my arm.

'Would you have gone to whoever your mother had approached to look into Helen's death and told them all this?' I asked her.

'Of course.'

On the far side of the marina, the yacht was finally lifted clear of the water. It swung slightly in its cradle. Men gathered around it, shouting instructions to each other.

Neither of us spoke for a minute. Pigeons scavenged at our feet.

'There's still no connection that I can see – other than Fowler himself, whose involvement with your sister three years later might have been entirely coincidental – between the loss of the shops and the drowning.'

'I know,' she said.

'Coincidences *do* exist,' I said.

'I always thought it was the first law of private investigations that the opposite was true.'

'We don't like them,' I said. 'But that doesn't make them go away. Sometimes they look good and lead to something; sometimes they just look too obvious; but mostly they just lead to a lot of wasted time because they promise to be something they never turn out to be.'

'It's all a bit complicated for me,' she said.

'And if I believed that,' I told her, 'then you'd probably consider firing me here and now and go looking for someone a little more willing to believe everything you wanted them to believe.'

'I could put my hand back on your arm, flutter my eyelashes, if it would help.'

'I don't see how it can hurt,' I told her. 'Will you tell your mother what you've told me?'

'She'll know already.'

Seeing that she was close to leaving – we'd been together for almost an hour by then – I asked her what she truly believed her mother hoped to achieve by my investigation.

'I think she's old enough still to believe in the notion of Peace of Mind,' she said. It was another evasive answer, and again we both understood that. 'It's the best I can do,' she said. 'Would it sound strange to you, Mr Rivers, if I told you that I doubt if I have ever loved anyone as much as I love my mother? I know we grew apart over the past fifteen years, and especially because of how I felt about Helen and what she was doing to us all, but my mother still matters more to me than anyone in the world. I often wish it were otherwise, but it isn't. I am what I am because of her, and the knowledge that she'll soon be gone – even the knowledge that our last few months or even weeks together might be spent in conflict over this – is painful for me. But if all she wants to do is to find out for certain what happened to her precious daughter, then that's fine by me. And even if she continues to choose to see only half of what was happening – what Helen had become – then that's fine, too.'

'Because soon none of it will matter?'

'Because soon none of it will matter.' She held my arm and butted her forehead once against my shoulder.

'A cheque would be better,' I told her.

'It's in my bag,' she said.

Across the marina, there was a sudden knock as the hull of the yacht finally touched the bed of the lorry and all the men who had been standing around for the past hour became suddenly busy with the cradle and the baulks of timber to support it.

We rose from the bench and she held me briefly. The gesture surprised me, so soon after meeting her, but I accepted it and reciprocated.

'I was wondering,' she said. 'Can we—'

'Can we keep each other informed of what's happening – that is, could I tell you everything I tell your mother?'

'I was thinking, *before* my mother.'

'She's my client.'

'I know. And she knows I'm here with you now, what I'm doing.'

'I'll talk to her about it,' I said.

She nodded her acceptance.

'She wept when she was telling me about remembering your office,' she said. 'If it's the same place, then I remember once being sat naked in the sink with the flowers as a baby.'

'Come back with me,' I suggested. 'Relive old times. It's only a hundred yards away.'

She laughed. 'I know exactly how far away it is,' she said.

7

At Humber Street there was a message waiting from Yvonne, returning my call of three days earlier and asking me to call her, which I did.

'*Qué pasa?*' she said.

'*Qué pasa* is half a dozen carefully folded newspapers packing out the Fowler file instead of what should actually have been in there, and which, presumably, had been stuffed in there by person or persons unknown to disguise the fact that whatever should have been in there no longer was.'

'It's a fair cop,' she said. 'I've got most of it here.'

'Where was it?'

'Somewhere else.'

'Until when?'

'Until you clicked your fingers for the file and Sunny jumped up with his tongue out and gave it to you.'

'Are you working on something to do with Fowler that Sunny doesn't know about?'

'I might be.'

'Something Sunny wouldn't approve of?'

'He might not.'

'How about if I plied you with drink at lunchtime?'

'Too early.'

'I know. But then again, any later and it might be too late. Especially if Sunny gets back before everything about your Woman Of Mystery routine is fully and unconditionally revealed to me.'

She swore at me, named a bar and a time, and hung up.

I arrived at Paull Holme an hour later. Hedon Road beyond the prison and the King George Dock was as congested as usual, but approaching the Salt End refineries and leaving the main road at the roundabout there, I found myself alone as most of the traffic continued into Hedon.

Helen Brooks and her unknown companion had drowned two miles further along the estuary. It would have been possible to drive closer to the place, but here, just beyond Paull Holme, was where Peter Nicholson lived.

It was my intention to park close to his home so that he might see me. There were no other buildings close by. I wanted our meeting to appear coincidental to him.

I turned at a field entrance a hundred metres from the house, got out and stood by the car for a few minutes. If there was anyone in the wooden-clad and dilapidated bungalow, then they could not have missed seeing me.

I waited by the car for a further fifteen minutes, walking back and forth, as though searching for something out on the open water, and making a show of unfolding and then folding a map I'd brought with me. I climbed back into the car, slamming the door.

A few minutes later, a man emerged and stood watching me through a pair of binoculars.

Pretending not to have seen him, I left the car again and walked in the opposite direction, still holding the map, and as close as I could to the low bank which rose above the mud and water below.

The man had a dog on a leash, and as I moved away from my car, I saw that he had approached it and was looking inside. I tried to determine if there was anyone else in the bungalow, but saw nothing. It was midday and the sun cast the interior of the low building into solid shadow. There was an unkempt and cluttered garden to the rear of the building, and at the front open land ran unbounded to the river. A few stunted and twisted thorn trees marked a boundary of sorts, and white stones marked the remains of paths in the overgrown grass.

The world was flat and open here, the land and the water only a few feet above and below each other. I could see Hull clearly to my right, and to the left the low curve of the Spurn peninsula stretched away into the North Sea.

The man by the car finally left it and continued walking towards me.

He wore only shorts and sandals, naked from the waist up. He released the dog from its leash, and the animal immediately ran from side to side ahead of him.

I waited where I stood, looking from the map to the water as he approached me. In my pocket I had the one clear photograph of Peter Nicholson printed by the papers. In it he was holding a commendation awarded to him for having participated in the rescue of a vessel that had lost its engine. He had still been a pilot on the river then and had been given the award along with three other men. The picture had been taken four years ago. He wore his uniform, his cap held beneath his arm. I imagined he himself had given a copy to the papers after the drowning.

In one of the reports, there was a photograph of him standing at the river's edge, holding a pair of binoculars and pointing out over the water. Peter Nicholson, the pose said, was a man of purpose, a man of dependable expertise gained through long experience. He was fifty-two, had lived in Paull or close by all his life, and he was married.

Waiting until he had approached to within twenty yards of me, and as his dog arrived in advance of him, I turned and pretended to see him for the first time. The dog nudged my feet and moved in a close circle around me. I bent down to stroke it.

The man's chest and arms were heavily tanned. He was wiry, and the outline of his breastbone was visible on his chest. He had lost most of his hair, but his chest and forearms were white with it. He wore sunglasses, and as he reached me he raised a hand to shield his eyes and study me.

Just as Simon Fowler's timetable for the day Helen Brooks had drowned seemed too conveniently complete and endlessly verifiable, so there were aspects of Nicholson's own account which, when repeated often enough, seemed equally too complete and worthy of further investigation.

The dog finally left me and returned to him. He took off his glasses and wiped his forehead and eyes with a handkerchief. His shorts were tight at his waist and fell almost to his knees. He wore socks beneath his sandals. His shins were covered in the same white hair, and he looked at least ten years older than he had done on the occasion of his award ceremony.

I went to him.

'Nice day,' I said. 'I didn't see you there.'

'I live here.' He motioned over his shoulder to the bungalow.

'I'm not trespassing, am I?' I said, feigning concern.

He said nothing for a few seconds. 'No, you're not trespassing.' He indicated the map I held. 'You looking for something?'

'Not really. Well, I am, but I don't even know if I'm in the right place.'

'What were you after?'

'You must know the river well,' I said.

'What were you after?'

'There was a young couple drowned somewhere out here about a year ago. Apparently, their boat ran aground and they died trying to get ashore.'

'And your interest in it is what?'

'My cousin went missing about the same time. Nobody had seen him for some time before that, but we heard from a relative that he was living in Hull. I was in the city on business and I promised his mother I'd ask around. He used to enjoy sailing, but he never owned a boat.'

'It was a yacht.'

'A yacht? It said in the papers that no bodies were ever recovered.' I looked back out over the calm and sunlit water. 'It seems hard to believe, looking at it now.'

I expected some response to this, but he said nothing. He was clearly wary of me. He put his glasses back on and continued watching me. I was uncertain how much of what I'd told him he'd believed, and what I might now gain or lose by telling him the truth.

'There were two of them,' he said. 'And, no, the bodies were never found, and that was because people who don't know this river only come out here on days like this and can't imagine it any other way.'

A line of tankers waited in position along the far shore.

'You sound as though you know it well,' I said.

'I was a pilot,' he said. He, too, looked across the water to the waiting vessels.

'A pilot?'

'A Humber pilot. We brought the vessels in and out of the ports and channels, up and down the Hull Roads. I'm retired.'

I could still hear the resentment in his voice and felt encouraged by this.

'There must be people drown out here all the time,' I said.

'There are,' he said. 'And you can drop the act. You've not come looking for anybody you knew. No bodies turned up then, and they're not going to turn up now. I've seen corpses in there wash up almost intact after a month in the water, and I've seen others picked out after only a few days that were unrecognizable.' He looked directly at me as he spoke.

'Are you Peter Nicholson?' I said.

He shook his head at the question. 'You know I am,' he said. 'You went to enough trouble getting out here and attracting my attention.'

I folded up the unwieldy map and stuck it in my belt.

'And if you know who I am, then presumably you also know that you're not even looking in the right place or that—' He stopped, assessing how much more I might already know.

'You were the only witness,' I said.

'Was I? And so that gives you the right to come round after all this time with your stupid questions, does it?'

'I don't understand your hostility,' I said.

'Hostility? Perhaps it's because I'm sick and tired of all the pointing fingers, perhaps that's why I'm so *hostile*.'

'You claim to know why I'm here,' I said, 'and yet you still came out to me.'

'Only to stop you from thinking up some excuse to knock on my door and harass me in my own home.'

'Is your wife at home?'

'My wife? You want to check your facts a bit better. My wife walked out on me a year ago. It's none of your business, but that's what happened. Been coming for years. And now that she's finally done it, I wish she'd done it years earlier, or that I'd had the nerve to tell her to go.'

'I see,' I said.

'I bet you do. Who are you working for? The girl's mother? What a surprise.'

'She wants to know for certain what happened to her daughter.'

'She *knows* for certain what happened. And even if she doesn't know every tiny little detail by now, then that's because it's the sea, and that's how things work in the sea. How much does she really want to know about how somebody drowns? One second they're an inch above the water, the next they're an inch beneath it, and after that they're gone for ever. Look at it. Even on a day like today, how far down do you imagine you can see? A foot? Two? More like two inches. It's as much mud and silt as it is water, and out on Foulholme it's ten times worse. At least here, the water's moving. Out there, it just settles and then occasionally stirs itself around now and then.'

I'd let him go on because talking about the river was clearly what still animated him.

'Has Alison Brooks ever approached you herself?' I asked him.

'During and just after the inquiry, all the time. As though I had more to tell her, as though I hadn't already gone over every tiny detail a hundred times already. Look, I'm sorry for what happened to her daughter, but that's all I was – a witness, and even then I saw little enough. It was dark. The yacht was beached a long way off. All I saw was a vessel where it shouldn't have been. In fact, Foulholme Sands was the *last* place it should have been, especially on that tide and at that time of year. It's all down there in my statement.'

It was the least of what his statement contained.

'Can you think why Alison Brooks might have thought there was more to learn?'

The remark put him back on his guard. 'Why she

accused me of lying, you mean?' he said. 'I'm sick of it. I told her eventually that it would have been better for me if I'd just carried on walking and said nothing to anybody about what I'd seen.'

'Why do *you* think the bodies were never recovered?' The emphasis was another appeal to his vanity.

'Why do *I* think they were never recovered? Because no one going into the water where they were would have stood much chance of being pulled out, that's why. Not without someone being able to get to them from the centre of the channel, and we all know how long it took the lifeboat to arrive.' There was a particularly cold edge to this last remark.

'*You* raised the alarm,' I said.

'I know I did. And thirty minutes later, there they were.'

'And in the meantime, in those thirty minutes, Helen Brooks and whoever was with her tried to save themselves and were lost.'

'See? It's *that* simple. So why don't you go back and tell *her* that and leave me in peace. I've got a busy day ahead of me.'

'Didn't it strike you as strange that the people on the yacht tried to escape from it *before* the lifeboat arrived? Were they in any danger just sitting tight?'

'Perhaps they thought they'd beached on solid land and that they could just climb overboard and walk ashore to carry on their party there.'

'Party?'

'Whatever. Whoever they were, they weren't serious sailors. Like I said, no one who knew the first thing about the river would have been where they were.'

'Perhaps they'd had engine trouble and drifted.'

'It was a yacht. They still had sails.'

'Perhaps things just got out of hand.'

'Tell *her* all this,' he said. 'Not me. I've heard it all too many times before.'

'I assume your wife saw nothing.'

He looked at me for a moment before answering. 'Is that a trick question? It was two miles away. I was out with the dog. I called the emergency services from a farm at Thorney Crofts. She'd have been sat in front of the television like she was every other fucking night of her life.' He regretted the profanity as much as I appreciated it.

'How long were you married?'

'Thirty years. Most of which was a complete waste of time.'

'Do *you* have any idea who the other people on the yacht might have been?' I asked him the question while the sour taste of his departed wife was still in his mouth.

'People? There was just another one.'

'Right. I meant the other one.'

'No you didn't. No – no idea whatsoever.'

'You said in your account that it looked like a man.'

'If that's what I said, then that's what it looked like.'

'But it *could* have been a woman. A woman in waterproofs with the hood up?'

'My impression is that it was a man.'

'And he did nothing to prevent Helen Brooks – you're certain *she* was a woman – from climbing overboard and, presumably, being the first of them to be lost.'

'I only told them what I saw.'

'I know. It's just that you seemed more convinced of some things than of others.'

'What's that supposed to mean?'

'Nothing,' I said. 'I'm just trying to understand what we know for certain and what, so far, everyone's been guessing at.'

' "We" being you and her, presumably.'

'So far.'

The remark made him cautious. I had deliberately avoided all mention of Fowler.

'When did you finally discover who owned the yacht?' I asked him.

'I don't know. The next day, day after.'

'Presumably there would have been some means of identifying the vessel from a distance.'

'Her sails were down. I couldn't see any name at that distance. And even then I wouldn't have known who she belonged to.' He swatted at the small flies which circled us in the heat.

'And there was no distress signal given, no call for help on the radio?'

'Tell me something I don't already know.'

'Did no one think that was strange at the time, especially seeing as how at least one of the people on board was uninjured and moving around?'

'What do you mean?'

'I mean why didn't they fire off a flare or something? You also said in your account that the person sitting at the stern of the yacht appeared to do little to prevent the other one from climbing overboard.'

'I never said anything about them being injured.' He seemed less certain of himself, about precisely what he'd said.

'Perhaps I just assumed it was what you meant. But that would be the implication, wouldn't it? Perhaps it was why Helen Brooks climbed overboard in the first place. Perhaps she was trying to get help. Perhaps that was why she didn't think she could afford to wait until the lifeboat arrived. After all, if they hadn't sent out any distress signals, how would they even know that help was on its way? Perhaps this injury was connected to the reason they'd drifted onto the bank in the first place.'

He doubted most of what I had just suggested – probably as much as I doubted it.

'You could speculate like that all day,' he said.

'And still be no closer to the truth? I know. But perhaps that's where the truth lies. Perhaps it was something as simple and as irrevocable as that, and perhaps if Alison Brooks had been able to convince herself of that at the time of the inquest, then she wouldn't still be worrying at it now, and I wouldn't be out here raking over all this old ground with you.'

'Or you could have done the honest thing to begin with and knocked at my door. I'm not the—'

'What contact did you have with Simon Fowler once the yacht had been identified?' I said, deliberately interrupting him.

'What do you mean, what contact did I have with him?'

'It's a simple enough question. You knew I was going to ask you eventually.'

'Of course I didn't *know*. What's *he* got to do with anything? He wasn't anywhere near. You'll be telling me next that you think *he* was the man on the boat with her.'

It was an impossible suggestion. He was clearly concerned by this unexpected inclusion of Simon Fowler in our conversation.

'Simon Fowler's alibi stands up to the closest scrutiny,' I said.

'Why would he need an alibi?'

'I mean his account of what happened — Helen Brooks taking his yacht and everything.'

'*Has* something new come up?'

'Not that I know of. Well?'

' "Well" what?'

'What contact did you have with Fowler once the yacht had been identified as his? You clearly know the man.'

'I met him once or twice, that's all. During the investigation, at the inquest. She was his girlfriend, that's all. We don't all make bad choices and then sit on our arses doing nothing for thirty years. They had pictures of her; she was a looker.'

'I know. Did he ever come out here?'

'Out here? Simon Fowler?' If the answer had been 'No', he would have said it immediately.

'Perhaps just to see where it happened,' I said. 'Or to see you and thank you personally for all you'd done.'

'He came out once,' he said. 'And like you said, to say thanks for what I'd done.'

'I'm surprised he wasn't as keen as Alison Brooks was — then and now — to find out exactly what happened to Helen.'

'Perhaps he was just more realistic. Perhaps he knew a bit more about the river than she ever did. I knew he wasn't a sailor, not really. He told me he hadn't been able to stop his girlfriend from going out,

81

and that he'd have to live with that fact for the rest of his life. Perhaps if her own mother had known as much about what she was up to, then perhaps *she* might have been able to have done something. I got the impression from the investigation and everything that the girl was practically out of control — spoiled, got what she wanted or else. That sort.'

Most of which would have come from Fowler's testimony.

'Perhaps if her mother had stepped in sooner,' he went on, 'then she wouldn't be trying to make up for her failings now.'

We were distracted by the noisy arrival of a van beside his bungalow. His dog ran back there immediately.

'More visitors?' I said.

'They're late.'

'Who are they?'

'Double-glazing people. Come to do properly what they should have done in the first place, hoping I'd let everything slide until the guarantee was out. They're trying to tell me that the salt air's corroded the fittings. They're bastards, and if they can see a way to cheat you, they will.'

The van drew up at the rear of the bungalow and two men climbed out. They stood for a moment to look at Nicholson standing with me. It seemed a pointless exercise fitting new windows into such a dilapidated structure.

'I'd better get back and keep an eye on them,' he said.

We walked together to my car. He pointed out a track which would take me to a farm lane leading back to the road to Paull.

'Will you call me if anything else occurs to you?' I said. I gave him one of my cards.

'Such as?'

'Perhaps if Alison Brooks tried to get back in touch with you,' I said.

'She'll not be back,' he said. 'Not after all this time. It might take a week or it might take a decade, but eventually everybody who's lost somebody drowned and never recovered comes to terms with the fact.' He paused and looked back over the water as he spoke. 'Either they come to terms with it or it eats away at them and turns them into a different person. And when that happens everybody else stops listening to them anyway.' He tapped a finger to his forehead – but whether to suggest the intuition of the person who knew or the madness of the person who didn't, I couldn't tell.

'You might be right,' I said.

'No "might" about it,' he said.

He left me and walked to where the two men were unloading pieces of equipment from their van. I heard him call to them, one of the men call back, their voices carrying on the warm air.

8

At five, I met Yvonne in the Sandringham bar. She was there before me, waiting alone in the far corner. It was a long, narrow bar, and few people ventured in there by chance. It didn't sell food, and it had a cased noose on the wall which proclaimed itself to be the noose used to hang the last man put to death in Hull Prison. There was no mention of the man's name, or of his crime, or of the date the noose was slipped around his neck. No one who drank in the bar knew if it was genuine or not. The rope looked old, and stiff where it had dried and warped in the tobacco-rich air.

Yvonne saw me enter, drained her glass and came back to the bar, ordering our drinks.

'Busy day?' she said.

'Sunny home?'

'Tomorrow.'

We carried our drinks back to the table. Little natural light penetrated into the Sandringham, even in the middle of summer, and the glass wall-lights were on above us.

'I probably don't want to hear this,' I said.

'Lose the amateur dramatics,' she said. 'I borrowed what was in the file and I put the papers in the folder to keep it looking full simply to avoid having to tell Sunny what I was doing.'

'Meaning it's not agency work?'

She clapped once. 'Meaning it's not agency work.'

'Is someone else interested in Simon Fowler, or are you using the stuff yourself?'

'Why should someone else be interested?' She drank the foam from her glass.

'Who is it?' I asked her. 'Did either Alison or Louise Brooks come to you and Sunny before me? And did Sunny say no and you said yes because—'

'I've never met either of them other than at the inquest and immediately afterwards.'

'It just seemed a bit too much of a coincidence – me wanting the file and you already having rifled through it and taken half of it for yourself.'

'I took out all those pieces which were concerned solely with Fowler's property dealings.'

'Why?'

'Because Simon Fowler owns – and this is a conservative estimate—'

'Meaning you're guessing.'

'Meaning some of us have done our homework properly, and we know that Fowler owns at least a hundred and eighty private houses, nearly all low-quality stock, which he rents out to anyone desperate enough to need them. And high on the list of these desperate people are the growing numbers of asylum-seekers being sent here. Fowler has an arrangement with the city council and with various of the agencies set up here to help them. He gets his money without having to chase it, he gets a steady and dependable influx of tenants, many of them short-term, which suits him because it keeps the rents high, and all he has to worry about is the upkeep – ha ha – of his properties.'

'And this has nothing whatsoever to do with Alison Brooks or what happened to her daughter?'

'Nothing at all. Except, of course, insofar as Simon Fowler is involved.'

'Except insofar as that,' I said. 'You said "we" and "us". Was that a slip for "I" and "me" or is someone else involved in whatever all this is about? Which, incidentally, and despite your breathless recall of a few, possibly spurious, and at best not-all-that-interesting, relevant or unusual facts, you have yet to actually tell me about.'

'I have a friend who works with the asylum-seekers,' she said. 'Some of them have accused Fowler of using threats and violence against them over disputes concerning their tenancies.'

'Accusations levelled against Fowler himself?'

'Against the men who work for him, his agents and contractors.'

'So they might, in fact, be men employed by some-one else entirely – a letting agency, say – and might not even know who Simon Fowler is.'

'If you'd heard some of the allegations—'

'I don't doubt that the allegations exist, or that the people who make them haven't got every right or reason to make them, all *I* need to get straight here is whether or not Simon Fowler is personally involved – if he even *knows* about any of this – and what bearing, if any, this has on my own interest in him.'

'Typical,' she said. 'The poor little rich girl.'

'You're the second person to suggest that to me today.'

She signalled her apology for the remark. 'And what you're thinking now is that the two things must somehow be connected because how could they *not* be,' she said.

'No – but I am prepared to accept that there are those parts of Simon Fowler's very extensive and ever-expanding property empire into which I personally need not go a-wandering in my eternal quest for truth and justice.'

'If I thought there was the slightest possibility of a connection, I'd tell you,' she said. 'I would have told you in the agency.'

'No you wouldn't. That's why you didn't say anything about Fowler to Sunny. You thought he might have opened the file. It's why you followed me outside.'

'I was going to tell you then that part of the file was missing, but Sunny would have heard.'

'Where is it?'

'Somewhere safe.'

'Is this the "we" and the "us" part again?'

She nodded and drained her glass.

I asked her if she'd heard from Sunny during his long weekend in Scunthorpe.

'When he's sober he calls every hour to remind me of whatever it is I should be doing. He leaves me lists of people to contact.'

'And when he's not sober?'

'He just calls to remind me of what he's already told me.'

He loves you, I wanted to tell her. But she knew that already.

'He just feels responsible,' I said.

'Is that what it is – responsibility?'

'He can't say no to these things,' I said.

I went to the bar and bought more drinks.

Looking back at her, she looked lonely in her corner beneath the dim light and the framed noose.

I went back to her.

'If you and Sunny *did* decide to get married,' I said, 'I'd be best man and I'd compose a speech without a single lewd reference or joke at your expense in it.'

'No you wouldn't,' she said. 'That's what you'd tell me, and then you'd do exactly the opposite.'

'I remember when nothing I ever said or did would have embarrassed you.'

She smiled at me and slowly shook her head.

Her phone rang. She checked to see who was calling and then switched it off.

'Are you helping someone compile a list of complaints against Fowler in connection with his asylum-seeker tenants?'

'Something like that.'

'But not something you're doing through the agency?'

'You know what kind of asylum-seeker news sells in this place.'

The phrase most commonly used was 'These People'. As in 'These People' are sponging off the state and are too idle to either find work or even learn the language. As in 'These People' are here for no good reason and ought to be sent back where they belong, wherever that is. As in 'These People' are pushing up the crime rate and making the city-centre streets unsafe at night. There had already been some outbreaks of violence at the end of those summer nights. Everything could be proved or disproved depending on your point of view. Some opinions, however unfounded, were vastly more popular than others. And with each repeated accusation, the chorus of condemnation grew louder.

'Who is it?' I asked her.

'Her name's Irina Kapec. She's a Croat. She has an eight-year-old daughter, and she's been in Hull for three years. She speaks perfect English. Along with French and Italian, and she was once a professor of Literature at Zagreb University.' She spoke quickly, as though I might have been about to challenge everything she said, and when she stopped speaking, she seemed suddenly tired, grateful for my silence.

'How long have you known her?'

'Over two years. She lives only a few minutes' walk from me. I met her through one of the dispersal agencies.'

'I never knew you were involved in anything like that,' I said.

'There's lots of things about me you don't know.'

'No there aren't,' I said, which was true, and which was why hearing her talk about her involvement with the asylum-seekers came as a surprise to me now. 'What's in the file that's so important to you?' I asked her.

'Not much, as it happens. A few old reports from the time when Fowler wasn't afraid to get his own hands dirty, when he had less of a shining reputation to lose. All we ever really wanted was to get everything together, to compile as complete a dossier as possible on him.'

'Is it very profitable for him?'

'A hundred properties, six people in each on average, the Government, via agencies too numerous to mention, paying him a hundred pounds a week for each one of them. It's not exactly *un*profitable.'

'A hundred a week?'

'Something like that. Sometimes more. Rent, community charges, guarantees, something to cover repairs which never get done.'

'Fowler would say he was responding to a humanitarian need.'

'He does. At every opportunity. He houses them, he provides work for them, he—'

'He provides work?'

She shrugged. 'He employs contractors who always need cheap labour, and presumably the cheaper the better.'

The more she told me, the more I realized that her own interest in Fowler now had nothing to do with those events of fifteen months earlier.

'I'm sorry for the remark about Helen Brooks,' she said.

'I think her mother had a somewhat distorted view of her,' I said.

'What else would you expect?' Her own two teenage sons lived away from home – one with his father, and the other at university, where he was studying politics.

She felt their absence keenly; it was why she worked such long hours at the agency. Her son at university had left home two years earlier and returned to Hull only two or three times a year. Her younger boy she had lost following a court case in which the boy's father had proved that she could not provide a suitable or stable environment in which to raise and care for him. Her business had just collapsed; she was a hundred thousand pounds in debt and her home had recently been repossessed. The boy's father had taken advantage of all these things to press his claim.

I told her about my visit from Louise Brooks.

'Sounds a real charmer,' she said, responding more to my tone than to what I said. 'You're a smart man,' she said. 'I'm sure you won't let yourself get caught between them, and that you won't believe one of their painted pictures over the other.'

'Does Sunny know about Irina Kapec?' I said.

'I once suggested a few articles looking into the actual backgrounds of some of "These People", seeing where they came from, why they were in Hull, what they had sacrificed to get there, who and what they had lost. Make them more understandable, less of a threat, that kind of thing.'

'And?'

'And he agreed. Great idea in principle.'

'Meaning nobody else was interested?'

'Certainly none of the local rags, and all of the Nationals already had their own angles on the "problem". I think we might even have lost a bit of other business – advertisers – as a consequence of even suggesting the articles. I once heard Sunny on the phone, talking to an editor who told him how little he thought of the idea, and who then went on to tell Sunny what he thought of *him* for having come up with it. Bread, buttered, and sides and all that.'

'What did Sunny say?'

'For a start, he never let on that the idea hadn't been his to begin with, and then he told the man what a small-minded, vicious little moron he really was. Those were his exact words. There were others, but I was outside on the landing, waiting until he'd finished before going back in.'

'What did he say to you?'

'Nothing. I asked him what all the shouting had been about, and he said one of our advertisers was trying to force his rates down. I never let on to him that I'd overheard.'

'You just quietly dropped the idea as far as the agency was concerned.'

'Something like that. It embarrassed Sunny to be spoken to like that by someone he'd known for ten years. I won't ever do that to him again.'

We sat together for a further hour. The bar emptied and then filled again. A man sitting, barely moving, on a stool by the pumps became almost invisible.

When it was time for us to leave I asked her if she would introduce me to Irina Kapec.

'Because you want to know what Fowler is really like before you pluck up the courage to go and see him by yourself?'

'I'm braver than I look,' I said.

'Which is probably a good thing,' she said.

She was half-drunk, but the half of her that was sober still saw everything as clearly as she needed to see it. And she knew as well as I did about those coincidences, about all those unlikely and unpromising connections which kept things moving.

9

Alison Brooks called me on my mobile the next morning. I'd just arrived at Humber Street and was on my way back out again. I'd called the agency earlier, but there was no one there.

'Louise told me she'd been to see you,' she said. 'I didn't want her to get involved in any of this.'

We both knew how unlikely that was.

'She came back here to be with you,' I said.

'Thank you for that reminder, Mr Rivers. I never asked her to. I want her to live her own life, not to keep getting bogged down in all this. When I'm gone, she'll be the only one of us left. Two husbands, two daughters.'

'She asked me to keep her up to date on everything I uncovered,' I said.

'She thinks she's protecting me.'

'I know,' I said. 'But *you're* my client. Tell me what *you* want.'

There was a pause. 'She'll find out anyway,' she said. 'Anything you can tell me, you can tell her.'

I asked her if she knew Helen had started sailing on the river on Fowler's yacht.

'He used to entertain on it. Business associates. Nothing too grand. She'd never done anything like it before. But she always wanted to be different, so I assumed that's what it was to her – a way of being different. Louise's father was a trawlerman, so Helen became a yachtswoman. Of sorts. She might have done it for all the wrong reasons, but it made a kind of sense.'

'But she wouldn't have been able to handle it alone?' I said.

'I doubt it. I think the socializing and what the yacht represented were more important to her. I daresay Louise has already told you things about Helen that perhaps I alone had trouble coming to terms with.'

'Why didn't you tell me about Fowler and the florists?' I asked her.

I left Humber Street and walked across the Dock Basin Bridge, from where I could look out over the river.

'I didn't want you to confuse the two things.'

'Is that what *you* did?'

'I couldn't help it. But I didn't want you to think that all this was me just trying to get my revenge on Fowler for what happened then. The business with the shops was a long time ago, four years.'

'It must still have hurt you to discover that your daughter was associated with the man.'

'What does that mean – "associated with"? I know what she was to him, Mr Rivers – at least I know what

95

she fooled herself into *believing* she was to him. And if you're about to suggest to me that she might have even thrown herself at him knowing exactly who he was and what *I* thought of him, then I won't deny the possibility of that, either.'

'I just need to be certain that we're all starting from the same point, that's all,' I said.

'Louise will have told you that she and her sister weren't particularly close. I know they were half-sisters, but that was never how *I* thought of them – never how I allowed them to think of themselves – and they were never treated any differently, whatever Louise might believe. Their upbringings were different, that's all. Louise sometimes looks back with too fond an eye to those early days.'

'She suggested you transferred your affection to Helen, that Helen was spoiled, indulged.'

'That was her father more than me. My business was thriving by then; I could afford to indulge her. I would have done exactly the same for Louise if I'd been able to. She knows that. She was the only friend I had in the world during the years after her own father's death.'

I heard the change in her voice and was reminded of her illness.

'Do you think Louise might have her own reasons for wanting Fowler implicated in all this again?' I said.

'Such as?'

'I don't know. I'd hate to think that she sees a connection between what happened to Helen and what's happened to you since then.'

'I'd be lying if I told you she hadn't suggested something of the sort to me. But it's not what she truly believes. What's happening to me now would be happening to me with or without Simon Fowler. She's an intelligent woman. If she did want there to be a connection, then she wouldn't remain convinced of it for long. Apart from which, if it wasn't for what's happening to me now, I would never have decided once and for all to try and find out what really happened to Helen.' She cleared her throat. 'Have you contacted him yet?'

'No,' I said. 'Do you think it likely that Louise would have approached me with the same request?'

'And told you to keep it from me?'

'Yes.'

She considered this. 'It's possible, but she's respected my wishes so far. She'd certainly have come to you – or someone like you – after I was dead.'

'Because she'd acquired another good reason for finding out?' Perhaps her only reason.

I left the waterfront and walked towards Queen Street in the direction of the Guildhall.

She avoided answering the question. 'Do what you have to do, Mr Rivers,' she said. 'But, please, don't do anything on the grounds that you'll be protecting *me* from any unpleasant truths, that you'll be sparing *my* feelings. It's far too late for any of that. Do what you have to do because it will get you to the truth of the matter, and for no other reason. And even if the truth turns out to be hardly any more than we already know, then still do it.' She asked me if there was anything else I needed to know before I attempted to see Simon Fowler.

'How long have you known John Maxwell?' I said. The question surprised her and she paused before answering. 'Forty years, longer,' she said eventually.

'And he told you to contact me.'

'I didn't even know he'd left Hull. I heard his wife died, but that's all. I almost went to her funeral, but thought it best to stay away.'

'Was there something between you?'

'We were close before he got married.'

'And afterwards?'

'There were one or two complications, and after a while it was just best for me to stay away. I used to see him occasionally, by accident, chance, and I always felt some affection for him. You won't believe how quickly forty years can pass. I knew he'd left the force and set up his own business. When someone told me he'd gone, I remembered where he'd been raised and rang directory inquiries. You could ask him all this. When the news of Helen's drowning was in the papers, he wrote to me. He gave me his address, but I never wrote back, not then. Perhaps I should have done. Far too late now, of course. He told me you were the only man he'd trust to do what I wanted.'

'He called me,' I said.

'To tell you?'

'I think that was his intention, but he never got round to it.'

'I told him I'd like to see him again, for old times' sake, but he said it was the worst reason in the world for wanting to see someone.'

'Have you spoken to him since?'

'I think about ringing him every day.'

I arrived at the Guildhall.

'Simon Fowler will tell me you're a vindictive old woman, perhaps a vindictive old woman with a vindictive, revenge-seeking daughter, out to stir up trouble for him.'

'I'm sure he will, and I'm sure it's something you've already given consideration to. Simon Fowler is a powerful man with friends in high places. What Simon Fowler wants, Simon Fowler usually gets. But I'm equally certain that you've already heard things about Simon Fowler – things that neither Louise nor I have told you – that lead you to believe there's another side to him, and one worthy of your efforts. I'm not flattering you, Mr Rivers; I'm just doing what you want me to do. You can see how my options were reduced once John Maxwell told me that you were the only man he trusted to help me.'

'Call him,' I said. 'Let him know what's happening.'

'Perhaps I will,' she said, and hung up.

I called the agency again, but there was still no reply.

In the Guildhall, a room had been given over to an exhibition displaying graphics and models of the various projected city-centre developments. These ranged from the massive Ferensway project – almost a decade of work and a complete rebuilding of that part of the city – to the rejuvenation of the Old Town and the lanes and alleyways along the River Hull between the new aquarium and the Scott Street Bridge; to the redevelopment of individual buildings throughout the city centre. The Dock and Quay developments were shown, along with their projected extensions; the work about to start around the marinas and Kingston Wharf; and the expansion of the new 'villages' south of Garrison Road and Island Quay.

Looking at some of the plans, there seemed to be

more of the city centre undergoing change than was staying the same.

Display boards around the room listed the developers and agencies involved in this coming transformation. Piles of neatly arranged brochures lay along a table at the rear of the room. Above one of the models was an enlarged photograph of a crowd of local dignitaries, all of them wearing hard hats, gathered around the mayor, who was pretending to dig into the ground with a shining silver spade. All the men wore grey or blue suits, and everyone was smiling.

Everyone was also identified in a key along the lower edge of the photo. I saw Fowler's name and found him in the picture, standing at the front of the group. He was the shortest of all the men, and he held rather than wore his helmet. His features were indistinct. He stood beside one of the two women in the picture. He was listed as the chairman of Fowler Holdings and as either a major shareholder or board-member of several other companies.

I gathered up a collection of the brochures. Several leasing agencies and housing associations were also listed as participating in all these changes.

I looked for Humber Street in the plans and models, and saw that once again it had been marked for outline development, although nothing any more specific had yet been drawn up or planned. The tenants who had already lived with these threats and promises for a quarter of a century remained convinced that the changes would never come. Old plans which had come to nothing ten years ago were displayed again with just as little expectation of anything happening in the future. Everywhere else everything changed, but not along the charmed and run-down length of Humber Street.

A bored guard stood in the entrance as I emerged.

'Seen what you want to see?' he asked me.

I showed him the brochures I'd collected. 'You have to move forward,' I told him. 'You need to have a vision of the future.'

'You need money,' he said. He was perhaps twenty or twenty-one, and his day consisted of standing around, directing people, answering the same four or five queries over and over, and trying to look as though his badly fitting uniform meant something to him.

'"Men without Vision might as well be blind",' I said to him, quoting from the front of one of the brochures. 'William Wilberforce.'

'If you say so,' he said.

Back at Humber Street I read the brochures in closer detail. I made two lists – one of all the private companies involved, and one of all the publicly funded and Government agencies concerned.

I called the number for Fowler Holdings, and was presented with an electronic list, which ended with the possibility of speaking to someone. After a minute, a woman apologized for having kept me waiting and then asked how she might help me.

When I said that I wanted to speak directly to Simon Fowler, she told me immediately that that was impossible, but that if I could possibly tell her the reason for my call – its connection to a particular project – then she would do her best to communicate this to Mr Fowler.

'I don't want to waste your time,' I said. 'I need to

101

talk to Mr Fowler directly and personally. My name is Leo Rivers and I would like to talk to him in connection with the death, fifteen months ago, of Helen Brooks.' I gave her my number. She seemed shocked by what I'd said, as though, in that world of ungrammatical and softly spoken evasion, any form of directness was a threat.

'I can only communicate your desire to speak to Mr Fowler to one of his personal assistants,' she said.

'I'd appreciate that very much,' I said. I repeated my name and number for her, thanked her and hung up.

Then I dialled the numbers given for those other companies in which Fowler had some involvement and went through exactly the same routine.

After an hour, I'd sent nine messages to Simon Fowler, and if the first of them he received felt to him like an unwelcome but gentle jab in the chest, then the ninth would certainly feel like something a little more forceful.

I knew Alison Brooks had contacted him immediately after the coroner's inquest, but I was still uncertain how conscious he had been of her grievances in the time since then. It was unlikely that she would have avoided all contact with him, but equally unlikely, following that first brief inquiry, that he would have felt either intimidated or threatened by her scattered accusations.

I considered it equally unlikely that Louise Brooks hadn't also tried to contact him since her return to the city, and that she may have done this without the blessing or knowledge of her mother.

These were all peripheral considerations.

My nine messages had already started their journeys towards Simon Fowler.

As I considered what kind of man he was, the phone rang. My immediate reaction was that it was the first of my requests being answered.

But it wasn't; it was Sunny.

'How was Scunthorpe?' I asked him.

'Use your imagination,' he said. 'You called here earlier.'

'I saw Yvonne,' I said.

'Is this still to do with Simon Fowler? Don't tell me – you got the file home and found it stuffed full of newspapers because she'd taken the contents to show one of her new friends.'

'She thinks you don't know.'

'I know she does. I know everything.'

'She overheard you on the phone when her asylum-seeker articles were being turned down.'

'Ah. I didn't know *that*. Is that why she agreed to drop the idea – to spare my feelings?'

'And to stop you using abusive language on the phone.'

'It wasn't a bad idea, but—'

'Its time wasn't right?'

'Time, place, focus, allegedly misguided sympathies.'

'To say nothing of upsetting your advertisers.'

He let the remark pass. I hadn't intended it to sound so critical of him.

'So you already know about Fowler's arrangement with the city council, leasing to the asylum-seekers they've been landed with by our caring, sharing Government. What else have you found out about him?'

'Nothing yet. I left a message asking him to call me.'

He considered this. 'And *if* that happens?' The tone of his voice had changed.

'What are you telling me?' I asked him.

'Not over the phone.'

'You always say that as though you believed someone was listening in.'

'And you know for certain that they aren't, do you?'

'Absolutely,' I said.

'I'll get back to you,' he said, and hung up.

I waited in my office for the rest of the day, but there was no call from Simon Fowler.

Louise Brooks called and asked if we might meet. She suggested dinner at a nearby restaurant the following evening. She also told me she'd found photos of Helen and Fowler together and that she wanted me to see them. I asked her what else she still possessed of her sister's, and after a moment's hesitation she told me she had everything.

'Not that it's much,' she said. 'Just her stuff from the university, the few bits and pieces from the house where she was living with other students when she met Fowler. There are a dozen or so boxes. Clothes, her cameras, bits and pieces of equipment. It's like—' She stopped abruptly.

'It's like what?'

'I was going to say that it's like one life ended and another began,' she said absently. 'She changed, that's all.'

'It was what she wanted,' I said. 'No one forced her.'

She was about to refute this, but checked herself. Something sounded in my ear and she told me she was being paged. She told me she was looking forward to seeing me, and went.

10

The man in charge of the perfunctory investigation into Helen Brooks's disappearance fifteen months ago was Detective Sergeant Andrew Brownlow. His name had appeared in the reports both Sunny and Alison Brooks had given me. He'd appeared as the police witness at the inquest.

I called him, told him who I was and what I was doing, and asked him if he'd see me. At first, he was reluctant, saying that, technically, the case remained open for as long as the coroner's own open verdict remained. He asked me if I had any new evidence to give him and I told him I hadn't, but that I wanted to make sure that his own reading of the events of that night tallied with everyone else's.

I offered to meet him closer to Tower Grange, where he was based, but he said that he was in the city all morning and that he'd come to me.

He arrived soon afterwards and made it immediately

clear to me that he was there unofficially. He said he didn't believe that I would uncover anything new regarding Helen Brooks's death, and that he would soon find out if anything I did discover was withheld from him. I let the contradictory remark pass.

He paced from one side of the room to the other and then came back to me where I sat.

'Fire away,' he said.

'What did you know about Simon Fowler before it transpired that it was *his* yacht and *his* girlfriend involved?'

He considered this before answering. 'That's still the unofficial line, is it – that she was his *girlfriend*?'

'Not necessarily. But it suited him at the time to let everyone believe that's what she was. It gave him an excuse for all those crocodile tears and heartfelt pleas to be left alone. I don't remember you or anyone else on the force saying anything to shatter the illusion.'

'Such as? Tell her sick mother that, in all likelihood, her daughter was probably no better than a common prostitute, and that Fowler was using her just as he used all his other women *associates*?'

'Of which there were many?'

He shrugged. 'To begin with.'

'Until he started getting a taste for respectability, you mean?'

'Something like that.'

'You also missed out the bit about her drug use,' I said.

'Pure speculation.'

'Because without the body nothing could be proved?'

'Ditto.'

'So, again, you were only acting in the best interests of the mother?'

'You'll be telling me next that *she* had no idea of what her precious daughter was up to.'

'I think she probably knew all along,' I said.

He clicked his lips and offered me a cigarette. 'It still wasn't the time or the place to rake it all up and feed it to the press,' he said.

'Until you were able to do so with some certainty and conviction when the two bodies finally showed up.'

He laughed coldly. 'Which everyone else involved kept insisting would soon happen. Most do, apparently. Ask the lifeboatmen; they'd know better about it.'

'Or Peter Nicholson?' I said.

'Who?'

'The man who raised the alarm. You interviewed him the next day.'

'Oh, him. And?'

'Nothing,' I said. 'I'm just saying – he was an expert on the river, its channels, tides, all that nautical stuff.'

He closed his eyes for a second. 'He was a pilot.'

'Ex-pilot.'

'Whatever. I remember him. A bit full of himself. He probably only told me what he'd already told the men the previous night. I only found out what had happened when I came on duty that morning.'

By which time it was already the tragic and wholly understandable accident it had remained ever since.

'Simon Fowler,' I said, wondering if he had deliberately diverted me from the man.

'I know what you're going to say,' he said. 'And, yes, we more or less knew about *him* from the start, from when he first arrived, and as whatever bits and pieces of what he'd been involved in down there followed him up here.'

'None of which stuck to him?'

'Not as far as we knew. He'd been here over two years before the girl died. He'd kept his hands clean. It did strike some of us as a bit of a coincidence – him being who he was and then it being his yacht and everything, but the more you think about it, the less sense it makes. Two years spent cleaning yourself up and turning yourself into one of Hull's worthies, and then that. Whatever happened that night – and whatever *you* might know that you're not telling me – it still made no sense for him to be so suspiciously or even so conspicuously involved like he afterwards became.'

'Except he wasn't involved, was he?'

'Not—'

'Not in the eyes of the law?'

'We got no complaints from the coroner. We kept Alison Brooks informed of everything we were doing on her behalf. And if you want the unofficial truth of it, yes, I for one was disappointed that everything was left hanging like it was.'

'Did you have *any* suspicions of your own?'

He fanned himself with one of the brochures on the desk. 'Not really. And certainly nothing that I would have repeated at the inquest or so that Alison Brooks would get to hear.'

'But?'

'But I knew that *something* had happened.'

'And when the bodies turned up, you'd have a better idea of what?'

'Something like that. I didn't like the man, still don't. Perhaps it was just that simple.'

'Any specific reason?'

'Just the way he was. Buying himself into things. He was an arrogant little fucker – there, I've said it, and you can imagine what that would have sounded like if I'd said it at the time.' He stopped fanning himself, looked more closely at the brochure and then put it down without remarking on it.

'Were you under pressure to get things done quickly?' I asked him.

'No more than usual. It was last April, remember.'

'What do you mean?'

'We'd just had three hundred new asylum-seekers delivered to us, some of whom weren't exactly keen to be here. They were mostly Kurds, from Turkey, Iran and Iraq. They certainly weren't from Kurdistan, because Kurdistan had long since ceased to exist.'

'And they found themselves living side by side and weren't able to get on?'

He laughed at the euphemism. 'Something like that. The small private landlords had no idea. The council always did the best they could with the few they housed directly, but the other landlords didn't seem to give a toss who they put next door to each other.'

'Fowler included?'

'He wasn't the only one. And they all pleaded ignorance, saying that so many new arrivals were stretching them to the limit. Privately, of course, they were all buying up whatever they could get their hands on and refitting it to take advantage of the windfall.'

'Are you suggesting that all this might in some way have been connected to what happened on the river at the same time?'

'You're not listening to me,' he said. 'I'm saying it put pressure on *us* to keep things under control. We had our work cut out for the best part of that summer.'

'So no one on the force would argue against the open verdict delivered on Helen Brooks and whoever was with her.'

'It was one less thing to worry about. Two years earlier I'd been in charge of an investigation into the deaths of two small girls who'd disappeared. One minute they were on the foreshore near Stone Creek, the next they'd vanished. Seven weeks it took for them to wash up. Fifty yards from where they'd been lost. I'm telling you – given the choice of seeing her daughter looking like either of those girls or—' He stopped talking, overtaken by the memory. 'I'd only just arrived here. It was one of my first jobs. There have been one or two others since.'

'But you'd still have been happier if the bodies *had* turned up?'

'Of course. I remember one of the lifeboatmen saying that the chances were good. He couldn't believe that at least *one* of them wouldn't show up. The real problem then was that there was never any dependable time limit on that happening. Which was why all the coroner could do was return his open verdict.'

'Would that be changed if more evidence came to light?' I asked him.

He looked at me, assessing what I might be about to reveal to him. 'Such as?'

'Such as discrepancies in the accounts of what happened.'

He laughed again. 'That's the whole point. We don't *know* what happened. Only what people *think* they saw or *think* happened on the night. It was late, it was dark, it was a dangerous place to be. And if you're going to try and convince me that all that sounds just a little too convenient, then you're right. But I come back to my original point – why, if Fowler was involved in some way, would everything be made such public knowledge? If he wanted rid of Helen Brooks – for whatever reason – then there were lots of other, considerably less obvious ways of going about it. I can think of one right now.'

He was referring to what Louise Brooks had already suggested to me – that Fowler provided her sister with the drugs she used.

'Did any of this get mentioned at the time?' I asked him.

'It got speculated upon, yes.'

'Only not in front of the coroner?'

'No. They play to very specific rules. Without the bodies, anything we'd attempted to introduce would have been inadmissible. All that would have come later. It might even have jeopardized what little we did have to go on. At least this way – the open verdict and everything – things are left where they can be picked up again. Which, I assume, is where you come in.'

'How likely is that?'

'Without the bodies, practically nil. Probably worse than practically nil. Believe me, whatever Alison Brooks wants from you now, you might not be doing her any great favours by bringing all this back out into the open.'

'Because the police might appear not to have been as thorough as they should have been?'

'No, not because of that – because this time round, and now that he's over all his grief and wailing in public, Fowler might decide to get a little more pro-active. I take it that's what this little get-together is all about – him, and not Alison Brooks or her dead daughter.'

I conceded this in silence.

'Then you're on a fool's errand, Mr Rivers,' he said.

'Who would have the authority to reopen the case?' I asked him.

'Not me, that's for sure. Is that what you're banking on – turning something up that gets *us* interested again?'

I shrugged.

'It won't happen. Fowler will say what he said after the inquest last time – that he was being harassed with no just cause.'

'And whereas last time he was prepared to let the accusations pass because both he and the two women were mourning the loss of Helen, this time he might not be so blinded by his tears?'

'I'm glad you understand that as well as I do.'

'And that if I'm already withholding something from you, it might not be any good as evidence if I don't reveal it to you until later, until it suits *me* to do so?'

'I seriously doubt that you could come up with anything that would make any difference at any time.'

He looked at his watch and said he had to leave.

'I appreciate you telling me everything you just told me,' I said.

'Only because it confirms everything you already knew about the inquiry and our involvement,' he said. He gave me his card. 'For when you turn up the bodies.'

'Or anything else?'

He pretended to think about this. 'No – just the bodies.'

11

The woman sitting beside Yvonne watched me closely from the moment I entered the bar until I sat opposite them. I had arranged with Yvonne to meet the pair of them close to where she lived in the Avenues to collect the missing material from the file.

The bar was usually popular with students, but it was summer and most of them were away. It was mid-afternoon and there were few other drinkers. An old couple sat and watched a silent horse race on a high television. The sunlight thickened the smoke rising from their cigarettes. There was a second room behind the bar and the voices of men playing pool filtered through.

I collected more drinks and sat with them.

'This is Irina Kapec,' Yvonne said. She spelled the name for me.

Irina Kapec held out her hand to me. She remained suspicious of me and did nothing to disguise this. She drank water. She took the slice of lemon from the glass I put in front of her and ate it.

I asked Yvonne if she had the press cuttings with her.

She motioned to the bag beneath the table. Another stood beside Irina Kapec, and she frequently reached down to quickly touch this to ensure that it was still there.

'I'm pleased to meet you.' I spoke slowly and clearly.

Irina Kapec looked at Yvonne as though she did not understand me.

Yvonne spoke in the same slow and exaggerated manner to me. 'Irina, she speaka the perfect English. In facto, she speaka the English better than you.'

Irina Kapec smiled at me.

I apologized.

'It's Yvonne who should apologize,' she said.

'To him?' Yvonne said. 'He'll have to be on his knees first.'

'I usually am where you're concerned,' I said. 'Sunny's back.'

'I know. He told me you'd called.'

I wondered how much else she knew about what he knew, and how much of what neither of them revealed of these shared understandings was all a part of the unspoken and perfectly understood intimacy between them. She watched me for a moment, perhaps guessing at my own uncertain conjectures.

Sensing this slight tension between us, Irina said, 'Yvonne tells me you're investigating Simon Fowler and his affairs.'

'I'm looking into the circumstances surrounding the accidental death of someone who was connected to

115

him. I haven't even met the man yet. I don't want to mislead you into thinking he's the sole focus of my inquiry. As far as I'm currently concerned, Simon Fowler exists only insofar as he was associated with Helen Brooks when she died.'

'And the rest,' Yvonne said.

'I'm not questioning your motives, Mr Rivers,' Irina Kapec said. 'But when I learned from Yvonne that you, too, were involved with Simon Fowler . . .'

'*I* persuaded her to see you,' Yvonne said. Her eyes remained fixed on me as Irina spoke.

'I do understand that a man like Simon Fowler has many interests,' Irina said. 'And that wherever one might look, so he might appear.'

'That's a very convoluted and all-inclusive remark to make for someone who speaks perfect English,' I said.

She smiled at me again.

'I won't lie to you,' she said. 'I won't deny that I have no sympathy for Mr Fowler – quite the opposite, in fact – and I won't pretend that I don't have my own agenda where he and his unfair property dealings are concerned.'

'No one else says they're unfair,' I said, hoping to provoke her into saying more.

'Anyone you care to speak to will tell you the same.'

'Depending on who that is?'

'Of course.'

'The implication being that, whatever discoveries I might make, whatever wrongdoing on the part of Simon Fowler *I* might bring to light, then those revelations might also be of some interest to you?'

'Of course. And the more you know about Simon

Fowler to begin with, then the more ways you might have of approaching him.'

It was something I'd already considered when agreeing to meet her. We'd circled each other and come back to our starting point.

'And, unlike you, I myself *have* met Mr Fowler. On several occasions. I've met him alone, and I've met him in the presence of his agents, his *employees* – never forget that that is what they are – and I have met him on several public occasions. If you ask Mr Fowler, he will go to great lengths to avoid calling me a thorn in his side. But that is what I am. I daresay there are also several councillors who feel the same about me.'

'That's a lot of sides for one thorn,' I said.

'Simon Fowler once referred to me as his "worthy adversary" when talking of me to a local reporter about the substandard housing in which he was accommodating new arrivals. He said he was pleased to have someone looking out for the rights of these unfortunate people, that my concerns were his concerns. And all the time he was putting people into cold, damp housing. Houses unsuitable for small children and babies. Houses unsafe in their electrical wiring and gas supplies.'

'I daresay the asylum-seekers aren't the only people who live like that,' I said again, knowing how provocative the remark would sound.

'Of course they aren't. And those other people should stand up for their rights, too. Simon Fowler owns almost two hundred properties. Half of them are rented out to private tenants. My interest is in my fellow countrymen and -women. There are few other English speakers among them. Most have been

117

through a terrible ordeal. That is why they are here. I refuse to see them abused and intimidated any further by men like Fowler, who never once—' She glanced at Yvonne and stopped talking. 'I'm sorry, Mr Rivers. You do not deserve my tirade.'

'Tirades are his speciality,' Yvonne said.

'Can you be more specific about Fowler's properties?' I said to Irina. In the Guildhall, the charts and models showed only the most prestigious or prominent of his current holdings and developments.

Irina reached beneath the table and took a large, folded sheet from her bag. She looked around us as she laid it on the table. The old couple remained silently watching the racing.

'I asked her to make you a copy,' Yvonne said. 'You never know . . .'

Irina unfolded the paper to reveal four taped-together sheets showing a map of Hull, upon which a scatter of coloured dots had been made.

'Simon Fowler owns all this?' I said.

'These are the ones we know about for certain,' Yvonne said. 'The yellow ones are the properties let to asylum-seekers. The red ones he lets elsewhere and then quickly converts them for asylum-seeker use when the need arises.'

'All of which you can prove beyond all reasonable doubt.'

'We can also prove that he intimidates and threatens those tenants handed to him on a plate by the council. I have the testimony of dozens of people,' Irina said.

'Told to you?'

'Does that make it any less valid?' she said.

'No, but it might make it unproven or unverifiable.

118

It might make it little better than hearsay. It might give someone else – Simon Fowler or his lawyers, for instance – cause to say that it's all a matter of inter-pretation, and that some people—'

'Some people what? Some people deserve less than others and should keep their mouths shut and just be grateful for what they're given because they've only been given it under sufferance? Is that what?'

'I was going to say that some people might say that Simon Fowler had the chance not to get involved in any way whatsoever. Some people might say he was doing the city council a big favour.'

'They do,' she said. 'And usually it's the council members themselves patting him on the back and offering up their thanks.'

'The same men who'd allowed their own housing stock to become so dilapidated that when they were called upon to provide it for the asylum-seekers, they were found wanting,' Yvonne said.

'And who knew what hostility this allocation would cause among those of their own tenants already suffer-ing from years of neglect,' Irina said. 'We're a long way from Westminster and the European Court of Human Rights, Mr Rivers.'

'Was that another tirade?' I asked her.

'That was nothing,' Yvonne said.

'What are the blue dots?' I asked Irina, drawing her attention back to the map, and still uncertain of its true value, if any, to me.

'Properties Fowler appears to keep empty.'

'For any reason?'

'Perhaps because even he knows they're beyond redemption. Or perhaps because he knows that the areas in which they stand are earmarked for demolition and redevelopment. You'd understand better if you saw some of them.'

The majority of these blue dots were scattered around the edges of the city centre, some between the dual carriageway along the river and Anlaby Road, some along Holderness Road to the east; and a few, I saw, scattered along Spring Bank on either side of the agency, and reaching west towards the bar in which we sat.

'Fowler buys cheaply,' Yvonne said. 'He's bought most of these properties in the past three years. He began the day he arrived. He bought from other land-lords and owners who'd already squeezed the tenancies dry, and who'd done nothing themselves to the properties for years. No one else was going to buy them or spend the money needed to bring them up to all the new safety standards. I imagine most of the original owners snatched Fowler's hand off when he waved his money at them.'

'And is that what you think the council did when he made his offer to them?'

'You tell me. An additional bonus of that particular little arrangement to Fowler, of course, was that the council itself went on to undertake or pay for the most urgent of the repairs needed to make the properties habitable.'

'Presumably on the grounds that it would be cheaper than doing it to their own run-down properties.'

'And without antagonizing their own long-suffering tenants.'

I studied the map more closely. Fowler appeared to

have acquired property wherever it had become available to him. I searched the area around Humber Street and saw the coloured dots there, too.

'He probably doesn't even know what he owns,' I said.

'Yeah, right,' Yvonne said. She left us and went to the bar.

'I understand that all this must be far beyond the scope of your own interest in Simon Fowler,' Irina said to me. 'But when Yvonne mentioned his name in connection with your work, I felt it was important that you should at least have a realistic understanding of the man you were dealing with. My daughter and I lived in one of his properties for six months. Until he decided he wanted it vacating and he wanted us out.'

'What did he do?'

'It doesn't matter what he did. Although *he*, of course, did nothing but express his surprise and regret when I told him what others were doing on his behalf.'

'How old is your daughter?'

'Rosemary. She's eight. My husband was killed and we were forced to leave our home. Believe me, I am not here by choice.'

Yvonne returned and she stopped talking.

It concerned Irina to keep the map on the table, and so Yvonne refolded it and slid it into the folder of cuttings.

'What do you expect me to do with it?' I asked her.

'I don't expect you to do anything with it,' Yvonne said. 'Or perhaps you could roll it up and then stick it in Fowler's eye when you finally see him.'

'You're being unfair,' Irina told her.

'It's what he understands,' Yvonne said.

I'd disappointed her, but she, too, could not have been convinced that I would so readily acknowledge any real connection between my inquiry into Helen Brooks's death and her own interest in Fowler as part of Irina's campaign for fair treatment for asylum-seekers.

'Tell me about the girl who drowned,' Irina asked me after a few seconds of awkward silence.

I told her in outline what I knew.

'And was she one of Fowler's *girls*?' she said when I'd finished.

'Too many people have suggested the same to me for her to have been anything else,' I said.

'I only ask because one of Fowler's cronies once approached some women I know and suggested that they too might like to work for him, to attend a few functions he was organizing. They were offered money, new clothes.'

'And did they accept?'

She hesitated before answering. 'Some did. This was eighteen months, two years ago.'

'And since?'

She shook her head. 'Not that I'm aware. Although, of course, there are those who no longer confide in me, who no longer come to me for assistance now that they're making their own way in the world again.'

'Were the women who took him up on his offer ever coerced against their will to do anything?'

Again she shook her head. 'It was never my intention to tell you any of this simply to prejudice you against Simon Fowler,' she said.

'Everyone I mention his name to does the same,' I told her. 'I was told that Fowler and his contractors might also be exploiting people as cheap labourers.'

'They do. A lot of people do.'

'Do you know anyone personally who works for Fowler in that capacity?'

'I can ask around,' she said, meaning she already knew, but was unwilling to tell me until she trusted me.

'It might be of some use to me,' I said.

'Perhaps you could employ Irina as your interpreter,' Yvonne suggested.

'Few of them bother to learn English,' Irina said. 'They're like me – always going home tomorrow and never coming back.'

'They'd be labourers,' Yvonne said. 'What do you think they'd know about Fowler?'

'I don't know,' I admitted. '*You're* the one insisting everything's connected to everything else.'

She slapped the folder into my lap. Our meeting was over.

I asked her if she was going back to the agency.

'Probably,' she said. 'Catch up with all the exciting things that have been happening in Scunthorpe.'

Irina was the first to stand. She held out her hand and thanked me for having listened to her.

'I hope the girl's death *was* an accident,' she said.

'Me, too,' I said.

Outside, we parted and they walked away together in the direction of Yvonne's home.

12

Upon my return to Humber Street there was a message waiting for me from Louise Brooks to say that she'd booked a table at a restaurant other than the one she'd mentioned earlier. There was still no return call from Simon Fowler.

I called directory inquiries for a number for Peter Nicholson, but was told he was ex-directory and that no number was listed.

'Is that the same thing?' I asked the operator.

I heard her working at her keyboard.

'The number was listed and then Mr Nicholson asked for it to be removed.'

'Do you know how long ago?'

'I'm not at liberty to say,' she said. 'Our records indicate only that the request was made some time within the past twelve months.'

'So the number might still be listed in an old directory?'

It was a possibility, she said.

I thanked her and hung up. I added finding the number to my growing list of things to do.

I unfolded the map Irina Kapec had given me. I knew what a precious thing it was to her, but was still not certain where its true value lay. I pinned it on the wall beside my door.

I spent the next hour reading the articles and smaller news items Yvonne had given me. They told me little that I didn't already know. They spanned a broader timescale than those articles left in the file, and some of them dated back to the time of Fowler's arrival in the city. There was nothing to suggest that he might be anything but an honest and wealthy visionary with only the interests of his newly adopted city at heart. Several of the writers suggested that his past remained something of a mystery, but there was no suggestion of anything illegal or even suspicious in either his background or the zeal with which he had arrived, announced himself and begun to establish himself in Hull.

There was nothing, for instance, which suggested to me why either Yvonne or Irina Kapec might find the articles of interest. I trusted Yvonne's judgement, but I began to wonder if it hadn't been clouded now by her friendship with Irina.

There were more photographs of Fowler in the company of those other men of vision in the city. He denied that he had any political ambitions, but in language that suggested otherwise. His pleading, where it existed, wasn't special, merely predictable.

There were two articles concerning the death of Helen Brooks and Fowler's response to what had happened. The word 'grief' was used a lot. There wasn't the slightest suggestion in either article that he and Helen Brooks had been anything except extremely close, or that his loss at her death was anything other to him than what he said it was. No one reading the articles could have inferred anything else from them unless they already knew something the articles themselves did not reveal.

Despite her obvious sincerity and commitment, I also began to wonder about the extent to which Irina Kapec's own judgement was being affected by her loathing of the man. I wondered, too, if either she or Yvonne had made copies of the complete file, and if there were parts of it which I alone had not yet seen.

I took the largest of the photos of Simon Fowler and pinned it to the map.

In the accompanying article, Fowler spoke about his ambitions in the city, about what he had yet to contribute to the place that had welcomed him with open arms, about the place that Hull was destined to become now that forward-looking men like himself were being given the golden opportunity to participate in the city's re-birth.

Among the brochures on the desk, I doubted there was a single one which did not include the phrase 'Vision of the Future'.

13

Simon Fowler and another man were waiting for me in my office when I arrived there the following day.

Fowler was a short, slightly built man with a drawn face, and lines around his mouth ten years too early. His ginger hair was closely and neatly cut and perfectly groomed. He wore a dark suit, a white shirt and no tie. Despite the heat, the cuffs of his shirt showed half an inch beneath each of his sleeves. He was sitting in my chair, facing the door as I entered.

The man with him was ten years younger, taller, and more heavily built. The clothes he wore showed off his physique, which was the point. He was deeply and too evenly tanned, and with a precisely clipped goatee – a line of black hair running from each corner of his mouth to the point of his chin, and a third, shorter line of hair running from beneath his bottom lip to the same point. He spent a lot of time stroking this arrangement. He was standing at the mirror as I entered.

I recognized Fowler immediately.

'Mr Fowler,' I said.

'Mr Rivers,' he said.

I crossed and opened the window, filling the room with noise and the voices of the men working below.

The man at the mirror came to stand beside me. He leaned out of the window and looked each way along the street.

'I appreciate you taking time from your busy schedule to come and see me,' I said to Fowler.

'I don't care what you appreciate,' Fowler said. 'What I *don't* appreciate is the way you went about contacting me.'

'You visionaries are busy men. I needed to get your attention, that's all.'

'Not like that, you didn't. No matter. Let it pass.' As though it were of no consequence to him.

I put a chair close beside him and invited the other man to sit down. I sat opposite him. Both Fowler and the man at the window were uncomfortable with the suggestion.

'Marco prefers to stand,' Fowler said.

'Sitting crease his jacket?' I said.

'Marco is extremely image-conscious,' Fowler said. It was hard to tell if he was being serious or if he was mocking the man.

'Marco?' I said, turning to him. 'Italian? Spanish?'

Fowler laughed. 'About as Spanish as you and me.'

If the remark angered Marco, then he didn't let this show.

'So why the cheap, orange salon tan and funny little beard?' I said.

Marco walked from one side of the open window to

128

the other and then back again. He looked at his feet as he walked. His shoes made no sound on the bare boards. He made the short and pointless journey seem like a declaration of intent.

'And *Marco* is here in what capacity, exactly?' I said. 'Is he one of your legal team, one of your business associates?' I knew he was neither.

'Marco drives my car. Like you said, Mr Rivers, I'm a very busy man.'

I lit a cigarette and blew smoke across the desk at him.

'I'd prefer it if you didn't smoke,' he said.

'I'm sure you would.' I blew the next plume of smoke towards where Marco stood at the window.

Fowler pushed the empty chair I'd placed beside him away from him.

'Technically,' I said, 'you and Mark – sorry, *Marco* – being here could be construed as unlawful entry.'

'Could it?' Fowler said. 'You call me nine times in an hour saying you need to see me urgently, and so I pay you the courtesy of coming to you at the first opportunity, find the door to your' – he looked slowly around him – 'office wide open, and so, assuming you to have just gone out for a moment, I do you the further courtesy of coming in and waiting for you. Plus, of course, I have a witness to all this.'

'You usually do,' I said. 'In addition to which, you probably own master keys to your properties which will get you through any fifty-year-old lock.'

'I certainly wouldn't carry all those keys around with me,' he said. 'Now that would ruin the cut of a man's jacket.'

At the window, Marco laughed.

'I wouldn't do anything that might be misconstrued, Mr Rivers, believe me.'

'Meaning you've probably got all nine of those phone calls on tape somewhere for when I get too close to you and whatever part you played in the death of Helen Brooks and you need someone with a bit more clout than Marco here to stand around looking threatening.'

Fowler turned to Marco. 'Marco, did you ever hear me tell you to stand around looking menacing?'

'He said "threatening",' Marco said.

'Either will do.'

'No, never, Mr Fowler,' Marco said.

'Of course I've got a record of them,' Fowler said to me. 'You never know where this kind of thing might lead.'

'And you're here today why?'

'Not because you shouted "jump", that's a fact.'

'And yet that's what you've done. You could just as easily have told one of your lawyers to send me a letter telling me that you've been through enough, that you'd been fully exonerated in the death of Helen Brooks and that you wanted me to stop harassing you now.'

'You're not harassing me, Mr Rivers. If you want the letter, you can have it. I came here today because I thought you'd appreciate being able to talk face to face on the subject. And because it's gone on for too long now. Fifteen months. I assume it's the mother who's put you up to all this. No disrespect, but she really did ought to learn how to let go, especially now, all things considered. What happened to Helen was an accident. I know what you think of me, Mr Rivers – I know what half the people who shake my hand and smile in my face think of me – but nothing will change that one simple fact: Helen Brooks drowned because she was somewhere she shouldn't have been, and because she was incapable of taking care of herself once things got out of hand. Whatever I say is going to sound harsh or unfeeling – I got all this from the mother and the other sister at the inquest. Can you honestly tell me, knowing what you know of the mother, that she wouldn't be better off directing her energies elsewhere and not endlessly raking over this old and painful ground?'

'If she chose to drop the inquiry, then I daresay Helen's sister might want to pursue it instead.'

'She'd be too busy working out how to spend her inheritance,' he said. He glanced at Marco, and Marco laughed again.

Fowler knew exactly what Alison and Louise Brooks were to each other, and the extent to which the older woman was now responding to her daughter's urging.

It was only then that I remembered the map and the photo I'd pinned by the door. I glanced at it, and Fowler saw this.

'I was wondering when we'd get round to that,' he said. 'Marco.'

Marco took a small silver camera from his pocket.

'You don't mind, do you?' Fowler said.

Marco took several shots of me where I sat with the map and photo on the wall behind me.

'Don't forget the brochures,' Fowler told him, indicating the pamphlets which still covered my desk. Marco took two more photos and then slid the camera back into his pocket. 'You can have copies, if you like,'

Fowler said to me. 'Marco, make sure Mr Rivers gets copies, will you.'

'There's nothing here that wasn't already in the public domain,' I said.

'The "public domain". Is that right?'

'You like getting your picture in the papers,' I said. 'You're good at it.'

'You don't live in the world I live in, Mr Rivers. These things matter.'

'I don't doubt that. But that's only because they matter to men like you, and because men like you are greedy and, possibly, corrupt; and because men like you like other men like you because you know where you stand with them.'

'Was that bit of cleverness an insult?' he said when I'd finished.

'Call it a statement of fact,' I said, feeling as unconvincing as I sounded.

'No, I'll call it an insult.' He paused. 'I'll be straight with you, Mr Rivers. I honestly thought that you and I might be able to sit down here today and get a few things straightened out before you wasted any more of your time, and before that poor, sick old woman caused herself any more unnecessary grief.'

'And how were we going to do that? By you telling me what you told the police and then the coroner and then the papers?'

'Perhaps. Because it was the truth. But perhaps there were things I could have told to you – man to man – which no one – least of all me – saw fit to mention at the time.'

It was another calculated move on his part. It occurred to me only then that he might have known where the map had come from. It also occurred to me that I had called him before seeing Yvonne and Irina Kapec and that he might have known of our meeting.

'Such as?' I said.

'Such as all the noise that was made about the bodies never being recovered, and the fact that this above everything else was what caused the coroner to bring in his open verdict. If anyone wanted those bodies recovered, then it was me.'

'Because it would reveal to the world who Helen Brooks had taken with her on the river?'

'No – because it would have revealed it to *me*. And because I imagine any autopsy performed on her would have brought one or two other interesting little things to light. Things which might have led to a different verdict entirely, and which would have cleared my name from the very start. And something which might not have painted *her* so squeaky clean. That was the story, remember – tragic death by drowning of promising student with the world at her feet. That the line the mother and sister keep on spinning, is it? The world at her feet? The world went up her nose or into her arm most days. Ask them – they knew that as well as anyone. Ask the mother. According to her, *I* was the one who was forcing her precious daughter to do it all. She didn't need my help, Mr Rivers. I never gave her anything. I never encouraged her in what she was doing. I never—'

'You never tried to stop her.'

'No, I never tried to stop her. You didn't know her. I did. Ask Marco. He met her on a few occasions. Tell him, Marco.'

'Absolutely out of control,' Marco said.

'World at her feet?' Fowler repeated. 'She hadn't been to any classes or lectures or whatever it is they do these days for the best part of a year. Go and check. Go and find out for yourself from the people who were about to kick her off the course she was supposed to be on.' He stopped speaking and composed himself. 'I'm sorry,' he said. 'I lost my temper. But I kept my mouth shut about a lot of things where that woman's precious daughter was concerned.'

'She had your permission to take the yacht,' I said.

'I didn't say no. There's a difference. She'd grown up spoiled. Her and the older one, chalk and cheese. You said "No" to her and she either did or took what she wanted anyway; or she wheedled and whined until you grew sick of listening to it all and said "Yes".'

'All the reports made out that the two of you were close.'

'Not all of them. And we were. Had been. To be honest, she was becoming a bit of an embarrassment, a bit of a liability at times. I won't lie to you. It was practically over between us.'

'And Nikki was already waiting in the wings?'

My mention of the name surprised him. 'Nikki didn't happen until at least six months later. Nikki had nothing to do with Helen.'

'You could have mentioned the drug abuse at the inquest.'

'You're joking, right? I was already being painted blacker than night by that family. You seriously think I'm going to open my mouth about something like that? Like I said, if the body had shown up, it could all have been proved and I would have been vindicated.'

'What would you have done – pretended to have been trying to get her to stop?'

He shrugged. 'Something like that.'

'You gave the police your phone records of the day, including recordings.'

'I gave them everything they asked for. Most of the calls were of me calling her and going unanswered. I hadn't seen her for three or four days. I first called her at home an hour or so before we were due to meet for lunch. My main concern, knowing she intended going out on the river, was to find out who she was taking with her. She was about as much use out on the water as I was.'

'And you saw her at lunchtime?'

'Marco drove me to the restaurant. I had to wait for her. She was half an hour late in getting there. Not that timekeeping was ever one of her strong points.'

'And afterwards?'

'Afterwards, Marco drove us all to the marina, where we dropped her off, and then he took me to a meeting at the Guildhall, which had been arranged a month earlier. I told him to go back to the marina and keep an eye on her, to try and persuade her one last time not to take the boat out; or, if she insisted, then to at least let him go with her.'

'Can he sail?'

'It's one of his few genuine talents.'

'What happened?' I said to Marco.

'When I got back there, the yacht was gone and her with it.'

'How long between dropping her off and then getting back to find her gone?'

He shrugged. It was the kind of question someone

might easily and accurately guess at. It was only half a mile from the marina to the Guildhall.

'Twenty minutes?' he said.

'Perhaps a little longer,' Fowler added. 'There was someone I needed to talk to – man called Webster – outside, before the meeting started. We waited in the car five or ten minutes before he showed up.'

'Were you late for the meeting?'

'Why should I be late?'

'You said Helen was late arriving at the restaurant.'

'No, I wasn't late. I never am. The meeting didn't start until three.'

'Did you know she intended being out on the river all day?'

'I didn't know *what* she intended.'

'But you had another restaurant booking for that same evening.' Two reservations in one day after not having seen her for the three or four preceding days.

'For eight. I didn't think she'd be out anywhere near that long. But, like I said, she was never the most reliable of people.'

'An "embarrassing liability" was what you called her.'

'I didn't mean it like that.'

I turned back to Marco. 'So what did you do?'

'What did I do when?'

'When you got back to the marina and found the yacht and Helen Brooks gone.'

'I hung around for about an hour, trying to make sure she'd taken somebody with her. Mr Fowler's right – she was next to useless on the yacht. Especially in her state.'

'Was she drunk?'

'Well on the way.'

'It was one of the reasons why I was so concerned for her to have someone else on board,' Fowler said.

'Which she must have done,' I said. 'Otherwise she wouldn't even have been able to leave the marina. Did you never consider that the yacht might have been taken out earlier and that she was never on it in the first place?'

Fowler laughed. 'Of course it occurred to me. Everything occurred to me. And then I heard the testimony of the man in charge of the marina, of the people she passed on her way out, of the people she called to on the quayside, of Mr whatsisname out walking his fucking dog, of all the others who'd gone out on the river and seen her. You can even hear the noise of the yacht – of the wind and the water and the gulls – in the background when she was on the phone.'

You could hear all that sitting outside the Baltic Wharf bar with a glass of sparkling water in your hand.

'And after you'd hung around for an hour?' I said to Marco.

'I went to the gym.'

'Of course you did.'

'He didn't need to pick me up until seven,' Fowler said. More leading remarks.

'I got back to the Guildhall at about quarter to, and waited,' Marco said.

'He was there when I came out,' Fowler said.

'Did you give anyone a lift, hold any more private meetings in the car?'

'No. I came out, he drove me home, and then he went home himself.'

I continued looking at Marco as Fowler spoke.

'And when you realized Helen wasn't going to keep your evening appointment?'

'I called her and she was still on the river.'

'She answered you?'

'She turned on her phone, presumably saw who was calling and then switched the thing off.'

'That can't have pleased you.'

'I was used to it with her.'

'So you cancelled the restaurant.'

'I forgot,' he said. 'They called me half an hour after we were due to be there. They know me. It was no big deal.'

'And in the meantime, Marco did what?'

'Mr Fowler told me to go back to the marina and wait for her coming in. He was concerned. It was getting dark. He wanted to know who'd been with her, what she'd been up to.'

'I was more angry than concerned,' Fowler said.

'After which?'

'After which I suppose I just assumed that she was in capable hands and that she had never had any intention of joining me for dinner.'

'Did you see Marco?'

'Yes, I saw him. He came to my home. I was trying to make alternative arrangements to see some other people. People who'd been at the meeting. I might have needed him to drive me. In fact, he was with me later — him and Webster — when the police called me to say they'd been alerted by the coastguard to a beached yacht.'

'And you were able to confirm its identity for them?'

'Of course I was.'

'After which, everything became public knowledge.'

'Public knowledge, accusations and allegations.'

So far, and from what I knew of the day's events from elsewhere, he had told me nothing new, nothing which didn't tally with all those other converging stories and recollections. It still intrigued me to see how meticulously his every move of that one day had been recorded. The alarm of the beached yacht did not reach him until nine, almost seven hours since he had last seen Helen Brooks.

He seemed surprised at having told me so much.

But most of what he'd just outlined still depended on Marco for confirmation, and much of what Marco had just confirmed, he had been led to by Fowler.

We were unable to speak for several minutes because of the noise of a lorry below reversing into one of the loading bays, its exhaust and engine noise amplified in the narrow space.

'They should look at a purpose-built market,' Fowler said when the engine was finally silenced.

'I'm sure you've already suggested it,' I said.

'Several times. I've already built two. One in Silvertown. That's East London to you. And another in Ipswich. Did everybody a favour and made myself another not inconsiderable fortune into the bargain.'

The recently built Hull Fish Market was losing money every day it traded. The covered market place was empty. The old open market had been landscaped and filled with seats and was also empty.

'Retail parks,' Fowler said. 'Proper access, proper communications with the rest of the country. Space.' He gestured to the street outside. 'This is conversion and loft-living territory. Leave up a few old frontages for character, rip out everything behind. Keeps property values up, keeps people interested in investing here, keeps local tax revenue up.'

'Save it for your Guildhall meetings,' I told him. 'I've seen the brochures, remember?'

He smiled at me. 'Pity you don't actually own this place,' he said. 'You're not the man I need to talk to.'

'And we all know how far down the food chain tenants like me come in your estimation of things,' I said.

He pretended to be offended by the remark. 'Oh, we're back to that, are we? The map. What the – what, really, does all that have to do with anything? And please, don't disappoint us all by saying you'd hope *I* was going to tell *you* that. As far as I can see, you're spreading yourself too thin, listening to too many people.'

'You included?'

'Perhaps. Listening to too many people and not knowing which way to jump next.'

'Perhaps. But the way I see it, there are still more unanswered than answered questions surrounding the circumstances of Helen Brooks's death. The biggest and most obvious of which was why no one has ever been able to discover who was with her on the yacht. You can tell me as often as you like that you'd have been happier with the washed-up bodies so that they might have been properly identified and autopsied, but the fact is, your story of what happened that day is still the only one available. The facts – *your* facts – fitted, and so everyone believed you. Why wouldn't they? As far as I can see, the reappearance of the bodies might have done you no favours whatsoever.'

He had grown angry listening to me. 'The story –

and that's your name for it, not mine – fits because it happens to be the truth.' He motioned to the phone. 'Go on, do us all a favour and call the mother and ask her how long she'd known about her daughter's drug abuse. Ask *her* what *she'd* done to try and stop her. All this – all this now, her coming to you, you dragging a stick through it all, it's conscience money, that's all. She could have done something earlier, but she didn't. She could even have taken a civil case out against me, but didn't, because she knew how far she'd get with it before she was laughed out of court. And then all of a sudden, it's too late. The other daughter's no different. There was certainly no love lost between her and Helen.' He fell silent after that, and neither of us spoke for a moment.

'I also know about the florists,' I said eventually.

'You know what the pair of them told you,' he said.

'I know you cheated Alison Brooks.'

The accusation did not concern him. 'I gave her five times what she paid for them in the first place, and more than the business was worth according to her own books.'

'You intimidated her staff.'

'Says who? Oh, that's right – says she. I'll tell you something, Mr Rivers: I used to respect that woman. I didn't know who she was when I first put my bid in. It was only after I met Helen that I put two and two together. Her mother knew who *I* was immediately, of course. Which, incidentally, you might want to consider as another reason for all this harassment now. And I'd been seeing Helen for a couple of months before anything clicked, so if you were thinking I'd somehow sought her out and manoeuvred her into my

141

evil clutches just to go on persecuting her poor old mother, then you'd better think again.'

'You said you respected her.'

'I did. She was like me. Self-made. Everything she'd got, she'd earned. She got sick of the life others had mapped out for her and so she got off her arse and did something about it. She bought a shop, made a go of it, bought another.'

'She wanted something better than she'd had for her daughters.'

'Very noble, very commendable.'

I regretted having made the remark.

'She did what I did. You sneer at a word like "vision", but what do you think happens when there's no one around who possesses it?'

'Pass me one of your pamphlets,' I said. 'The answer's probably in there.'

'There you go again. Sneering. It's easy enough to do.'

'I'd have more faith in all these so-called "visionaries" if their first and foremost concern wasn't lining their own pockets.'

'There's nothing wrong with money. You can put it to a lot of good uses.'

'I was talking about greed, power, that kind of thing.'

'That *kind of thing* goes hand in hand with money. You get one, you acquire the rest, whether you pretend to want it or not, whether you actively pursue it or not.'

'And that's exactly what I think you do,' I said. 'Hence all the photogenic women and glossy brochures and self-serving PR.'

'That's just your opinion,' Fowler said.

'I know. But *I* just happen to be the one who thinks

there's a lot more to Helen Brooks's death than you're prepared to admit.'

At the window, Marco took a step towards us.

Without turning, I said to Fowler, 'Next thing you know, he'll be cradling his fist in the palm of his hand and looking menacing again. He might even take off his jacket to show me his tattoos. Biceps would be my guess. Something vaguely Celtic-looking.'

Fowler glanced at Marco, who dropped his arms.

'Grow up,' he said to me. 'Is that what you want from me – threats of violence? Would that make everything a little bit easier for you to understand? Would you feel a little more confident, a little more *justified* in what you're doing?'

'I was beginning to feel that with the beginning of your rags-to-riches story,' I said. 'I'd like to hear it in full some time, though not necessarily from you. See what gets left out and what gets rewritten and polished up for all your brochures.'

Behind me, Marco coughed to attract Fowler's attention.

'I'm expected elsewhere,' Fowler said to me. I imagine it was how he ended every meeting he attended. He had referred to his meals with Helen Brooks as 'appointments'. 'I appreciate having had the opportunity to put my side of things – my "story" as you call it. I hope you'll be able to convey something of what's passed between us here today to your client. And I sincerely hope that she, in turn, might begin to reconsider her own position and motivation in all of this.'

He rose and went to look more closely at the map of his properties.

'I'm going to forget all about this other stuff,' he said.

He rested his finger on one of the coloured dots and then moved it to another. 'It seems remarkably accurate. Of course there are always those deals, acquisitions and negotiations which one might prefer to keep reasonably confidential – commercial advantage and all that – but I daresay they're no more or less than the secrets *you* keep, Mr Rivers.'

'What happened to the yacht?' I asked him.

He glanced at Marco. 'Sold it for scrap. It was badly damaged when she ran it aground. Beyond repair. I sold it to the firm who salvaged it for me. It's all there in the inquest records. Don't tell me you haven't read them. Besides – you might say it held too many painful memories for me. I only bought it in the first place because someone suggested I should. I'd been wanting rid of it for a long time. Marco here used to take it out now and then, but that's about all. After what happened with Helen ... Marco, dig out the receipt from the salvage company and show it to Mr Rivers.' He turned back to me. 'I meant what I said about you passing things on to the mother.'

'I know you did. Something about what had "passed between us here today".'

'I'm serious. The pair of them ought to give some serious consideration to what they're getting themselves into.'

'I doubt if the revelation of Helen's drug use will come as much of a surprise to anyone.'

'I wasn't—' he said, and then checked himself. 'I wasn't making a threat.'

'Yes you were,' I said. 'Everything you say is a threat of one sort or another.' I stood to one side and opened the door.

He waited where he stood for a moment, as though debating whether or not to offer me his hand in parting, but then decided against the gesture and walked out.

Marco followed him.

'Bye, *Marco*,' I said.

Marco was about to say something in reply, but Fowler called to him. He caught my upper arm with his elbow as he went.

He passed with his face close to mine. I could smell his cologne.

'Better run,' I said, my voice still low. 'We don't want to keep Mr Fowler waiting, do we?'

I stepped back and closed the door.

14

Louise Brooks was waiting for me at the restaurant when I arrived. She was talking on her mobile and waved me to her as I went in. It was the same restaurant, overlooking the marina, at which her sister had failed to keep her appointment with Fowler on the day she had died. She held the phone a few inches from her cheek and pulled a face as I joined her.

'I'm seeing to all that. It's done. Yes. Stop worrying. I told you.' She fell silent for a minute, and then said, 'In which case, there's not much more to be said, is there?' and clicked the phone shut. She switched it off and laid it beside her.

'Problems?' I said.

'Not really. Work. Discussions about meetings about arrangements.'

There was a half-empty bottle of wine in a cooler at the centre of the table.

She stood up and kissed me on the cheek.

'Are we here because this is where Helen was due to eat with Fowler?' I said.

She looked around her. 'Of course.' She poured me a drink and we drank a silent toast to her dead sister.

It was cool in the restaurant. We sat at the centre of the room. Traffic flowed continuously past outside, but the glazing kept out all sound of it.

I asked her if she'd been there long.

'Happy hour,' she said. 'Forty minutes. I came straight from the hospital. My mother's been in bed at home since yesterday morning. She has someone with her. She insisted I didn't go home.'

'Has something happened?'

'It's how it works – some days you'd hardly know there was anything wrong with her, and a day later she can barely find the strength to stand upright.'

'I take it she visited me on a good day.'

'She'd been building up to it. I'm afraid she wasn't a hundred per cent honest with you.'

'I usually work closer to fifty,' I said.

'Even with me?'

I fluttered my hand and she laughed.

She refilled her own glass and signalled to a waiter for another bottle.

'*Did* she lie to me?' I said.

'Only about herself. She first refused treatment four months ago. Like I said, there are good days and there are bad days, but overall things aren't getting any better.'

'What did her doctor say four months ago?'

'He said what they all say – that he couldn't tell her anything for certain. You only have to see the figures for her kind of cancer to quickly stop listening.'

147

'So she's—'

'So, yes, she's probably further along the road than she led you to believe.'

'Was there a specific reason for that?'

'She thought that you might be unable to do what she was asking of you if you thought there wasn't so much time; or, worse still, that she wouldn't be able to put on the show she managed and that you'd end up doing what you did out of pity for her rather than any good reason.'

'I told her I knew about John Maxwell's recommendation.'

'It was important to her.'

The waiter brought our wine. He was opening it when he recognized Louise. She watched him closely, making him feel even more uncomfortable.

'Nice to see you again,' she said.

'You, too,' he said. He finished drawing the cork and poured the wine into her glass. She ignored it. The man stood the bottle in the cooler and took out the empty one. He left us as quickly as possible.

'You know him,' I said, already guessing closer to the truth, and beginning to feel uncomfortable myself.

'He gave his testimony at the inquest. He used to work at the Scale Lane restaurant. He was the one who told the world that Helen *appeared* to be drunk, that her behaviour was *beyond* the *acceptable*. You can imagine how that particular piece of information helped to sway everyone's opinion.'

'If that's why we came here, then I think we ought to leave,' I told her. I looked to where the man stood watching us from the edge of the room. Another stood beside him, both of them glancing towards us.

'I'm sorry,' Louise said. 'It wasn't my intention. I didn't even know he worked here until I arrived. It just brought things back, that's all.'

'Because he was telling the truth?'

'No. Because it was *him*, and not Simon Fowler, who pointed it all out to the coroner. Because he was all "Mr Fowler this" and "Mr Fowler that", and because when the coroner asked Fowler why *he* hadn't seen fit to mention my sister's drunkenness he put on his Because-I'm-a-Gentleman act and apologized. Even when the coroner criticized him for having let Helen go out on the yacht knowing what condition she was in, he managed to evoke some sympathy. I saw the two of them – Fowler and the waiter – in the street afterwards, shaking hands.'

'It was – probably still is – one of Fowler's favourite restaurants. He probably knows the man well. He might even have felt bad about what he'd just been asked to do.' I knew this was unlikely, but it was as likely as anything she might have wanted to believe now.

I told her about Fowler's visit earlier in the day.

'What happened? I want to know everything.'

'He came to give me his civic-minded, persecuted, law-abiding-citizen-with-friends-in-high-places speech.'

'Was he alone?'

'I get the impression he seldom does anything alone,' I said.

'Without witnesses, you mean?'

'While all this is happening, yes.' I told her about Marco.

'Another one who was word-perfect at the inquest. By the time everyone had finished telling their stories, you'd have been forgiven for thinking that Helen *deserved* to drown.'

'I doubt that,' I said. 'But it certainly made it easier to bring in the open verdict.'

'Made everything more convenient, you mean. Made everyone feel that little bit better about themselves and their own part in what had happened to her because after all that testimony she was made to look like an accident waiting to happen.'

I waited until she'd calmed down before saying, 'He told me about her drug use.'

She made no response to this.

'He also told me that he knew that there was no love lost between the two of you and suggested that there was a lot about your sister you resented. He implied that you'd pushed your mother into hiring me for reasons of your own, and that you're motivated now primarily by your vindictiveness towards him. He said you hounded him at the time and that you're doing it again.'

'Please,' she said eventually, smiling and raising her glass to me. 'Don't bother to spare my feelings.'

'Most of what he said made sense,' I said.

'And most of it you already knew from listening to me at the marina. Do you hear me denying any of it?'

The second waiter approached us and took our order. When we'd given it, Louise asked him to convey her apologies to the first man.

'Is vindictiveness not a good reason, then, for wanting some kind of justice – or, seeing as we're not exactly pussyfooting around here, some kind of revenge, for the killing of your only sister?'

'I have no problem with that just as long—'

'As it's clearly understood by all parties from the beginning?'

'Something like that. *Did* you push your mother into coming to me?'

'I suppose so. And, yes, I'm doing it as much for myself as for her, and as much to see Fowler exposed for what he is as to clear Helen's name.'

I'd already told her how unlikely that was to happen. I didn't feel like telling her it all again.

She started to laugh and held a hand to her mouth.

'What?' I asked her.

'I even thought I might be able to work with you, the pair of us, together, righting wrongs and avenging unspeakable evils. Walking down those mean streets together.'

'You'd need more sensible shoes for that,' I told her.

'I know. That's why I abandoned the idea.' She put her hand on my wrist, and when I left my hand where it lay, she started drawing circles with her forefinger.

'I leave most of the avenging of unspeakable evils to the magistrates' courts,' I said.

The first of our food arrived and she withdrew her hand.

We talked for an hour about her childhood, about her time alone with her mother before the arrival of Helen's father and then Helen. It had been a happy time for the two of them, and her regret at all the changes which had followed her mother's remarriage was evident in everything she said. They had lived together in a small terraced house on Linnaeus Street, off Hessle Road, and then been rehoused – upon the wholesale demolition of the area – in one of the

Orchard Park flats. She spoke fondly of the life they had lost there.

She told me of the times she and her mother had shared together, the hardships they had endured before the florists took off. They had only ever rented their homes, and had twice been evicted and thrown on the mercy of relatives and friends. At one point, telling me the story of how her mother had suffered from pneumonia following a winter working nights in a flower market, she started to cry.

I gave her my handkerchief, which she took.

'I was eight or nine,' she said, able to speak again. 'The woman who was looking after me told me I had to be prepared for the worst in case my mother died. She said there was a strong possibility of it. My mother was in hospital for a month.'

'But she recovered,' I said.

'Yes, she recovered. But it was a big blow to her. One of the evictions happened while she was in hospital. It knocked her confidence.'

'Who would have cared for you?'

'The State, most likely. Hull was full of Children's Homes.'

'It must have made the appearance of Helen's father—'

'It did.' She took a deep breath, pinched the bridge of her nose and gave me back my handkerchief.

'I've never told anyone all that before.'

'Probably because it'll make you cry every time,' I said. It was the blaze in which she had been tempered and burnished.

I told her about my own childhood to regain some balance. We had grown up less than a mile apart. She was two years younger than me. We had in common what a million others growing up in the same place at the same time had in common. It was enough.

She was drunk by then, and relaxed.

She wondered aloud if we might order a third bottle, and then held up the empty bottle to signal before I'd had a chance to answer her.

'Do you talk about all this with your mother?' I asked her. My own mother lived completely in the past, endlessly retreating and remaking it as she went.

'I try,' she said. 'On occasion. But *she* thinks we should live more in the present. Ironic, really. To be honest, she's probably already having doubts about what she's asking you to do.'

'What will you do if—'

'If she dies before anything's resolved?'

I nodded.

'I don't know. It only makes sense, I suppose, because she's still alive.' She looked directly at me. 'Do *you* have any serious doubts about what you're doing?' she asked me.

'I doubt you'll get the coroner to change his mind. And I doubt you'll ever get anyone to reopen the inquiry without something drastic happening, something no one can ignore.'

'I mean doubts about the circumstances of Helen's death,' she said. 'About Fowler's part in it.'

I thought about this. It was something I would rather have considered perfectly sober.

'I think Simon Fowler told me a pack of lies this morning, but that he's got so used to saying the same thing over and over that even he probably isn't entirely certain of what happened.'

'Don't you believe it,' she said, her voice low. And then she laughed and filled both our glasses from the new bottle.

It was ten o'clock, and the sun had set. Across the road, mostly empty now of traffic, the lights of the marina stretched in wavering lines into the darkness of the river beyond. The sodium streetlights made everything look clean. Warehouses rose in stark outline against the brightness of the night sky. Those that had already been converted stood revealed in the lights of their windows.

She saw me looking. 'It's a different world,' she said. She meant from the years of our childhood. 'Christ, listen to me,' she said.

I asked her if she wanted to call to check on her mother.

'She forbade me,' she said, surprised by her use of the word. She repeated it. 'She knows where I am. I normally call her through the day, and in the evenings if I'm working or out. My social life is not exactly the merry-go-round I once imagined it might be. I talk to her when I – when we—' She stopped speaking and looked at her distant reflection in the window.

'What?' I asked her.

'I'm not even going home afterwards, after this. I've booked into the Holiday Inn for the night. She insisted.' She nodded towards where the name floated in its curved yellow letters beyond the road and the water. 'I've done it before. She has someone to sit with her all night. She insists I need time away from her. It's difficult for her to sleep right through. Sometimes she wakes in pain. She probably thinks I don't know, that I don't hear her.'

'And you don't tell her?'

'Something like that. She thinks I should have gone back to Birmingham after the inquest. She thinks I should be taking care of myself. As opposed to pretending that I'm taking care of her. Instead of forcing her into having to pretend that it's what she wants from me. A week before Helen was killed, she and Helen had an argument. Something about what Helen was doing to herself – you can imagine what was said; the thing followed its usual, predictable course – and somehow the subject of grandchildren came up – I can't remember how – and Helen laughed in her face and said that *I* was the one my mother ought to be addressing that particular question to. I had a termination when I was twenty-three. My mother never knew about it.'

'Did Helen tell her?'

'Not *tell* her, exactly.'

'Just drop enough heavy-handed suggestions so that you had to tell her yourself?'

'My mother said she wished I'd been able to confide in her at the time. It really hurt her that I hadn't told her. She said she would have gone along with whatever I'd wanted, that she would have helped and supported me through it all.'

'But you would have known all the time that she disapproved of what you were doing?'

'Of course she would have disapproved. It was why I didn't tell her – I knew it would have done something to us. Helen was still a small girl.'

'And the father?'

'Disappeared the instant our scary little spree was over.'

'And you never saw him again?'

'Or heard from him, or wanted to.'

'Did Helen regret having done what she'd done?'

'I don't know. None of us ever got the chance to find out.'

Something else unresolved. Another confused ending.

We left the restaurant thirty minutes later.

We crossed the road and sat overlooking the water. The air was still warm. The shapes of hovering gulls came and went in the darkness above us.

She asked me if I'd go back to the Holiday Inn with her, and I said I would.

I thought she might want to leave immediately, but instead she remained where we sat. We talked until she fell asleep. I left her with her head against my shoulder for ten minutes before waking her.

She rubbed her face and asked me whether I'd said yes or no to her invitation.

She stood up, took several paces towards the water and then reached down and took off her shoes.

She held my arm and we walked around the old dock to the hotel.

A conference was being held there and the bar was full of men wearing laminated identification tags long after they'd had the opportunity to remove them.

I waited with her at reception while she collected her key. The receptionist told her there was no one to help her with her luggage. She had none, she said. A group of men sat at nearby tables with their drinks, talking loudly and calling out to the people who passed them.

Louise watched them while we waited. Several of

the men raised their glasses to her. One of them patted the empty seat beside him and invited her to join them. It was something she might have done if she'd been alone. She was still carrying her shoes.

In the lift up to her top-floor room, she closed her eyes against the bright light.

She'd asked for a room overlooking the marina, and I saw again the exact shape and outline of the evening we had just spent together. At some point in the near future she would come with me to the bank of the Humber overlooking Foulholme Sands. And after that, perhaps, her journey would be complete.

She opened the window and looked out over the water. She emptied the minibar of its contents and lined up the small bottles on the dressing table.

She took off her jacket and fell backwards onto the bed, her feet still on the floor. I sat beside her.

'Don't worry,' she said. 'I'm not going to disappoint you by telling you that I don't *usually* make a habit of inviting strange men back to my hotel rooms.'

' "Strange"?' I said.

'Different,' she said quickly, and I accepted the compliment for what it was.

She held my arm and I kissed her.

'Is this going to work?' she said as our mouths parted.

'I don't know,' I said. 'You've probably given it more thought than me.'

'You think I planned it?'

'I hope so,' I said. 'It's been a long time since I was anyone's object of desire.'

'How long?'

'A year, perhaps longer. You?'

'A few months. But "object of desire" would be stretching a point.' She drank the miniature of brandy.

I helped her to sit upright and we sat together looking out over the yachts below.

She fell asleep again soon afterwards, and I laid her on the bed and lay down beside her.

The muted sounds of the city centre carried into the room on the night air. The yachts rattled at their moorings. I could still hear the voices of the celebrating men four floors beneath us.

I fell asleep wondering whether or not to leave her there.

I woke in the morning to find her sitting at the window in one of the hotel's white robes.

She spoke to me without turning. 'Saturday morning,' she said. 'Does the pursuit of evil never cease?'

'Sometimes,' I said.

She left the window and came back to the bed.

'I woke a few times in the night,' she said. 'I'm glad you stayed.'

'You promised me a full English breakfast,' I said.

'As temptresses go, I'm certainly up there with the best.' She looked to where the miniature bottles had been lined up.

'I put them all back,' I told her.

She lay on the bed beside me, her hands clasped over her stomach, looking up.

'What else did I promise you?' she said.

'There were no promises.'

She turned to face me. 'Would it have spoiled anything?'

'By which I take it the moment's probably passed,' I said. I feigned disappointment.

'You don't have a code of ethics, then?'

'Somewhere,' I said.

Her robe fell open to reveal part of her breast and she covered this up.

'You'd be feeling compromised by now if we had slept together,' she said.

'And wondering about your motives for having done it?'

'Something like that. When the truth of it is—'

'I know,' I told her.

She brushed my hair with her fingers and held her hand against my head.

I took her other hand. 'You're supposed to say, "Perhaps one day, when all this is over",' I said.

She considered this. 'Happy endings. It's not really a choice we ever get to make, is it?' She was talking about her mother, and so I said nothing in reply.

'What next?' she asked me.

'Which answer do you want?' I said.

She kissed me on the forehead. I could smell the soap with which she'd washed herself clean of the night before. I let my nose and mouth rest in the hollow of her throat, my lips against her neck. I closed my eyes. She held my hand in both her own, as though it were something precious to her and she had only just realized this.

15

We spent the morning in the hotel and then had lunch together at the Minerva. She walked with me back to Humber Street, but then stopped and drew away from me as we approached the doorway leading to my office.

The fruit men had all gone and the street was deserted. It still smelled of peaches. Other fruit – rotten and trampled strawberries and kiwi fruit – lay in the gutter.

'I'd better be getting back to my mother,' she said. I guessed she was already several hours late. She'd checked her phone: there had been no messages from the woman sitting with her mother.

'Can we do this again?' she asked me.

'I'd like to.'

'Seriously?'

'Unless I find the booklet listing all that ethics stuff,' I said. 'I'd still like to look through the possessions you've retrieved from your sister's flat.'

We held each other on the empty, sweet-smelling street. Then she kissed me and walked away. I could hear the dancing feet and grunted punches of the boy boxers training in the gym.

I'd been in my office only a few minutes when Sunny rang me.

'Good night?' he said.

Uncertain what he meant, I said nothing.

'I've been trying to call you since yesterday evening.'

'I've been busy,' I said.

'Right. You still interested in rattling Fowler's gilded cage?'

'I've already pushed a stick through the bars.'

'And?'

'Same old predictable snarls.'

'Come round,' he said.

'When?'

'Last night would have been good. Believe me, you've got nothing better to do.'

I told him I'd be there in half an hour and hung up.

The city centre was crowded with afternoon shoppers. The owners of the pubs and bars had lined the pavements with tables. People sat around the walled rose-beds, drinking. Policemen and -women walked among them in short-sleeved shirts pretending to be their friends.

I arrived at the agency to find the door locked. I called inside and Sunny opened it.

'Are you expecting someone else?'

'Not particularly. I just wanted to do this without Mother Teresa casting her disapproving looks at me.'

He locked the door behind me. The room was again made cool by the fans. He poured me a drink from a bottle of wine standing in front of one of these.

'Out all night?' he said.

'Most of it.'

Seeing that I was not prepared to be drawn, he said, 'As long as you realize and never forget that you're only there to do her dirty work for her.'

'Whose dirty work?'

'I'll pretend you didn't say that,' he said.

'Whatever you think you know or understand about her, her sister was still up to her neck with Fowler, and she still died in what you groundbreaking journalists like to refer to as "mysterious circumstances".'

'Ouch,' he said. 'And I'll assume that's "mysterious" as in "unexplained". You know, like flying saucers.'

'What have you got on Fowler?' I asked him.

'Has it never occurred to you that you might need someone watching your back on this?'

'You, for instance?' I said, and he shook his head as though I had misunderstood him completely.

I told him everything about my encounter with Fowler and Marco.

He asked me to describe Marco, which I did. He took faxed photos of several men from an envelope, but none of them was Marco.

'Fowler?' I prompted him.

'I spoke to an old friend who did a stint on the *Evening Standard* crime pages. He was there five years ago, same time that Fowler was making a name for himself in that neck of the woods. He sent me this.' He patted a pile of papers in front of him. 'Fowler used to work with four or five other developers. None of them

162

national players, but all of them with enough cash, local clout and know-how to make their various killings on what we groundbreaking journalists like to refer to as a buoyant and ever-rising property market. Some of them built from scratch; some of them re-developed; some of them built only to sell on, some to rent, and some solely to build up their own little empires. Some worked as complete independents and some had public sector contracts and backing to keep everything safe as well as profitable on those rare occasions the market dipped.'

'And Fowler was what?'

'Fowler was a bit of everything. That's the point. They all worked together. No bidding against each other, no undercutting. It was a cartel. If one took on a job he couldn't handle, the others helped out.'

'And they shared the profits accordingly?'

'Something like that. And all of it perfectly legal and perfectly suited to what was needed. Every house they built, they could sell three times over. Every property they converted, they had a waiting list a foot long. It's how Fowler made all the money he brought up here with him.'

'You said crime pages.'

'I'm coming to that.' He emptied his glass and refilled it. 'It was suspected that Fowler and these others were using illegal – as in cheap, no taxes, no national insurance – labour.'

'Illegal immigrants?'

'Among others.' He paused after that, allowing me to consider what he was telling me. 'Qualified labourers are a large part of the cost of any build. Even cutting that cost by ten or twenty per cent saves you a small fortune.' He searched the pile of papers and pulled out a sheet he'd already highlighted. 'In 1999, Fowler's companies – seven are listed, though my contact thinks there were over twice that number – built almost seven thousand homes. Seven thousand. The cheapest of which sold for eighty-five thousand pounds, the most expensive for over two million. Working on the basis that he was operating on profit margins of between twenty and thirty per cent, that's a lot of profit. And that was just for one year. To my friend's knowledge, Fowler was part of this unofficial syndicate for at least three years prior to that.'

'And is your friend convinced that Fowler and the others were actively recruiting this labour?'

'It gets better. He's convinced that Fowler was some-how involved in bringing the men into the country in the first place. Between them, those companies employed a lot of labourers.'

'And his proof of all this?'

He clicked his tongue, meaning he had none. 'The Department of Immigration carried out raids on companies they suspected of employing the immigrants illegally. Fowler and the others were always too far removed from everything to ever get their own hands dirty or to be caught themselves. The ones who did get caught – those lower down the chain – admitted liability, paid their fines and promised to keep a closer eye on who their own unscrupulous minions employed in the future.'

'And then they walked away from it all.'

'With hardly a backward glance.'

'And the men who were caught working or living here illegally?'

'Dropped into the system. Most of them were probably sent home.'

'Adding weight to the suggestion that it would have paid Fowler to keep his workforce topped up from a dependable source.'

'A source he exercised some control over, yes. Either that, or find a way of avoiding losing the men in the first place. This was where my contact first got interested in it all. There was a trial of two Met detectives who'd been accused of taking money to keep one of the other men in the syndicate tipped off about the work they were liaising on with Immigration and Customs.'

'And if they were accused of tipping off one of the men, presumably they were tipping off them all.'

'Whether they knew it or not, yes. Three years was a long time for something like that to operate without something going seriously wrong.'

'What happened at the trial?'

'It collapsed. The CPS handled it badly. Usual story. Insufficient evidence, unsafe procedure, unreliable and withdrawn testimony.'

'Meaning Fowler and the others knew as much as anyone about what was happening.'

'They never seemed particularly alarmed by it at the time. Nothing was ever traced to Fowler or the others at the top of the pile which would have convicted them.'

'Meaning they probably paid or hung out someone further down that pile to bear the brunt of everything.'

'They did. But, like I said, it didn't amount to much. Fines, suspended sentences, revoked licences.'

'What happened to the two detectives?'

'Suspended and then kicked out. The trial might not have proved anything, but everyone knew what they'd been up to. Presumably someone – Fowler or one of the others – made it worth their while to leave the force.'

'And Fowler himself was never actually convicted of anything in the whole of this?' I said.

He shook his head.

'But you still think it was one of the reasons he left London and came to Hull?'

'Who knows? He arrived less than six months later. The impression my contact got was that the trial shook the syndicate up more than a little, revealed a few weak links – men some of the others felt they could no longer trust – and that their cosy little set-up all began to come unstuck.'

'Leaving everyone looking for their own way out. And presumably when that happened, there'd be others ready to muscle in on things.'

'There were plenty waiting to do it,' he said.

'So Fowler might have decided to come somewhere he could start again and go on operating without all this unwelcome competition.'

'Or police attention, yes.'

'And none of the others attempted to follow him?'

'Not that I know of. Some of them took the close call of the trial as a warning shot and decided to retire from the work. Most of them were older than Fowler. Presumably, they'd already amassed more money than they could ever spend.'

'What do they think happened to the networks or organizations bringing the immigrants in?' I said.

'When the trial collapsed, Immigration turned its

attention to tracing and blocking as many of the routes as possible. A lot of the evidence might have been inadmissible in court, but it was still there and they acted on it.' He searched for another sheet of paper, which he gave to me.

It was a report of a man's body that had been retrieved from the Thames.

'A worker?' I said.

'Better. He was one of the original syndicate. According to my contact, he was the first to panic when the Met and Immigration got too close.'

I read the article. 'According to this, he waited until a month after the trial had collapsed and then took his own life.'

'I know. How convenient was that?'

'Was he killed?'

'It says the balance of his mind was disturbed by all he'd just been through. His wife had left him and he thought he was about to lose everything he owned.'

'How could Fowler or any of the others make that happen?'

'Use your imagination,' he said.

'Did they think he was going to change sides to save himself?'

'I doubt it. Otherwise he would have "committed suicide" a lot sooner.'

'And after all the dust had settled?'

He shrugged. 'My contact left the *Standard* soon afterwards. He started working freelance. When asylum-seekers became big news he wrote a series of articles on how they were getting here, and on what happened to them after they arrived. He called me up a couple of years ago. We went for a drink in Howden.'

'Why there?'

'He was there to interview someone who'd moved there after previously working in the Met.'

'Someone involved in the trial?'

'I'm not entirely certain. It seems likely. He told me he was chasing cold trails. A week before I met him, he'd been offered a job in Canada. I think he was more interested in that than whatever he was in Howden for. He said that if he'd known about the job sooner, he would never have come.'

'Who was the man in Howden?'

'I don't remember. It might be in this lot, somewhere. I haven't read it all.'

We sat without speaking for several minutes, considering all that he'd just told me.

'Do you think Fowler's involved in something similar up here?' I asked him eventually, knowing that this was the conclusion towards which we were both moving.

'Illegal immigrants, asylum-seekers? Yvonne says he employs them, but the scale of his work up here is nothing compared to what he was involved in down there.'

'It's still a big coincidence,' I said. 'Plus everything is about to get much bigger once all the city-centre redevelopment gets under way.'

He shook his head, unconvinced. 'He's not the same man he used to be. Up here he's all Mr Respectability, Scion of Society. Down there he was somebody fighting his way up through a crowd of other fighters and not worrying too much about his tactics or what was required of him. He's made his money. What interests him now are all those things his money can buy here that it couldn't buy him there – prestige, respect, some standing in the business community, respectability.' He closed his eyes and turned his face into one of the fans. 'Practically nothing of what happened in London all those years ago ever became public knowledge up here. At least not in the circles Fowler started moving in. And besides, who'd care? You've seen him. You know what kind of man he is. He's re-made himself.'

I considered what he was telling me.

'All of which adds up to why both you and Yvonne think the idea of him being somehow involved in the death of Helen Brooks is ridiculous?' I said.

'All *I'm* pointing out to you is that it makes no sense – that whatever he might be involved in up here, she played no part in it – meaning he had no *reason* to kill her – and anything that attracted *that* kind of publicity to him he'd want to avoid like the plague. Not only because of what it might do to his reputation – his new reputation – and his credibility or standing here, but because of everything in his past it might then go shining a light on.'

It was an imperfect explanation, as most were. But even in its imperfect way, everything he said made sense. It was what Andrew Brownlow had already suggested to me.

'Tell me some more about Marco,' he said.

I told him everything else I remembered, but he still didn't recognize the man.

Then he cupped his face in his hands and said, 'Did you sleep with her?'

'There are rules and regulations,' I said.

He shook his head.

'No, I didn't sleep with her,' I said.

'But you were still close enough – she *allowed* you close enough – for it to have been an option?'

'Leave it,' I said.

'And you still don't think she's more motivated by her own feelings in wanting to see Fowler prosecuted than simply because she wants to see justice done? And for that she needs to keep you on board. You're not seeing any of this straight.'

'So everybody keeps telling me,' I said.

'I know that, despite current appearances, you're not that stupid, so tell me what little bit of all this you are seeing clearly.' With the wine finished, he took the whisky from his drawer and poured an inch into the same paper cup. 'Perhaps we could start with the mysterious, unidentified man.'

'What about him?' I said.

'Don't.'

'Don't what?'

'Don't pretend that you haven't already worked out that he's in the middle of all this somewhere.'

'They tried for weeks afterwards to try and find out who he might have been,' I said.

'And Fowler, naturally, absolutely and always that little bit too emphatically, denied he had ever known who he was. Might he have been somebody Helen Brooks was seeing at the same time she was arm-hanging for Fowler?'

'What, and Fowler found out and the night on the river was his way of letting them know their relationship was over? Like you just said, I can think of better, less conspicuous ways of telling her. And if the man *had* been known to her beforehand, then there's a chance they would have identified him by now.'

'Perhaps he was just a local business rival,' he said, equally unconvinced. 'A new and unsatisfactory partner?'

'After all you've just told me, I imagine Fowler had had his fill of unreliable partners to want to take on any new ones up here. Besides, he's a wealthy man – he doesn't need them. He likes to give the impression of working completely independently.'

My own cup was empty and I held it to him for a refill.

'So who does the dutiful daughter think the mystery man might have been?' he said.

'She hasn't said anything so far.'

'Don't you find that a bit strange? She seems to have an opinion on just about everything else where Fowler is concerned.'

'Perhaps if her only sister hadn't drowned alongside him, perhaps then she'd have given the matter more thought.'

He smiled. 'Meaning you think it's just as strange as I think it is. Or were you intending to ask her last night before the pair of you sat beneath the moon and the stars and did all that stuff people sitting beneath the moon and the stars do?'

'Keep pushing,' I said. 'As far as all this is concerned, you know as little as I do.'

'Debatable,' he said. 'I was, however, the first person to interview Peter Nicholson.'

'I read it. Very insightful. When did you see him?'

'The morning after. Got most of what I wanted from the police story-tellers and the lifeboat log. But you know the public – they do like a local hero every now and again.'

'And Nicholson fitted the bill? Raised the alarm, did all he could — which didn't amount to a great deal — and not being in possession of a video camera, he at least had the presence of mind to stand and watch it all? All you had to do then was blur the boundary between man-stands-back-and-watches and have-a-go-hero and let the story run its course.'

'Why do you think it mattered what he was or wasn't able to do? You've only got to look at the facts — there wasn't anything anyone could have done for them once whoever was on board had decided to try and save themselves. The lifeboatmen said it. The police said it. The helicopter pilot said it.'

'And so you said it? That must have made things nice and easy for you.'

'It did. Christ, how much expert opinion do you want? OK — if you're looking for a conspiracy which includes the invisible man, then you're going to come unstuck if all you've got to go on are the events of the night in question. But the reason everyone involved had an expert opinion is because that's what they were — experts.'

'And all of which was more than enough for the coroner,' I said.

'Of course it was.'

Neither of us spoke for a moment. He knew as well as I did how much easier all this expert opinion and testimony had made things at the time of the inquest.

'Was it obvious to everyone by the time you saw Nicholson that whoever had been on the yacht wasn't now likely to be found alive?' I asked him.

'Pretty much. There was talk about the bodies being found eventually, somewhere — Paull itself is where

172

they normally wash up – but that was about the best anyone involved was hoping for.'

'What did Nicholson think?'

'That they'd turn up eventually. They already had a small inflatable going in and out of the creeks on both sides of the estuary.'

'Was he optimistic?'

'Not particularly. The lifeboatmen seemed to think we wouldn't have to wait too long, but Nicholson said they were wrong.'

'He was proved right,' I said.

He swatted at a fly which landed on his chest. 'Are you getting at anything in particular here?'

'Twelve hours passed between Nicholson spotting the yacht and him talking to you.'

'So? He'd already told the same story to the police and the coastguard. He might have embellished it a bit for me, played up his own part in it once I'd flattered him with the local-hero angle, but that was all. I did *check* with the police and the coastguard. All the facts of the matter remained the same. No one saw any strange, hovering craft in the night sky or heard gun-shots and screaming on the water.'

'I went to see him,' I said. 'A few days ago. His wife left him.'

'So? Would *you* want to live out there?'

'Plus he bears a grudge against the Associated British Ports people for sacking him as a pilot.'

'He resigned. They all did. It came to a stand-off and the Ports won. Most of the men went back to work under new contracts. Perhaps Old Man River Nicholson was just too stubborn for his own good. As far as I'm still concerned, he was just a man in the right place at the right time. That's all. You can't have it both ways – if Fowler was somehow involved in what happened to Helen Brooks and her sailor friend, then the last thing he'd want was a witness. Without Nicholson raising the alarm when he did, none of this might have been discovered until the following day, which would have suited Fowler – *if* he had the faintest idea what was happening – much better.'

Again, everything he suggested made sense.

We started to search for the name of the man who lived in Howden, but were interrupted by a call from Yvonne, who shouted at him to pick up the phone. She told him she'd already called my office and that I wasn't there.

He picked up the phone. 'He's here with me,' he said. He put her on the public speaker, which distorted her voice, and which picked up other voices alongside her. I heard another woman and the sound of someone crying.

'I think Fowler knew you'd arranged to see me and Irina,' she said to me.

'You were the one who arranged it,' I told her. 'Why?'

'Did you speak to him before you saw us?'

'I left a few messages, that's all. The morning before I saw the two of you. I'm certain I wasn't followed, and he didn't get back to me until the next day.'

To Sunny, she said, 'Tell him how pathetic he sounds.'

'She's right,' Sunny said. 'Just because all this isn't unravelling in front of you, it doesn't mean to say that things aren't happening elsewhere now that Fowler knows you're sniffing around.'

'I'm at twelve, Walmsley Street,' she said. Less than a hundred yards from the agency. 'Tell Sherlock it's one of Fowler's properties.' She paused. 'You're supposed to say, "Don't move. We're on our way",' she said, and hung up.

'You contacted Fowler and *then* you went to see Yvonne?' Sunny said to me disbelievingly.

'She wanted me to meet Irina Kapec.'

'I bet she did. Good move. Helen Brooks plus her mother plus Louise Brooks plus you plus Yvonne plus another of Fowler's sworn enemies. No wonder he saw fit to visit you to find out how it all fitted together. After which, and quite coincidentally, of course, you spend the night with Louise Brooks, *after* spending the evening at a restaurant known to be frequented by Fowler, wherein are possibly employed some of his favourite waiters who might every now and again top up their miserable wages by selling information to him. And then, the day after, you come here. I can see you're really getting the hang of this undercover investigating business. What next – a skywriting plane?'

'No one followed me,' I said.

'Keep saying it,' he told me.

'You think they might be outside now?'

'Your guess is as good as mine. Though judging by that call, my guess is that, once again, you've grossly overestimated your own abilities, and Fowler is already, oh, three steps ahead of you.'

We left the agency and climbed over the rear wall of the yard into the ten-foot alleyway beyond, where we parted. I turned left, he went right. We emerged into side streets and made our separate ways to Walmsley Street.

None of which would have fooled anyone who had followed me there, and who was now watching either the agency or the address on Walmsley Street where Yvonne was waiting for us.

16

I arrived at the end of Walmsley Street to see Sunny already standing on the far corner and looking out for me. I walked from one side of the street to the other, making it obvious to anyone who might have been watching that I was searching for a particular address. I arrived at number twelve and knocked.

Yvonne answered the door, holding it on two chains as I spoke through the gap to her. She opened it. The noise of the crying woman came from a room at the end of the narrow hallway, surrounded by the foreign voices of others. Three children sat side by side on the uncarpeted stairs and looked down at us.

I followed Yvonne into the room where Irina Kapec awaited us.

'I've called the doctor,' she said to Yvonne. Her glance at me was brief and hostile.

I began to explain to Yvonne what I thought had

happened concerning Fowler and our meeting two days earlier.

Irina Kapec interrupted me. 'What has happened is this,' she said.

She stood aside to reveal a young woman, no older than twenty, sitting on a threadbare couch holding her arm in her lap. Her hand was bruised and swollen, and lay at an uncomfortable-looking angle to her arm. The swelling on her wrist was black and her thumb lay at too wide an angle to her forefinger. She gasped for air and cried out each time one of the three other women in the small room tried to comfort her. She looked up at my arrival. One of her eyes was closed, swollen and discoloured, and both her cheeks were bruised.

'Who did it?' I asked Yvonne, who shook her head once and said nothing. She went to the window and looked through the net curtains to the street outside.

'We don't know who did it,' Irina said. She spoke reassuringly to the woman on the couch.

'Don't we?' Yvonne said, her back still to us.

'She ought to go to the hospital,' I said.

'The last place she needs to go is the hospital,' Irina said. 'That would involve perhaps a little too much form-filling and perhaps one too many pairs of prying eyes.'

The injured woman had looked up at me in alarm at the word 'hospital'.

A doctor was due to arrive shortly, but it seemed unlikely to me that the injuries to the woman's wrist and face could be fixed without proper attention.

The other women in the room were all young and similarly dressed in long skirts and with their blouses fastened at their necks. Two of them wore headscarves. I knew from their lowered voices and their glances that they were discussing my arrival.

Yvonne finally turned from the window and came past me without speaking. She went to the front door and opened it.

Sunny joined us a moment later.

Irina said something to the other women and they rose and left us.

A portable television lay smashed on the floor beside where they had been sitting.

'Three men came to the house demanding to see a man they insisted lived here,' Irina said. 'She answered the door to them. The man they said they were looking for has never lived here. No one here has ever heard of him. She thought if she let them in to see for themselves that he wasn't here then they'd go away. As you can see, they didn't much care for what she tried to tell them. She's Iraqi.' She turned back to the injured woman, making it clear to me that this was as much as she was prepared to tell me.

'Any idea *why* they wanted to see him, what they were after?' Sunny said.

Yvonne shook her head. 'I called you three times,' she said to me.

'Because you didn't want me involved?' Sunny asked her.

'Something like that. This isn't the time or the place for that particular discussion.'

'She thinks the men who did this were lying about the man they were looking for,' Irina said, having spoken again to the injured woman.

'If searching for the man was only a pretence to get

in and to intimidate the women, why would they hang around?' I said.

'Just her bad luck, then, that she was the one to open the door to them,' Yvonne said angrily.

'We just need to get a few things clear,' Sunny said to her. 'You're not angry at me or him, or if you are then it's not because of what's just happened here. If this has any bearing whatsoever on what he's looking into concerning Fowler, then we need to understand it properly and to be able to see it for what it really is.'

But Yvonne was neither convinced nor placated by this, and again I sensed her resentment at my involvement. She closed her eyes and held a hand over them.

Irina left the injured woman and stood beside her.

'I called you last night,' Yvonne said to me. 'Your phone was switched off.'

'He was *otherwise* engaged,' Sunny said.

She considered the remark for a moment. 'Louise Brooks?'

'She wanted to tell me about her mother and her sister,' I said. 'I needed to get a few things clear.'

'All night?' she said.

'I can do without this,' I told her.

Sunny signalled to her to let the subject drop.

'So what did you discover?' she said. 'Or was that just you justifying something to yourself?'

'You weren't there,' I said, regretting the remark immediately. I felt uncomfortable being confronted by her like that in front of Irina Kapec and the injured woman. 'We can talk about this later if you like,' I said.

'You'll probably be too busy trying to get things clear.'

I let the remark pass.

'I'm sorry,' she said.

'Not as sorry as I am for first having called Fowler and then having come to see you and Irina,' I said.

She looked to Irina, who was growing impatient at the delayed arrival of the doctor she'd called.

'There was some violence in the city centre last night,' Yvonne said to me. 'Asylum-seekers and locals. Usual stuff.'

I remembered the sirens I'd heard as I sat overlooking the marina with Louise.

'A few arrests. Irina was up all night translating for the men she could help. A few of them are being held and investigated.'

'Could what happened here be connected to that?' I asked her.

'I don't know. I doubt it, but . . .'

'But every time an asylum-seeker gets involved in something like this, someone somewhere starts making the connections?'

Sunny came to us, and Yvonne left me and went with Irina back to the injured woman.

'Eight people live here,' he told me. 'Five adults – all women – and three kids. And even if she hadn't opened the door to them, whoever came knocking wouldn't have had too much trouble getting in.'

'It might be useful to find out about the man they said they were looking for,' I said.

'None of them had a little beard, if that's what you're thinking. Only one of them spoke Iraqi, and none of the women who live here had seen any of them before.'

'Meaning what?'

He shrugged. 'I don't know. That they were

181

newcomers? That they were sent knowing they wouldn't be recognized?' He lowered his voice. 'It also occurred to me that there was no one here watching the place afterwards because that wasn't what mattered to them. What if they were watching the agency, and all they really needed to see was me and you going down the fire-escape?'

I thought this unlikely, but said nothing.

'And what if they beat her up' — I too lowered my voice in the presence of the woman — 'because they knew she was here illegally and that no one was going to call the police and tell them what happened? We don't even know what the police line is on this kind of thing.'

'It varies. Irina would know more about it. Ask her.'

We were interrupted by a knock at the door.

Irina left the sofa and went to the window. She nodded to Yvonne, and Yvonne went to the door.

The woman who returned with her was the same age as Irina and Yvonne, and wore a sari. Her wrists were covered with silver bracelets. She embraced Irina and looked at the rest of us.

'I was at a wedding,' she said. She told the injured woman to hold up her arm and to bend it at the elbow. The woman attempted this and then screamed at the pain it caused her. The doctor put down her bag and examined her other injuries. Her face betrayed nothing of what she saw. The gentlest of her touches produced another scream from the woman. She took a syringe and a phial from her bag, filled the syringe and injected the woman in her forearm. Several minutes later she wrapped the woman's hand in a thick foam cuff and fastened this with a sling around her neck.

She asked the woman several questions, which Irina translated for her.

'I've given her something to reduce the worst of the pain,' she told us. 'But there's not much more I can do here. She has a broken wrist, a broken thumb, and at least one broken finger. Whoever did this to her knew what they were doing. The bruises on her face are from being held tightly between someone's finger and thumb. Her swollen eye is painful, but it looks worse than it is. There is no damage to her vision that I can see. I imagine she was punched just for good measure. She would have screamed a lot because the pain from something like that would have been intense.' Again, she betrayed no emotion in this brief and workmanlike assessment.

'They kept the others in the back room while they did it to her,' Irina said. 'And they told them that they knew there were children in the house.'

The doctor shook her head. 'I know someone who may be able to help her. A colleague. He may be able to undertake the necessary resetting in his own surgery. But a general anaesthetic is out of the question.'

'It would still be preferable to taking her to the hospital,' Irina said.

'I understand that.'

'I know you do. And I'm grateful for everything you've been able to do for her here today.'

'A temporary measure.'

'I understand that, too,' Irina said. 'Some of us seem to live our lives moving from one temporary measure to the next.'

'I can make no promises,' the doctor said. 'The man I spoke of is at the wedding I just left.'

'It would be very reassuring to know that he felt himself able to help her,' Irina said.

They were speaking to each other in a language by which each perfectly understood the other, and in which not even the slightest superfluous detail was revealed.

The doctor gave Irina a packet containing five further phials of anaesthetic and a handful of sealed hypodermics. 'The first injection will wear off in an hour or so. I have no more to leave you, so use them wisely.'

'Wait until the pain becomes unbearable again, you mean?'

The doctor nodded once. 'I'm sorry. I'll talk to my colleague as soon as I get the chance.'

Irina gave the woman her phone number. 'I'll stay here with her,' she said.

Yvonne looked alarmed at this suggestion, and though she said nothing in the presence of the doctor and the injured woman, it was clear that she wanted to try and persuade Irina to leave the house in case the men returned.

'Yvonne can look after my daughter,' Irina said firmly, pre-empting Yvonne's unspoken concerns.

The doctor left the house.

I watched with Sunny from an upstairs window to see if anyone paid any attention to her departure. The cars along the street were closely parked and none followed the woman.

We went back down to Yvonne and Irina.

The injured woman lay on the sofa with her eyes closed. The phials and hypodermics had been put out of sight.

'I'm staying here with them,' Irina told us. Her daughter stood beside her. She spoke to the girl and she went to Yvonne and took her hand. She clearly knew Yvonne and was happy to do as her mother told her.

Yvonne asked her about the other children, offering to take them, too. But Irina told her that the women would never agree to the children leaving the house without them.

I heard the children running on the landing above us.

The woman on the sofa spoke to Irina.

'She says she can feel the pain in her wrist again.'

The anaesthetic had lasted only half an hour.

Irina kissed her daughter and told Yvonne to take her.

Sunny and I followed them out of the house, waiting until the last of the locks had clicked and the chains been pulled into place behind us.

We parted from Yvonne and Irina Kapec's daughter at Prince's Avenue, having walked with them past the agency in the direction of Yvonne's home. Yvonne and the girl walked ahead of us. She kept the girl's hand firmly in her own. When Sunny and I paused and then turned back, she pretended to look in a shop window. She glanced at us and nodded.

We waited where we stood until the pair of them were lost amid the other shoppers.

Back at the agency, I asked Sunny if he thought that whoever had attacked the woman might now do the same to either Yvonne or Irina.

'I suppose it would all depend on who was intended to get the message that was being sent,' he said.

'Or on who was sending it?'

'Fowler? Unlikely. It might even be something we've all missed – something like a bad debt or an avenged insult, something we've all overreacted to because we want it to be more than it actually is.'

'And we're only involved because Yvonne is involved in trying to help Irina?'

He shrugged. He seemed suddenly exhausted, unwilling to prolong our speculation. He stood in the centre of the room, distracted. He looked around us.

'What?' I asked him.

'Someone's been in here.'

'Are you sure?'

He sat at his desk and turned to face the fan which still swung back and forth on the window sill.

'It's been moved,' he said. 'Someone's picked it up and put it back down again in a slightly different position. Look.' He indicated a calendar on the wall. At its furthest reach, the air from the fan lifted the calendar's pages slightly. 'I moved it so it wouldn't do that. It was getting on my nerves. The fan's been turned by an inch.' He looked closely around the rest of the room as he spoke.

I told him about the map Fowler had seen on my own wall. 'Perhaps he thought you gave it to me,' I said.

'Why should that bother him? It's hardly a secret that he owns the properties.'

'The Walmsley Street house would have been on it,' I said, uncertain what, if anything, this signified.

'Along with two hundred others.'

'If you're convinced someone's been in here, then it

might mean that we were lured away deliberately,' I said, confirming what he'd already suggested to me at Walmsley Street.

'I don't imagine the woman on the sofa will feel any better for knowing that. Apart from which, they could have got me out of here a dozen other ways or simply have waited for me to leave, all of them considerably less obvious.'

He went to a filing cabinet, checked that it was still locked, unlocked it and slid open the bottom drawer. He searched through the files it held, took one out and gave it to me.

'Has anything been taken?' I asked him.

'I'm not certain. I'm not even entirely certain of what was in there.'

The file contained a variety of articles concerning the regeneration of the city centre.

'All I know is that somebody's had it out of the cabinet while we were away. I was looking through it this morning. I put it back in the wrong place because you arrived earlier than I expected you. When I went just then to look, it was where it belonged.'

'Where anyone who'd taken it out to read it would have put it.'

'They probably switched the fan off while they were looking through it to stop the loose sheets from being blown around.'

He looked more closely at the contents of the file, but could still not determine what might or might not have been taken from it.

Eventually, he put it back in the cabinet and turned off the fan.

I asked him for the name of the man who had

transferred to Howden and he found this and wrote it down for me.

He asked me if I had plans to see Louise Brooks again.

'No plans,' I told him.

'And you're still saving your breath by not trying to persuade me that I've got completely the wrong idea about the two of you?'

'I won't lie to you,' I told him.

'So what now?'

'I go to see the others who were involved one way or another in what happened to Helen Brooks that night. So far, all I've got is one eye-witness account and Fowler's own neatly packaged and expertly corroborated little story. What about you?'

'I'll call Yvonne. Make sure everything's OK.'

'Why did you insist on telling her about me and Louise Brooks?' I asked him.

'Right,' he said. 'Like she didn't already know.'

'Are you serious?'

'She knew, or she guessed, or she was just waiting for it to happen. What difference does it make?'

I made a gun out of my fingers and shot him where he sat.

'I'm a dead man,' he said, and he slumped backwards in his seat.

17

Three days passed before I was able to visit Michael Ellis, who worked as a lifeboatman, who had been involved in the abortive rescue attempt at Foulholme Sands, and who had given evidence on behalf of the coastguard service. I'd seen the report submitted by the coastguard, but it contained little other than the details and timings of their own involvement. The first call was logged at eight-fifteen, and an inflatable craft was launched eight minutes later, arriving at the beached yacht at eight-fifty. The rescue helicopter was not alerted and requested until nine-twenty, half an hour after the lifeboat had arrived at the yacht and it was already known that there was no one left on board.

It was important to me to understand the precise sequence of these events and these degrees of involvement. Everything that had been reported afterwards had followed on from them.

Michael Ellis lived in one of the houses built to replace the original dwellings at Spurn. I drew up in front of these and he came out to me. He suggested we walk on the expanse of sand stretching either side of the lifeboat station, which was built out into the estuary on the inland side of the promontory. The pilot station rose from the brambles and dunes behind this. Further along the beach stood the abandoned black and white tower alongside the sand-covered road I had followed along the peninsula.

We walked beneath the old wall, a layer of fine white shells crackling beneath our feet.

'Is this where either of the bodies was likely to have washed up?' I asked him, indicating the beach on either side of us. There were a few other walkers there, but most had climbed the dunes and gone down onto the seaward beach, where the sun shone more directly. The voices of playing children could be heard.

'Here?' he said. 'Not very likely. Not on those tides.' He indicated the far shore. The tower at the entrance to Grimsby dock was visible to us through the haze. Beyond that, the flatlands of northern Lincolnshire ran invisibly to the Wolds, which were no more than a faint blur on the horizon. Terns and gulls filled the pale sky above us.

'What exactly is it you want to know?' he asked me. He raised his hand to the man on the gantry above us. The lifeboat sat at its end, on calm water.

I told him I was working for Alison Brooks.

He remembered her. 'I spoke to her when it was all over. She came up to me, her and her other daughter, and thanked me for what we'd tried to do. I told her I wished we'd been able to get there sooner.'

'You seem to have responded and arrived quickly enough,' I said.

'I mean I wished we'd been notified as soon as the yacht ran aground, while she was still in some water that might have allowed us to get closer to her.'

'The tide had receded too far by the time you arrived?'

'Too far for us to be able to do anything, even in the inflatable. It surprised us all to see her so far from the deep water.'

'Meaning what?'

'Meaning that according to our tide tables, for her to have been that far from the water's edge meant that she'd been there for at least an hour, perhaps longer. Our understanding from the call-out was that she'd only just run aground. We worked out where she'd be, and how far from the shore. You wouldn't want anyone trying to set off across that on foot.'

'Was there anything apart from the tides which caused you to think she'd been aground longer than you'd been led to believe?'

He thought about this. 'I don't know. It might have been something Peter Nicholson said.'

'You sound as though you know him,' I said.

'I do. We all do. He applied to Trinity House, but they knocked him back. Too old.'

'To become a coastguard?'

'Coastguard, lifeboatman, anything they were prepared to offer him. To be honest, I don't think even he expected to be successful, but he did it anyway. We're a permanent, paid station here. There's a waiting list. I think he thought that his working knowledge of the river would swing it for him. It was after all that bother with the Associated Ports.'

'When he was fired?'

'That was certainly how *he* saw it. He came down here to the pilot station, accused some of the men there of selling out. ABP kept them on, see.'

'What did Nicholson do after he was fired?'

'I'm not sure. He used to turn up here reasonably regularly, offering to do voluntary work – work on the boathouse, maintenance, that kind of thing. It wasn't allowed. Everything's regulated.'

'Did he make a nuisance of himself?'

'Some thought so. One or two of the wives said he gave them the creeps. He just used to come and watch, hang around.'

'His own wife left him soon afterwards.'

'I know. The fact is, the offer from ABP stayed on the table for a long time after he'd told them to stuff it.'

'Would they honestly have taken him back?'

'I think so. Whatever anyone thought of him, he used to be good at what he did. It frustrated him to think that all his knowledge and experience were going to waste.' He smiled. 'Believe me, he was in his element when he saw that yacht aground.'

'Excited enough to suggest that he'd actually seen it run aground?'

'Possibly. Not that even he would have seen too much, of course.'

'Because he was too far away?'

'Because it was a dark night. He must have been at least eighty metres away. It might not sound like much, but there was no light whatsoever where he was. Yet to hear him tell it, he saw everything that happened.'

'He described the woman climbing over the rails, and

the man sitting in the stern of the yacht and making no effort to stop her,' I said.

'I'm not saying that he didn't see *something*,' he said. 'All I'm questioning is that he saw everything as clearly as he *said* he saw it. Even in the clear light of day you'd be hard-pressed to tell a man from a woman in a life-jacket at that distance.'

'Did anyone at the inquest question what he said he saw?'

'I don't think so. I don't really suppose it mattered. All that mattered then was that he'd seen the yacht and raised the alarm. Like I said – in his element. Man of the hour. He certainly got his face in the papers for the next few days.'

'And that might not have happened to the extent it did if he hadn't built up his own part in the events?'

'It's what one or two of the lads thought at the time. Especially after there was some criticism of us on account of how little we were able to do.'

'How close could you get?' I asked him.

'I'd say about forty or fifty metres. Not much closer than he was on the other side of her.'

'Did *you* see anything to suggest that the people on board had left her and tried to make it across the mud?'

'Nothing. Besides which, they would have sunk into it up to their waists.'

'And then gone under and been lost?'

'It was a common enough suggestion at the time. They searched. No, there was nothing to show that anyone had left the vessel where she was stuck.'

'What do *you* think happened?'

He stopped walking and sat on a rusted oil drum

protruding from the sand. Empty crab shells lay scattered at his feet. He picked up a few of these and crushed them in his hand, scattering the debris over his knees.

'I don't know,' he said. 'Perhaps they got out into a dinghy while they were still in deep enough water. Perhaps that's what we should have been looking for all along instead of wasting our time trying to get close to the yacht. Perhaps they were caught by the tide, carried out to sea and lost there. It's as good a reason as any to account for why they never showed up afterwards.'

'No dinghy was ever found.'

'I know.'

'Do you think Nicholson might have gone too far and actually have lied about what he saw?'

He considered this. 'Like you said – he probably blew up his own part in it, that's all. Let's just say he always had a better opinion of himself than anyone else ever had.'

'Other than the publicity, I don't really see what he'd have to gain by it,' I said, hoping the remark sounded sincere.

'Perhaps it was just meant to be one in the eye for us, for having rejected him. Perhaps it was just his way of getting one over on the whole world.'

'I saw him,' I said. 'That's how I know about his wife.'

'Jane,' he said. 'Some of us knew her. She and my wife were friends. What neither of us ever did understand was why she put up with him for so long. Where did she go, do you know? No one here ever heard from her after she'd gone.'

I didn't have an answer. I asked him if he thought there might be a connection between the events of that night and the timing of her departure.

He shook his head. 'She'd been threatening to do it for years. And all that time, he'd been telling her to go. There was never any love lost between them. Who knows – perhaps all his bragging and preening was the last straw for her. With a bit of luck, she'll divorce him soon and he'll be forced to sell the house. Christ knows why, but it's his pride and joy, that house. You'd never get the planning permission these days to build something that close to the water, especially not an eyesore like that.'

'He didn't seem particularly upset that she'd gone when I spoke to him,' I said.

'I remember him at the inquest. All over the mother and sister, telling them how sorry he was about what had happened.'

'And by which time you and your colleagues had started to have your own doubts about his story, about exactly what he'd seen?'

He nodded. 'Nobody was exactly in a position to call him a liar, but anyone who knew that part of the estuary and who knew how the tide was running would be aware that there was something wrong with what he was saying.'

He left his seat and we turned back along the beach towards the houses.

'Does he still come out here?' I asked him.

'Not recently. I haven't seen him for months. Some of us even thought he'd already been forced to sell the house and move into Hull.'

'Did his wife work?'

'Used to, a few years back. Somewhere in Hull. She didn't drive. It was hard for her to get there and back each day for her shifts. It might have suited *him* living in such an isolated spot, but she was never too keen. Find her and ask her,' he said. 'She'll tell you everything. Though if she's any sense, she'll be as far away from him now as it's possible to be, and letting her solicitor get on with all the dirty work.' He shielded his eyes to look at the distant houses.

We parted back at the wall and I returned to my car. I'd parked it in the shade, but it stood now in full sunlight, and the door and the steering-wheel were hot to the touch.

18

I drove from Spurn to the marine salvage yard beyond Hessle Haven, to where Fowler's yacht had been towed when it was finally released by the police.

I found the entrance to the yard and knew immediately that I'd come too late. The business had closed. A rusted chain was looped and padlocked around the gates. Beyond, a slipway was filled with the blocks and baulks of timber upon which vessels had once rested. A massive corrugated-iron shed stood to one side, and the space between this and where I stood was filled with small broken hulls and all the other detritus which, once so vital, had suddenly become so much worthless dead weight. I rattled the chain and my hands came away stained red.

I remembered having been taken by my father to see the working trawlers in Saint Andrew's Dock, dozens of vessels being unloaded through the night and across each other's decks under the glare of arc lights.

I'd gone back with him only a few years later to see the same vessels moored side by side and abandoned, rusting like the hulls in the Hessle yard, not even worth the effort of dismantling them.

A noise at the far end of the yard, where the slipway gate stood closed to the Humber, alerted my attention, and I saw a man in overalls walk from the rear of the shed towards a mound of discarded chain and tackle.

I called to him and he came over. He stood on the other side of the padlocked gate and asked me what I wanted.

'I was looking for whoever was in charge,' I said.

He looked around him. 'In charge of this? That'd be a desperate man.'

'Do you work here?'

'*Worked*,' he said. 'And if you're about to accuse me of breaking and entering, then you're wrong. I've just got a bit of welding needs doing on a trailer, that's all.' Meaning he was there illegally.

'When did it close?'

'Six months back.'

The yard looked as though nothing had been done there for a decade.

'I'm making enquiries about a yacht that was broken up here about a year ago,' I said.

'What sort of enquiries?'

'You might remember it. A couple of people drowned further down the river. The yacht was too badly damaged to be repaired. I understood that this was where it was brought to be broken up.'

He looked at me closely. It was clear to me that he knew what I was talking about.

'I'm authorized to pay for any assistance I might receive in making my enquiries,' I said.

He directed me along the chain fence to where a flap had been cut and folded back, and he held this clear for me as I ducked through.

'I worked on dismantling and burning that boat myself.'

'Burning?'

'That's why I remember it. They wanted all the fittings ripping out and burning. Yacht like that, there's usually a bit to be made by selling on the fittings. It wasn't a big vessel, but there would still have been enough to make a tidy sum selling stuff on to the Sunday sailors.'

'Who insisted on it being burned?'

'Don't know. Owner, presumably. We reckoned at the time that it was an insurance job – that he didn't get his money until the thing was properly gone. We always considered it to be a bit of a borderline case.'

'How did the yacht get here?'

'We used to have a recovery boat. An old river tug out of Goole. They had the yacht at the marina. We only got word to take it away after everybody else had finished with it.'

I followed him to the rear of the shed, and into the cavernous space. He went to an oxyacetylene torch on a trolley and turned off the flame. A rack of other gas tanks stood nearby.

He saw me looking. 'A drop left in each of them,' he said. 'Shame to waste it.'

'Tell me more about the yacht,' I said.

'The boss offered to buy it, but nobody wanted to listen.'

'Was it badly damaged?'

'Not too bad. Some harm had come to her keel fitting. She'd got a few dents – nothing that couldn't have been straightened out – and some of her rail had gone. Usual stuff. Inside was the bigger mess. She must have had her engine full on when she ran aground, or had all her sails rigged.'

Nicholson had said she was showing no sail when he'd spotted the yacht.

'What sort of mess?'

He filled a saucepan with water from a tap and turned the torch on to it, offering me tea, which I accepted.

'Used to be thirty of us working here at one time,' he said.

I told him I was surprised the place had survived for so long.

'Me, too,' he said.

I took out my wallet and gave him forty pounds.

'Do you want me to sign for it or anything?' he asked me.

I told him I didn't. He kissed the notes and slid them into his pocket.

The water in the saucepan began to boil and he poured it into two cups.

'Is that why the interior fittings were burned – because they'd been knocked about?' I said.

'Might have been. But it was still a waste. That's what made us think it was an insurance job.'

The milkless, sugarless tea tasted bitter.

'I was the first in there, so if anyone should know whether it was worth saving or not, it's me.'

I asked him if he could describe it for me.

'This was four or five months after it had run aground, remember. Might even have been longer.'

'Presumably all the personal possessions had already been retrieved by the police,' I said.

'I imagine so. I know there were still one or two charts in the chart-drawer. The story we were told was that the owner couldn't bear to have anything to do with it because of what had happened on it. That's right – we were told to destroy it because he couldn't bear to think of anyone else using it. He even sent somebody, or the insurers did – I can't remember which – to make sure that we did what we were told to do. There's always a bit of unofficial reclamation and resale goes on in a job like this, if you know what I mean.'

'Can you remember what the man who was sent to oversee the destruction looked like?'

He described Marco. 'Arrogant little shite. Acted like he owned the place. Boss told us to do whatever he said.'

'Meaning he'd probably already been paid to comply.'

'Something like that. She was just sat up here for a few days and then this guy turns up and starts telling us what to do. The boss even pulled some of us off other jobs to get the work finished in his presence.'

'Which it presumably was.'

'She was a yacht in the morning, and a pile of broken pieces and a mountain of ash in the afternoon.'

'Was everything burned?'

'Mostly. I imagine we took the charts and a few other bits and pieces off her – instruments, gauges, that sort of stuff. Whatever the police hadn't already taken. We used to put everything in lockers just in case the owners came back. Leave it a few months and then sell it on and share the proceeds.'

'Will anything you took off still be here?' It seemed unlikely.

'Doubt it. Not after all this time. I'll look if you like. Place was more or less finished by then and we all had a lot more on our minds than a few perks.'

'Tell me what you can remember about the inside of the yacht,' I said.

'Below deck? Bit knocked about. Nothing in its proper place. But, like I said, that could have happened at any time. Everything unsecured had gone flying at one point or another. Something had obviously gone with a knock against one of the cabin walls because there was a bloody great hole. I remember that well enough on account of it being smack in the middle of a lovely bit of panelling.'

'How big?'

He joined the forefingers and thumbs of both his hands together.

'What do you think had caused it?'

He shrugged. 'Looked just as though someone had swung a sledgehammer into it, so it must have been either something heavy or something fast-moving.'

'In such a confined space?'

'I'm only saying what I saw. It's not as though there was ever any blood or anything like that in there.'

'Was it an actual hole?' I said. 'Or was the panelling all still there in pieces?'

'Proper hole. I could put my fist through it.'

'Would it have affected the seaworthiness of the yacht in any way?'

He laughed. 'Nah. Thing like that you could have

had patched in an hour. It was only an interior panel.'

I asked if he remembered anything else from the time the boat was delivered to its destruction.

'I remember there was a list taped to the back of the door of all the stuff the police and whoever had taken away. I read it. There was drink, cases of wine, spirits. A few cartons of cigarettes. They'd taken glasses, plates, ashtrays, stuff like that. Probably for that forensic thing.'

'Probably,' I said. Whatever the police had found on board, none of it had helped them to identify Helen Brooks's companion.

He sat for a moment with his elbows on his knees and his face in his hands. 'The girl's mother came,' he said. 'Turned up with her other daughter. They wanted – you know – to see where she'd . . .'

'Did they get there in time? Before the yacht was destroyed.'

'They came the day before tin-pot turned up. It wasn't really safe for them to go on board – she was just resting against another wreck – but the daughter insisted it was what she wanted. She had a bunch of flowers with her, said she wanted to leave them where her sister had died. What could we say?'

'And so she went on board?'

'Somebody fetched her a ladder. I told her I'd go with her, but she said she wanted to do it by herself. To be honest, and now that I remember, she was a bit sharp with me. I went back down to keep the mother company. She apologized to me for the way her daughter had been with me. She said she appreciated us letting her see the yacht. She tried to give me some money, but I wouldn't take it. I've lost a child of my own. There are lots of emptinesses in this world, but there's none like that.'

'Did *she* ask if anything had been retrieved from the yacht?'

'Asked the boss. He told her everything was long gone. To be honest, he had a lot of other things on his mind at the time.'

'The closure of the yard?'

'That, and putting twenty men out of work. To say nothing of finding a buyer for the land without it being a going concern any longer. I remember wishing there was something more I could have done for her.'

'How long was the other daughter on board?'

'Not long. You could hear her clattering about.'

'Do you think she was looking for something?'

'She might have been. Perhaps she just wanted something for the pair of them to remember the dead girl by.'

'Perhaps,' I said. 'Did the owner or the man who supervised the destruction ever come back?'

'Not that I know of. What for? Job were done. I remember the boss trying to sell him another yacht and the man laughed in his face. Said he'd had enough of the sea for one lifetime. Understandable, really.'

'I suppose so,' I said.

He drank the last of his tea. Sparrows flew in and out of the high girders above us. Holes had already appeared and pieces of the fallen roof lay around us. From where we sat, we could see distant vessels on the river.

'It's why I come,' he said, looking. 'You miss that kind of thing.' He motioned to the trailer on which he'd been working. 'That's just a piece of junk belonging to a neighbour. I told him I'd sort it. It's not worth ten quid and I've been working on it for a week already.'

'I appreciate what you've been able to tell me.'

'I wish there was more,' he said. I gave him one of my cards and he wiped his hands before taking it. 'I can't think that I've missed much out,' he said. 'Who are you working for — the mother?'

I nodded.

'Was it more than they said it was at the time?'

'No-one's sure,' I told him. 'You said there might still be some charts or instruments.'

He rose and motioned me to follow him. 'Don't get your hopes up,' he warned me. 'The scavengers have been over this place a fair few times.'

I followed him up a narrow open staircase to a small room above the shed entrance.

'Used to be the office,' he told me, forcing the stiff door open.

Inside stood a desk, a chair, several filing cabinets, their drawers missing, and a row of cupboards. A calendar on the wall was already two years out of date.

'All the paperwork's long gone,' he said. 'Creditors, people like that.'

He went to one of the cupboards and opened it to reveal a box full of rolled charts. He spread these out on the desk.

I began looking at them. They were all of the Humber in its various reaches.

'We used to keep them here so we could be exact about where we had to pick a vessel up or drop it off,' he said. 'The soundings on most of them will be out of date by now. If there's anything here that was taken off your yacht, it'll probably have its name and registration numbers in the top left-hand corner, but, like I said, don't get your hopes up.'

I saw the name as he was still talking. I pulled the chart from the others and held it up to him.

'That was a chance in a million,' he said. 'Show it me.' He took it from me, glanced at it and made a disparaging noise. 'It's just a general chart,' he said. He stretched his fingers apart and measured the scale. 'Runs practically from Goole to the sea. They won't have had much use for it, and they certainly won't have used it for plotting their course.'

'Not much use for a yacht sailing close to Foulholme Sands?'

'None whatsoever. You'd need to be a lot more accurate than this for that sort of close work. A foot of water one way or the other can make all the difference in that place. They'd only have this on board to get a general idea of where they were going and to see where the main shipping channels ran.' He showed me the dotted blue lines.

'Was there ever any suggestion at the time that the yacht might have been in a collision with something bigger, and that that was why she'd run aground?' I said.

He shook his head. 'There was no sign of anything like that.'

He looked through the remainder of the rolled sheets, but there was nothing else from the yacht. I took out my wallet, but he refused to take any more money from me.

'Take it,' he said. 'It might help.'

I thanked him and told him I'd tell Alison Brooks

that he'd remembered her and that he'd helped me.

He took a rubber band from another of the charts and gave it to me, and it was only as I rolled and secured it that I saw the writing along its lower edge. Someone had written, in biro, the name LULU over and over – LULULULULULU – until it came to resemble a pattern around the edge of the sheet. I finished rolling the chart without showing this to him.

He walked with me back to the gap in the fence.

I asked him what would happen to the yard in the future.

'The future?' he said. 'What's that?' And then he turned and walked away from me, absently raising his hand as he went.

19

Four days had passed since I'd seen Louise. On Wednesday morning she called me at Humber Street and left a message to say that her mother's condition had deteriorated and that it was difficult for her, Louise, to see me. She was taking some time off work, she said. She asked me to call her.

I rang a few minutes later.

Alison Brooks answered, and it was immediately clear to me that, despite her efforts, it had grown harder for her to speak in anything other than a dry and painful whisper. She paused after every few words.

I told her about the man I'd seen at the salvage yard and she said she remembered him. I didn't tell her yet about the chart I'd found in case it turned out to be of some significance and I needed to hold onto it.

Louise had just gone out, she said. She said her daughter would be sorry to have missed me. She asked me not to visit her until she was feeling stronger, and then she apologized again for having misled me with regard to the advanced state of her cancer.

After only a minute, it was impossible for her to continue speaking, each word now accompanied by an airless rasp which threatened to choke her. I told her I'd talk to her soon, and hung up.

I rang directory enquiries for the number of the Howden police station, dialled and was put through to the desk sergeant. I asked for James Salter, the man who had transferred from London at the collapse of the trial there, and who, according to Sunny's contact, had known of Fowler and his dealings prior to his arrival in Hull.

The desk sergeant asked me what I was calling in connection with.

I didn't want to tell him. 'I was given the number by the Hull police,' I lied.

'If it's to do with his neighbourhood watch stuff, I'll put you through.'

'That's right,' I said. 'Neighbourhood watch.'

I waited a minute while the connection was made.

'Salter,' he said.

I told him who I was and the case I was working on. At first, the name Helen Brooks meant nothing to him, and it was only when I mentioned Fowler that he showed any interest in what I was telling him.

'Who are you?' he asked me again.

I told him I'd been given his name by Sunny, and that my enquiries into Fowler had led me to the collapse of the case the Metropolitan Police had tried to build against Fowler and the others in his syndicate.

He remained silent for a minute. 'I don't want to discuss this on the phone.'

I told him I'd meet him wherever he liked. He considered this and then asked me if I knew of the old Ouse Ferryboat Inn upriver from the new motorway bridge. I knew it, and we agreed to meet there at eight that evening. Then he said, loudly, 'Of course I can come and give you a talk. That's my job. Right. Eight o'clock. I'll be there,' and I knew someone had arrived beside him.

It was a little after midday.

I left Humber Street and walked to the dock. The marina office was suspended over the inner-lock gates leading out into the river. I went up the steps and rapped on the glass to the man inside. I told him who I was looking for and he said, 'You've found him. But what you've found is a busy man, so make it quick.' He'd been sitting with his feet up, reading a paper when I'd arrived.

'I just wanted to find out from the people who were actually there, actually involved, what happened on the day the yacht ran aground,' I said.

He came to the glass and slid open a small hatchway.

'Already told everybody who asked everything I saw,' he said.

'I know. I've read all the reports. A lot of people got to have their say in one way or another, but there were very few actual witnesses, very few people who actually saw the yacht leaving here, or who saw Helen Brooks on it.'

'It was her, all right,' he said.

I was uncertain whether he was referring to the yacht or to Helen Brooks.

'She waved to me. Always did. Always took the time to wave. Terrible what happened, terrible.'

'How did she seem to you?'

'What do you mean, how did she seem?'

'There was some suggestion at the coroner's court that she might have had too much to drink.'

'I know. Well, if she had, it wasn't particularly noticeable. She was that kind of girl.'

'Was she at the tiller?' I said.

He smiled at the remark. 'I can't ever remember once seeing her at the tiller. No, the man was at the tiller.' He motioned to the water behind me. 'That's how far away they were.' It was twenty yards. Far enough for some things to remain uncertain.

'Some of the other witnesses said there might have been some doubt. He was wearing waterproofs and—'

'I *know* what he was wearing,' he said, angry at having been contradicted. 'I watched them getting ready, casting off. Everything going in and out has to come through here. And if they have to come through here, then they have to do it through me.'

'How long did they take to get ready and then leave?'

'As long as it takes. They were there about half an hour, I suppose, before finally getting under way. They berthed at the far side.' He pointed to the distant corner of the marina.

'Did the man do or say anything?'

'Such as?'

'Such as wave to you, acknowledge your help, talk to you.'

He thought about this. 'Not that I can remember. He was concentrating on steering them through the other yachts. Apart from which, *she* was shouting to me. Went on shouting until long after I could properly hear her. It still brings me up short when I think of her and what happened. I'd helped her out with a few things one or two days previously.'

'Such as?' There had been no mention of this in his testimony to the court.

'Nothing, really. Deliveries. Carried a few boxes for her. Food, drink, that's all.' Meaning she'd flirted with him and he'd been flattered by her attention.

'Did you see her on the yacht with Mr Fowler on occasion?'

'Of course I did; it was his yacht.'

'And when the two of them went out together, was he the one at the tiller?'

'Mostly he had someone else to do all that for him. More often than not a younger guy, small beard.'

'Would you say it was the same man with Helen Brooks when it was just the two of them that day?'

He became suddenly suspicious of me, as though I'd tried to trick or confuse him.

'If you thought as much of Helen as you say, you'd tell me,' I said.

'I don't need people like you telling me what I should or shouldn't do,' he said. He waved to a man on a passing yacht. 'Mr Fowler came to see me afterwards. Asking the same questions you're asking. Wanting to know who the man was, if I recognized him. So no – in answer to your question – it couldn't have been the same man. Satisfied?'

He saw none of the obvious flaws in this reasoning, but I said nothing.

'Did Fowler come after or before the inquest?'

'*Mister* Fowler. Before. And I told him what I told you – that it was a man, but that I didn't recognize him. *He* seemed satisfied with everything I was able to tell him – especially considering all he was going through – so why aren't you?'

'And you said the same at the inquest?'

'Of course I did. It was the truth. They said all sorts of things about her in the papers afterwards. Mister Fowler didn't deserve all that.'

'He got rid of the yacht fast enough,' I said.

'So? Wouldn't you?'

'I mean he had it broken up, burned, completely destroyed.'

He hadn't known this. 'I suppose I assumed he'd just sold her,' he said. 'Anyhow, what difference does it make? He cancelled the berth here once the police and everyone had finished with it.'

'You saw the condition the yacht was in when they towed it in from Foulholme Sands. Would you have said it was beyond repair?'

'Like I told—' He stopped abruptly.

'Told who?'

'The men from his insurers. Like I told them: it hardly mattered whether or not *I* thought it was or wasn't beyond repair, because whatever was decided, he was going to get rid of it regardless, whatever it cost him. He cancelled the berth booking with three months' notice. That's the minimum we allow. Plus, he told me himself that it was what he intended doing. Too many unhappy associations.'

'And you assumed he meant he was going to sell it?'

'Naturally.'

'But if he'd sold it, wasn't there a chance it would

213

have continued to be berthed here, a constant reminder to him?'

'Not necessarily,' he said, but again uncertain of himself and of where my questions were leading. I wondered why he was making so many excuses for Fowler, why everything he said was based on the premise that Fowler and not Helen Brooks had been the one to suffer and lose the most in that night's events.

'Thanks for your time,' I said.

'Is that it?'

'Like I said, I really only wanted to hear from the few people who actually saw Helen that day. So far, all I've heard is what everybody said at the inquest. I was hoping for something new, some insight, something to tell Helen's mother.' It was a pitch at his own self-importance.

'I don't know what you expect me to tell you,' he said. But I could see that he was considering something.

'You could tell me that you knew for certain that she was drunk,' I suggested. 'I can understand why you might be trying to protect her memory, but you're doing no one any favours by keeping things uncertain or half-hidden.'

'All right,' he said angrily. 'If it makes you happy, yes, she was probably drunk. Perhaps even worse.'

'Drugs?'

'I don't know. Something. I know we're all supposed to know about these things, but I don't. OK?' He paused. 'I told you – I'd helped her once or twice, carrying and fetching for her. Most of what I'd carried on before they sailed was drink. Like they were

214

preparing for a party. It's what Mr Fowler used the yacht for. Perhaps they were just celebrating being able to get back out on the river after a long lay-off, who knows?'

'A party for just the two of them?'

'There was enough food and drink for a dozen, more. She actually told me they were stocking up for a little private party. Those were her exact words. She was grateful for my help, chatty. I wasn't even certain if she meant for that day or some time later.'

'It wouldn't have been much of a party – not with the man at the tiller presumably having to stay perfectly sober,' I said.

'I'm only telling you what she said.'

'I appreciate your assistance,' I said.

'She always waved,' he repeated. 'Some of them don't even bother to look up and acknowledge you on their way in and out.'

I left him and walked to the tables set out on Dock Street. A man with a guitar and a dog sang 'In the Summertime' over and over. He'd trained the dog to carry a plastic bowl and collect money from his small audiences.

20

I arrived at the Ferryboat Inn at seven-thirty. Since the coming of the motorway and the mile-long span of the new bridge, the box-girder construction a quarter-mile upriver on the Ouse had been largely abandoned by all but local traffic. It had once been on the main route between the cities of south Yorkshire and the east coast, and five-mile-long traffic jams had been commonplace most summer weekends.

I waited in the car park for a few minutes, watching the few passing cars.

James Salter arrived at eight, parked close to the exit facing the road and came to me.

I went out to him.

He held out his hand to me, and the instant I took it, he said, 'All this is off the record. I mean it.'

'There isn't a record to be *on*,' I told him.

He looked pointedly at my jacket and I took it off and threw it into the car.

We walked together to the bridge and looked along the Ouse. A line of fishermen sat high above the water along the far bank.

He was younger than I had anticipated, in his late twenties.

'Tell me exactly what it is you're looking into,' he said.

I told him about the death of Helen Brooks, the open verdict and all the unresolved questions this had left in its wake. I told him about her dying mother, about the motives of her sister, and about Helen Brooks's involvement with Fowler. I finished by admitting that I might have so far got everything wrong, and that Helen Brooks's death might have been the accident that almost everybody else wanted it to be, and that her involvement with Fowler beforehand had been purely coincidental.

'You don't believe that for one minute,' he said. 'And neither do I. Otherwise, the pair of us wouldn't be here.' I felt encouraged by the remark. He leaned forward to watch the dark, sluggish water beneath us. 'If you didn't believe Fowler was in some way responsible,' he said, 'then you would have kept your distance from me.'

'Not once I'd learned from Sunny what happened in London.'

He relaxed at the mention of Sunny's name. Sunny, via his contact on the *Standard*, was our guarantor of confidentiality, and we both understood this.

'The more I find out about Fowler, the more chance I have of making the few connections he hasn't already taken care of ahead of me,' I said.

'What Fowler's good at where connections are concerned, is severing them,' he said.

I asked him if he'd like to go into the bar, but he said he'd prefer to remain outside a little longer. He'd been working since six that morning.

'How were you involved with Fowler?' I asked him.

'I joined the Met six years ago, straight from UCL. They had a graduate recruitment scheme – fast-tracking – but part of the deal was that you spent a couple of years at the bottom, learning the ropes. I can't pretend it was much of a success or that I ever really fitted in. A degree in medieval history? Big deal. You can imagine the attitude of everyone else slogging it out the hard way. There was a lot of resentment. They always made a big thing about how the culture' – he drew quotation marks with his fingers – 'of the force was changing, but I never saw any signs of it. If your face, your behaviour and your prejudices fitted, then you were in. Otherwise . . . I first came across Fowler when I was sent to East London for three months. There was a big operation being undertaken with Immigration and Customs – illegal immigrants being brought in and employed as cheap labour.'

'Fowler's syndicate.'

'It was never *his*, exactly. He was just one of the lucky few getting rich on the backs of others. It stank from the start.'

'The operation? How?'

'Because half the men working out of the stations involved talked about Fowler as though he was their best mate. They respected him. They wanted what he'd got. They treated the immigrants like animals, but whenever Fowler or any of the others were mentioned, it was as though they were aristocracy. Fowler lapped it up.'

'Do you think he was paying any of them?'

'My so-called colleagues? Nothing was ever proved.'

'But it's what you believed.'

'Yes, it's what I believed. We spent months watching some of the building sites, taking pictures, checking up on the faces working there, tracing their records or their families' records through every database available. And then on the day we picked to turn up and arrest everyone, the sites would be full of legitimate, tax-paying, national insurance number-owning labourers.'

'Meaning the contractors had been tipped off.'

'I didn't need the medieval history degree to work that much out.'

'What did you do?'

'Nothing, at first. And then I was approached by one of the men who put me on to the fast-track scheme, my mentor, and he asked me to tell him what I'd seen and worked out for myself. He told me he was asking me in confidence, that nothing I told him would ever find its way back to the station chiefs. He was an honest man; I trusted him. But somewhere down the line, everything became common knowledge.'

'What happened?'

'I told him of my suspicions, of the men I thought were involved with Fowler and the others,' he said.

'And?'

'And nothing. The CPS set up a case against two of them, but the whole thing fell apart for want of evidence, and because – surprise, surprise – of a whole litany of procedural irregularities while they were awaiting trial.'

'Irregularities perpetrated by others involved?'

'I doubt if anybody ever said as much to their faces.'

'The outcome of which was to shift the focus of the inquiry away from Fowler and the syndicate to the team investigating him,' I said.

'And of which Fowler and the others took swift and full advantage.'

'In what way?'

'In every way they could. They'd had a close call. I was never personally convinced that any of the dirt would stick to those at the top – they had their sub-contractors and sub-subcontractors for all that little-people stuff. Fowler and the others were per-fectly respectable businessmen who pretended to be horrified and angry when it was pointed out to them that men had died in accidents on building sites ultimately controlled by them.'

'What happened to the men who were caught work-ing illegally?'

'Everything about them was illegal. It was what made them such easy prey for men like Fowler in the first place. I bet he could hardly believe his luck, having left London and come to Hull, to discover that the Government had chosen the city to relocate thousands of asylum-seekers away from the south-east. Only this time, Fowler could make his money legitimately by getting hand-in-glove with all those other agencies, and rent his properties to them having employed cheap labour to renovate those same properties in the first place. He couldn't have gained more from the arrangement if he'd written the rules himself.'

'So everything he was once doing illegally in London, he now gets to do up here with more or less everyone's blessing?'

'More or less. And you'd worked that much out the minute you met him. I'm assuming you have met him,' he said.

'Once,' I said. 'It was probably enough.'

'It was,' he said.

'What happened to you?' I asked him.

'The day after the trial collapsed, my flat was searched by the Drug Squad. Acting on information received.'

'And they found what?'

'The few pieces of dope I had there.'

'Just that?'

'If they'd planted anything, I'd have put up a fight. This way there was nothing I could do except put up my hands.'

'But you weren't kicked off the force.'

'The man I'd spoken to about my suspicions came back to see me. He was angry that it had all come to nothing. He was catching some of the flak for that himself. He was angry that I'd allowed myself to be compromised the way I had. There wasn't much he could do for me, he said.'

'And you told him that if he didn't try, if you were kicked off the force, that you'd make all your suspicions public.'

'Something like that. I wasn't particularly proud of it, but the whole thing was raining back down on us all by then. Nobody knew who to trust. I don't think I'd have survived for very much longer under those circumstances.'

'And so you made a choice while you still had one to make.'

'I was told that any request for transfer that I made

would be granted, preferably a long way from London, and that I'd got a week to do something about it. I was given a list of vacancies. I grew up in York.'

'And the fast-tracking?'

'In Howden?'

'And, meanwhile, while all that dust was settling, Fowler and the others began to dismantle and to distance themselves from being prosecuted.'

'You'd be surprised how easy that was. Immigration and Customs were certainly in no hurry to work with the Met again. They blamed us for everything that had gone wrong. According to them, the collapse of such a major case would only encourage others to get involved in exactly the same sort of thing.'

'Do you think Fowler stayed connected to any of it?'

'No idea. You might say I lost touch with things. The impression I got at the time was that everybody involved, on both sides, was anxious to put it all as far behind them as possible.'

'Because they'd made their money and escaped prosecution? Is that what you meant when you said Fowler was good at severing connections?'

'There were a few messy ends, but I think Fowler and the others got themselves far enough away from anything that was likely to stick.'

'And presumably the men on the force who'd escaped prosecution wouldn't be too keen to go back after everyone again.'

'It wouldn't have been up to them. They'd have been kept well away from it all a second time round. But by then there was no appetite for it. Everybody had been embarrassed by the extent of the alleged involvement and corruption. It wasn't the kind of shitpile you'd want to kick over twice in the same week.'

Beneath us, one of the anglers caught a fish, which he stood up to play, and which swam back and forth in front of him, invisible beneath the brown surface. He held his pole high, eventually raising the exhausted fish's silver head out of the water. We both watched as he netted it.

'You said there were some messy ends,' I said. 'What did you mean?'

'Just that others further down the pecking order weren't quite as lucky as Fowler and his friends.'

'Were there some successful prosecutions?'

'A few of the contractors were fined, but that's all. I was referring to some of the others involved – men Fowler probably never even knew about.'

'What men?'

'The traffickers who brought the asylum-seekers into the country in the first place.'

'No one's ever seriously suggested that Fowler was actively involved in that side of things beyond stimulating the demand,' I said.

'No one ever proved that Fowler was involved in *anything*,' he said.

'Do *you* think he was?'

'I don't honestly know. But it certainly paid him and the others to have a steady supply of men coming in who weren't all held in Government detention camps, and who *they* then had some hold over. At the very least he must have known about the trafficking operation. The men on the force who escaped prosecution certainly knew all about it. Immigration and Customs knew all about it. I don't see how someone like Fowler *couldn't* have known about it.' He paused and smiled.

'What?'

'When I first read about Fowler being in Hull – I wasn't even sure at first that it was the same man; not until I saw a photograph of him shaking dicks with the mayor – it occurred to me then that he was there, that he'd come to Hull specifically—'

'Because of the asylum-seekers starting to arrive?'

'It made as much sense as anything.'

The thought had already occurred to me, and while I hadn't dismissed it completely, I considered it unlikely.

'Were any of the traffickers caught?' I asked him.

'Most of the main players in that particular set-up were from Eastern Europe and the Middle East. Someone might have warned Fowler and the others what was about to happen, but I imagine the word only ever went so far down the line. That was how it was *supposed* to work; that's how Fowler and the others protected themselves. It was always more a part of the Immigration brief to deal with the traffickers. The Met were meant to tie up the illegal-working side of things.' He held his hands apart, cupped them and drew them together. 'Chop things off at both ends, leave everybody in the middle.'

'Instead of which . . .'

'Instead of which, three or four days after the first of our failed raids, some of the traffickers actually turned up in London and were arrested.'

'Why did they come?'

'It was all a big mystery. They were deported and sent for trial in the countries they'd come from. There were some from Albania, some Croatians, one or two from places most people here had never heard of. The thinking at the time was that they'd come on one of their regular visits to the country. Some thought they were there to set up their own little slave markets, and some that they were there to connect with the people here who could take care of the new arrivals for them, so that the risk to themselves was reduced. Everybody could stay at home and do what they did. The only people moving and exposed would be the illegal immigrants themselves.'

'Surely, someone could have warned the traffickers to stay away?'

He shrugged. 'Perhaps them coming and getting caught was all a part of the syndicate's plan. At least that way Immigration got something out of it.'

'What happened?'

'To the traffickers? No idea. I was long gone by the time any of it happened.'

'Meaning they'd all probably be back in business soon enough.'

'It's not as though the trade's become any *less* profitable.'

'And by which time, Fowler himself was also long gone.'

'Washing his hands for three years and then holding them up to show everyone how clean they were.'

We left the bridge and walked back to the inn.

Dusk was falling, and bats flew among the cross-pieces above us. We both stopped walking to watch.

'Would Fowler ever have had any idea what happened to you, what part you might have played in it all?' I asked him.

'What part *did* I play? Fowler wouldn't have known I even existed.'

We went into the inn and sat at a corner table. Music played. Photographs of vessels passing the bridge and of men holding fish hung above the bar.

'What was she like?' he asked me when I returned to him with our drinks.

'Someone who got caught up in something she didn't have the sense to stay away from,' I told him.

'Whatever she did, she didn't deserve Fowler,' he said.

'What do *you* think would have happened if all the trials had gone ahead and succeeded?' I asked him.

'If Fowler and the others had been convicted and locked up, and if my esteemed colleagues had then been convicted and imprisoned on the evidence of people like me, you mean?' He pretended to consider his answer. 'Then by now I'd probably be watching my back and sitting in a shitty little bar somewhere in the middle of nowhere with somebody who was about as lost as I was. All being well, I'll be a desk sergeant in five years, and after that I'll be one for another twenty years.'

'You could always take up fishing,' I said.

He laughed. 'I did.'

We left the bar an hour later, by which time the darkness was complete. Lights stretched away on all sides of us. The illuminated motorway rose high into the night. The men along the riverbank continued fishing by the light of lanterns.

21

The following morning I went to Humber Street early, at seven. A line of lorries waited to be unloaded. The Cutter had opened its doors and some of the drivers sat out on the pavement, drinking. I spoke briefly to the men I knew. In the warehouse opposite my door, a consignment of melons was being unloaded. The owner called to me and then presented me with two. He told me to eat them with yoghurt for my breakfast. I knew for a fact that he himself ate three fried meals a day with sandwiches in between. I took the melons and thanked him.

I called Louise and asked how her mother was. I'd hoped to catch her at home and speak to Alison Brooks at the same time, but I knew from the background noise – banging, the voices of others and distant traffic – that she was outside somewhere. I had difficulty hearing her, and she me.

'I'm on the roof,' she shouted.

I asked her what roof.

'The hospital. I've been here an hour. The air conditioning in two of the operating theatres waited for the heatwave to go on the blink. The Buildings Manager is on holiday. I've been up here with the engineers since six.' She told me to wait while she put some distance between herself and the banging. It made little difference.

'I wanted to talk to your mother,' I told her.

'Fine. But leave it until later. The doctor's going to see her at ten, and a nurse is going in after that. She's in bed, but I'm sure she'd like to see you. Anything in particular?'

'I just wanted to bring her up to date,' I said.

'Has something turned up?'

'I'm not sure,' I said. 'It's all to do with Fowler's past. It might have some bearing, or it might not. I just thought it would be easier to see her than to write it all down. I'd still like to look through what you have of Helen's possessions,' I reminded her. We both knew she had delayed arranging this for me. Then I told her that I wanted to visit the students with whom her sister had been living at the time of her death.

'What are you hoping to gain from that?'

I asked her for the address and she gave it to me. I also asked her if she could remember any of the names of these others, but she was unable to.

'There was a Chinese girl,' she said. 'Laura something. Lee, I think. I only remember her because she was on the same course as Helen. I think they worked on things together. Anyway, won't they be away for the summer?'

I wrote down the address and the name.

Someone called to her and the background banging ceased.

'I have to go,' she said. She asked me if I was free that evening. I said I was. Whoever had called to her, called again, and the line went dead.

I put the piece of paper with the name and address on it in my pocket, and I was just about to leave when there was a single rap on my door, after which it was pushed open to reveal Fowler and Marco.

'What a pleasant surprise,' I said to Fowler. 'You do like your little entrances, don't you? You were probably ignored a lot as a child. I'll be with you in a minute. Get Marco to wipe a seat clean for you and sit down.'

I pretended to study several of the blank sheets on my desk, and then I carefully folded these and slid them into a drawer.

Fowler and Marco came into the office and Marco closed the door behind them.

Fowler sat directly opposite me at the desk. He looked at the melons.

Marco went to where he'd stood at the window during their previous visit six days earlier.

'Tell him to sit down,' I said to Fowler. 'Unless, of course, being the busy man that you are, this is only a flying visit.'

'I'm in no hurry, Mr Rivers. Especially not at this time in the morning.' It was not yet half past seven.

'Speaking of which,' I said. 'Where were you waiting?'

'Waiting?' Marco said.

'Just off Sewer Lane,' Fowler said. 'And, please, don't say "How appropriate".'

'How appropriate,' I said. I turned to Marco. 'Me come office seven in morning. You come office twenty minutes later. Me put two and two together. I don't know if I can make it any easier for you.' I looked back to Fowler. 'He's giving me one of his menacing looks again,' I said. 'Does he get a bonus for each one?'

'Play all the pathetic little games you like, Mr Rivers,' Fowler said. 'But, please, try not to over-estimate your own position in any of this, or my interest in you.'

'You're interested enough to be here this early,' I said. 'And all these calm and measured remarks you keep making – there's just a tiny whiff of them having been a little overrehearsed. Either that, or . . .'

'Or what?' he said.

'Or you're as predictable as you always were. But, then again, that suits me just fine. Because like all pre-dictable men, you're the only one who would ever deny it.' I turned to Marco. 'Am I right, Marco? Is Mr Fowler a predictable man?'

Marco said nothing.

Fowler took an envelope from his pocket and laid it carefully in front of me, placing it squarely between the melons.

'I wonder if *you* predicted this?' he said.

'It's the letter from your solicitors,' I said, sitting back in my chair. 'And, yes, if you recollect, I did predict it. It's the letter telling me to stop harassing you. And which also points out to me that you've suffered enough because of the tragic death of Helen Brooks, and that what I'm doing now is tantamount to defamation of character. In their opinion. Allegedly.' I paused briefly. 'And, should I see fit to pursue these enquiries – especially those which point out to the world what a thieving, murderous, self-serving, greedy little bastard you actually are – allegedly – then further action may be considered necessary.'

Marco came away from the window at the 'greedy little bastard' part.

I continued looking directly at Fowler.

'I doubt they'll have actually said "greedy little bastard" or "self-serving",' I said. 'I'll take full credit for that. But, roughly speaking, I imagine that's the gist of it. So you see – there's being predictable and there's being able to predict. And before you go running back to whoever this particular paid lackey might be, wringing your hands and thinking you're giving him any more ammunition against me, I said "murderous" and not "murdering". I thought you might appreciate the distinction. But, who knows, perhaps later, when I've managed to see a few more things a little more clearly – the mists of time and all that – that might change as well.'

'Just read it,' Fowler said.

'Later, perhaps. I'm busy today. That's why I made such an early start. What have you been doing – going round after me and trying to find out who I've been talking to and what I've been told?'

I waited for him to insist again that I read the letter before picking it up and opening it.

It was exactly what I had said it would be.

I wondered how he'd known to come to Humber Street so early, and could not dismiss the possibility that someone was watching my home.

I finished reading the letter. There was a sentence or two outlining Fowler's grief and regret at what had

231

happened. Followed by his sense of injustice that the matter was being brought back to light again for no good reason. Surprise was expressed that I was unable to accept the findings of the coroner's court, and that my behaviour in doing what I was now doing suggested a callous indifference bordering on malice with regard to Fowler's feelings.

'Ouch,' I said. ' "Callous indifference"? I'd say I was far from *indifferent* to the outcome of all this.'

'I think that part refers to my feelings on the subject,' Fowler said.

'That's good,' I said. 'Because I don't give a toss about *them*.' I folded the letter along its creases, slid it back into its crisp cream envelope, tore it slowly in half and then half again and dropped it into the bin at my feet.

'You can have one of those every day for the next year,' Fowler said.

'I don't doubt it. And I shall remain as callously indifferent to all three hundred and sixty-five of them. It's a letter. It doesn't tell me anything I don't already know. And, to be honest, I'd expected it the morning after you and the monkey here last came throwing your weight around. You knew I'd tear it up, calculate what it meant, and then wait for the next one, and the one after that. I'm only trying to save you the time and trouble of coming round on all those other mornings. In fact I'm surprised you're here at all – knowing how desperate and uncertain it makes you look, I mean.'

'You're still looking for evidence of something that didn't happen,' he said.

'There you go again,' I told him. 'Predictability. A bit of word-play, second-guessing and circling each other and then you go and spoil it all by cutting to the quick. I *know* why you're here. Next you'll be thinking about offering me ten times what Alison Brooks is paying me to work for you instead of her.'

'And you talk about insulting *my* intelligence,' he said.

'Meaning what? That you're going to disappoint me even further by telling me that everyone has their price and that you know what mine is?'

'It's true,' he said.

'And something I'd do well to remember?'

'Something like that.'

I looked back to Marco. 'What about you, Marco? Is that what you believe, too?'

'Nothing to do with me,' Marco said.

'Just because you say something, doesn't make it true,' I said. 'Soon – very soon, perhaps – you might have to decide exactly where you do stand in all of this.'

'Meaning what?' Fowler said.

I stopped talking. This vague warning had served its purpose. To have said any more would only have exposed my own uncertainties.

'Perhaps I could get my solicitor to write to your solicitor refuting all these slanderous claims of slander,' I said to Fowler. 'Perhaps that's what I'll do. And then there'll be no need for you to keep interrupting your own busy schedule to come round here and make your threats in person. It seems pointless for you to have your snarling all dressed up and nicely worded, and then for you to feel you have to come round here and do it the way you know best.'

'Stop pretending you know about me,' he said. He'd said something similar on his previous visit.

'I suppose I know as much about you as anyone,' I said. 'I know, for instance, that you came to Hull thinking you could draw a nice thick line under everything that had happened to you beforehand, and that you thought you could start to invent yourself anew.' It wasn't much of a revelation and it did nothing to unsettle him.

'I hope you're listening to all this, Marco,' he said. 'More slander and innuendo.' He leaned towards me. 'Everybody knows I have a past, Mr Rivers. Just as everybody knows that I was never charged with, tried or convicted of a single thing.'

'Which means nothing,' I said. 'Unless, of course, you've managed to convince yourself that you were never charged, tried or convicted of anything because you were completely innocent. But I doubt that. You were never charged because you were wealthy enough to keep your own hands clean, that's all. There was always somebody else standing in front of you. And when they were knocked down, you stood somebody else up, ready for the next fall.' I turned to Marco. 'I hope you're getting all this, too,' I said to him. 'All this stuff about Mr Fowler using other people to keep all the bad stuff well away from him.'

Fowler laughed at the transparency and simplicity of the suggestion. 'He's talking about London,' he said to Marco.

'Right,' Marco said.

'You got away, the trial collapsed and you left everything behind you,' I said. 'But it's my guess that there's still something, however small, however seemingly

234

inconsequential to everyone else, that keeps you connected to it all.' And even if that too was simplistic and unverifiable, it still felt like the right thing to jab him with at that particular moment.

'Oh, and what little thing would that be, then?'

'I don't know,' I said, still guessing and trying to read his own guarded response. 'But my next guess would be that it's something you never completely wiped off your shoe.'

He laughed again. 'Is that it? Something that happened years ago that was never properly resolved? How do you do it? You're practically clairvoyant.'

Marco smiled at the remark.

'Christ, Marco,' Fowler said. 'We're wasting money on solicitors' letters. Perhaps we should have done as I suggested in the first place and gone straight to old woman Brooks.'

'Threaten a dying woman?' I said. 'That'd look good.'

'There you go again. Nobody's threatening anybody. All I'm doing is making my own feelings clear. And if—'

'Marco,' I said, deliberately interrupting him.

'What?'

'Was there a dinghy on the yacht that day?'

'A dinghy?'

'A dinghy. On the yacht. That day.'

'Of course there was a fucking dinghy,' Fowler said.

'No one in the marina remembers seeing it,' I said. It was a lie.

'Well, they're wrong,' he said. 'It's regulations. They all have to have them.'

'Perhaps people didn't see it because they were so accustomed to seeing it,' I said.

'Yeah, perhaps that's it.'

I turned back to Marco. 'Well?'

'Well, what?'

'I asked you if there was a dinghy on the yacht. Fowler butted in before you could answer me.'

'He just told you,' Marco said. 'Of course there was a dinghy.'

'So, once again, you're telling me what he's telling me,' I said, my meaning clear to Fowler at least.

He raised his palms an inch and let them drop onto the desk. 'Take it from me,' he said. 'There was a dinghy.'

'I only asked,' I said. 'Perhaps Marco could tell me about the salvage yard instead.'

'What about it?' Marco said.

'I just wondered why you went there in person to supervise the destruction of the yacht. It struck me that you might have been there to look for something, or perhaps to ensure that no one else who might be looking found anything.'

Across the desk from me, Fowler relaxed, and I knew immediately that they were the wrong questions.

'Tell him,' Fowler said.

'I went because Mr Fowler was concerned that they might try to repair it and sell it,' Marco said.

'Imagine what terrible memories seeing it again would evoke,' Fowler said. 'Me still grieving for that poor young woman and everything.' His smile had returned. He moved the melons apart and then back together.

'So you'd have no idea whatsoever why Alison and Louise Brooks were at the yard in the days between it being delivered there and finally being destroyed?'

'No idea at all. Because she wasn't there,' Fowler said. He looked at Marco, who shrugged. 'Who says she was there?' Fowler said.

'They both told me,' I said, not wanting him to know that I'd spoken to anyone at the yard.

'The place has been shut down for six months,' Marco said.

'Good to know that you still show an interest in the place,' I said.

'Perhaps they just wanted to see it,' Fowler said. 'I'll say it again, Mr Rivers – you're working for two very vindictive women who refuse to see the truth of the matter. And whatever you believe now – however much you might have confused your own uncertain motives for doing what you're doing with their own very definite ones in employing you – let's see how long you go on believing it when the old woman dies. Let's see then how long the other one manages to string you along. Ironic, really – the mother losing her voice and getting the daughter to go on doing her dirty work by spreading all these rumours and lies about me.' He looked at his watch. It was almost eight. 'So what do I tell my solicitor?' he said.

'Tell him I tore his letter up because I understood how you were using him and because I wouldn't want him to be embarrassed by his weakness or slavish compliance any further when all this reaches its grand finale and the truth of what really happened that night, including your own dirty little part in it, is finally revealed.' It was another clumsy and unsustainable jab and we both understood that.

'He'll not appreciate it,' he said.

'He's not meant to. And something else he'll not appreciate is the copy of my report which I'll make sure he receives at the same time as Alison Brooks and DS Brownlow.'

He considered this. 'I can't imagine the law's going to be too pleased – having everything they did wrong or perhaps missed the first time around rubbed in their face.'

'I appreciate that "perhaps",' I said. 'It shows you're thinking. And despite what I might have said earlier, I imagine the true purpose of your letter here today was so that you'd have it on file when you eventually went to the police to complain of my harassment. Perhaps they won't be keen to go back over old ground, but I'm sure there must be someone somewhere who'll show a little bit of interest – enough, say, to reopen the investigation regardless of whether or not any new forensic evidence turns up. Especially now that most of that seems to have conveniently been either washed out to sea or burned to ashes.'

'You're clutching at straws,' he said. 'Just as long as you can live with yourself when all this is over and the old woman is dead. Because, like I said – when she dies, all this dies with her.'

'You seem very convinced of that.' It was something else he'd made a point of telling me at our previous encounter.

'I am,' he said. He rose from his seat and glanced at Marco, and before I fully understood what was happening, Marco had crossed the room behind him, gone to the map of Fowler's properties pinned to the wall, taken a lighter from his pocket and had set fire to its bottom edge. The flames rose quickly up the taped sheets.

Fowler continued looking directly at me, only pretending to turn and see what was happening as I, too, rose.

'Marco,' he said. 'Look what you've done. How could you be so careless?' He looked at the burning map for a second, and then said, 'Quick, put it out, these old properties go up like straw.'

Marco extinguished the flame with his hand. Pieces of burning paper fell to the floor and he ran his foot over them.

Fowler turned back to me. 'I'm so terribly sorry, Mr Rivers. I don't know how that could have happened. Perhaps he just couldn't contain his anger any longer at all your insults to his intelligence. I will, of course, pay for any damage incurred. It doesn't look too serious. Lucky he realized the error of his ways and acted so promptly. Perhaps the whole place might have burned down, and us – or perhaps only you – with it.'

I was about to comment on the gesture – destroying a map of which countless copies might already have been made, but I thought better of this and said nothing.

'Perhaps Louise Brooks could give you a photo of herself to pin up there and hide the scorch mark,' he said. 'Perhaps if you've got a camera, she'll even let you take a few pictures of your own. I'm sure we understand each other, Mr Rivers. And whatever you consider my motives to be in coming here today, I feel certain that you'll take into account the concerns I've expressed here and act accordingly.'

'Tell your solicitor he'll get that report at the same time as the police,' I said again. 'None of this changes anything.'

'You're wrong there,' he said. 'Very wrong.' He gestured to Marco, and Marco opened the door for him.

I waited until the two of them were in the corridor, the door still open behind them, before shouting, 'Well done, incidentally.'

Fowler came back to the door alone. 'Go on,' he said. 'I'm listening.'

'I just said "Well done". For not having once mentioned or made the slightest reference to Helen Brooks's mystery companion.'

'Is that all? Why would I mention him? Nobody has the faintest idea who he was.'

'Nobody?' I said. 'Somebody somewhere must know, don't you think?'

'Play all the games you want,' he said.

'Like I think I said earlier, things don't always go away just because you want them to.'

He laughed. 'For me they do. It seems to me that your biggest problem is working out what things have *already* gone away and what things were never even there in the first place.'

'And some things go away without anyone ever knowing they've gone?' I said.

'There's always that possibility.'

'I'll bear it in mind.'

'You do that.' This time he closed the door behind him.

I waited a few minutes and then took the remains of the map from the wall. I folded it and put it in an envelope. I also took down the photo of Fowler I'd cut from one of his brochures. I tore this into small pieces and let them scatter over the charred remains on the floor. It was a pointless gesture, but I felt better for having made it.

22

I arrived at Park Grove on the edge of Pearson Park two hours later. It was where Helen Brooks had been living at the time of her death, and where she had lived for the first eighteen months of her life as a student, before meeting Fowler.

I followed the doors to number 19 and knocked. The ground-floor curtains were drawn. Through the pane of pebbled glass, I could see cycles in the hallway. I stood back from the door and looked up. If the rooms were occupied separately, then perhaps someone upstairs or in one of the converted attic rooms might have heard my knock and looked down.

Nothing. I knocked again and called through the letter-box.

I walked back to Prince's Avenue, wishing I'd driven there instead of walking. I had no number to call to confirm if anyone would be in.

At the junction of the two roads I passed a Chinese

girl carrying an art folder and two carrier bags. She turned along Park Grove. I crossed to the far side of the road and followed her.

Arriving at number 19, she leaned the folder against the wall and unlocked the door.

I called to her and she turned.

She put the carrier bags inside the hallway and watched me as I went to her.

'You're late,' she said.

'I can't be,' I told her.

'You're here about the exhibition, right?'

'What exhibition?'

She went to retrieve the folder.

I asked her if she was Laura Lee.

'Lei,' she said. 'Pronounced "Lie".'

'I'm sorry. I was told Lee.'

'That's what most people think. It makes things easier.'

'But only for them.'

'Precisely. Besides—'

'The Rhine maiden,' I said.

'Hm. I wouldn't mind, but it's not even as though my parents knew what they were doing.'

I picked up the two carrier bags and followed her into the cool of the house. 'I'd like to ask you a few questions about Helen Brooks,' I told her. I watched her closely. She showed no sign of surprise or alarm at what I'd said.

'That's what I was expecting,' she said.

'From whoever was supposed to be here in connection with the exhibition?' I wondered if we were again talking at cross-purposes.

'Right. You're probably like the rest of them and

think I'm jumping on the bandwagon, exploiting what happened to Helen.'

'I don't even know what you're talking about,' I told her. 'I was given your name and address by Louise Brooks.'

She pulled a face at the name, suggesting to me that perhaps Louise was one of her accusers.

She asked me for a cigarette and led me out into a small yard filled with pots of geraniums, and tall daisies long past their prime in the heat. She filled a watering can from a plastic butt and watered them. When she'd finished, we sat together on two of the plastic chairs stacked against the wall.

'Tell me about the exhibition,' I said.

'You can come and see it for yourself. It opens tomorrow. The *Yorkshire Post* was supposed to be sending someone today to interview me. That cow – Helen's sister – said she wasn't happy with my exhibit, said it was in bad taste and called for it to be withdrawn. She said it was disrespectful to the memory of her sister. Ha.' She delivered the last remark like a blow.

' "Ha"?' I said.

She smiled. 'It's Chinese.'

'And you think the opposite,' I said.

'Who cares about respect? I told her I could have exhibited it last year, but that I hadn't, that I'd withdrawn it then out of respect – whatever – for Helen, not to protect *her* stupid feelings.'

'Can I see it?'

She shook her head. 'It's already set up. I've got some photos you can look at.'

'Louise said you worked on things with Helen.'

244

'We did. Not much. We worked on this together, but it was mostly me, even though she's the subject. You'll see what I mean.' She left me and went back into the house, returning a few minutes later with a photograph.

She gave it to me.

It showed the life-size model of a woman, any woman.

'Is it meant to be Helen?' I asked her.

'Of course it is. It *is* her.'

I asked her what she meant.

'You have to look closely. You need to see the real thing to get the full effect.'

I looked again at the picture. Different parts of the figure were composed of different objects, but it was difficult to make out what these were.

'Her lips,' she said. 'Those are her old lipstick cases and broken lippies. Her eyes, mascara brushes and liner cases.' She pointed to the woman's breasts. 'That's one of Helen's bras, and her chest is stuffed with the cigarette packets she'd saved for a year. You can lift the bra up, and inside there's a pair of lungs made of all the tabs she'd collected for that year. There's not enough of it, but she saved all her hair trimmings so I could make a wig. If you look inside her stomach there are tins and packets of all her favourite foods. That's what I meant when I said it was her. We saved for over a year to get enough stuff together.'

'And that's what Louise took exception to – that Helen's death and disappearance gave the exhibit a new and painful significance?'

'That, and the fact that the model's pants are filled with used sanitary towels. Helen even donated a few pubes and all her nail clippings. We wanted originally to put bags of her piss and her shit in there, but I couldn't get the bags to stay properly sealed.'

I was beginning to understand why Louise might have objected to the exhibit.

'She even saved me the dirt from between her toes and the sand from her sandals. If you open the mouth, there's one of her teeth in there – she'd kept it since she was a kid – and a small tape recorder with recordings of her crying and laughing. You activate it by pressing the tongue. We worked on getting everything together in time.'

'Did Louise ever see the finished exhibit?' I asked her.

'No. I've only just reassembled it for the show. Fifteen months ago, everyone agreed with her. That was why I withdrew it then.'

'I can understand why she might want you to withdraw it again,' I said.

'I daresay you can, but it was Helen who told me to ignore what anybody might say – especially her mother and her sister – and to go ahead with it. Even when she lost interest in her own work and started missing more and more classes. She still wanted *me* to carry on with it. She even gave me stuff to carry on adding to it. She said we should never compromise.'

'What kind of stuff?'

She hesitated before answering me, pointing to the photo. 'There's a panel in her arm. You have to know how to open it. It isn't obvious.'

'She gave you hypodermics?'

She nodded.

'Empty ones?'

'Like I said, she didn't want any of it to be compromised. Some are empty. Some still have something in them, and—'

'And some still have her blood in them?'

She nodded.

'Did Louise know about them?'

She thought about this and shook her head. 'Not as far as I know.'

'Because if anything was going to get the exhibit banned now, then that almost certainly would?'

She nodded, remembered something and smiled.

'What?'

'If you do come to see it, don't go sticking your finger up her nose.'

She left me again and returned with two cans of cold drink.

I asked her if I could take a copy of the photo with me.

'Sure,' she said.

'Did you see much of Helen in the days before she drowned?' I asked her.

'We had adjoining rooms up in the attic. She was here up until three or four days before she died. I tried calling her, but I kept getting that unable-to-connect message.'

'Did she talk much about her boyfriends?'

'Simon Fowler, you mean. A bit. I listened to all that crap at the inquest, but that wasn't how she told it. She knew what kind of man he was right from the start.'

'I doubt that,' I said.

'He bought her stuff, took her to places she'd never been.'

'Her mother gave her money,' I said.

'I know, but that was part of the problem. Mummy and big sister telling her what to do all the time.'

I asked her how often she'd met Louise. I remembered how uncertain or evasive Louise had been when telling me of her.

'A couple of times. She came round a few days after Helen drowned, saying she wanted everything that belonged to Helen put into bags and boxes so that she could take it all away.'

'Was there much?'

'Her clothes, books, bits and pieces. All her photographs and equipment. Not that she'd used it much recently. She even took all the pictures of Helen's own project.'

'Which was what?'

'We'd always intended setting them up side by side.'

'What was it – a model of you?'

She smiled at the suggestion and shook her head. 'She called it her Fuck Up Collage Kit. FUCK for short. I'll show you.' She went back into the house and returned with another photo, which she gave to me. 'This wasn't the finished thing; she was always adding to it, shuffling the pieces around, trying to make better sense of them.'

In the photo, three tall free-standing screens stood hinged at their inner edges. The two outer boards were covered in photos of all shapes and sizes, starting with a number of white-bordered black and white ones in the top left-hand corner of the left-hand screen, and finishing with what appeared to be digital printouts at the bottom right-hand corner of the right-hand screen. The middle board contained only two vertically arranged photos with a black outline marked beneath the lower of these.

'Almost five hundred pictures,' Laura said. She looked closely at the photo and sipped from her can.

'Her fucked-up life?'

'That's what she called it. From baby photos right through to the pictures taken and sent days before she died.'

I looked hard at the bottom right-hand corner, the end of Helen Brooks's life. 'And Louise took everything?' I said.

'The lot. Helen and I put everything up on the boards and endlessly rearranged it. When we got things where we wanted them, we numbered them so we knew where they went. Disposables, Instamatics, badly exposed or developed pictures, the lot. Technology through the ages. Everybody – and especially her sister – kept on telling her how she was fucking up her life, so that's what she decided to put on show – her fucked-up life.'

'And her mother and sister said it with increasing frequency after she'd met Fowler?'

'Something like that.'

'How late were the last pictures?'

She shrugged. 'She sent me some via digital camera and her laptop during the days she wasn't here. That was all part of it – taking and either posting or emailing the pictures as soon as possible after they were taken.'

There were several internet cafés within easy reach of the marina.

'She sent you pictures during the days immediately before she died?'

She nodded and held the cold can to her forehead.

'Can you remember what was in them?'

'Just close-ups of her face. She looked pretty fucked. She was taking them herself. You could tell. Exactly what she needed for the end of the collage.'

'Did *you* ever try and dissuade her from seeing Simon Fowler?'

'Why should I? Plenty of others for all that.'

I pointed to the central screen with its two pictures and outline. 'What was this meant to represent?'

'The top picture was Helen when she was about five or six and the one beneath it was taken at her last birthday.'

'When she'd already met Fowler.'

'I think it was intended as a sort of message to her mother and sister.'

'And the outline beneath it?'

She shrugged. 'I was never sure. Perhaps that's all it was ever meant to be – an empty outline, a blank. I never saw her stick anything in there.'

'And you're certain that Louise took away everything that was going to be on display?'

'Everything except the boards. Helen was pretty methodical about the thing. Once everything had found a place it was carefully filed away in boxes. There are a few pictures on the left-hand screen of Helen and her mother, and of Helen and Louise together.'

'What did Louise say when she knew what Helen was planning?'

'Guess.'

'I can imagine,' I said.

'She told me again that she was only thinking of Helen's memory and of her mother's feelings.'

'But you got the impression her concerns were a

little closer to home? What do you think she was afraid of finding?'

'I don't know. It wasn't a particularly good time for any of us.'

'Did Simon Fowler ever come here?' I asked her.

'Here? Him? No, Helen always went to him. I think that was the point. I told her she shouldn't be at his beck and call so much, but she told me not to worry, that things weren't as one-sided as they might look.'

'What did she mean?'

'I don't know. I just took her word for it.'

'Did you know he was the one providing her with the drugs?'

She looked away from me. 'None of my business. If she took them from him, she knew what she was doing. Is that what Little Miss Perfect Sister was doing when she came round here demanding to be given everything of Helen's – making sure there was nothing like that lying around to blacken the family name even further?'

'Possibly,' I said, regretting even that half-lie. 'When did you last talk to Louise?'

'She was round here a couple of days ago threatening to close the entire exhibition down. A few of the administrators said she had a point, but my tutors stood up for me. If I withdrew under any kind of pressure, they said – hers or the administrators' – then they'd recommend everyone else withdrew. I suppose they thought it would cause an even bigger stink.'

'It's Art,' I said. 'Nobody would either notice or care.' I asked her how much Louise had taken away with her.

'A carful. A dozen black bags, a dozen boxes, all the equipment. She was here for two or three hours, making sure she got everything.'

'And you probably neglected to tell her that you'd already been through everything and removed any incriminating evidence.'

'Probably. It made me angry to see how she treated Helen's stuff – like it meant nothing, like it was worthless, and all *she* cared about was protecting herself and her mother. Helen used to go on about how close the two of them were – her mother and Louise – about how Louise tried to exclude her from things. She said that Louise was more like an aunt to her than a sister. Will you repeat any of this to her?'

'Some,' I said. 'Perhaps.'

'Good. And before you ask me – no, I didn't take any of Helen's photos from her boxes before Louise got her hands on them. Everything's still there. I told her to show a little more respect.'

'And she told you to mind your own business.'

'I told her to give the photos back to the university, that Helen's exhibit might be shown posthumously.'

'What did she think to that idea?'

'About as much as me using the used tampons and towels,' she said. And then she admitted to me she had kept several photos of Helen and herself together. These pictures hadn't been part of the exhibit. I asked if I could see them and she fetched them for me.

There were only half a dozen of these, and I looked closely at each one. I saw Helen Brooks as I'd never seen her before. She was either laughing or grinning broadly in each of the pictures. In one, she held Laura Lei round her waist and lifted her off the ground. In another, the two of them sat in their underwear blowing smoke at the camera.

'That was only a month before she died,' Laura said.

I looked at her and saw the tears running down her face. She wiped them with her hand and took a deep breath.

'She once told me that she wished *I* was her sister,' she said.

I put my arm round her shoulders.

'I miss her,' she said.

It was the first time I'd heard anyone say it.

I asked her for details of the exhibition and promised her I'd go.

'If you come tomorrow,' she said, 'I'll be there. You could ask me some intelligent questions.'

'About Art? I doubt it.'

I took my arm from around her.

'Is the exhibit for sale?' I asked her.

'Of course it is. Ten million pounds. Just come. I'll show you everything there is to see of her. Just—'

'Don't bring Lulu?'

'Who?'

'Louise,' I said. 'It's the title of an old song.'

We were distracted by someone knocking on the front door.

'Your date with destiny,' I said.

'My appointment with the *Yorkshire Post*,' she said. 'There's probably a difference.' She kissed me on the cheek and asked me how she looked.

'Inscrutable,' I said.

She said, 'Ha,' again.

23

I called Sunny and told him I'd seen James Salter. He already knew; Salter had spoken to him. I also told him about Fowler's second visit to Humber Street.

'I was going to call you about him. I heard one or two interesting things after a council meeting last night.'

'About Fowler?'

'Some of it. Mostly about the next bright new future that's about to dawn, and in which, naturally, our man Fowler remains a major player. It might be something and it might be nothing, but you should probably know about it. In fact, gumshoe, it's what you should probably have found out about a fortnight ago.'

We arranged to meet later that afternoon.

I called Alison Brooks and told her I'd appreciate being able to see her. She seemed keen for me to visit her. The doctor was still with her, but he would soon be gone. Her nurse was not due to arrive for another hour. Louise had told her about my earlier call. Louise, she said, had wanted to stay at home with her for the next few days, but there were mounting problems at the hospital and she had insisted on her daughter returning to work.

'The air conditioning,' I said.

'Among other things.' Her voice sounded stronger than the last time I had spoken to her.

I told her I'd be with her in thirty minutes.

When I arrived, she was alone.

I spoke to her through an intercom at the door and she let me in. The locking device had been recently installed and its cable still lay along the hall floor.

Her bed was in a downstairs room with a view over a well-kept rear garden.

She was sitting up, the sheets drawn neatly across her waist. She turned off the radio beside her. On a table at the bottom of the bed was a television. A CD player stood on a cabinet to one side.

She wore a pale lambswool shawl over her shoulders. Beside the CD player stood an array of dark bottles and packets. Closer to her was a covered bowl.

She saw me looking at all this.

'We've tried to make it as little like an actual hospital room as possible,' she said.

But that was precisely what it looked like.

She indicated one of several chairs, and I drew it close to the bed. She asked me to open the door over-looking the garden.

She breathed deeply. 'Honeysuckle,' she said. 'A late-bloomer early because of the heat.'

I couldn't smell anything, and wondered if she could.

'Have you come to tell me what you've found out about Helen?' she said, her eyes still closed.

'I'd hoped Louise might already have told you most of what there was to know.'

She opened her eyes. 'Is that what you think – that she's watching you, following you, and using you to get to Fowler herself?'

'The thought had crossed my mind.'

'I called her when I knew you were coming. She told me to pay you.' She opened the cabinet drawer and took out a cheque.

My first thought was that I was being paid off.

She gave me the cheque. It was for two thousand pounds.

'It's too much,' I said. She'd already given me one for the same amount.

'Louise was concerned in case you saw me like this and convinced yourself that you weren't going to get your money.'

'I imagine that's your interpretation of whatever it was she actually said,' I said.

'It is.'

I made no move to take the cheque, and she put it back in the drawer, which she then left open.

'Is that honestly what you thought I'd think?' I asked her.

She shook her head.

'Because of everything John Maxwell told you about me?'

She nodded. 'That, and perhaps because of what he's told *you* about me.'

I told her I hadn't spoken to him after his late-night call before her appearance, that it was something I'd put off doing ever since learning that he'd recommended me.

'The money's not important,' she said. 'We just want this thing seeing through.' She hesitated. '*I* want it now more for *her* sake than for either Helen's or my own.'

'Because she's the one who's going to be left with all the details, all the pieces?'

'When I'm dead, yes.'

I apologized for the insensitive remark.

'Don't,' she said. 'You know as well as I do that there isn't time for that.'

'Why *did* you leave it so late?' I asked her.

'Because I tried for too long to convince her to let everything go.'

'And she couldn't do that?'

She shook her head. 'She'd been trying to persuade me for months – as soon as all this was confirmed – to find out about Helen. We were both already more or less certain that Simon Fowler had played some part in her death.'

'But Louise was more convinced than you were that he might now be made to acknowledge or to pay for that?'

She bowed her head. 'It seemed callous of me to be less interested than she was in what had happened.'

'And so you felt you owed it to her to go along with what she wanted.'

'"Owed"?' She understood me perfectly.

'Louise told me she felt neglected after you remarried, and certainly after Helen was born.'

'I suppose she was. We were so close after her own father died, and while I was establishing the business.

Later, when Helen was four or five, Louise accused me of sacrificing her happiness for my own.'

'And agreeing to what she wanted you to do now was your way of making amends?'

'We've grown close again,' she said. 'That means a lot to me. She gave up everything after Helen was killed to come back here to be with me. I'd be lost without her now.'

And she without you, I thought.

'Is that why you agreed to come and see me in the first place?' I said.

'After talking to John Maxwell, yes.'

'And because you knew that if I refused to take the case, all you'd have to do was mention his name.'

'It was my insurance,' she admitted. 'But I knew that once you started looking into things you'd come across all the discrepancies and unanswered questions Louise and I have lived with for the past fifteen months. John Maxwell told me you were good enough not to have to be told everything, that you'd probably be suspicious of my motives if I'd tried.'

'In addition to which, you'd already done some research – you knew how long I'd been at Humber Street, and you assumed I knew all about the developers' previous attempts to redevelop the warehouses there.'

'Louise said you'd probably know all there was to know about Fowler and the others and that you'd resent them for what they'd tried to do.'

'Is that also why you removed most of the clippings from your file before giving it to me – all those clippings which referred to your own accusations and allegations against Fowler at the time of the inquest?'

We sat in silence for a minute.

She started to cough, and the effort was painful for her. She held her throat and then took the cloth from the bowl beside her and held it to her lips. She tried to spit into it, but again the effort of this made her flinch with pain. I went to stand beside her, supporting her as she leaned forward, my palm between her shoulder blades.

She finally dislodged the saliva from her mouth and put the bowl back on the cabinet. I let her back onto her pillows. She covered the bowl. I took a tissue from a box beside the radio and gave it to her. She wiped her lips.

She lay with her eyes closed for a moment, regaining her breath.

'The doctor needs his specimens,' she said eventually, in a tone which told me she considered this demand unnecessary. Then she smiled. 'The last time, when I agreed to their treatment, I lost most of my hair, and Louise insisted on gathering it all together and saving it for me.'

Just as Laura Lei had gathered up and saved her other daughter's hair.

'She bought me a new brush and used to collect what had fallen out each day.'

I told her I'd been to see Laura Lei.

'I know all about it,' she said.

'Are you as offended as Louise appears to be by the exhibit?'

She shook her head. 'I met Laura soon after Helen was killed. I know how fond they were of each other.'

'And suspected that Louise was jealous of that affection?'

'I think there was a time, then and now – and perhaps for all the obvious reasons – when I saw things a little more clearly than Louise. I think her own true feelings about Helen remained unresolved at the time of Helen's death.' It was another imperfect understanding, but one perfectly suited to its purpose.

'And that's another reason for acceding to her wishes now?' I said.

'I asked her to leave you alone, to let you get on with things. I knew that if she did or said too much, you'd get suspicious.'

'Suspicious of her reasons for wanting Fowler exposed?'

'Possibly. Or of mine for lying to you about my illness or the extent of Louise's involvement. I think sometimes she underestimates people.'

'Do you think she underestimated Helen and her relationship with Fowler?'

'I think she never gave Helen enough credit for knowing her own mind, for being in control of what she was doing. Louise sacrificed a lot to come back here, Mr Rivers, and I have to give her credit for that. Without her, I'd have no choice but to be hospitalized. Not just yet, perhaps, but the day may not be too far away. And after that, I may require hospice care. She's adamant that neither of those things is going to happen to me.'

'And you?'

'I can't deny that this is far preferable to either. It may not, when the time comes, be possible, but given the choice it's where I would prefer to die.'

'I hope you can manage it,' I said. I remembered John Maxwell's unsuccessful fight to keep his own terminally ill wife out of hospital. I'd been with him the night she died. I knew what a difference it had made to him for ever afterwards.

She asked me for a glass of water and I gave her one. She sipped at this, barely wetting her lips.

'Swallowing hurts just as much as coughing,' she said, her voice becoming even fainter.

Waiting until she'd finished, I asked her what she'd hoped to find at the salvage yard.

'You're as thorough as John Maxwell said you'd be,' she said. 'I don't know. Not much. The yacht had been impounded for months, searched and searched again. Louise just wanted to go to where Helen had last been alive. I don't think we were actually *searching* for anything. We just wanted to go because we thought that we'd be close to her. Fowler had already made clear to us his intention of completely destroying the thing.'

'Did you ever doubt his motives?'

'Louise did. To be honest, I wasn't sure that it wasn't what I wanted, too. Like I told you – I come from a family of trawlermen, Mr Rivers, not yachtsmen.'

We both smiled at the remark and all it signified. Laughter was beyond her.

'And *did* you feel close to Helen, seeing it in the salvage yard?'

'In a way, yes, I did. I spoke to her. I told her I wished I'd been able to do more for her in those last few months. With the death of Helen—' She stopped abruptly and put a hand to her mouth.

I told her not to talk.

She caught my glance and held it for a moment, and after that she looked away from me and back to the garden.

'Shall I tell you what I once considered doing soon after Helen died, and after I'd been to where she'd been living . . .'

'You considered buying Laura Lei's model from her,' I said.

She closed her eyes and nodded.

'Until Louise persuaded you otherwise.'

'She said it was the last thing in the world I should have considered doing. She threatened to go to a solicitor to prevent it from ever being seen. She said I'd regret it for the rest of my life – which, under the circumstances, was probably true.'

'Because it would have come between you?'

'Because it would have confirmed all Louise had ever accused me of where Helen was concerned.'

I told her I intended visiting the exhibition and seeing the model for myself. I told her about the photo Laura Lei had given me and promised to send it to her.

'If you see her, give her my regards,' she said.

'And tell her that whatever Louise might accuse her of, you don't necessarily share her views?'

'You took the words right out of my mouth.'

The inadvertent irony of this remark made us both smile. By then her voice was no more than a hoarse whisper and the gaps between her words had grown longer.

'I need to go,' I said.

'What next?' she mouthed.

'Next I take the cheque from the drawer and bank it against the further days it pays for.'

'Good.' It was all she could say. She held her hand out to me and I took it. She wanted to tell me a great deal more about her own unresolved feelings, perhaps, and about all those regrets and failings and omissions of her own which she would not now have the opportunity of acting on. Her fingers tightened weakly around my hand.

24

We sat at the back of the Old White Hart. I'd suggested taking our drinks outside, but Sunny said he wasn't an outdoor drinker. Too Continental. Too hot. Too many children. Too many other people drinking outside. Too hot. Too many children. Too many wasps. Too hot.

'Two years ago, a year after his arrival, Simon Fowler did the city council a big favour by offering to go into a kind of unofficial partnership with them and provide them with the properties in which to house their unexpected windfall of asylum-seekers,' he said.

'I think that may have been one of the reasons he chose to come here after everything blew up in his face in London,' I said, though still not entirely convinced of this. 'I think whoever kept him informed about what the Department of Immigration were up to in the south-east also told him about the Government's plans to start sending people elsewhere. I think he came to Hull because it offered him the *legitimate* opportunities he never had in London.'

He, too, was sceptical. 'Whatever,' he said.

'He came for the scenery and the nightlife?' I said.

'Shall I go on?' he said. 'Whatever his reasons, he came. And whether or not he knew about the burden the council was shortly about to have to bear, he did what he did and made himself a lot of very influential friends.'

'What he did was buy up as many near-derelict properties as possible and then milk them, and everybody, dry. They were properties that had practically no value whatsoever until the asylum-seekers turned up.'

'Granted. But the council didn't have much choice. They weren't going to be a council for much longer if they started doing up their own long-neglected stock and filling them full of unwanted, unwashed and undeserving foreigners.'

'Of which Fowler also took advantage.'

'OK – of which Fowler also took advantage. But the interesting thing about that little deal, I discovered last night, is that it was only signed for two years. Renewable, of course, but no one thought then that the "problem" would actually last this long. The best estimate at the time, apparently, was that the people would be here for a year, tops, while they were being assessed and processed. After which, they'd either be sent home or somewhere else. Most, it was assumed, would *want* to go home as soon as it was feasible for them to do so. Happy days. In addition to which, there was always pressure from those happy shiny people planning Hull's redevelopment to get rid of them soonest. Image, see? Unfortunately, once the first few

265

hundred were settled here, it became easier to send the next hundred and then the next. Apparently, these things reach a kind of critical mass.'

'If things can't get any worse, then just go on doing what made them bad in the first place?' I said.

'Something like that.'

'And as the numbers grew, so did Fowler's opportunities for legitimate money-making?'

'And the council gave him more and more support.'

'Tell me more about this two-year deadline,' I said.

'According to my source—'

'A disgruntled council employee who probably had one too many grudges and five too many drinks inside him paid for by you.'

'Her. And there are no grudges. Let's just call it an increasing awareness of the inherent injustice of the overall situation.'

'Nothing like being specific.'

'And five fizzy waters won't buy you anything these days, even with a thin slice of lemon in each one.' He raised his empty glass into my face and I went to the bar.

'The deadline,' I prompted him on my return.

'I'm coming to that. Eighteen months ago, the council unveiled the latest of its city-centre regeneration plans. You probably remember the fireworks. They commissioned a sea-shanty in honour of them. And once those plans were unveiled with a view to seeking tenders, Fowler expressed considerably more than a passing interest in becoming involved. It was his first real opportunity to become a major player here.'

'What did he do?'

'He didn't really have to do anything. Not just then. There was lots of consultation and lots of planning and lots of image-making still to be done. All Fowler or anyone else who was interested had to do then was to pledge their support and to show they were serious by showing some proof of the financial nature of their commitment.'

'Meaning this could only go ahead with Government funding if it attracted the same amount from the private sector. What was Fowler's bid?'

'Have a sip of your drink,' he said. 'Twenty million.'

'Has he got it?'

'Not the point. He offered it, and it brought him into the game. If the contracts he's after go to him and his companies, then he stands to at least triple that amount in seven years. He's the Golden Boy. Who on the council is going to start asking awkward questions about whether or not he's actually got it in his hand? Whether or not he has it in his hand is beside the point – the point is that it would be up to *him* to raise it, not *them*, and certainly not the Government. That way the risk is spread across the board. Fowler's particular interest was in the redevelopment of the Old Town, High Street to the river, over the dual carriageway to the Humber. Housing, bars, restaurants, IT industries.'

'Including Humber Street?'

'Eventually. The total cost was estimated at four times what Fowler was prepared to put on the table.'

'Made up by Government money and the other investors.'

'He wouldn't even have to find all the up-front money to begin with. He'd be required to deposit a bond and then most of the rest would be swallowed up

267

by the cost of the building work itself – labour, materials, compulsory purchases.'

'Top to bottom. Fowler's speciality.'

'Exactly. But the point you're missing here is that to come up with his initial buying-in bond, Fowler would at least have to be sure of getting his hands on enough of the money to convince the council of his good and honourable intentions. There were one or two who thought he was already overstretched with all his buying up of properties to fulfil his asylum-seeker obligations.'

He let me consider this for a moment.

'And now the two years is up,' I said, 'you think he wants to offload those properties and concentrate instead on his considerably more upmarket future?'

'Makes sense to me. He knows how to read the signs. However maliciously greedy you might want to paint him, he does at least know that things change, and that men like him need to keep their money moving. He knows when one good investment has run its course and when a much better one has presented itself. This has nothing to do with the death of Helen Brooks. This is purely and simply Fowler doing what he does best. And the sweetest part of it for him, of course, is that for possibly the first time in his life, everything is miles above board and he himself is completely beyond reproach. For the first time in his life, he's got people practically begging him to do exactly what he himself wants to do. The asylum-seeker rentals might have been profitable, but they were never exactly his cup of tea in terms of the new image he wanted to create for himself, the reputation he hoped to establish.'

'So the bond was promised how long before Helen Brooks was killed?'

'January before last. Three months. You're still not listening to me. This has nothing to do with her.'

'Perhaps. But I doubt if the death of his so-called girlfriend and all the publicity that attracted to him did him any favours.'

'It got him the sympathy vote from a few of the waverers. And his injunctions put an end to anything he didn't want to hear.'

I refused to accept this, but said nothing. 'Has the story moved on from the bond guarantees?' I said.

'That's the whole point. In just over two weeks' time, the contracts for all the good stuff are signed and everything finally gets under way.'

'And everyone who signs is committed to action?'

'Either that or they lose everything they stood to gain. Along with their name and their reputations.'

'Will Fowler definitely be among the signatories?'

'According to my source, he's itching to be the first off the blocks. Can't wait to get started.'

'Which tells us what?' I said.

He shrugged. 'That his financing's in place, that his money isn't all tied up, and that he's got it in his hand ready to invest. The sooner everything's done, the sooner he reaps his reward and the eternal praise and thanks of the people of this pioneering and rejuvenated city.'

'And after that?'

'King of Hull?'

'Are you serious?'

'My source was.'

'Even after five sparkling waters?'

'Five fizzy waters, five slices of lemon and a bucketful of my charm.'

'I was forgetting that,' I said.

He went to the bar, leaving me to consider all he'd just suggested.

'If Fowler's turning his attention to the finer things in life,' I asked him on his return, 'then what's going to happen to everything he's ploughed his money into so far? He's hardly likely to be able to offload all those run-down properties; some of them aren't even inhabitable.'

'Fizzy water said the same. She thinks he's faced with something of a dilemma, but that there are already rumours circulating of him having found someone prepared to take them off his hands, leaving him free to concentrate on the loft apartments and Pacific Rim restaurants.' He paused to light one of his cigars.

'Are there any names attached to these rumours?'

'Man called Webster? Him and Fowler have collaborated on a few things in the past. Webster's an old name.'

I tried to remember where I'd heard or seen the name before. The most likely place was at the Guildhall, above one of the models or in one of the brochures.

'There is, however, one more tiny little piece of information of not completely totally and absolutely unrelated significance. It seems that our esteemed and highly regarded Deputy Prime Minister is shortly to announce his beloved Government's intention to increase the urban housing stock of the country following two decades of Tory misrule.'

'Which ended ten years ago.'

'Don't quibble.'

'And as part of which policy, it is their stated aim that at least eighty per cent of all this new housing should be built on brownfield sites.'

'Of which Hull, presumably, has more than its fair share.'

'And a good many of them—'

'Owned by Fowler.' All of those blue dots on Irina Kapec's map. The map Fowler had told Marco to burn.

'So will he sign another deal with the council for them to slap compulsory purchase orders on his properties to fulfil their obligations?'

He shook his head. 'Unlikely. That would take years. And there are already those who think he's benefited enough from his earlier deals.'

'And you're certain the council's two-year unofficial arrangement to house the asylum-seekers won't be extended?'

'Definitely not,' he said. 'Fowler himself insisted on it.'

'Meaning the rumours of a buyer for everything he wants to off-load are probably true.'

'And that whoever it is, is taking the properties off Fowler with the intention of evicting the tenants and then using the properties or the land as part of this brownfield plan. Probably even more profitable, but over the longer term.'

'And leaving Fowler with the cash in hand to get on with the Pacific Rim restaurants.'

He drained his glass. 'He'll have an even closer eye

on Humber Street after everything you've done to antagonize him over the past few days.'

'He's already made that clear to me. Do you think what happened at Walmsley Street was the same thing moving in another direction?'

'Fowler firing his first shots? Proving to his buyer how easy it is to empty the properties? I doubt it. One more thing fizzy water let slip was that the council will shortly be looking to demolish a few thousand of its own derelict properties – along with a few not so derelict ones – out on the estates, and that they'll then be looking to sell off all this prime development land to private developers.'

'So Webster, or whoever takes over Fowler's asylum-seeker tenancies, might be able to cut himself a slice of that particular pie, too?'

'I wish I had your way with words,' he said. 'What's important now is that all these events are linked and all the rich men involved who look set to become considerably richer are dependent on each other, and on things working out exactly as they want them to work out.'

'I wish I'd known all this before I met him,' I said.

'Why? Because it would have made you feel better about his threats?'

'That. And because I'd have known the size of the boat I was rocking. And because I'd have known that he was starting to sweat himself.'

And because I'd just remembered that the man Fowler had had a private meeting with in his car outside the Guildhall on the day of Helen Brooks's death had been called Webster. The man who had provided Fowler with his unnecessary alibi for later in the afternoon. The man, in all likelihood, whom Fowler had arranged to meet later in the evening upon the non-appearance of Helen Brooks.

'What is it?' Sunny asked me.

I told him.

'Like I said, Webster's been here a long time. Him and Fowler are well matched by all accounts. I'll ask around.'

He knew as well as I did that the meeting and Fowler's plans now cannot have been purely co-incidental. He asked me what else I'd come up with and I told him about Laura Lei and her exhibit. He already knew about the short-lived outrage the exhibition had caused locally.

'It looked to me like something blown up out of all proportion because of the publicity it would attract,' he said.

I asked him not to add to this by writing about the exhibition. As a favour to me.

'I wasn't aware I owed you any favours,' he said. 'Especially not after all I've just told you.'

'Then as the decent thing to do where Laura Lei's concerned,' I said.

He repeated the word 'decent' as though it were an unfamiliar taste in his mouth. 'OK, I promise,' he said. He licked a finger and drew a cross over his heart.

I also told him I'd arranged to see Louise Brooks again.

'So she can tighten her blood-sucking grip on you?'

'We know where we stand,' I told him.

'No, you don't. You're still confusing what you feel for her and what happened to her half-sister with what

you feel about Fowler and what you think *he* did to
the dead girl. Added to which, there's the history with
the mother and your blind allegiance to John Maxwell
to throw into the equation.' He pretended to think.
'Oh, and the fact that the mother's dying.'

'So you think I should tell them I've done as much
as I can for them and that nothing new is going to
come to light?'

He sighed dramatically. 'No, I'm not saying that.
You wouldn't have come this far if you didn't think
there was *something* left to discover. All I'm saying is
that you should make sure you know why you're
doing what you're doing.' He stopped speaking
and signalled his apology to me. 'So what now?' he
said.

'Let Louise Brooks tighten her blood-sucking grip on
me?' I said.

'Keep laughing about it,' he said.

We left the bar and walked together to the taxi rank
in Victoria Square.

For a year after his estranged wife and thirteen-year-
old daughter were killed in a road accident, he had
allowed no one close to him. And at the end of that
year, Yvonne, having considered sufficient time had
passed, moved in with him for a month until he
sobered up and was able to look at himself again in a
mirror. He accused her of interfering in his life and
called her every name he could think of. He even
looked in a dictionary for names to call her. And of
everything he afterwards regretted having done during
that year of unrelenting grief, that was the thing he
regretted the most. When he tried to apologize to her a
few months later, she told him she'd already forgotten

most of the names. Then she listed for him the ones she remembered.

He offered to share the leading cab with me, but I told him I preferred to walk. He made no further attempt to persuade me. He told the driver to take him home, and the driver pulled out into the traffic before asking him where that was.

25

The following morning, crossing Queen's Gardens, I saw Irina Kapec sitting on one of the walled flower beds there, her face raised to the sun, her eyes closed. Her daughter, Rosemary, sat beside her.

Neither Sunny nor I yet had a plausible explanation for why the assault on the woman at Walmsley Street had taken place, why it had happened so publicly, or how whoever had orchestrated it had known that Yvonne, Irina, he and I would all be drawn there. But it was the closest of Fowler's properties to the agency, and I remained convinced that this played a part in explaining the assault.

I approached Irina where she sat. Rosemary saw me first and rose beside her mother. I spoke to her and Irina jumped at the sound of my voice. The girl looked suddenly terrified of me and clutched her mother's arm.

Irina also rose, and shielded her eyes to identify me. Then she put her arm around her daughter and said something to reassure her. But Rosemary continued clinging to her, staring at me with her face pressed into Irina's side.

'Were you looking for me?' she said.

I told her I'd spotted her on my way across the gardens.

She considered this for a moment, as though she believed I might have lied to her.

'Yvonne didn't call you?' she said.

'What about?'

She looked around us and then down at her daughter, who was still holding her arm. She took some change from her pocket and told the girl to get herself an ice cream. A van stood at the junction with Guildhall Road. At first the girl was reluctant to go, but Irina insisted.

'I received these,' she said when we were alone. She took several photos from her pocket and gave them to me. They were of a house and of her daughter standing at the door. 'It's where we live,' she said. 'Look on the back.'

The rear of the photos contained nothing but the date on which they'd been taken, and a serial number, which I assumed identified something connected to their processing.

'Taken yesterday,' I said.

'They arrived in a plain, unaddressed envelope this morning. They were there when I went downstairs.'

'Do you think it's some kind of warning?'

'I don't know. It must be *some* kind of message to me, otherwise why would anyone take them and send them to me with no explanation of their purpose or intent?'

That would come later, I thought, but said nothing.

'And you told Yvonne about them?' I said.

She looked at her watch. 'She's meeting me here.'

I looked around us. There were people sitting on most of the other low walls and seats, some of whom – a dozen or so scattered men – were clearly asylum-seekers.

She watched her daughter at the ice cream van, leaning to one side when someone walked across her line of vision.

'Is there a reason why you're still here after so long?' I asked her.

'Why do you ask? Because I'm a Croat, and surely it is safe by now for all Croats to return home?'

'It wasn't a criticism,' I said.

She considered this, her eyes still on her daughter.

'I was given Exceptional Leave to remain. By the Home Office. My husband was killed by the Serbs at Srebrenica, where all three of us had gone in an attempt to persuade his elderly parents to leave their home and come to live with us in Zagreb. He was a lecturer in physics at the same university where I taught. For weeks we had seen what was happening, what atrocities were being committed. He said he would go alone and see his parents, but I insisted on accompanying him. Rosemary was only a baby then. There had been such awful tales of what had happened to young men who had been seized and questioned. I thought that the three of us travelling together would be safer for him.

'Besides, shortly before we departed the UN declared its intention of creating a safe haven at Srebrenica. His parents lived only eight kilometres away. If the worse came to the worse, we told ourselves, and the Serbs did arrive and try to drive everyone out, then at least we would receive *some* protection. And failing that, then perhaps the roads out of the town and back to Zagreb would be kept clear.'

She stopped talking as her daughter returned.

'We were successful in persuading Peter's parents to accompany us, but then we were stopped by the Dutch soldiers of the peacekeeping force. We were forced to spend the night in an empty school. The following morning, they told us, they would be leading a convoy of all the vehicles out of the town. That night, the Serb soldiers came to the school and took away Peter and his father. We never saw either of them again. Peter's father's body was formally identified four years ago. Peter has yet to be officially identified. His mother died a year after leaving home.

'You can imagine my feelings when, having applied to leave, I was finally accepted by and given a home in Holland. I lived there, Delft, for three years. After which, I was granted permission to come here. Rosemary was christened in Delft.'

'Rosemary for—'

'Remembrance, yes. We made a new home for ourselves there.'

'Why did you leave?'

'Because when Milosevic was finally taken there to stand trial, I was approached and asked if I would become a witness against him – tell everyone what had happened to Peter and his father at Srebrenica. Having agreed to do this, I was then told along with a dozen others that it was no longer considered safe for me to go on living there.'

'And so you were relocated here?'

'And so I was sent here, yes.'

'Are you still going to give your evidence?'

'When they are finally ready for me, yes. The trial has only just begun. Kosovo first.' She looked around us at the rapidly filling space. 'I doubt if anyone here would even be able to point to it on a map.'

I asked her if she thought that what had happened to the woman in the house on Walmsley Street had anything to do with her own presence in the city.

'I gave it a lot of thought,' she said. 'I've been here over three years. It makes no sense. The same with these.' She took the photos from me.

I was about to suggest tracing the pictures to their developer, when she looked beyond me and waved.

Yvonne joined us. She kissed Irina and then picked up Rosemary and hugged her. She wiped the last of the ice cream from the girl's mouth.

'ESP?' she said to me.

'I was passing.'

'I showed him the photographs,' Irina said.

Yvonne took them from her and studied them.

Irina showed her the envelope, which revealed nothing.

Yvonne suggested that the four of us walked around the rose beds and fish pond. She told me to make a show of leaving them, and then to double back to see if anyone was following them.

I did this, but saw no one acting suspiciously as they started to walk. I crossed from one side of the garden to the other. There was still no one, and I went back to them.

'Who do *you* think sent them?' I asked Yvonne.

'I'd have thought that much was obvious,' she said. 'Someone who wants to intimidate Irina.'

'To make her do what?'

'Leave.'

'In connection with the trial in the Netherlands?'

'That would be my guess.' But she was as unconvinced as I was by this. 'OK,' she said, 'what's your take on it?'

'I don't know,' I said. 'But I imagine it's the timing of the thing we ought to concentrate on.'

'Could this be about Fowler?' she said.

'I don't know. I think Walmsley Street was. I don't see there's any connection, though. And I don't understand what he'd stand to gain from something like this if the sole purpose of the pictures was to intimidate Irina.' I was reluctant to repeat what Sunny had told me about the imminent transfer of property from Fowler to Webster.

I asked Yvonne what she and Irina intended doing. I offered her the keys to my home, but she declined.

'I'd hate to turn up there and find you'd turned one of the rooms into a shrine to me,' she said.

'Top of the stairs, second on the left. As far as I know, none of Fowler's sidekicks are following me.'

'As far as you know,' she said dismissively.

I turned to where Irina stood with her daughter. 'I'm sorry this has happened,' I told her. 'But I honestly don't know if it's connected to Fowler and my own enquiries into him.' Behind me, I heard Yvonne mimicking me. 'And if it is,' I said to Irina, 'I'll find out about it and do whatever I can. Tell Yvonne that she, you and Rosemary are always welcome at my home if there's nowhere else for you to go.'

'Unless, of course,' Yvonne said loudly, pausing for effect, 'you're entertaining Mata Hari there.'

'She means Louise Brooks,' I told Irina.

Irina put her hand on my arm. 'I know,' she said. 'I think she's jealous. Also a little concerned for you.'

'I can take care of myself,' I said, again largely for Yvonne's benefit.

She came to join us.

Irina withdrew her hand.

'So what next?' Yvonne asked me.

'A few more loose ends? I don't know.'

'*Are* you seeing Louise Brooks?'

I told her about the contents of Helen Brooks's flat in Park Grove that I still wanted to see.

'Perhaps the two of you could sit on a rug in front of a fire and go through everything together,' she said.

'I'll suggest it.' I kissed her. 'I'll let you know.'

'Just be careful,' she said.

'I always am.'

'Whatever.'

'OK, what do *you* think I should do? Apart from staying away from Louise Brooks and mistrusting everything about her.'

'It might be about time to start doing what you do best,' she said.

'Go on, I'm listening.'

'Start pulling on a few of those loose ends. Barge in where you're not wanted, pretend you already know everything there is to know and then start making wild and unfounded accusations, get yourself laughed at and kicked out, and then wait to see who laughs the loudest at it all.'

'Great idea,' I said.

'I'm serious.'

I said goodbye to Irina and her daughter, and left them.

'Farewell, Superman,' Yvonne called after me.

I turned, and all three of them waved at me in a single, perfectly synchronized gesture.

26

The exhibition opened at four that afternoon.

I spent the day at Humber Street working out what to do next. Most investigations came to no great conclusion; some petered out in small confessions and revelations and disappointments; and some – by far the majority – died quiet, unnoticed deaths due to exhaustion and unhappy compromise. This was how I was beginning to think Alison Brooks's case might end.

I wasn't entirely certain why I was going to see Laura Lei again, except that I knew she had loved and cared for Helen Brooks as much as anyone else, and that she and Helen's mother might gain some small measure of comfort from each other before it was finally too late.

I finished work early in the afternoon and walked to the Minerva Pier. The cobbled square was full of drinkers. Out on the Humber, a succession of barges made their way upriver, their wake barely breaking the surface of the flat brown water. I could hear the churning of their engines as they came close to where I stood.

The new footbridge over the River Hull was down, and people lined it to look over the estuary and into the mud below. On the opposite bank, the sides of the aquarium reflected the sun in blinding copper sheets. Queues stretched along the building as people waited to get inside to press their faces against the glass walls, beyond which the sharks came and went with flashing menace in their giant tanks.

At four, I walked back through Queen's Gardens to the university site on Wilberforce Drive. Posters announced the exhibition all along the front of the buildings and on the advertising hoardings there.

I followed the signs along a paved court to a door at the rear and entered a building overlooking North Walls.

At the main door a model of Ronald McDonald sat astride a headless cow, the head of the animal being under Ronald McDonald's arm. He was sucking the fingers of his other hand and there was blood all around his mouth. The creator of this – a boy with an impressive display of piercings around his nose and mouth – handed out catalogues for the exhibition inside.

I asked him what the sculpture represented, and he gave me a disappointingly predictable answer. I tried to look interested.

There were already thirty or forty others in the room beyond – most, I assumed, connected with either the organization or the press coverage of the exhibition. I saw the Lord Mayor surrounded by half a dozen councillors I recognized from their frequent appearances in the local press.

Laura Lei and her model of Helen Brooks stood at the far end of the room. A chain of rope had been placed around the exhibit. She was standing alone, a wad of brochures and photographs in one hand and a glass of wine in the other.

She saw me and smiled. She poured me a glass of wine and gave me another photograph and one of her brochures.

'I'm pleased you came,' she said.

No one else in the room appeared to be showing much interest in her exhibit; most preferred the giant paintings arranged along the longer walls.

The model of Helen Brooks was impressive. One of her hands was held out towards me – a gesture not apparent from the photos.

'I went to see her mother,' I told Laura.

'She's ill, isn't she?'

'Cancer of the oesophagus. I told her I'd take her one of your photos. I know it's little consolation, but I think she has a far better understanding of what you're doing and of what Helen meant to you than Louise has.'

'Like that would be difficult. Sorry.' She drained her glass and refilled it, pulling a face at the cheap wine.

Elsewhere in the room, photographers from the *Mail* and other papers took pictures of the mayor standing beside the exhibitors and their work. The majority of the pictures would not appear in the *Mail*, only in its office windows, for sale to the proud parents of the exhibitors at exorbitant prices.

A plaque beneath Laura's model said 'Young Woman, 1983–2004', and the bluntness of this, and of the dates, made me realize perhaps for the first time that Helen Brooks had been little more than a girl when she had died.

As though reading my mind, Laura said, 'We were born only four days apart. We used to celebrate our birthdays together.' She raised her glass to the model and I did the same.

I asked her how long the exhibition lasted.

'Usually a week, but this year probably only four or five days.'

'What will happen to her after that?'

'Dismantled again, I suppose. And then they'll probably ask me to make my own arrangements to take her away.'

'Back to Park Grove?'

'Perhaps. I'm applying for jobs. Come and visit me again, if you like, and have a closer look.'

I told her I would, though we both knew this was unlikely.

A woman with dyed pink hair came to us.

'Laura,' she said loudly, holding out her arms. She reached me and stopped. 'Laura is one of our *star* students,' she said. 'We *all* have so much *faith* in her.'

Behind the woman, Laura pulled a face.

'It's a thought-provoking exhibit,' I said.

'So *potent* about all it *reveals* to us about *today's* young woman. I know. About the consumerist *ideologies* in which she is *nurtured* and *moulded.*'

Laura closed her eyes.

'You took the words right out of my mouth,' I said,

but rather than make the woman suspicious of me, the remark served only to encourage her.

'You do *know*, of course,' she said, her hand on mine, 'that there was *pressure* placed on Laura to withdraw her exhibit from the show.'

'I had no idea,' I said. 'I think it's the best thing here.'

' "Best"?' she said, finally looking disappointed. 'I'd rather such *qualifying* assessments were kept *out* of our discussion. But I must say I agree with you.'

Behind her, Laura opened her eyes and raised them. I caught her glance and drained my glass.

All the time the woman was with us, the mayor and the photographers had been moving closer. The woman saw them, too. The other exhibitors had all been asked by either the mayor or one of the councillors to say a few words concerning their work. The photographs were usually taken while they were still talking.

'Did you know Helen Brooks?' I asked the woman.

'Helen Brooks?'

'Laura's model.'

'Oh, *Helen*. No, not *personally*. She was a close friend of *yours*, I believe, Laura, right?'

'Right,' Laura said.

I thought she might respond angrily to the woman's ignorance, but her attention was now elsewhere, beyond the mayor and the photographers. She looked back at me and I turned away from the woman.

At the other end of the room, Louise Brooks stood in the doorway.

'What is it?' the woman asked me.

'Someone I have to go and see,' I said. I told Laura I'd be back.

I put down my wine and crossed the room to where Louise stood.

She was reading from the catalogue as I reached her. I knew she'd seen me approaching her, but she pretended to be surprised by my arrival beside her.

'I don't know why I came,' she said.

'Because your mother told you I'd be here?' I said.

'Perhaps. I worked through lunch so I could have an hour off. I tried calling you. Have you been here long?'

'Ten minutes.'

'Have you spoken to her?'

'The girl you pretended hardly to remember? Yes.'

'There's not much on display, is there?' She studied the distant exhibit as she spoke.

'It's somewhere for the mayor to spend an idle hour.'

'Are there any reporters here?'

It occurred to me only then that she might have come because she believed Simon Fowler might also have been present.

I asked her if she thought he would want to see it, and the suggestion surprised her.

'Did *you* think he might be here?' she said.

I shook my head. 'This is the last place he'd want to be.'

She looked hard at the model, and at Laura Lei standing beside it. 'Seeing it – her – again – I don't know—'

By 'her' I wondered whether she meant Laura or her sister.

'Perhaps I ought to go over and say something to her,' she said.

'And perhaps that would be the worst idea in the world.'

By now, the mayor and the photographers were alongside Laura.

If Louise *had* come to the exhibition either to cause trouble for Laura or to repeat publicly her feelings concerning the model, then she could hardly have chosen a better moment than the arrival of the mayor and his entourage.

She took several steps into the room and I grabbed her arm.

'What?' she said.

'Don't do it.'

'You think I'm going to create a scene?'

'I don't know. But you might get there and then not be able to help yourself. Don't. Everyone else here sympathizes with you. They wanted it less than you wanted it. Think of Helen. And remember, whatever you think of Laura, she thought a lot of your sister, and Helen of her.'

Across the room, Laura Lei continued watching us. The woman had moved away from her to join the mayor.

'Let's go,' I said to Louise, waiting.

'You're probably right,' she said eventually.

I raised my hand to Laura and she waved back.

Outside, in the foyer, alongside Ronald McDonald and the headless cow, Louise started to cry.

'It's not that bad,' I said.

She looked at the cow. 'It is,' she said, and wiped her face.

The pierced sculptor came out from the hall and asked me if it was his exhibit that had caused Louise to cry.

'She's an animal lover,' I told him.

The studs in his top lip spelled out a short name, but I couldn't make this out. Those beneath his mouth were pointed and became splayed when he spoke.

'I could explain the concept, if you like,' he said to her.

'I'd rather you didn't,' Louise told him.

We left him and went outside. There was still no queue. In an hour it would all be over. It was already too late for the exhibition to be featured in that day's *Mail*, and by tomorrow it would be old news.

'That's probably the last you'll hear of it,' I said to Louise.

'You don't have to,' she said. 'I know I'm being stupid. My mother told me to stay away, said I was hurting no one but myself.'

I gave her one of Laura Lei's photos to give to Alison Brooks.

'She'll appreciate that,' she said. She put the picture in her bag without looking at it.

We walked together to the Drypool Bridge.

'I ought to get back to the hospital,' she said. 'Can I bring Helen's stuff to Humber Street later?'

I asked her if it wouldn't be more convenient for us to go through this where she lived with her mother.

'I don't want her to know what we're doing,' she said. 'I'll bring something to eat.'

We parted and she turned back in the direction we'd come.

I considered returning to the exhibition and continuing my conversation with Laura Lei, but by then the event would have been almost over, and perhaps Laura and the other exhibitors would be consoling themselves with the left-over wine at the poor attendance and at the little genuine interest their work had attracted.

I crossed the dual carriageway and walked back along the marina to Humber Street.

27

I called Sunny and told him I was going to see Peter
Nicholson again.

'Any particular reason?' he said.

'Yvonne told me it was time to start pulling at a few
loose ends.'

'Makes a change from endlessly searching for those
missing pieces of the jigsaw.'

'Not really,' I said.

'You think he was lying all along, don't you?'

'I'm certain he was,' I said.

'And so now you're going to try and find out why?'

'You're wasted reporting on record ice cream sales
and streets melting in the heat,' I told him.

He said nothing for a minute. 'So presumably you
already think you *know* why he's been lying.'

'How could I possibly know that?'

Another minute of silence. 'What else?' he said.

I told him.

Louise called me at seven.

She was parked immediately below. I went to the window and watched as two of the men from the warehouse opposite helped her to unload the boxes she'd brought. She stood with them for several minutes, laughing at what they said, and they in turn responded to the attention she paid to them. She'd come directly from the hospital and wore the same blouse and skirt. The men wore dirty leather aprons. One of them was in his early twenties, tanned and muscular; the other was at least sixty, pale and overweight. She paid equal attention to them both.

I went down to her and she introduced me to the two men. I knew them already, but neither of them revealed this to her. She insisted on giving the older man five pounds to buy the pair of them a drink. He tried to refuse, but when she told him she was leaving the money on the roof of her car, he took it. He offered to help carry the boxes up to my office, but Louise told him he'd done enough and that she and I would be able to manage from there on.

I knew from what Laura Lei had already told me that these could not be all Helen Brooks's possessions gathered from the Park Grove flat, and when I mentioned this to Louise she told me she'd brought none of the clothing she'd removed. I asked her to hang on to this, and she assured me that everything was safely stored at her mother's home, untouched since being taken there.

In one of the boxes were three bottles of wine, bread, cheese and packets of cold meat. The wine was already chilled, but she went to the waterless sink at the back of the room and stood the bottles in it. The same sink in which her mother had stood her flowers and her small, naked daughter almost forty years earlier.

'What are we looking for?' she asked me, and I told her I wasn't sure.

'Anything that might connect her to Fowler,' I said, knowing it was the answer she expected to hear. It was unlikely that she hadn't already done this, but she said nothing, and we began our search.

There were four boxes of Helen Brooks's photos, along with folders containing her notes and designs for her own three-screen exhibit.

It would have taken days to establish which of the photos intended for the finished piece remained in the boxes. I assumed Louise would have found this detailed montage, and all it implied concerning her relationship with her sister, as offensive as Laura Lei's model, and that either she alone, or she and her mother together, had already sorted through the photos and had retrieved many of them – either for their own use or simply to prevent them from ever being used in the way Helen had intended.

My greatest interest remained with the last of the photos – those taken and emailed to Laura during the days of Helen's absence before her death. I asked Louise about these and she showed me them. There were five in total, all of them hand-held self-portraits, deliberately unfocused and poorly lit – close-ups of Helen's pale face, her open mouth and dark eyes.

Disappointingly, they revealed nothing of where they had been taken, and there was no evidence of anyone else in them. Louise showed me the five pictures on one of Helen's plans, convincing me that all those final few photos were present.

'I was as disappointed as you are,' she said. 'What had you hoped for?'

Pictures of Helen on Fowler's yacht sitting alongside her mystery companion with a newspaper in her lap bought the day she died.

'It would have been far too much to hope for,' I said.

It was still possible, however, that Helen had sent Laura Lei more than these five pictures, but that these were the only ones included in her plans for the triptych.

'Perhaps there *were* others, and Laura took them,' she said.

'She'd have no reason to keep them from me.'

'*Did* you think Helen might have taken a photo of whoever was with her?'

'It would have been a start,' I said. And it would have been a good reason for everyone wanting to search the yacht at the first possible opportunity once the police had finished with it and it had been taken to the salvage yard.

'Do you have any idea at all who it might have been?' she said.

I shook my head. It was another lie – or half-lie – but it would have served no real purpose to have started making wild guesses to her before I'd seen Peter Nicholson again and had the first of those guesses confirmed.

'You think she was blackmailing Fowler, don't you?' she said.

It was something else I'd considered, and something else that remained a possibility.

'Meaning she knew something, or she'd photo-graphed something or someone, either then – in those last few days – or beforehand – and that that was why she was killed?' I said.

She nodded, but with little conviction.

'Is that what you and your mother believed right from the very beginning?'

'I don't think *she* ever gave it much credence.'

'But you at least suggested it to her?'

'Once or twice,' she said.

'And did you raise it all again – the idea that Helen might have been killed by Fowler because of some hold she had over him – when persuading your mother to come and see me?'

She bowed her head and clicked her lips.

'How much have you taken from the boxes?' I asked her.

'About a third of everything. There were lots of pictures of the two of us together, of Helen and my mother together, of the three of us.'

'And you thought everything was now being degraded by the way Helen intended using them?'

'Of course I did. She might have been fucked up towards the end, but she wasn't always like that. She had no cause – no *right* – to use everything that came before then to promote or add weight to that one ridiculous and offensive notion.'

'Meaning you felt she implicated you and your mother in what she allowed to happen to her?'

'What she *did* to herself, yes.'

I went to the sink and opened the first of the bottles.

'You also think she might have hidden something on the yacht, don't you?' she said. 'You think that's what

Fowler went looking for – something either implicating him or identifying Helen's mysterious companion – and that that's why he had the thing completely destroyed when he didn't find it.'

I avoided pointing out to her that she, too, had gone to the yard in search of something.

'If you're keeping anything from me . . .' I said, handing her a glass.

'I'm not,' she said.

To release this sudden tension between us, I turned to the remaining boxes, most of which contained nothing but art books and catalogues and photographic magazines.

'There's nothing hidden in any of them, either,' she said. 'I looked.'

We sat together by the open window and drank the wine.

'You might be wrong about Fowler not having gone to Park Grove,' she said.

'What makes you think he might have done?'

'Guess,' she said.

'He owned it? Laura Lei never—'

'She never knew. She moved in when Helen moved in – cheap rent courtesy of her new boyfriend. Laura paid Helen and Helen paid Fowler via one of his leasing agencies.' Her tone was again cold and dismissive.

'I wish I'd known all this sooner,' I told her.

It perhaps explained why Fowler had told Marco to half-burn the map – to eradicate the dot on Park Grove and prevent me from arriving at the connection once I'd learned where Helen had been living at the time of her death. And if this were true, then perhaps he believed there was something hidden in the house which he needed to retrieve. Against all this obvious reasoning was the fact that he'd then had fifteen months to go on looking, and the fact that Laura Lei still lived there, presumably still unaware that Fowler was her landlord.

'He searched the boat and then he searched the house,' Louise said. 'It makes perfect sense.'

'It might not have been anything specific,' I said. 'Perhaps he just wanted to ensure that nothing remained in either place that might afterwards cause fingers to be pointed at him.'

'Like the drugs he was providing her with?'

'It's as good a reason as any,' I said.

'I know. It was the same conclusion my mother and I came to.'

'All of which added to your anger when Fowler came out of the inquest whiter than white, while Helen—'

'Became the All-Humberside Fuck-Up even she couldn't help calling herself?'

We continued looking through the photos.

There were whole sequences of pictures featuring only Laura Lei, some of which, like the ones she'd already shown me, revealed her naked or partially clothed.

'Do you think your sister and Laura were intimate?' I asked her.

'I wondered when you'd get round to asking that one,' she said.

'You could just as easily have kept the pictures from me.'

'Don't think I didn't consider it. There were too many of them. You'd have noticed. I asked Laura about it and she said they weren't. She loved Helen, she said, and Helen loved her, but they were never lovers.' She paused. 'If I'm being entirely honest with myself, Helen's affair with Fowler concerned Laura as much as it upset me and my mother. She knew about it from the very beginning, whereas my mother and I only got to hear about most of it afterwards.'

'And you resented that?'

'Of course we resented it.' By 'we' she meant 'I'.

'Is that partly why you feel as you do now about how Laura used Helen's life in her exhibit?'

She shrugged. 'It was probably just a focus, that's all.'

'It's understandable.'

'Well, that's all right, then.' She signalled her apology for the remark the instant she'd finished speaking. We'd covered a lot of ground in that last hour.

She spread the food she'd brought across the desk, and we ate most of it.

She sat on the window sill and the men below called up to her. They asked her for dates and she said she'd think about it. The older man she'd given the money to told her to ignore them, and she shouted down to ask him why *he* hadn't asked her out, adding that he was the only one she'd accept. He told her he'd been married for forty years. They were unloading a cargo of bananas, and like the smell of the earlier fruit, the distinct aroma of these now filled the air.

She opened the second bottle and we ate the last of the food. She said the sweet smell of the fruit made the shabby street seem exotic. She switched on my lamp and its yellow glow cast shadows across the detritus of her sister's life scattered all around us.

And an hour after that, and after we'd drunk the final bottle, we made love on the floor, with only my jacket between us and the dusty boards.

Afterwards, we both dressed and sat together back at the window. She unfastened her hair, brushed it out with her fingers, refastened it, and then began to cry.

I held my arm across her shoulders, but said nothing.

It might have been what she'd planned to happen eight days earlier at the Holiday Inn, but I doubt it's what she had intended then.

She asked me if I regretted what had just happened.

I shook my head.

'But in the morning you'll probably feel compromised by it, right?'

'Possibly,' I said.

She held a hand against my chest and kissed me. 'Would you feel doubly compromised if we did it all again?' she said.

'We could pretend we were both drunk,' I said.

'And that the dusky air was awash with arousal and the aromas of the night?'

'Bananas?' I said.

She cupped the back of my head in her hand.

'We *are* drunk,' she said.

' "Dusky air"?'

'I know.'

Afterwards, she fell asleep on the bare boards where she lay, her blouse and my shirt bunched beneath her head.

28

I slept where I sat, and when I woke at five the next morning, she was gone. Her sister's belongings had all been returned to their boxes and stacked by the door.

I couldn't decide whether I genuinely did feel compromised by what had happened, or if it was what I imagined I felt because it was how I was supposed to feel. I felt hung-over. The smell of the bananas lingered. Whatever small part of my conscience needed satisfying, I satisfied by telling myself that I was working for her mother and not Louise. I understood the self-serving reasoning of this, and knew that it would sound like nothing other than the excuse it was if I was ever forced to repeat it to anyone else. To Yvonne, for instance. Or Sunny. Or Fowler. Or Alison Brooks.

I waited until seven, and then went to the agency.

Sunny was already waiting for me at the top of the fire-escape.

We sat there together for fifteen minutes while he told me what he'd found out – which was considerably more than I'd anticipated – and then I left him and drove to Paull Holme to see Peter Nicholson again.

I arrived thirty minutes later to find Nicholson already up and in the untidy yard of his home washing a four-wheel drive.

He stopped at my arrival.

I left my car at the end of the track leading to his house, and walked first to the bank overlooking the estuary before going to him.

'Nice car,' I said. 'Is it new?'

'Second-hand. Two years old. I've had it—'

'Let me guess,' I said. 'You've had it a year. And you probably bought it with the money Fowler gave you for lying about what you saw on the night Helen Brooks went missing. The same money, in all likelihood, that paid for the double-glazing in this dump.'

'I don't know what you're talking about,' he said.

'I hear that said to me so often, I always ignore it,' I said.

'Are you accusing me of lying? I'm—'

'You're what – a dependable, honest old Humber pilot? Sorry – dependable, honest old *ex*-Humber pilot.'

'You can't just come out here and start accusing me of stuff like that.'

'OK, I'll go to the police and accuse you of it to them. What did Fowler tell you – that a coroner's court wasn't like a real court, that you couldn't perjure yourself?'

'I hardly spoke to the man.'

I clicked my fingers. 'That's right,' I said. 'I was

303

forgetting. You did it all through Marco.' I pulled one of the sheets Sunny had given me from my shirt pocket. 'That's a picture of you, in full uniform, protesting at a Ports meeting about the renegotiation of your contracts.'

'So what? They never even—'

'Please, let me finish. I don't care about what happened to you before or after you were fired. All I care about is finding out what happened to Helen Brooks. And when I say I know you lied about what you saw – or, most likely, *didn't* see – I mean it.'

He held the picture I'd given him without looking at it.

'Go on,' I said. 'Look at it. You and the other diehards standing firm against the offer.'

He opened the folded sheet.

'When was that – a week before their ultimatum expired and you were out on your arse?'

'Five days,' he said. He remembered everything perfectly.

'You and those final few others must have been very close by then. What were you – brothers forged in a common bond of grievance? Remember all their names, do you?'

'Of course I do,' he said.

'Of course you do. And let me guess which name you remember best of all. Well, no need to tell you, is there? Not really. There you are, the pair of you, standing shoulder to shoulder. Good old William Shaw. The same William Shaw who was standing beside you when you, he and two others received your commendations for rescuing a – what's the phrase? – a "stricken vessel". Standing beside you in the photo-

304

graph you gave to the *Mail* when they came back to hail you as the Man of the Hour following the beaching of Fowler's yacht. Though Christ knows what good you did on that particular occasion. Except for Fowler, of course. And yourself via his wallet. Good old William Shaw. Peter Nicholson and William Shaw, two diehards, firm until the end.'

'So?' The word was more of a reflex than a genuine question.

'Is that it — "So?" He's Marco's *father.*' It was what Sunny had discovered for me.

'Mark's father. So?'

'So that makes everything look considerably cosier than it ever did before, wouldn't you say? You, Marco, his dad and Fowler all tied up in a neat little bundle.'

'You're being ridiculous,' he said. 'I knew Bill Shaw for twenty years before I ever set eyes on Simon Fowler. We trained and worked together. We went through a lot, me and him.'

'I can imagine,' I said.

'I hardly ever even saw his son until—'

'Until he turned up with Fowler and asked you to do him a big, a really big, a really really *really* big favour.'

'I spoke to Simon Fowler once — *once* — at the inquest, to tell him how sorry I was.'

'But you knew Marco was working for him. You must have known that everything Marco asked you to do — let's make that *paid* you to do, shall we? — you were doing for Fowler.'

'He never—'

'Oh, hang on,' I said, pretending to think. 'I've got this all wrong, haven't I? You weren't doing it for Marco or Fowler — you were doing it because you and

305

Marco's father had been close all those years and you'd both been badly treated, and you, at least, saw a way of getting back at all those others who'd turned their backs on the pair of you and left you to rot out here in this dump.'

'Bill Shaw took his own life six months ago,' he said. I hadn't known this. 'I know,' I said.

'Left a note saying how worthless he felt.'

'Which made perfect sense to you because it was exactly how *you* felt.'

'Don't tell me what I felt, Rivers, because you know fuck all about it. And all you're doing now is throwing a lot of shit around in the hope that some of it will stick.'

'You've got me there,' I said. 'Is that what Fowler told you I'd do? What else did he tell you – that all you had to do was keep your head down and your mouth shut and everything would go away. Did he tell you what he's been telling everyone from the start – that without the bodies, nothing of what happened on that night was ever going to come back to haunt you?' I paused briefly. 'Well, things have changed, Mr ex-pilot Nicholson, and that isn't going to happen. I can see which of those two options might appeal to you the most – Fowler's and mine – but you're wrong.'

'Why? Because *you* say so?' It was the closest he'd come to a sneer, and I sensed some of his confidence returning. The everything-depends-on-the-bodies-washing-up scenario still carried a lot of weight, and we both understood that.

'No,' I said. 'Because I'm going to get the inquest re-opened, and then I'm going to get everything I've discovered in the past couple of weeks re-examined in

306

light of what I think happened. Either way, it leaves you and Shaw somewhat exposed.'

'Bill Shaw had nothing to do with any of this,' he said. 'Leave his good name alone. Let him rest in peace.'

'I was referring to Marco,' I said. 'I don't think his father had the faintest idea of what was happening. But I do think Marco used his father to get to you. The only thing I'm not entirely certain of just yet is the full extent of *your* complicity. Did he come to you because something went wrong on the night in question? Or were you involved before then? If anyone dragged Bill Shaw's good name into all this, then *you* did.'

He looked at me for a moment and then turned and walked away from me. Suds still covered half his car. The water which had spilled around it dried quickly in the heat.

I waited until he had almost reached the door before calling, 'And then there's your missing wife to consider.'

He stopped walking and turned to face me.

I went to him, walking slowly, giving him time to think about what I was suggesting.

'What's *she* got to do with anything?' he said. 'Besides, who said she was missing? She left, that's all. She's not *missing*.'

I took a second sheet from my pocket. 'You certainly never reported her missing,' I said.

'I just told you – she left me.'

'And you let her go? Just like that? After thirty years of marriage?'

'And?'

'I'm just curious, that's all.' I tapped my chin with

the rolled sheet. 'And you're right – Humberside police have no record whatsoever of her being missing.'

'It's got nothing—'

'But Leeds police do,' I said.

'What?'

'She went to live with her sister in Leeds,' I said.

'I know she did.' He looked hard at the piece of paper.

'But then she left there, too.'

'I know that, too.'

'Only, unlike you, her sister saw fit to report her departure. I wonder why that was.'

'Ask her, not me.'

'I intend asking her. In fact, I'll be visiting her very soon. There are one or two other things I'm hoping she'll be able to clear up for me.'

'Such as?'

'Such as why your wife just walked away from everything here without trying to take you to the cleaners. She knew how much this place meant to you. If things between the pair of you were as bad as you say they were for all those years, I imagine she'd at least want to hurt you by forcing you to sell the house as part of a divorce settlement. I imagine she'd want that as much as you wanted to hold on to the dump.'

'Ask her what you like,' he said, meaning his wife's sister. 'Ask her about the time I went all that way to see her, to try and reason with her, to get her to come back with me.'

'And?'

'And she'd already gone. I'd just missed her.'

'She'd gone, presumably, because she knew you were coming. I think, perhaps, that you'd under-estimated her loathing of you because you were too concerned with your own hatred of her and because of how much you stood to lose by her going. What did you do – phone her and make sure she knew you were coming? Keep her unsettled and moving, and hope that she'd just be glad to be rid of you?'

'Think what you like,' he said. 'You've got it all wrong.'

'Not about you being involved with Marco Shaw and lying through your teeth at the inquest, I haven't,' I said.

He wanted to contradict this, but said nothing, knowing that I was provoking him without any real evidence for what I was suggesting.

'I called the ABP people,' I said. Another lie.

'And?'

'And apparently you shouldn't have been wearing your pilot's uniform at the inquest. You were already on the scrapheap by then. Impersonating a Humber pilot. Perhaps *that* might be the key to getting the inquest re-opened.'

'I told them I was an ex-pilot,' he said.

'I know you did. You told anybody who'd listen. Over and over. Over and over and over. They must all have been sick of the sound of your voice by the time the coroner brought in his verdict.' Something else occurred to me only then. 'I suppose even you guessed a long time ago that you were their second choice as key witness.'

'Nobody *chose* me. I was there. I saw what I saw.'

'Of course you did. Just a pity that William Shaw

was in the middle of his breakdown at the time, otherwise Marco could have done everything Fowler told him to do *and* have kept it in the family.'

'You're making some serious allegations here,' he said.

'And you've waited until now to point that out to me. Waited until you more or less knew what I knew so that you could tell Fowler everything I'd said and stick your hand back into his wallet. You were the only one at the inquest who expressed doubt about the bodies turning up. Everybody else seemed reasonably convinced that they'd reappear, and soon. I wonder why that was.'

'Because I knew more about the river and its tides and channels than anybody else they asked.'

'So you keep saying. But you still sowed those seeds of doubt, didn't you? And, even more crucially, everything everybody else said, speculated on and reported afterwards was based on the testimony of what you said you'd seen that night.'

'Not everything,' he said.

'Everything that mattered. I bet even you can't remember the number of times you used the phrase "tragic accident".'

He smiled coldly at the remark.

'None of which really matters, I suppose,' I said. 'Because it was exactly the same conclusion everybody else was going to come to anyway until the bodies turned up and were autopsied to reveal what everyone had so far missed. All you were doing, having laid the foundations for everything which followed, was telling people more or less what they wanted to hear. You probably even convinced yourself

310

that you were doing it all to spare Alison Brooks's feelings.'

'It was what she—'

'Not that *I* believe any of that,' I said. 'And I'm also not convinced that you were doing it solely because of any allegiance you felt to William Shaw, or even a desire to get one over on everybody else – although I can see how something like that might appeal to a jumped-up, bitter little man like you who—'

'Call me all the names you like,' he said. 'It won't alter the facts.'

'I know it won't. And I also know that no one's come anywhere near those *facts* yet. What I was going to say is that you probably agreed to do what you did in providing and insisting on your false evidence for the same reason most other people in the same position do it – greed. Perhaps you even used the money to pay your wife off and hang on to all this. Perhaps her leaving her sister's in Leeds was all part of that same deal. You're right – I don't know everything yet, but I know more than you or Marco or Fowler ever imagined I'd discover, and regardless of what I do or don't know for certain regarding those facts, I know that the last thing any of you wants now – especially Fowler – is for me to start making all these half-formed explanations and connections public. Like I said, you're in a very exposed position – all three of you.'

'You're all talk,' he said, and moved closer to his open door.

I shrugged. 'Have it your way.' I started walking away from him.

'You can tell her from me,' he shouted after me. 'Tell her I gave her every chance to get things sorted out.'

311

I resisted asking him if he was talking about his wife or her sister.

'No you didn't,' I said. 'You just pushed your wife further and further away. Why don't you go in and put your uniform on and stand waving at the boats. Perhaps somebody might wave back.' I heard the door slam behind me.

I drove to the end of the track, turned towards Hull and pulled into a parking space a few hundred yards beyond the junction.

Less than five minutes later, Nicholson passed me on the road heading in the same direction. I let two cars get between us and then followed him.

He stopped in Hull opposite the King George Dock and went to a phone kiosk.

He left the kiosk and went back to his car, pulling it onto the edge of a vast building site. He stood beside it for several minutes, and then climbed back inside and waited there.

I was parked on Elba Street, facing away from him, watching him in my rear-view mirror.

Twenty minutes later, Marco arrived in a minicab.

The two men spoke in Nicholson's car for fifteen minutes while the cab waited.

When Marco finally left the car, Nicholson followed him and walked a pace behind him to the waiting cab. Marco turned on him and pushed him away. He pointed back to Nicholson's car and Nicholson stopped walking.

Marco returned to the cab and it left in the direction of the city centre.

Nicholson waited where he was for several minutes

longer, as though deliberating what to do next, and then he returned to his car and drove back in the direction of his home.

I continued my own journey back to Humber Street.

I had intended visiting Leeds and talking to Jane Nicholson's sister immediately after my visit to Paull Holme, but there was no answer from the number Sunny had given me.

I called the number listed on the list of missing persons issued by the Leeds police and told the woman who answered that I thought I'd seen Jane Nicholson. After a moment's delay, she told me that my sighting was the first to go into the file. I asked her why she thought there had been no others, but she was unwilling to speculate. She wanted to know how certain I was that the woman I'd seen was Jane Nicholson. I said I was 90 per cent certain and heard the sag in her voice as she went on taking details. I asked her if it was unusual for there to have been no sightings whatsoever in the year the file had been opened. Not particularly, she said.

Later, I tried calling the sister's house again, and again there was no answer.

Sunny called me in the middle of the afternoon and asked me how the visit to Nicholson had gone. I told him what I'd said to Nicholson and about his hurried meeting with Marco.

He asked me if I'd seen that day's paper yet, and I told him I hadn't. Get one, he told me. Pages three and nine.

I walked to Silver Street and bought an early edition from the vendor there.

On page three was the announcement of yet another

display of all the about-to-be-announced plans for the rebuilding of the city centre. This was to be held in the Banqueting Hall at the Guildhall, and everyone concerned was to be on hand to answer the public's questions about the work. Afterwards, a reception was being held, and the contracts for the work were to be signed in public. I saw both Fowler's and Webster's names among those participating. The meeting was scheduled for a week's time, and whatever else it was intended to achieve, it was primarily just another PR exercise.

I turned to page nine, and at first I thought Sunny had made a mistake. The page was mostly adverts. A new boutique was opening. All the other boutiques wished it luck. A woman in Driffield had given birth to triplets having expected only twins. Protests were building over the recently introduced Sunday car-parking charges. Vicars and others were flexing their muscles and raising their voices in more than prayer. And in Hessle, in a disused salvage yard, awaiting sale, an as-yet unidentified man had been killed in an accident when a rack of empty gas tanks had fallen on him where he knelt working. In addition, he had suffered burns to his chest and face in the accident. The incident was being investigated by both the police and the fire service. No one else was involved.

29

Louise arrived an hour later to retrieve her sister's possessions.

I showed her the announcement of the Guildhall presentation and she asked me what it meant. She remained less convinced than I was that this was the line Simon Fowler was drawing beneath the past and the future. She asked me why I thought this still mattered – especially to a man like Fowler – and said she was also not convinced that the death of her sister fifteen months ago and Fowler transferring his money and his interests now remained connected. I said nothing to try and persuade her otherwise.

We arranged to meet for an early dinner, after which she had promised to return to her mother, who had spent several painful and sleepless nights.

'Is that why you left so early this morning?' I asked her.

'I went at three. There was someone with her. A nurse, but . . .'

I told her I understood.

'I don't expect you to have to understand,' she said.

'I understand that, too,' I said.

'You can be *too* understanding,' she said, and kissed me.

I helped her with the boxes to her car.

Afterwards, I called Yvonne and told her what had happened the previous night.

'None of my business,' she said.

'I still wanted you to know,' I told her.

'So I'm what – your confessor, your analyst, what? When's the wedding?'

'You'll be the first to know,' I said.

'I'll be on holiday.'

'Whatever else you think I'm doing wrong, I'm not confusing the issue here.'

'Yes, you are,' she said. 'But you don't need to try and convince me otherwise. Sunny thought it had happened long before now. She's an attractive woman. You're absolved. Just remember – there's no "i" in louse.'

'I'll laugh at that piece of cruel cleverness later,' I said.

'Sunny told me about Nicholson,' she said. 'Are you going to get to Fowler through him?'

'Unless Fowler decides to do something about it first.'

'Like he did with the old guy at the salvage yard?'

'Accident, they say,' I said.

'Glad you can live with that. Do you honestly think he knew something about what had happened on the yacht and that Fowler had paid him to keep quiet, but that he couldn't trust him to go on keeping quiet now that he was out of a job and because you'd turned up to see him waving money in his face?'

'I gave him one of my cards,' I said.

'It just gets better and better,' she said. 'Forget about being absolved.'

'I went to see him four days ago,' I said.

'And Fowler followed you straight to him.'

'Thanks for making me feel better about it all,' I said.

'That's not what I'm here for. You've got other people for that, remember?'

'Well, thanks anyway.'

'You're welcome. Have a nice day.' She hung up.

Going to the police and repeating anything she'd just suggested would serve no one's interests. If I could prove Fowler's part in what had happened on the yacht, then the connection to the salvage yard and the man who had died there would become obvious to everyone, and Fowler could then be tied to that far more securely than I could ever connect him to it now with more of my unfounded accusations.

I wondered about the card I'd given the man. Perhaps it had been burned when he was killed. If the police had found it they would let me know soon enough. And if Fowler or Marco had found it, then that too would soon become evident to me.

I met Louise two hours later at the same restaurant overlooking the dual carriageway and the marina.

We talked about her mother and I told her about the death of John Maxwell's wife, about how he too had tried to care for her at home, and how he'd been beaten by the severity and the duration of her illness and been forced to relinquish his care of her. Following two years of suffering, she had died five days after being taken into hospital.

'I won't let the same happen to her,' she said. She asked me to check with her before next visiting her mother and I promised her I would. 'There are some things you wouldn't want to walk in on,' she said. 'There are some *days* you wouldn't want to walk in on.'

We ordered our meal.

The waiter she'd antagonized at our previous visit was not on duty. The restaurant was only a quarter full.

By nine we'd finished and we rose to leave – she back to her mother, and me back to Humber Street.

We parted at the dual carriageway, and as I kissed her, someone called to us.

In the centre of the road I saw Marco, and beside him a blonde-haired woman whom I recognized as Nikki, the woman photographed with Fowler six months after Helen Brooks's death.

Marco called to us again and then the pair of them came to stand beside us.

I'd said nothing to Louise about my visit to see Peter Nicholson.

'Very touching,' Marco said. 'Bit late for people your age still to be up.' Both he and Nikki laughed at the remark.

'Perhaps he was kissing her goodnight and they were both off to bed together,' Nikki said.

Marco looked hard at me. He knew that I'd been to see Nicholson, but not that I'd seen the two of them together at the King George Dock twenty minutes later.

'Delivering her to Fowler, are you?' Louise said to him, holding the woman's gaze as firmly as Marco held mine.

'You want to keep *that* out,' Nikki said, tapping the side of her nose. Her nails were long, straight at the tips, and varnished translucent and white. Her skin was as evenly tanned as Marco's, and she wore a dress which revealed most of her assisted cleavage and all of her legs.

'Unless, of course, Marco here is helping himself to a slice of the same sugary cake himself,' Louise said.

I saw Nikki tense and then release her hold on Marco.

'Try it, sweetheart,' Louise said.

I saw her stance change slightly, her feet move apart and her hands come up to her chest.

Marco saw this too, and understood better than I did what it meant.

'Leave it,' he said to Nikki. He grabbed her arms and pulled her back a step. Nikki protested at this, but he kept his grip on her. Eventually, she relaxed.

'Clever girl,' Louise said. She opened and then closed her fingers.

'Why don't we just say goodnight. You go one way and we go another,' I said to Marco.

'Nicholson says you accused him of making it all up,' he said.

'I accused him of worse than that. What's it got to do with you?'

He glanced first at Nikki, and then at Louise, who said, 'Well?' to him.

Nikki was about to speak, but Louise turned to her and told her to shut up. 'We know what you are in all of this,' she said. 'So the less said about that, the better, eh?'

Considering what she already professed to know about her sister's relationship with Fowler, it was a dangerous remark to make and Nikki took advantage of this.

'I'm more in any of this than that stupid fucking little tart was,' she said. 'At least I'm doing something useful instead of lying around stoned out of my skull all fucking day ready to jump up and open my legs when somebody tells me to.'

Marco told her to shut up. I saw his concern at what she might be about to say next, but before she could speak, Louise slapped her hard across her face and Nikki fell back against the roadside railings.

She quickly regained her balance and laughed. She held a hand to her cheek. 'That's assault,' she said. She looked to Marco for support.

But Marco, considering all the implications of what was happening – especially having encountered me so soon after Nicholson had repeated my allegations to him – was reluctant to say anything that might encourage her further.

Louise took a step towards Nikki, who raised an arm to protect herself.

'Next time you want to say anything about my sister, make sure I'm out of hearing first. And if you think for one second that this is an end to anything, then think again, stupid.'

'You just going to stand there?' Nikki screamed at Marco.

'If he's got any sense, he will,' Louise said. 'Besides, I'm betting he's not too sharp at thinking for himself.

Probably one of those men who are better at doing what they're told to do rather than thinking something through for themselves.' She turned to Marco. 'Am I right?'

She wasn't, but I said nothing.

Then she turned to me and said she had to go. She kissed me quickly and then crossed the road to where her car was parked.

'She really ought to watch her mouth,' Marco said when she'd gone.

'Tell *her* that,' Nikki shouted at him, still angry at his lack of support for her. 'Slag. Her and her precious fucking sister alike.' The remark was intended for my response, but I said nothing. Misinterpreting this, Nikki said to Marco, 'See, *he* knows what I'm saying. He knows I'm telling the fucking truth.'

Marco grabbed her arm again and pulled her away from the railings. It occurred to me that they might have been meeting Fowler at the restaurant, and that, despite what Louise had suggested, there was nothing between the two of them, that Marco was simply delivering her there.

As they left me, I said, 'I'm sorry for what happened to your father, but you were the one who decided to use him because of his closeness to Nicholson.'

He thought about this for a moment. 'I haven't got the faintest what you're talking about,' he said. 'Either say something you can back up for once, or just fuck off.'

'Fair enough,' I said. 'Just so long as *you* know that I know.'

'What's he talking about?' Nikki said.

Marco came to me until our faces were only inches apart.

'You just don't know when to leave well alone, do you,' he said.

Then he stood back from me, ran his hands down the front of his jacket, and walked away from me and into the restaurant.

Angry at being left like this, Nikki shouted after him and then ran to join him.

I waited until they were both inside before leaving and walking back along the dockside to Humber Street.

30

Two days later, I was finally able to talk to Jane Nicholson's sister.

The first thing she told me was that if I had anything to do with Peter Nicholson then she had no intention of speaking to me. I told her I was interested only in tracing and talking to her sister, and that I would not reveal her whereabouts to Nicholson. She remained suspicious of me, reluctant to talk on the phone. She told me eventually that she had no idea where her sister had gone after leaving her home, and that other than report her departure to the police, she had done nothing else to try and find her. She told me they had never been particularly close, and that they had grown even further apart since her sister's marriage to Nicholson. She spoke as though all this had happened three, and not thirty years ago.

I asked her if I could visit her. It was her day off, she said, and she gave me her address.

I left Hull and diverted before Southfield to revisit the empty salvage yard.

I parked on the side of the road and crossed a foot-bridge over the traffic to look down at the salvage yard. I met a man there who, when he saw where I was looking, said, 'A terrible thing to happen.'

I pretended not to understand him.

'One of the old workers there was killed yesterday. He'd been laid off, but he still used to turn up every now and then to work in the shed.'

'What sort of work?'

'Bits and pieces of welding.'

'What happened to him?'

'As far as they could tell, he was pulling down a tank from a rack and they think he dislodged another and it fell on to him. Crushed his skull. Killed.'

I remembered the stack of near-empty tanks along the shed wall.

'Thing is,' he went on, 'he had his torch already lit, and when he fell it went on burning into him. Burned his clothes. There was a fire. The new owners are try-ing to sort it all out with the insurers. The place has been running down for years. Should have sold up long since. Piece of land like that, right on the river, worth a small fortune.'

I asked him if he knew who the new owners were, but all he could tell me was that they were local. It was something I should have found out following my first visit to the place. Perhaps Fowler had seen the potential of the yard when his yacht had been taken there. Perhaps – along with Walmsley Street and Park Grove – it had been another of the dots on the burned map. Anyone living in an apartment overlooking the river there could be in the city centre in fifteen minutes.

The man left me alone on the bridge, and a few minutes later I returned to my car and continued my journey to Leeds.

I called Sunny as I drove and asked him if anything more had come to light concerning the accident. It was old news, he said. Everything would now go quiet until an inquiry was completed, and then it would be even older news.

I knew that what had happened to the man could not have been an accident, that the timing following my visit and conversation with him was too co-incidental. But if Fowler did turn out to be the new owner of the yard, then the last thing he would want now would be all the unwelcome attention surrounding the man's death.

I told Sunny what had happened outside the restaurant the previous evening.

'You think Marco's helping himself behind Fowler's back?' he said.

'They weren't being particularly secretive about it, and I daresay the waiters there would let Fowler know soon enough.'

'Perhaps Nikki's already last month's flavour.'

'And Marco trawls the rejects?'

'It's a thought.' He was talking about Helen Brooks.

I told him where I was going.

'I looked again through the files,' he said. 'She went, she was never reported, she never came back, she was never missed, end of.'

'Any reason why Nicholson would try to persuade her to go back to him?'

'After letting her go so easily and glad to see her gone? None that I can think of.' He paused. 'Do you think she's mixed up in all this?' He made it clear to me by his tone that it wasn't what he believed.

'By default, perhaps,' I said.

By then I'd left the dual carriageway and joined the motorway. I saw the Ouse Bridge ahead of me, and as I rose over its gentle sweep I looked down over the old bridge and the expanse of river-filled land all around it.

I arrived on the northern outskirts of Leeds an hour later.

Jane Nicholson's sister lived at the centre of a vast estate and I spent twenty minutes searching for the address she'd given me.

She was waiting for me when I arrived.

Her home was newly decorated and immaculately clean. She was younger than her sister. Pictures of her children lined the mantelpiece and the walls.

She offered me tea, which I accepted.

I asked her why she thought her sister had finally left Nicholson after enduring an unhappy marriage for so long, and why, considering that the two women had not been particularly close, she had chosen to go there upon her departure.

'That last one's easy,' she said. 'Because she had nowhere else *to* go.'

'She must have had friends closer to home, in Hull,' I suggested. I remembered what the man at Spurn had told me about his wife and Jane Nicholson.

She shook her head. 'Not that I know of. He put paid to all that.'

I asked her what she meant.

'He had ideas about what women should and shouldn't be and do. He wasn't like that to begin with, but he got worse. When they moved out to live at Paull she hardly saw anyone from one day to the next. She never learned to drive. He was never happy about other people being in the house. It was what they'd gone out there to get away from, he told her. He was obsessed with his job.'

'Losing it hit him hard,' I said.

'So what? He could have done what most of the others did and gone back on different terms. Anyway, him losing his precious job had nothing to do with how he was with her. That was something recent, and they'd been growing apart for years, ever since Alex.'

'Alex?'

She looked at me as though I'd tricked her into revealing something. 'He never told you?'

I shook my head.

'Alex was their son. Born twelve years ago. He would have been nearly thirteen now.' She went to the mantelpiece and took one of the framed photos from it. She gave it to me. In it, Nicholson and his wife stood with a baby held between them.

'What happened?' I said.

She took the picture from me and returned it to its place among the others, wiping the non-existent dust from its upper edge with her finger.

'Drowned,' she said. 'He was three. She was bad after the birth, but Nicholson behaved as though it was the best thing that had ever happened to them. One day, he took the child out with him. One minute he was walking along behind him, the next he was gone. Nicholson spent most of his time with his binoculars

327

glued to his eyes, watching the ships, the other pilots coming and going, forever talking about where he thought the ships were coming from and going to, forever pointing out which channels they were using.'

'And the boy drowned because he wasn't keeping a close enough eye on him?'

'Nobody ever said as much, but that's what happened. That's what *she* told *me* had happened. His little body turned up two days later.'

'And it forced them apart.'

'Further apart. I don't know why she didn't leave him sooner. Inertia, I suppose. That, and a kind of resignation. There hadn't been anything between them for a long time. It was a surprise to everybody when Alex came along.'

'And he was definitely Nicholson's child?'

'Spitting image. More's the pity.'

I remembered how Nicholson had spoken of people drowning in the Humber during our first meeting, how he had turned away from me to avoid my eyes and to look out over the expanse of water as he spoke.

We sat in silence for several minutes, after which I asked her if she'd been in the house when Nicholson had turned up to try and persuade his wife to return to Paull with him.

She'd been remembering the death of the small child and wiped her eyes before answering me.

'That's what he told you, is it? That he wanted some sort of reconciliation?'

'Why do *you* think he came?'

'I don't know. To let her know where she stood, perhaps? To scare her even further away? To leave her in no doubt that he had no intention of leaving or selling his precious home, if that's what she was after?'

'And was she?'

'She'd have been stupid not to get *something* out of him. She was entitled.'

'Did you try and persuade her to?'

'I told her to go and see my solicitor. My husband walked out on us six years ago – good riddance – and I've never looked back.'

'So did she set proceedings in motion?'

'Divorce, you mean? Never got the chance. He turned up, begging me – *me* – to persuade her to go back to him.'

'What did she say to him?'

'That's what I mean when I say she never got the chance. He phoned up and told her he was coming to see her, that he was coming *for* her, and she went before he got here. Coward that he was, he waited until I was home from work before turning up. None of the kids were here, thank God. He practically forced his way into the house and stormed round it looking for her. He accused me of having told her to go and wait somewhere else until he'd gone and I was able to give her the all-clear. I'd only been in the house a few minutes myself.'

'How did you know she'd gone?'

'Because most of her stuff was gone. Because I always rang her to say I was on my way home. Because if she was here by herself, she always kept the bolt on the door. She would never have opened the door to him if she'd been here alone. He phoned her two or three times the day before to say he was coming.

Devious bastard that he is, he told her he couldn't come until the weekend, Saturday.'

'And he turned up sooner?'

'On the Friday.'

'Then how did she know to leave before he got there?'

'Because he phoned her again on that same day. Said he'd been able to borrow a van and that it was big enough for everything she had with her. Christ, you'd have got everything she owned into the glove compartment.'

'So when she went, she wouldn't have had much to gather together?'

'Could she leave at short notice, you mean? She had to. Apart from which, whatever time *she* thought he was coming, he didn't turn up until three. I finished the early shift at two. To tell you the truth, I was glad she'd managed to get away. I didn't realize then, of course, that I'd never see her or hear from her again. I thought she'd give it a few days, wait for him to bugger off home with his tail between his legs, and then we could get back to normal. She'd started applying for jobs. She'd put her name on the council list for a flat. My kids loved her. Their only auntie. Given the chance, she would have been a good mother.'

'What happened to the divorce proceedings?'

'Died a death. She never turned up to sign any of the papers.'

'Which convinced you even further that that was why Nicholson had come in the first place?'

She nodded. 'She would never have gone back to that place with him, not the way he treated her. The only one who couldn't see that was him.'

'Did he say where he'd got the van from?'

'I never asked him. I was too busy trying to get him to calm down. He was running up and down the stairs, everywhere. He went into the room she'd been sharing with my youngest and practically tore it apart.'

'Do you think he was looking for something?' I asked her.

'Such as? And if he was, he never found it. He left this house empty-handed. I threatened to call the police.'

'How did he respond to that?'

'Told me to try it. Accused me again of helping her to avoid him, to hide from him.'

'And afterwards?'

'What do you mean?'

'Did he come back, call her again, make any more threats?'

'He rang once or twice. Even said he was sorry for how he'd behaved. He said he hadn't been thinking straight. I told him I didn't want anything to do with him. He told me to tell Jane that he was sorry for what he'd done. Perhaps he thought that if *I* believed him when he said it, then I'd try to persuade her to think the same way. I told him where to stick his apology. He even said that he knew he was being unreasonable, but that now – having lost his job and everything – he was prepared to talk to her about a divorce. I told him I didn't believe him, and that even if Jane did want to get in contact with him, I had no intention of acting as his messenger. After that, he stopped calling.'

I asked her if her sister had contacted her, and if she was keeping this from me now for fear that I might tell Nicholson.

'And you expect me to answer that?' she said.

'I wouldn't,' I told her.

'Unless it suited you to do so. Well, she hasn't. You can tell him he did a good job. Tell him I hope he's happy with everything. Tell him he got everything he wanted in the end.'

'What time did he leave?' I said.

'About an hour after he'd arrived. Said that whoever had lent him the van was expecting it back that night.'

'Did you see it?'

'It was parked where you are now. White, some writing on the side. Some kind of tradesman's van. If I could remember what was written on it, I'd tell you.'

In the hallway, the door opened, and two young children, a boy and a girl, ran into the room. She sent them upstairs to get changed.

'When their dad went they waited all night at the window for him to come back,' she said.

'Why didn't Jane leave him sooner?' I asked her.

'I don't know. She once told me that it was because Alex was buried in the local graveyard. What was I going to say against that?'

I thanked her for everything she'd told me. I gave her a card and asked her to contact me if she heard anything more from Nicholson.

'I thought at first,' she said, and then hesitated. 'I thought at first that somebody might have hired you to look for her. And then I thought it might have been him who was paying you.'

We were interrupted by the children running noisily downstairs. She sent them into the kitchen and showed me to the door.

'Will you let me know if you hear anything?' she asked me.

I promised her I would, but warned her that it was unlikely.

She held my gaze as I spoke and then left me before she found the courage to ask me if I believed her sister was dead.

I was caught in the traffic leaving the city centre, and I came back to Hull via York and over the Wolds.

They were harvesting in the fields, and the freshly cut stubble shone in the sunlight. On Arras Hill I passed a tractor carrying bales, a trail of chaff filling the road behind it.

Leaving Beverley, I phoned Sunny again.

Yvonne answered and asked me if I wanted a drink.

I told her I had work to do.

'Wrong answer,' she said, and told me where to meet her.

31

We met in a bar close to the agency.

As soon as I arrived, she took out a photocopy of a photo, showed it to me, and said, 'This is her, right?'

It was the picture of Fowler and Nikki together.

'Fowler's fast-track, sugar-coated diversion to help him get over Helen Brooks's death,' she said. She took out a second photo and laid it over the first. It was of the same woman. 'Her name's Nicola Fletcher. She had this one taken when she had aspirations — let's call them that, shall we — of becoming a model. She was winner, Miss Northern Dairies, two years running. Mark to Marco, Nicola to Nikki.'

'Proving what?' I said.

In the picture, Nicola Fletcher had her hair cut differently — though still dyed vividly blonde — and wore another strapless dress which revealed even more of her than I'd already seen.

'It's three years old,' Yvonne said.

'She looks much the same.'

'She looks exactly the same. That's the point. And she'll go on looking exactly the same for another ten years.'

'And then it'll all just disappear?'

'Along with her wit, charm, keen intelligence, winning personality and sense of humour.'

'Like yours did?'

'Like mine did.'

I wanted to avoid asking her why she was telling me all this.

'You'll be wanting to know why I'm telling you all this,' she said.

'I thought perhaps you just wanted to look at the woman who was prepared to have a go at Louise Brooks in the street.'

'It's the Hull way,' she said. 'And according to Sunny, who heard it all from you, little Miss Northern Dairies here wouldn't have stood much of a chance against little Miss Martial Arts.'

'It certainly looked that way.'

'I take it she hasn't tried to put a stranglehold on you yet?'

'I got a bit tired of the stranglehold approach to lasting relationships.'

'Funny, Sunny seemed to think the pair of you had turned a corner.'

'What made him think that?'

She took a deep breath. 'I love the smell of testosterone this early in the evening.' She held up her empty glass. 'Fetch.'

I went to the bar. The door had been fastened open and traffic fumes blew into the room.

When I returned to her there was something else on the table.

'I've been working hard on your behalf,' she said.

At first I thought it was another of Fowler's brochures, but looking at it I saw that it belonged to another company. It told me as much as any of his own self-congratulatory productions. Quality homes, quality lives, quality futures. Only this one belonged to a company owned by the man called Webster. The man Fowler was hoping to sell his scattered properties to in order to raise the finance for his considerably more prestigious city-centre developments. The man now vital to everything Fowler hoped to achieve.

'I know about him,' I said.

'Of course you do. You know *everything*.'

'I don't,' I said. 'I don't know, for instance, why you're still so keen for me to tie in what happened to Helen Brooks with what you think is about to happen to Fowler's old tenants when his deal with Webster goes ahead. Sunny told me all about it a couple of days ago.'

'I know something he didn't tell you.'

'Such as?'

'Such as Mr Quality Homes, Quality Lives Webster is the new owner of—'

'The Hessle Haven salvage yard.'

'From which Quality River Views will soon be available for anybody who's able to afford one and thus secure their Quality Future.'

'Has anything been finalized yet between Fowler and Webster?' I asked her.

'Not according to their websites. But reading between the lines, it's definitely about to happen. The share prices of all their companies have been rising recently in anticipation of all that's coming.'

'And your interest in this is what – that once Webster acquires the properties he'll empty them immediately – using whatever means he sees fit – and quadruple their value overnight?'

'They'd be worth *ten* times more once he started to redevelop them,' she said. 'It's what Irina's been predicting for months, ever since the end of Fowler's own cosy little arrangement with the council came into sight.'

'I still don't see how it connects to what happened to Helen Brooks,' I said.

'If you turn something up on Fowler then the deal might never be finalized and nothing would happen.'

Neither of us could believe in the simplicity of what she was suggesting.

'You know as well as Irina does that it's a done deal,' I said.

Her silence confirmed for me that she and Irina had already had the same unhappy conversation.

She slid the first photo she'd shown me – the one of Fowler and Nikki together – from beneath the glossier shot and brochure. 'Read the caption,' she said.

I read it. The man standing to Fowler's left, separated from him only by Nikki, was Webster.

'It's a Civic Society dinner,' I said.

'It's a reception held under the auspices of the Civic Society to welcome all these local men of vision to begin to prepare for all their wonderful work ahead.'

'Which was such a secret that they held the dinner at the Guildhall and invited every newspaper within a hundred miles to send someone to record the happy event.'

'Once again, he shoots, he misses,' she said. 'It means Fowler and Webster were together in this from the very start.'

'"Local Businessmen Plan Together For Brighter Future"?'

'Look at Fowler's hands,' she said.

I looked. They were clasped over his crotch.

'So?'

'And Webster's?'

One hand held a glass. The other was not in sight.

'And now look at Miss Cream 'n' Cheese's waist.'

Webster's fingers could just be seen there.

'Not held stiffly at her shoulder, note; not awkwardly linked through her arm and brushing ever so gently against her slightly palpitating bosom.'

'Fowler told the press that, following the death of Helen Brooks, he'd found happiness again. He mentioned Nikki by name.'

'Ah, how sweet. Next you'll be telling me that the picture proves nothing, that they were all drunk and delirious at the thought of their coming good fortune.'

It made as much sense as any other explanation, but I said nothing. I tried to remember what else Fowler had told me about Nikki and his relationship with her.

'Do you think he's using her like everybody seems to think he was using Helen Brooks?' I asked her.

'I'll assume your euphemistic evasions are the result of some ancient chivalric code to which you – and you alone – still cling. She's either bait, or she's a sweetener, but however you might want to see it, she's involved.'

'She could be working as Fowler's PA,' I said.

'Which would be another good name for it.' She looked at her watch and said she had to leave.

'Where did you get all this?' I asked her.

'It was with the stuff I took out of the file.'

'Did you put it back?'

'Not yet. Why?'

'Because it might have been what whoever broke into the agency once we'd all been decoyed to Walmsley Street was looking for,' I said.

But she remained unconvinced, still preferring to see the attack on the woman there as part of a plot being devised between Fowler and Webster to get rid of all their unwanted tenants.

'Why?' she said. 'Like you said, none of it was exactly a secret.'

'Is that why you wanted to see me?' I said. 'Just to make sure I wasn't missing anything. Or was it because you heard what happened between Louise and Nikki and wanted to make sure I was aware of what that implied regarding Helen Brooks?'

'I knew you'd work it out eventually,' she said.

'I knew about Helen Brooks from the beginning,' I said. 'Louise confronting Nikki like that didn't mean a thing. Whatever Nikki might have been about to tell me about Helen and Fowler in front of Louise, it wouldn't have been anything I hadn't already considered.'

'It just seemed to get very personal and very physical very quickly considering it was the first time they'd met,' she said.

'Implying it wasn't?'

She pursed her lips. 'You know her better than me. And in answer to your question – no.'

'No, what?'

'No, it wasn't why I wanted to see you. I learned something else that might be of interest to you.' She leaned closer to me across the small and cluttered table.

'Go on.'

'Fowler and Webster are having another little get-together. Tomorrow.'

'What kind of get-together?'

'I don't know. All I know is that they're meeting at a property Fowler is already developing on Lister Court. One of his flagships, apparently. Nothing to do with any of his other dirty little deals with Webster.'

'So?'

'So nothing. But whatever it is, it's important enough for one of the gutted rooms to have been cleared, and for food and drink to be laid on. A fair few of Fowler's tame little councillors will also be in attendance. I daresay even the Lo-fat Yoghurt princess herself might put in an appearance, doing what she does best in between handing out the canapés. Twelve o'clock.'

'How do you know all this?'

'One of Irina's spies works on the site.'

'One of her *spies*?'

'Someone who keeps her informed of what's happening.'

'Someone working illegally?'

'As opposed to what, exactly?'

'Working for Fowler?'

She shook her head. 'Fowler owns the place, but all the work's subcontracted. You're not going to get to Fowler like that again, not now, and certainly not here.'

'What else do you know about Lister Court?' I asked her.

'It runs to the river.' She meant the Hull, not the Humber. 'Prime development. Riverside views out on to the cement works. With a classy restaurant in the basement. Fowler's been developing it for eighteen months. The place is almost finished. Just the fixtures and fittings to go in.'

'Perhaps Fowler and Webster are simply getting together with a few of their friends to celebrate a job well done,' I said.

'And perhaps they're going to finalize everything they've concocted to announce at the Guildhall next week. It doesn't matter *why* they're getting together, just that they are.'

I was beginning to understand what she was suggesting to me.

'You want me to gatecrash?' I said.

'You invited Fowler to Humber Street, did you?'

'And do what?'

'Use your imagination?'

'You want me to confront Fowler with anything I might have got on him in front of Webster and all the others? Why?'

'I just thought it was about time you started pushing back, that's all.'

'You seriously think my accusations might unsettle Webster, that he might pull out of their deal?'

'It's worth considering.'

'No it isn't. Because it would never happen. They both stand to gain or to lose too much. Everything's too far down the line.'

'You could still throw everything you've uncovered

about Helen Brooks's death in Fowler's face in public,' she said.

'Great idea. Why didn't I think of that earlier.'

Neither of us spoke for several minutes.

'Whatever I might one day confront Fowler with,' I said eventually, 'I still can't prove any of it.'

'How many times do we have to have that particular conversation?' she said. 'Besides—' She started laughing.

'What?'

'I was going to say that you could always take the Karate Queen along to protect you.'

'Incisive, witty *and* hilarious.'

'You missed out the bit about me probably knowing you better than you know yourself,' she said.

I asked her if Irina Kapec had received any more photos or threats, but there had been nothing. I still had no idea who might have sent the pictures, or what purpose they were meant to serve. I knew that if I pushed her, Yvonne would say that they, too, were somehow connected to Fowler and what was happening now; but whatever she said, we both knew that this was unlikely.

I told her about the man at the salvage yard who had died.

'Sunny told me,' she said.

'Does *he* know about all this, about Fowler's gathering?'

'He offered to come with you. Batman and Robin.'

'Which one am I?'

'He's bigger and taller than you.'

'And I'd look better in yellow tights and a belted skirt?'

'You know you would.' She drained her glass and rose to leave.

I followed her outside.

'Whatever you do . . .' she said, holding out her arms to me.

'Be careful?'

'I was going to say don't mention my name if it gets messy or if there's any shooting.' She held me tightly. 'And no leaping from rooftop to rooftop.'

'Sunny?' I said. 'He can barely leap to a wrong conclusion.'

She released me, holding my shoulders until she was certain I understood what she was saying to me.

And then she stepped back from me and held up her hands as though she was about to karate chop me.

'Very funny,' I said.

'*I* thought so. Besides, you flinched.'

'I *winced*,' I said. 'There's a difference.'

'I'll tell Sunny you'll call him,' she said, and then she turned and left.

Upon my return to Humber Street, there was a message for me from James Salter in Howden, asking me to call him as soon as possible. His message had been waiting since noon.

'I've arranged for you to see Steven Rix,' he said.

'Steven Rix?'

'He works for Immigration. He was one of the liaison officers on the operation Fowler walked away from. I knew Rix beforehand. You can trust him.'

'Will he be able to tell me more about Fowler's part in it all?'

'More than anybody else will be willing to tell you. He can see us the day after tomorrow.'

'Where?'

'Peterborough station. It's an hour out of London for him and hardly twice that for you. I'll meet you on the train at Goole. He insisted on me being there. I told him you were paying all the fares.'

I sat for an hour in the fading light before going home.

In the street below, gulls fought over the remains of a recent delivery. I looked down at them and saw them running along the pavement in their efforts to get airborne, pieces of fruit in their wide beaks. And when the gulls had gone, a flock of starlings arrived to scavenge through what remained.

I went back to my desk and called Sunny. He answered on the first ring.

32

The following day, Sunny and I sat together in his car outside Saint Anne's church on High Street. The entrance to Lister Court lay ahead of us, already filled with parked cars. The River Hull lay to our left, beyond the half-demolished walls of a building site. The tide was out and the river was little more than a drain running through a valley of grey mud. A line of empty barges lay stranded by the departed water.

We'd been there an hour, watching the men arriving. We'd already walked around the surrounding alleyways several times to get our bearings.

The building Fowler was converting overlooked the river at the end of Lister Court. It had been a warehouse, empty for thirty years. Its crumbling red brickwork had been renovated and strengthened. Panels showed where girders had been fitted to reinforce the structure. Every window frame had been replaced, and fitted with tinted glass that revealed nothing of what lay inside. A developer's hoarding announced an eighty-seat restaurant and bar, and above this, sixteen high-quality apartments, eight with river views, and each of these with a narrow wrought-iron balcony overlooking the mud. I recognized the company's name as being one of Fowler's. It was clear, seeing the renovated property, why it formed no part of his deal with Webster.

'Tell me again what we hope to achieve here today,' Sunny said. The smoke from his cigar filled the car. All the windows were open but it still sank to the floor and settled there.

'Yvonne thinks I need to become more proactive,' I said. His remark had been intended to ensure I was clear in my own mind about why I was about to confront Fowler at a time and place where I was the last person he would want to see.

'She wants *me* to get a decent haircut and start dressing better,' he said. He wore a suit because I'd asked him to, and a tie with a small crest neither of us could identify. 'Perhaps she just wants you to go in there and get yourself beaten up or killed and that'll be her revenge on you for having fallen for the somewhat obvious charms of the daughter of your client.' He said the last four words slowly and evenly, leaving me in no doubt as to his own feelings on the matter.

'She'd never forgive herself if I was killed,' I said, my eyes still on the entrance to Lister Court, where a group of men I recognized from the city council had just arrived.

'She's got a diploma in Bereavement Counselling,' he said. He raised the camera from his lap and took a shot of the men. I'd asked him to bring the biggest camera and flashgun he owned.

'Fowler inhabits a world in which he calls all the shots,' I said. 'If he isn't in control, he doesn't go there.'

'And today *we're* in control? You should have said. Excellent.'

'No. But today we're going to prove to him that he can't always have things his own way.'

He remained sceptical. 'And how will that work?' he said. He took a second photograph of the men as they were greeted by others emerging from a taxi. I sensed his growing interest at the sight of these new arrivals.

'Who are they?' I asked him.

'Just the same old Great and the Good.'

He knew about my journey to Peterborough the following day with James Salter.

'Bereavement counselling?' I said.

'The diploma's got her name on it and everything. Perhaps she and Louise Brooks can hold a competition to see who can fill your grave fastest with their tears.'

'Directly or indirectly, Fowler is responsible for three deaths. And as much as he might want everybody else to believe that I'm undertaking some kind of paid and misguided vendetta against him, those three people are still dead, and, one way or another, the blood's still on *his* hands.'

He tutted and shook his head at the phrase. I'd already told him everything I'd learned in Leeds and my suspicions concerning Nicholson's wife. He remained unconvinced, but said nothing to undermine my reasons for doing what we were about to do.

I'd spent a mostly sleepless night trying to convince myself that I would still have turned up at Lister Court if he'd refused to come with me.

'We ought to go,' he said, tapping his watch.

We left the car and walked along Pease Court to the river, arriving at the warehouse from the opposite direction taken by all the others.

A man stood at the door welcoming the arrivals. I was relieved to see it wasn't Marco.

There was no checklist of the invited, and the man on the door said, 'Morning, gents,' and stood aside as we entered. The group of councillors stood ahead of us. A waitress brought a tray of champagne flutes to us. We each took one and walked through into the room beyond.

Though unfinished, this was to be the restaurant dining area with its views over the river and its sodden, crumbling wharves. The concrete floor was covered with a vividly red carpet. Tables of food were laid out, and on the walls giant photographs showed what this and other developments would look like when completed.

I searched the room for Fowler or Webster, but saw neither.

We walked from one table to another. We spoke to some of the others there, pretending to know them, telling them how good it was to see them again. It was what they were accustomed to.

After ten minutes of this, there was a brief round of applause in the doorway and Fowler and Webster entered together. They were accompanied by several others, including Marco and Nikki.

Sunny and I stood to the rear of the room, our heads

down, inspecting one of the models I had already seen in the Guildhall.

'They look pleased with themselves,' Sunny whispered.

'They walk into a room and people applaud them. It can't hurt.'

We'd already ascertained that there were no other members of the press in the room.

Seeing Fowler and Webster in the doorway, others began to applaud, and this grew until almost everyone in the room was clapping.

'You're right – that must do wonders for your self-esteem,' Sunny said. He flicked over a tree on one of the models.

Fowler and Webster went to the far side of the room, where a low stage had been built, and climbed to the microphone which stood there.

Fowler stood this to one side and announced that he didn't need it. Apparently, this was funny, and those standing closest to him laughed. He didn't intend making a speech, he said, just a few words of welcome followed by a quick run-through of all they were there to celebrate.

Fowler's welcome lasted fifteen minutes, and every-one in the room listened intently to what he said. When he'd finished, he introduced his partner, Webster, and there was more applause. Webster took Fowler's place at the front of the low stage and repeated more or less what Fowler had just said.

While all this was happening, I watched Marco, who stood to one side of the stage, beside the door. Nikki stood close by. She handed out drinks, flirting with the men who took these from her. Marco led the applause on several occasions, occasionally whispering to those standing around him. He had not yet seen either Sunny or myself at the rear of the room.

Webster concluded his own speech with a promise to the gathered councillors that, between them, he and Fowler had only one goal in mind, and that it was a goal they shared with everyone who lived in Hull, and with all those leaders who had only the best interests of the city and its people at heart. It was as specific as he was prepared to be, and he was rewarded by the longest bout of applause yet.

After this, both Fowler and Webster left the stage and began to move around the room shaking hands. After several minutes, seeing that Fowler was at last coming towards where we stood, I told Sunny to turn away from him, allowing our eventual confrontation to come without warning.

I heard Fowler talking to one of the councillors, telling him how pleased he was that the man had been able to find the time in his busy schedule to attend. Fowler motioned to Nikki, who came to them and exchanged the councillor's almost empty glass for a full one. He started talking about the model at which Sunny and I were standing, and the two men and Nikki came closer to us.

'Showtime,' Sunny said, and before I could tell him to wait, he turned, raised his camera and fired his flashgun directly into Fowler's face when he was only two or three feet away from us. This caught Fowler by surprise and he raised his hand to shield himself.

'We said no cameras,' he said. 'We were very clear on—' He stopped speaking when he saw Sunny, and he looked from Sunny to me as I finally turned to face him.

'No harm done,' the councillor said appeasingly.

Fowler looked at me without speaking for a moment, and then he asked the councillor to excuse him. He needed to have a quick word with me. He motioned again to Nikki, who understood him perfectly, and who slid her arm through the councillor's and led him away to another of the models.

I drank the last of the champagne in my glass and handed it to Fowler, who took it and then looked at it in his hand as though he had no idea how it had arrived there.

Sunny wound on his film and pretended to make adjustments to his camera, diverting Fowler's attention and leaving him uncertain about which of us to speak to first.

'You're not welcome here, Mr Rivers. You neither, Mr Summers.'

'We gathered that much,' Sunny said.

'So?'

'So I'd like you to leave,' Fowler said.

'Yeah, right,' Sunny said. 'I just need to take a few more shots. Perhaps one of you and Webster together, your arms around each other's shoulders. Perhaps I could even get one of the two of you licking each other's arses. You know, like dogs.'

Fowler looked back to me. 'I'm warning you,' he said.

'I know you are,' I said. 'You've been warning me ever since *you* broke into *my* office uninvited.'

'This is a private celebration,' he said.

'I know.'

'Anything you want to know, to ask me – to ask anyone – you'll get your chance at the Guildhall in a week's time.'

'Oh, well, in that case, we'll leave straight away and see you there,' Sunny said. He picked up the tiny tree he had toppled and snapped it in half. 'Oh dear,' he said. He waved to a passing waitress and exchanged his own empty glass for a full one, which he emptied in a single swallow. Then he picked up a small white car from beside the broken tree and pushed it back and forth across his palm making the noise of its engine.

'You *will* regret this, Mr Rivers,' Fowler said to me, his face close to mine, his voice low.

A group of men arrived beside us, and he turned to speak to them. I introduced myself, saying I was an interior designer specializing in restaurants. One man said he looked forward to seeing the finished thing. I pretended to be offended and told him that it was already finished and that the only thing left to do was to put out the tables and chairs. The man looked uneasy at my remarks.

'He's joking,' Fowler said, and sensing this sudden tension the man left us.

By then, Marco, alerted by Nikki, had come to stand a few feet behind Fowler.

'Marco,' I said. 'Good to see you. How's Nikki?'

'Nikki's fine,' Fowler said.

I ignored him, continuing my conversation with Marco over Fowler's shoulder. 'Good job this little get-together was scheduled for today. Because if it had been yesterday, I wouldn't have been able to make it. Had to go to Leeds, visit an old friend.'

'What's he talking about?' Fowler said to Marco.

'You don't have to pretend not to know what I'm talking about,' I said to Fowler.

Behind him, Marco looked suddenly and fleetingly anxious.

'What?' I said to him, exaggerating my surprise. 'You mean Mr Fowler here really doesn't know?'

'Perhaps if you told me what you were talking about, Rivers,' Fowler said to me.

'A minute ago, you wanted us to leave. Is Marco going to throw us out? In front of all these people?'

Beside me, Sunny raised his camera and fired the flash into Marco's face.

Marco said, 'Fuck,' loudly, and several of the men standing close to us turned and looked at him.

Fowler, too, cast him a glance, and Marco apologized to him.

'No,' Sunny said. 'You should apologize to *me*. Tell him, Mr Fowler.'

'Apologize,' Fowler said.

Marco stood without speaking for several seconds.

'He apologizes,' Fowler said.

'Wholeheartedly and unreservedly?' Sunny said.

'Of course.'

By then, Webster's attention had also been attracted, and he came to stand beside Fowler. He knew immediately that something was wrong, that Sunny and I were unwelcome in the room. He put his arm around Fowler's shoulders and asked him what was 'occurring'.

Fowler whispered to him behind his hand.

'What's "occurring",' Sunny said, 'is that Fowler's pet monkey here swore at me, and Fowler was just apologizing for that. You are? No, don't tell me – you must be monkey number two – Webster.'

Webster took his arm from around Fowler's shoulders and moved a step closer to Sunny. 'Mr

Summers,' he said in a whisper, 'play whatever stupid fucking games you want to play – you and your stupid fucking friend here – but don't fucking well play them with me or with my good friend Mr Fowler, because you're never going to win. You're a washed-up, useless fucking arsehole, and everybody here knows that.'

'Everybody but me, apparently,' Sunny said.

'A useless fucking arsehole who is going to find himself in the deepest fucking pile of shit he's ever found himself in if he doesn't fuck off out of here.' All the time he was speaking, Webster was smiling, and nothing he said was overheard by the men around us.

'Well, if you put it like that,' Sunny said, and fired his flash into Webster's face.

But Webster refused to be goaded by this. 'And you are?' he said to me.

'Me?' I said. 'I'm the man who's about to go public with the news that your good friend – your *partner* – here is responsible for at least two, possibly three, deaths. And that's "deaths" as in "murders". And what's more, Mr Webster, I'm going to do it either at or before – I haven't decided yet – your big announce-ment next week. Me and the washed-up, useless fucking arsehole here have a lot in common, and one of those things we have in common is our under-standing of exactly what kind of man your good friend Mr Fowler here really is.'

Webster considered this for a moment. 'What's he talking about?' he said to Fowler.

Fowler raised his eyebrows and shook his head. 'Not the time or the place,' he said.

'I asked you what he was talking about,' Webster said.

'The Helen Brooks thing. Rivers here is taking her mother's money to stir things up and pretend to her that her daughter wasn't the doped-up little slag everybody else knew her to be.'

'I remember her,' Webster said, smiling.

'You should,' Fowler said, his eyes still fixed on mine. 'I seem to remember you and her spent a fair bit of time together. Showing her the sights, were you?'

Both men laughed, but there was a cold, uncertain edge to their laughter.

'Is that seriously what all this is about, Rivers?' Webster said to me. 'Because if it is, you're second only in the useless fucking arsehole stakes to this tosser here.' He stopped his finger an inch from Sunny's chest. 'Make all the fucking accusations you like. Where's your proof? And what the fuck do you think that fucking mess has got to do with any of this? You're pushing your fucking luck, and you know it. You've got nothing on Fowler, nothing on any of us, and whatever you think you *might* have got, it's all too late to do you any good now, so why don't you do like you've been told to do and fuck off out of here and play your stupid fucking little detective games some-where else.'

I waited for him to finish speaking. By then his voice was raised, and several of the men standing around us had finished their own conversations to listen to him. Fowler saw this and turned to talk to them. He signalled for more food and drink to be brought over.

Webster's outburst suggested to me that he already knew what had happened to Helen Brooks all those months ago, and what it might imply regarding their current venture together. And he seemed as convinced as Fowler had always been that, whatever force my accusations might appear to carry, I still had nothing to back them up.

When Fowler had returned from the others, Marco whispered in his ear. Fowler, in turn, whispered to Webster.

It had surprised me to see how readily Fowler had given way to Webster, and how little he had done to try and restrain him.

'That's right,' Webster said to me. 'You're giving the other daughter one. Bit fucking underhand that, isn't it?'

'You mean "unethical" or "compromising",' Sunny told him. 'Not "underhand".' He continued to run the small white car back and forth across his palm.

'Thanks for clearing that up,' I said to him.

I turned back to Fowler. 'You didn't throw up your arms in complete surprise when I suggested you were responsible for, or complicit in, three murders,' I said.

'That's because you talk a load of crap,' Webster said before Fowler could answer me.

'Sorry, but I was talking to Mr Fowler,' I said. 'I'll try and make your part in all of this a little clearer when I've finished with him.'

'Why should I respond?' Fowler said to me. 'If you think you've got evidence, take it to the law. Let them deal with it.'

It was what he'd been telling me all along.

'I will,' I said.

Webster moved even closer to me, until our chests were touching. 'If you are giving the other daughter one, then that gives you and me something in common and—'

356

Fowler put a hand on his arm. 'Let me deal with this,' he said.

'You should have dealt with all this a long time ago,' Webster said angrily.

'Boys, boys,' Sunny said to them, and again he raised his camera and fired the flash.

'You take one more fucking picture and I'm going to ram that fucking thing down your throat,' Webster said. He pulled his arm from Fowler's hand.

I could see that he was finally close to being unable to restrain himself.

'Let's hope the police don't have to come searching through and then digging up too many of the properties Fowler is about to offload onto you,' I said.

'What the fuck are you talking about?'

'Searching for the bodies,' I said. 'They're probably hidden somewhere in or under one of his houses. Christ, that would be inconvenient, to say the least.' I was no more convinced of this than Webster was.

Fowler laughed. 'There are no bodies. They were lost at sea. He's just trying to wind you up.'

'I know what he's doing,' Webster said, but for the first time, he seemed uncertain, unconvinced by what Fowler was telling him.

'The evidence I take to the police may suggest otherwise,' I said.

I caught Sunny's glance; even he wasn't certain what I was suggesting or why I'd said what I'd said. But before I could say anything else, Webster grabbed me by the throat and forced me backwards until my head hit the wall. I had been completely unprepared for this and I lost my balance, dropping my glass and fumbling to get my hands around Webster's arm.

357

Beside me, Sunny took a succession of pictures.

Webster shouted at me as I struggled to free myself. Fowler, I saw, raised his arm, as though about to pull Webster away from me, but then thought better of the gesture and took a step backwards instead. Everyone else in the room stopped their own conversations to watch what was happening. Marco came to stand beside Fowler.

'I'm not going to tell you again.' Webster spat in my face.

Sunny stopped taking pictures. He grabbed Webster's hand and prised it from my throat. 'I think that was uncalled for, to say the least,' he said. 'And if I might give you a bit of advice – arsehole to arsehole, so to speak – I'd recommend you lay off the strong-arm tactics while half of the city councillors are looking on and somebody else is taking pictures of it all. Save all that kind of stuff for intimidating your tenants or your illegal workforce. Me and Mr Rivers, we're made of sterner stuff.' He relaxed his grip and Webster pulled his hand away and flexed his fingers.

I loosened my collar and struggled to catch my breath.

Fowler said something to Marco, who left us. Several of Webster's own employees now stood watching us, ready to respond to his orders.

'It isn't going to happen,' Fowler said to Webster. 'Trust me. There's nothing to look for, nowhere to look, and nobody to come looking. The law isn't going to lift a finger, whatever Rivers might want to believe. They weren't interested then and they aren't interested now. You have my guarantee.'

Marco returned to stand beside him.

I assumed he'd been sent to gather reinforcements, but he remained alone.

Nikki still stood at the centre of the men she'd been talking to when Webster had grabbed me.

I asked hoarsely if anyone in the room was still unsure about what was happening.

No one answered me.

Fowler turned to address the room. 'I can only apologize for this unseemly incident,' he said. 'This was meant to be a day of private and modest celebration for everything everyone gathered here today has achieved over the past months.'

Few responded as he'd hoped to this, even when Marco began to applaud.

'I'd shut up if I were you,' Sunny said to Fowler.

'He's right,' Webster said, and Fowler felt the remark like a blow.

Sunny flicked the small white car from the palm of his hand into Fowler's chest.

Elsewhere in the room, several men started to leave, and Fowler called to them to persuade them to stay.

They told him they had other appointments to keep, and left. None of the men tried to make their excuses sound convincing.

My throat still hurt where Webster had held it. I rubbed at it and he saw me.

'Sue me for assault,' he said.

'I think we can do better than that,' Sunny told him.

'Meaning?'

'Wait and see.'

'Fuck you,' Webster said.

'Louder,' Sunny told him. 'There are still a few people here who might not have heard you. And who knows – they might even be important people – people whose support or money you might shortly be calling in.' He looked at the men around us as he said all this. He turned to Fowler. 'I can see now why you always considered him to be a bit of a liability,' he said.

'You said that?' Webster said.

Fowler ignored him for a moment. 'He's winding you up,' he said.

'And that's not the hardest thing in the world, is it?' Sunny said to him, tapping his camera to suggest the pictures it now held. He turned to me and told me there was already a bruise on my neck. He told me to raise my chin and then took a shot of me. 'Have we finished here?' he said.

I watched as several others left the room ahead of us. Even those uncertain of what had just happened sensed that they did not want to be involved any further in the day's events.

'Perhaps Mr Webster might like to apologize for the remarks he made about Helen Brooks,' I said.

'Fuck you,' Webster said again.

Ever since Webster's assault on me, Fowler had been watching me closely, assessing what I'd revealed, and starting to guess at how much more I might already know. He understood as well as either Sunny or myself the purpose of our visit and the disturbance we'd caused. And he had clearly been shocked and dismayed by Webster's incendiary response to everything I'd said.

I held his gaze for several seconds, confirming the first of his guesses. He was right: I had no evidence whatsoever, only a tangled mass of supposition and guesswork held together by my own hopeful theorizing and the need to gain at least some small measure of acknowledgement or redemption for the people who had found themselves in Fowler's path and who had been pushed aside by him.

Sunny picked up the small white car from where it had fallen after hitting Fowler. He replaced it carefully on the model from which he had taken it. He then poured a glass of champagne over the model and said, 'Looks like rain.'

Neither Fowler nor Webster made any attempt to stop him.

By then there were fewer than a dozen other people in the room. The same number of opened and untouched bottles stood on one of the tables.

'Looks like the party's over,' I said to Fowler, my voice by then little more than a painful rasp.

33

We walked back to Sunny's car. On the way we passed several of the others who had been present at Lister Court, and who now stood on the far side of High Street and watched us pass. Sunny waved to them and then took their picture. One of them shouted something to us, but his words were lost in the noise of the traffic between us.

Back at Saint Anne's, the car was hot and we sat with the doors open.

Sunny lit another of his cigars, and I saw by the smoke which rose from it that his hand was shaking.

'Must be all the excitement,' he said.

He offered to drive me to the hospital to get my throat examined, but I refused. The bruising was becoming more pronounced, but my voice was already improving.

The men across the road watched us where we sat for several minutes – as though their presence alone might intimidate us – and then they continued walking back to the Guildhall. Sunny recognized some of them and the others were on film. Identifying them would be straightforward.

'So?' Sunny said eventually.

' "So" what?'

'The mysterious third corpse. I assume that was a not-too-subtle reference to the guy in the salvage yard. Although, I must say, and considering how touchy they were on some other points, neither Fowler nor Webster seemed particularly alarmed at having *him* tossed into the equation. I wonder why that was.'

'Because, like last time, they cleaned up after themselves,' I said.

'And yet another tragic accident enters the reports?'

'It's what they think they're good at.'

'Added to which, you can stop blaming yourself for having led them back to him in the first place.'

'No one followed me to him,' I said.

'Whatever it was, it wasn't an accident. Do you think he called Fowler to tell him you'd been to see him? Screwing Fowler for some more money by selling to him what he might have just sold to you?'

'He sold me nothing.'

'Right. Just a friendly little chat, and a few days later one of you gets his skull crushed and his face burned off.'

I'd still told no one about the chart the man had found for me.

'Would it have made things any easier if either Fowler or Marco *had* asked you who you were referring to?' he said.

'Perhaps. But the fact that they made the same false

363

assumption you made and then didn't throw up their hands in horror at the vile accusation tells me something.'

'What false assumption?' He let the smoke rise from his mouth into his eyes and over his forehead, which shone with sweat.

'There are four bodies,' I said.

He considered this. 'The fourth having something to do with whatever Fowler was involved in in London?'

I shook my head. 'Nicholson's wife,' I said.

'The one who left him shortly after his hero-of-the-hour walk-on?'

'The marriage had collapsed a long time ago, years. She blamed him for the death of their son. They went to live out at Paull Holme and she never settled. *He* might have been in his element – the house, his job, the river, everything – but she was never happy there.'

'And this is connected to Fowler how?'

'Whatever happened on the night Helen Brooks and her unknown companion died, Fowler was responsible for it. I don't yet know how, or why, but everything was too neat and tidy afterwards for him *not* to have been involved.'

'And you still think Helen Brooks was killed as some kind of diversion, that the unknown man was Fowler's real interest?'

'It's the explanation that makes the most sense so far,' I said. It was what I hoped to learn more about the following day in Peterborough.

'And Nicholson was what?'

'The perfect witness. So perfect that everyone believed him right from the start. And so that everything that was repeated afterwards was nothing more than a retelling of what he said he'd seen.'

'And he was lying from the very beginning?'

'According to the man from the lifeboat I talked to out at Spurn, Nicholson professed to having witnessed things he couldn't possibly have seen, not at that distance, not in that light, and certainly not in the detail he claims, however selective that might be. The tides were wrong, the depth of the water surrounding the yacht, the extent of the exposed mud.'

'So was he there by arrangement, do you think?'

'I didn't at first. I thought that perhaps he actually had been out walking his dog when he'd come across the beached yacht. After which, somebody, probably Marco, got to him and persuaded him to become a part of everything.'

'Persuaded him how?'

'Nicholson worked with Marco's father. They were both fired by ABP. Neither of them went back under the new terms. Nicholson harboured a grudge deeper and wider than the river.'

'And what – Marco threw in an additional cash incentive to help Nicholson over hard times?'

'All Nicholson ever cared about was his job and the house he lived in. The first time I visited him, he was having his recently installed double glazing repaired. The next time he was hosing down an almost new four-by-four. The money came from somewhere.'

'And if his involvement wasn't initially accidental?'

'Then Marco knew he was there all along, and the three of them – Nicholson, Marco and Fowler – worked something out together. Let's face it – it didn't take much for the coroner to return his open verdict and for all the press reports, yours included, to adopt the same old "Tragic Accident" angle.'

'Just Nicholson's expert testimony.'

'However he was involved, he was involved,' I said.

'And the involvement-by-arrangement theory somehow involves Nicholson's wife?' he said.

'Supposing she found out about what Nicholson had agreed to do – whether before the "accident" or afterwards, having witnessed it by chance – and supposing that was the last straw for her and she couldn't stand all his strutting around and preening – not knowing what she knew – and she finally left him. Perhaps she even threatened to expose what he'd done.'

'Nicholson always insisted she'd gone to live with her sister in Leeds.'

'Only when people pushed him for an answer. She did. And then she went missing from there.'

'Are you telling me you think Nicholson went after her and killed her?' he said sceptically.

'I think, encouraged by her sister, his wife was about to divorce him, and that, as part of the divorce settlement, he would have been forced to sell his precious home. He wouldn't have had a leg to stand on – not with her knowing what she knew about that night.'

'He killed her so he wouldn't lose the house?' He shook his head in disbelief.

'There had been nothing between them for a long time. I think Marco used his influence over Nicholson and then offered to help him out of an unhappy situation.'

'It would be an unnecessary and dangerous risk for either Marco or Fowler to take.'

'I'm not convinced Fowler knew anything about that particular little arrangement,' I said.

'It would still be a risk for Marco to take.'

'Not if it tied Nicholson even more tightly to them. Not if it ensured his silence concerning what he'd really seen on the river. Not if it solved all of Nicholson's problems at once. And not if it also gave Marco something over Fowler.'

'How did it happen?' he said.

'According to Nicholson's sister-in-law, Nicholson, after months of silence, called his wife asking her to go back to him, or at least to see him.'

'You think she'd mentioned her intention of divorcing him?'

'At the urging of her sister, yes. Apparently, Nicholson arranged to go and see her and then turned up a day early. According to the sister, he arrived shortly after she herself had returned from work and then rampaged around the house looking for his wife.'

'Suggesting what?'

'Suggesting he'd already been there. Still a day earlier than his wife was originally expecting him – and therefore able to avoid him – and at a time when he knew her greatest – her *only* – ally wouldn't be there to stand between them and witness everything that happened. By pretending to search for her all he was doing was creating a lie *and* covering up any of his earlier tracks. All the evidence – *if* anyone had ever been interested – would point to an angry man in a rage going from one room to another and not caring about what damage he caused. In addition, the two small children who lived there would also have been out of the way at school when Nicholson first arrived.'

'How did he explain his wife's disappearance to her sister?'

'He didn't have to. All he did was accuse *her* of poisoning his wife against him. That's what started me thinking – how would his wife have known to leave the house a day early in advance of his arrival if she believed he wasn't coming until the day after? She had nowhere to go. Her sister told me there was a call on the answering machine, from Nicholson, telling his wife he was coming a day early. The woman gave the recording to the Leeds police at the same time as she reported her sister missing.'

'And presumably Nicholson waited until *after* he'd been able to get into the house to her, abduct her – whatever – before making the call telling her he was coming.'

'I can imagine how reasonable he sounds,' I said.

'Do you think Marco was with him?'

'Perhaps Nicholson's wife had no idea who Marco was and perhaps she opened the door to him.'

'If the two of them were in it together, I imagine Marco led Nicholson by the nose,' he said.

'A toss-up who had the most to gain by her death,' I said.

'And yet you still think Marco managed to keep all this a secret from Fowler?'

I told him about the meeting I'd witnessed between Marco and Nicholson outside the King George Dock. 'They're like three men, each pointing a gun at the head of one of the others,' I said. 'One fires, they all fire. Except I'd rather be on the receiving end of Nicholson's gun than either Marco's or Fowler's. Fowler set the "accident" up, Marco was involved in making it all happen, and Nicholson was brought in to make the whole story stand up at the end. If one of them talked, they were all in trouble. Like I said, by involving Nicholson in the killing of his own wife, he was in as deep as either Fowler or Marco were in the killing of Helen Brooks and her companion.'

'Do you think Nicholson went on asking for more from Fowler to keep quiet?'

'It's a possibility. Perhaps Fowler even sanctioned the killing of Nicholson's wife as a way of cutting off the cash and yet still keeping Nicholson quiet.'

'And now that you're sniffing around, there's nothing either Marco or Fowler can do about Nicholson without giving their own part in it all away.'

'There's nothing any of them can do. They can't risk having the police becoming interested again, that's for certain.'

'Do you think either Fowler or Marco have plans for Nicholson?' he said.

'He was always going to be the weakest link.'

'What if Fowler only found out about Marco and Nicholson and Nicholson's wife after they'd killed her?'

I asked him what he meant.

'Supposing Fowler thought it was an unwise thing to have done – that, like I said earlier, it was an unnecessary complication, and something which, if the police did look at it too closely, might attract some more of that unwelcome attention to Fowler and all he's involved in now.'

'It would have been too late by then for him to have done anything about it,' I said.

'I know. But it might have changed his opinion of Marco somewhat. Fowler never struck me as the kind of man who appreciated his employees acting on their own initiative. And especially not at a time like this with so much depending on him smelling of roses.' He threw his half-smoked cigar to the ground and rubbed it out with his foot. 'Hence the reference to Leeds in front of both Fowler and Marco,' he said.

'Which seemed of considerably less interest to Fowler than to Marco,' I said.

'I'm serious in what I'm suggesting,' he said. 'Because the instant Fowler puts that particular little two-and-two together, you become the fourth man in that gun-to-the-head-and-who-fires-first scenario. And if that happens, I'd put you third after Fowler and Marco, though I wouldn't necessarily put them in that order.'

'And Nicholson?'

'He's the sap going to be riddled with bullets but left alive with an unfired gun in his hand. He's the sap going to be saved by the doctors and who will then be found guilty of murder and sentenced to Life.'

'And me?'

'Dying in the dirt and still trying to think of something either funny or profound to say about it all.'

We sat for several minutes without speaking. We saw Webster emerge from Lister Court and cross the road. A man walked on either side of him.

'Nice man,' Sunny said.

'It makes what Yvonne and Irina have been saying about his intentions regarding his newly acquired tenants considerably more plausible,' I said.

370

'Doesn't it just.'

We both watched as the three men walked up Chapel Lane towards Lowgate.

'Do you think he's having second thoughts about his deal with Fowler?' he said.

'I think he probably told Fowler to do something about you and me. I think the deal's far too lucrative for either of them to let go of it now.'

'And life's cheap?'

'Sometimes.'

'And it'll get considerably cheaper once Fowler or Marco realizes you know more than you're letting on about Nicholson and his wife,' he said.

'I know.'

He turned to face me. He reached out his hand as though about to grab my jacket, holding it instead against my chest.

'What?' I said.

'You know what. You're going to think of a way of using Nicholson to get either Fowler or Marco to reveal something about what happened to Helen Brooks. Either that, or you're going to stick her between them and lever them apart.'

'She's still my main concern in all of this.'

He shook his head. 'She's the reason you're getting paid,' he said. 'That's all. You stick Nicholson out in the open, and the first bullet fired is more likely to be fired into your thick skull than into his.'

'I need *something*,' I said. 'And until something better turns up, Nicholson and his wife are all I've got. Let's face it, the dead welder didn't appear to be the cause of too much sorrow or regret.'

'Perhaps. But whatever else you expect from

Nicholson, he isn't going to stick his own neck out as a favour for either Fowler or Marco. And the only thing that's going to worry either of *them* is if one or both of the bodies turns up, and that's not going to be much use to anyone after all this time.'

'It isn't going to happen,' I said. 'Not even in the foundations of one of Fowler's houses. The bodies were never "lost". That was what Nicholson saw and lied about. Fowler was never going to dump them in the river or the sea and then risk having them turn up to contradict the perfect little story he and Nicholson had concocted between them. Fowler's conviction that the case was long since dead and buried rested on his knowledge that the bodies were never going to reappear. He made that much clear to me right from the start.'

'So the remark about the possibility of the bodies turning up under one of the houses Webster was about to acquire?'

'Intended to get Webster thinking about Fowler, that's all. Whatever Webster did or didn't know about Helen Brooks when she was being used by Fowler, I don't think he had anything at all to do with her killing. I think that was a completely separate part of Fowler's past catching up with him.'

'Do you think Nicholson knows where the bodies are or how they were disposed of?'

'I'll remember to ask him the next time I see him,' I said.

He let the remark pass. 'He already ran straight to Marco, and Marco went to him alone – without Fowler – after your last little prod,' he said. 'Don't forget that. So make sure you consider all eventualities before you go shouting through *his* letter-box again.'

I smiled. 'I thought you could do that for me.'

He finally withdrew his hand. 'Tell me,' he said.

34

James Salter was waiting at Goole station. He saw me where I sat at the window and raised his hand to me.

A week had passed since our meeting at the Ferryboat Inn. Pulling out of the station, he told me about the man we were going to see. Salter had persuaded Steven Rix to talk to me because he, like Salter, felt aggrieved at the ease with which Fowler and the others had managed to avoid prosecution, and because months of work had been wasted upon the syndicate being tipped off by its informants.

He asked me about Fowler's arrangement with Webster – he had never heard the name – and said he'd seen announcements in the press concerning the meeting at which the plans for the redevelopment of Hull were to be revealed to the public and the press.

We arrived in Peterborough shortly after eleven.

Steven Rix was waiting for us in the buffet bar. He rose at the sight of Salter and shook my hand.

I told him I appreciated his help, and in response he gave me the receipt for his return ticket to London. His train back there was in less than an hour. I handed him the money. I started to offer him more, but he refused this. He took back the receipt and put it in his wallet.

He went to the counter and returned with more coffee.

'Ask me specific questions,' Rix told me. 'I still work for Immigration, and while the Fowler inquiry might be dead, I'm not going to compromise anything that might still be affected by what you want to know.'

I didn't entirely understand what he meant by this, and so my first question to him was to ask if Fowler was still in any way connected to the other members of the old syndicate, or if he still had any major financial interests in any of his previous developments.

'No and no,' he said. 'When he went, he went. Burned his bridges and vanished over the beckoning horizon.'

'Leaving others to shoulder the blame.'

'Is that a question?' he said. 'Forget "blame". Let's talk about answering charges. Not a single member of the so-called syndicate was ever charged with anything other than very minor misdemeanours. Employing illegal labour. Defrauding the Inland Revenue. It might sound big, but it isn't. Not a single one of them ever served any prison time. None of them even faced a proper trial – there were always plenty of the little people under them to do that – and whatever *they* were eventually fined, they paid out of their small change and walked away laughing.'

'Did any of the others feel betrayed or deceived by Fowler?'

'Enough to come after him, you mean?' He shook his head. 'Wrong tree. They all took care of their own insurance policies. When the time came to get beyond our net, not a single one of them was within our reach. Including the man we fished out of the Thames.'

'Leaving you to conclude that someone had tipped them off.'

'Someone on Salter's side of things, yes.'

James Salter confirmed this with a nod.

'And no one from the Met or Immigration or even Customs and Excise ever came after Fowler?'

'No one. The fallout from the collapse of the case was horrendous. We all spent three months chasing our own tails and trying to look better than we felt. I daresay we could have gone after some of them, but there wasn't much of an appetite for it once all the bollocking was over. Apart from which, without Fowler and the others squarely in the frame and surrounded by the evidence, there wasn't much chance of getting them on the charges we'd originally intended. You might say that we were overtaken by events.'

'Meaning?'

'Meaning that the illegal immigrants and asylum-seekers didn't exactly slow to a manageable trickle as some suggested they would once everything was sorted out in the places they were coming from. Yugoslavia, Albania, Iraq. Take your pick. The world never stops turning, Mr Rivers.'

'It stopped long enough for Fowler to get off,' I said.

'I know. And to be honest, some of us were just glad to see the back of him and the others.'

'Because after leaving London he became someone else's problem?'

'Something like that.'

'Did you think that Fowler and the others demanding reliable sources of cheap labour was actually stimulating the supply?'

'You sound like a politician,' he said. 'Of course he stimulated the trafficking. If we hadn't scared everyone off when we did, by now Fowler would have had his own little privately operated network of traffickers, routes and means to satisfy his demands.'

'So who *did* control all of that?'

He paused before answering me, exchanging a glance with James Salter.

'As far as we could tell, Fowler dealt mostly with a man called Innes who operated out of Folkestone. In turn, Innes made most of his money by arranging for the safe arrival and dispersal of immigrants from three brothers – we called them the brothers Karamazov – who operated in Iran and Turkey, and who brought people across Europe to Britain in as many ways as they could think of. When one route was closed, another two opened; when they were located and closed, four more were opened. And so on and so on.'

'What happened to Innes?'

'We arrested him. Apparently, neither Fowler nor any of the others had bothered to let him in on what they knew about that descending net. He's three years into a fifteen-year sentence.'

'Meaning he'll be in prison for what?'

'Another four or five years at least. He was our only big arrest. At least with Innes we salvaged something from the mess. Innes was always going to be one of our – Immigration's – targets. We wanted him and we wanted the network stretching back from him. Fowler and the others were always in the frame for the Met, not us.'

'What did Innes tell you regarding Fowler?'

'Not a thing. Never heard of him.'

'Did the syndicate buy his silence?'

'They might have done, they might not have done. Nothing was ever proved. When we finally went looking through the banks for Innes's assets, we found almost four million stashed away, some of it irretrievable. He wasn't the kind of man who did anyone any favours.'

'Meaning Fowler and the others would have paid him up front.'

'There were plenty of others demanding his services. I don't know about your part of the world, but house-building down here isn't exactly a dying trade.'

'And *did* you close the network down?'

'Temporarily, yes. Stopping an operation that size completely would have been too much to hope for. We tend to have become a little more realistic recently.'

'And the traffickers in charge of things on the other side?'

'You make it sound so simple and straightforward. The Channel might as well not exist. Forget it. As far as we know, one of the three brothers is still in prison and the other two have subsequently been killed.'

'As a result of what happened here?'

He looked again at James Salter.

Salter said, 'We were less concerned than perhaps we should have been with that side of things. It was one of the reasons Fowler and the others were able to make their clean breaks. The Met pulled everything in from this side, and Immigration pushed everything back from their side of the line.'

'So everywhere you look, there's a divide of sorts?'

'A point at which the lines of communication are more easily severed than elsewhere, yes,' Steven Rix said.

'Who prosecuted the traffickers?' I asked him, conscious that half our time together had already passed, and that I was still no closer to discovering who, if anyone, might have followed Fowler to Hull.

'They were caught here and then deported and prosecuted in Albania,' Rix said. 'They were Albanians. They had most of their assets there.'

'They were caught here? Were they here often?'

'No, not often. They sometimes came to see how things were being done. Sometimes they just came on holidays. They were very wealthy, violent and powerful men. There was never usually any risk involved for them. They always came on bona fide visas. Always plenty of documentation giving them every right to be here. Sometimes they even brought their wives and kids for a week or two.'

'So why were they arrested?'

'Because for the first time ever, we had them in the frame along with Fowler, the syndicate, Innes and the dozens of others who profited by the supply of cheap labour they provided. We didn't arrest them simply because they were here, but because, finally, we had something which would stick. Innes might have been a nice catch, but those three were pretty good consolation prizes.'

'And all three of them came together?'

'Why not? They weren't exactly the most trusting of

men. According to information received afterwards, we now think that they were there in an effort to streamline the procedure, to ensure that the people being brought in were even more profitable for them than before. Sangatte was about to close. Things were about to change and they needed to be involved in making those changes to ensure they weren't being taken advantage of or being left out in the cold.'

'Was there ever any evidence to suggest that they were smuggling people to order, depending on what Fowler and the others needed?'

'That was the theory, but even brain surgeons can turn their hand to digging foundations. There was another theory.'

'Which was?'

'That the three of them were there for a face to face with Fowler and the others either because they were owed money or because they were going to demand a bigger share of the profits now that the people they were trafficking were worth more at this end of things. Or perhaps they just wanted to cut out the middleman. Just because property values rise by twenty or thirty per cent in a year, it doesn't mean the wages of an illegally present and illegally employed labourer keep pace.'

'Does that sound likely – that they were going to demand more from Fowler?' I asked him.

'It's feasible. It had happened elsewhere.'

'But there was never any solid evidence to prove that this was why they were here?'

'None whatsoever. And, like I said, the three of them were arrested, deported and prosecuted at home before they even got the chance to talk to Fowler. They were thugs. In addition to the trafficking charges, they were also charged with extortion, robbery with violence, assault and murder. All three of them were sentenced to Life. We know for a fact that one of them is still alive and doing time, and that another, the youngest of the three, was killed during a fight less than a year into his sentence. The last we heard concerning the third was that he was dead, too, but we never received any official confirmation on that.'

'Which means what?'

'Which means he might be dead, but that he's just as likely to be still rotting in prison somewhere.'

'Why can't you find out for certain?'

'Because, like the past, Albania is a foreign country and they do things differently there. By all accounts, the prisons govern themselves. He certainly hasn't shown up on any active case reports since he was arrested.'

'And, presumably, if he was assumed to be locked away in prison for the rest of his life, then no one anywhere would have any reason to be looking for him?'

'We've got enough on our plates dealing with the men who took over the operation once the brothers were in the bag and on their way to court.' He looked at his watch. His train left in fifteen minutes. 'That's it,' he said. 'I don't know what more I can tell you.'

'Do you think Fowler and the others let the traffickers walk into your operation the same way they left Innes in the middle of things?'

'Something for us to concentrate on while they walked away unnoticed? It was one of the possibilities we considered. We were certainly grateful to get our hands on *something*. Their supply lines collapsed for almost three months after they were arrested.'

'Ridding Fowler and the others of three increasingly greedy suppliers *and* providing a smokescreen behind which they themselves were then able to disappear.'

He rose from his seat. James Salter rose beside him and the two men shook hands. They spoke of getting together again, but neither spoke with any genuine enthusiasm, and even as they said it, each man knew that the encounter would never happen, that what little remained of their friendship had long since been blighted by those events five years ago, and that this blight remained today and would remain for ever.

James Salter and I waited in the buffet until the London train pulled in and then departed. When it was no longer in sight, we left and crossed the tracks to await our own train back to Hull. The station was briefly crowded, and then quickly empty again.

35

I was back at Humber Street by mid-afternoon.

James Salter left me at Goole, from where he would drive back to Howden. He stood on the platform watching as the train pulled away from him.

I called Alison Brooks and told her I'd like to see her.

She was barely able to speak and asked me if I'd talk to Louise instead. I knew not to persist. I called Louise and arranged to meet her later that evening.

My understanding now of what had happened to Helen Brooks fifteen months ago remained imperfect, but even though incomplete and inferential in places, it was a valid and plausible understanding, and one I hoped would satisfy Alison Brooks, allowing her some late and necessary ease before her own death.

I had been aware throughout the investigation that there was a symmetry of kinds in the two deaths, a beginning and an end, and that the nature of both – Alison Brooks's no less than her daughter's – had played their own unmistakable parts in the uncertain shape and direction of my enquiries.

The radio was on and the weather forecaster announced that today was likely to be the hottest day in the city for fifty years. The hottest day of my life in the place. It was already thirty-two degrees, and expected to rise even higher. Further inland, away from the cooler air of the estuary and the coast, that same temperature had already been reached by noon.

I made a list of all the points I wanted to communicate to Louise – partly to solicit her own opinion and beliefs concerning what I had uncovered, and partly so that she might afterwards repeat them to her mother in an equally credible and unadorned order.

There was no time to compile a comprehensive report, and perhaps now there was no need for one. Perhaps now all that was needed was for everyone's fears and suspicions to be confirmed, and for any final, lingering hopes to be finally laid to rest.

I moved my desk out of the glare of the sun and finished writing.

I waited for her at the Baltic Wharf, outside, overlooking the water.

She was almost an hour late. I tried calling her but her phone was switched off. I bought a paper and searched for any news of what had happened the previous day at Lister Court, but there was nothing.

She arrived finally in a cab. She came to me and sat opposite me at the small table. She kissed me and drew her chair closer to mine. She looked exhausted. It was the first time I'd seen her without make-up, and catching my glance, she acknowledged this.

'I was up all night with Mum,' she said. It was the first time I'd heard her use the word, and it made her a girl again. 'The nurse was there until midnight, and then I sat with her for the rest of the night and most of today.'

'Is it worse?'

She filled her glass from the bottle I'd bought and drank it before answering. 'The doctor wants her to go into hospital for a few days. She refused.'

'What do *you* think?'

'I want whatever she wants,' she said, but without conviction. 'I don't know. She equates going into hospital with staying there until it's all over. And all *he* can talk about is "pain-management", about "readjusting" her medication until some new kind of balance is reached. "Balance" – that's a laugh.'

'Does he think she's close to dying?'

'It's not the kind of question I'd ever ask him,' she said. 'Though more for my own sake than for hers, I suspect.' She gazed for a moment without speaking at the distant Holiday Inn, perhaps remembering our night there. 'He thinks that soon she might not be in a position to decide for herself what she does and doesn't want. I told him that when that happened, then *I* would know what she wanted and make sure she got it. He told me I didn't fully understand what I'd be taking on, what a responsibility it would be to bear.' She mimicked the man's voice.

'And?'

'And I told him she was my mother and that the only responsibility I had was to her. I told him to stick to all his useless predictions and endless tampering with her painkillers and every other God-knows-what drug she's been given. He made me angry. I absolved him of all responsibility. He'd said what he had to say and his own conscience was clear. I must have sounded like the worst kind of ungrateful bastard after all he'd done for her. He apologized and then I apologized. He even asked me if there was anything *I* needed. He told me I was taking too much on, even with the nursing care. He knows about all this, too, about Helen, though he's careful not to mention it, of course. He's been my mother's doctor for twenty years. He helped her through all the earlier bouts. When she told him she didn't want to endure any more of his or anyone else's treatment this time round, he agreed with her and supported her. He wants what I want — what's best for *her* — so why do I antagonize him at every opportunity?' She refilled her glass.

'Perhaps because there are things you haven't told him?' I suggested.

'What things?'

'Perhaps he thinks you've made plans which don't include him,' I said.

She finally understood what I was saying. 'Perhaps they're the same plans he'd make and undertake in a perfect world.'

'Talk to him,' I said.

She shook her head. 'This is between me and her,' she said. 'Me and her.'

I took the folded sheet of paper from my pocket and laid it on the table.

'Do you know what happened?' she asked me. She touched the tip of her finger to the paper, but left it where it lay.

'Three things,' I said. 'I don't want to keep anything

from your mother that I believe is directly related to Helen's death, and I'd appreciate it — however you choose to tell her — if you did the same.'

She nodded her agreement at this. 'And two?'

'That all three of us accept that this is a less than perfect or complete understanding of how or why Helen died, but that it's probably as close as anyone is going to get after all this time.'

'That sounds like an excuse,' she said.

'It probably is, but it's what your mother asked of me.'

'And three?'

'That we also accept that there may be no way forward from this.'

'I don't understand.'

'I mean that however convinced *I* might be that what I've discovered concerning Helen's death is a plausible version of events, I still have no solid evidence to back it up. We can make all the allegations we like, throw as much mud at Fowler as we like, but none of it's going to change that fact. And for your mother's sake—'

'We should adopt the non-mud-slinging option?'

'I was going to suggest that first and foremost we consider what *she* needs to gain from all of this. Revenge was always the least of our options.'

She considered this, looking for the first time at the bruise on my neck, which was at its most impressively coloured. She touched it as tentatively as she had touched the sheet of paper, and as gently as she had touched my face only four days earlier.

'In the line of duty,' I said.

'Fowler?'

I shook my head. 'Nor Marco. Just somebody else I managed to upset.'

She was still considering the third of my stipulations.

'How convinced are you that what you've uncovered is the truth?' she said.

'As convinced as I can be without a full confession from anyone involved, and I doubt very much if that's ever going to happen.'

'From Fowler, you mean?'

'And others.'

'But Fowler's definitely implicated, right?'

'More than.'

She relaxed slightly. She asked me if I had a scale of charges for various injuries.

'I'll consider compiling one,' I said, anxious not to divert us from the single, narrow and painful course ahead of us.

She finally picked up the sheet of paper, unfolded it and read it. And then she refolded it and put it back down. 'Go on,' she said.

I told her about my meeting with Steven Rix that morning, and about the syndicate in London. I told her about the collapse of the inquiry and what everyone involved had lost and gained from this. I told her about the three traffickers, especially the one who had gone missing from his prison in Albania. I told her that the man was convinced either that Fowler still owed him money, or that Fowler and the others had deliberately allowed him and his brothers to walk into the same trap they themselves were already walking away from. On top of this, I said, he probably also blamed Fowler for the death of his youngest brother in prison.

She understood all I was telling her.

'And you think this man traced Fowler to Hull and followed him here.'

'Either to get his money or his revenge for what had happened, yes. Probably the former, possibly both. Or possibly Fowler had talked him out of the revenge option with an offer of more money.'

'And he was the one on the yacht with Helen?'

'No one ever knew who he was because he was already missing and there was never any record of him ever having returned here – let alone to Hull – after he was deported, tried and imprisoned.'

'Is that why their bodies never turned up?'

'Fowler would never risk the man being found and identified. It would tie him too securely to everything that had happened in London, to everything he'd come here to leave as far behind him as possible. The trafficker was the final thread that needed severing.'

'And Helen was killed why?'

But I knew by the way she said it that she was already beginning to work out her sister's part in what had happened.

'Fowler used Helen to lure the man on to the yacht. He was probably no more of a sailor than she was,' I said.

'Lure?' she said absently.

I waited a moment before going on. 'Fowler's story of what happened that day only works because the only ones ever telling it were the solitary eye-witness and then Fowler and Marco afterwards. It worked because it was all anyone ever had to go on, and because there was never any plausible alternative for anyone to consider. Once Fowler's minute-by-minute alibis were firmly in place, and after Nicholson had told everyone what *he* had allegedly seen, then there can't have been any reason for anyone to go on asking questions. If there were any doubts to be aired, then that didn't happen until long after the inquest and even then they were never made public.'

'Especially after everyone had more or less agreed to wait for the bodies to show up before going any further,' she said.

'Everything Fowler said to me, he said because he knew that that was never going to happen. He wanted everyone looking in the same direction, waiting for the same impossible event.'

'And after a while, everyone, including the coroner, lost interest.'

'There was no other course open to him,' I said. 'It was what Fowler knew would happen.'

'But why kill Helen if she was only doing what he was telling her to do?'

'I can't answer that honestly. I believe the man the marina officer saw on the yacht with Helen was Marco. We only have Fowler's word that Marco returned to him after delivering Helen to the marina. I believe the trafficker was already on board. I believe he'd been there a few days and that Helen had been with him. I think she went from the yacht to her lunch with Fowler. The yacht was certainly well provisioned, and no one would notice one new strange face with the new sailing season getting under way and people coming and going all the time. Plus the yacht was moored about as far from the marina office as it's possible to be. Marco knew how to sail. It's my belief that he took the yacht out, careful not to reveal himself to anyone on the way.'

'And all the time, Helen was below with the other man?'

'Until she was required to show herself and let the marina officer see her so that he could positively identify her afterwards, yes.'

'So despite all the reports and accounts always referring to there ever only being two people on board, there were three.'

'Reports based on what people here at the marina saw, and then afterwards based solely on what Peter Nicholson *said* he saw. Both of which allowed Marco to do what he had to do, then get back to Fowler in time for their alibis to mesh – and, remember, they were never exactly *suspects* in the first place. Fowler grieved loudly and publicly and let his perfect alibis be uncovered and joined together, and Marco walked around in his shadow. With Nicholson's testimony there was never any need to go looking for suspects – suspects for what? – only the need to try and better understand what had led up to the terrible accident in which Helen and her companion had lost their lives.'

'It still doesn't explain *why* she died,' she said.

'It may never have been part of Fowler's plan,' I said, this being the least likely and least convincing of all the alternatives I had considered.

'I find that hard to accept,' she said.

'Perhaps because it's what you don't—'

'Don't patronize me,' she said angrily, immediately lowering her voice, putting her hand on mine and apologizing.

'OK,' I said. 'The only other answer is that Fowler wanted rid of her as much as he wanted rid of the man he had lured on to the yacht using her. He told me he hadn't seen her for four days prior to their lunch appointment on that day, and Laura Lei told me she hadn't been back at the house on Park Grove during those same four days. Perhaps she was on the yacht all that time.

'Perhaps the trafficker had shown up and Fowler had made his deal with him, and while the man was waiting for his money, and while Fowler was making his preparations to get rid of him, the man and Helen were staying on the yacht together.

'The man had nowhere else to go, and Helen was there solely to keep him occupied and to make sure he didn't wander. The marina master told me there was enough food and drink on board for a dozen people.'

She moved her hand back and forth over mine as I said all this.

'Fowler lied to me,' I said. 'He said he called her at Park Grove because she was late for their lunch date. He knew all along that she was on the yacht. It always struck me as strange that, not having seen her for four days beforehand, Fowler had arranged for them to have both lunch and dinner together on the day in question. The dinner date and his uncancelled reservation were all part of his alibi.'

'And lunchtime?'

'So that Fowler could ensure she was drunk, and so that he could reluctantly suggest the same at the inquest. So that everything that happened took place in a restaurant full of people who knew him well.'

'It all makes sense,' she said.

'As much sense as the alternative explanation.'

'Which is?'

392

'That Fowler never intended to kill her at all, that something went wrong with the holding and the killing of the trafficker, and that Helen was just in the wrong place at the wrong time.'

She shook her head at this.

'He made *sure* she was on that yacht,' she said. 'And he made sure she was never able afterwards to tell anyone what happened there. He could just as easily have kept her off it. She was there to keep the man on board, and then she was killed, and that way Fowler kept everyone more interested in what had happened to her than in the man who had died alongside her.'

'He still might have considered her a loose cannon,' I said.

'He *used* her,' she insisted. 'To keep everyone looking away from where they might otherwise have been looking. The death of Helen was connected to Fowler here and now. The killing of the trafficker took everything back to London all that time ago.' She was shouting again, and stopped abruptly, looking at the people around us who were watching her.

'Whatever else Fowler did,' I said, 'he certainly wasn't stupid enough to want to leave any new loose ends lying around – especially not after all the trouble he'd gone to to get rid of those old ones.'

'So – two birds, one stone,' she said.

We sat without speaking for several minutes. I wondered if I'd told her anything she hadn't already imagined a thousand times over.

'So what exactly happened out on the river?' she said.

'Marco killed the man, and then – by design or accident – he killed Helen and—'

393

'Don't say it like that,' she said.

'Like what?'

'"By design or accident." It makes you sound as mealy-mouthed and evasive as the rest of them.'

'I'm just telling you what little I know for certain and filling in the blanks,' I said. 'He killed them both and then ran the yacht aground on the Foulholme Sands.'

'Where good old reliable Nicholson was waiting to witness the whole thing,' she said absently.

'Except Nicholson's story never tallied – the tides, the timing, the darkness, the depth of the water. Perfect in itself, but it never quite matched up to what everyone else said and expected. It's my belief that everything happened at least an hour – perhaps two – sooner than Nicholson said it did. Giving Marco time to get ashore with the bodies in the dinghy, possibly guided and then helped by Nicholson, who, once Marco was safely on his way back into Hull, went back to the shore to raise the alarm, perhaps at a signal from Marco.'

'He could have been back in the city centre in twenty minutes,' she said. 'So *everything* Nicholson said he saw was a lie?'

'Everything was made into a lie by the timing.'

'That, and him being the perfect expert witness,' she said. 'Why did he do it?'

'Because Fowler offered him a lot of money?' I said. 'Because Nicholson harboured a grudge against all the others involved? Perhaps both. Greed *and* getting one over on everyone else.'

At the start of my investigation I had not even been convinced that Nicholson himself hadn't been accidentally or unwillingly involved in the whole thing, and that, having witnessed the beaching by chance, he hadn't then been coerced by Marco into helping him. It was a plausible theory, especially in light of the friendship between Nicholson and Marco's father. But the more I had subsequently discovered, the more convinced I had become that Nicholson had been involved from the outset.

I remained less convinced that the abduction and killing of his wife had been sanctioned or even known about by Fowler, and felt that this had been wholly concocted between Marco and Nicholson alone. It seemed equally unlikely to me, however, that Fowler would not have learned of this afterwards – perhaps when Marco convinced him of Nicholson's lasting silence – but by then it would have been too late. The third man and his loaded, pointed gun had already joined the circle.

The marina master had said that Helen Brooks had diverted his attention from the man at the wheel as they left the marina that afternoon, suggesting that she was aware of what was about to happen to the man out of sight below, even if not of her own precise part in those proceedings. I still considered it likely that Fowler had had her killed because he could no longer trust her to keep silent – either about the appearance of the man or his eventual murder.

Equally likely was the fact that the only way Fowler had been able to placate the trafficker upon his un-expected appearance was by using Helen Brooks to take him to the yacht and then to keep him company there while Fowler and Marco worked out how to get rid of him. Perhaps they persuaded him that he would have to wait while Fowler collected the money he was demanding. Whatever the truth of the situation, Helen Brooks's fate was sealed the instant Fowler started using her.

In all likelihood, the trafficker had been drugged and unaware that they were even leaving the marina that day, and it would be difficult to believe that Helen Brooks had played no part in that particular part of Fowler's plan.

And contrary to what Andrew Brownlow had suggested to me about everything having taken place so publicly, it was precisely this open and public nature of the accident which had kept everyone focused on the death of Helen Brooks and not her companion.

And whatever Fowler's reasons for killing Helen Brooks, he had afterwards used her death to create sympathy for himself, and to suggest to anyone asking questions that the man had most likely been someone she had known, rather than anyone connected to Fowler himself. Certainly, there was speculation at the time of the deaths that the man might have been romantically attached to Helen. I think I'd known that this was not the case from the outset, from the moment Fowler, knowing the bodies would never again be seen and examined, had dropped his guard with me and revealed the thin, cold snarl behind his smile.

Whatever his reasons for killing her, Helen Brooks's life had meant nothing to Fowler, and whatever might or might not be proved in the future with regard to the trafficker, it was because of this – the killing of Helen Brooks – that I most regretted that nothing of what I had so far revealed to Louise might be used to re-open the police investigation into the two deaths.

She understood this as well as I did and was no less disappointed by the realization.

'Do you have any idea at all where the bodies might have ended up?' she said eventually.

'He went to a lot of trouble to get rid of them in the first place. I doubt he'd take any chances once they were off the yacht and away from the river.'

'How do you think Marco killed them?'

'The man at the salvage yard showed me a hole that had been smashed in one of the panels in the cabin. I think Marco shot them and then smashed the panel to hide the bullet hole at its centre. I think part of the need for a delay in what Nicholson said he saw was so that there were no obvious signs of what had happened. I think Marco took the bodies ashore in the dinghy – the marina officer definitely saw one on board, and Fowler was adamant that all the safety and rescue equipment was serviced and present. I think that was why Nicholson was told to include it in his story – suggesting that it was launched but that it drifted beyond reach and was lost.'

'Even when, according to others, the yacht was at least fifty metres from open water by then?'

'Everywhere you look, there are discrepancies in his story.'

'Why don't the police go back to him and tell him they know he was lying?' she said.

'Because they have no good cause, no proof, no enthusiasm to re-open the case. And because Nicholson would tell them exactly the same story. *They* found no discrepancies, nothing wrong with it on the night in question. They're hardly likely to find anything new – or even to look too hard – fifteen months later. Besides, he's not likely now to confess to having lied at the coroner's inquest.'

'So nobody says anything, nobody goes asking, and Helen stays dead all because Fowler wanted to leave everything behind him, to sever that one last link with his past before he started to turn himself into Mister Wonderful here?'

I put my hand on her arm.

And the Albanian trafficker stayed dead. And Jane Nicholson stayed dead. And the man in the salvage yard, whose name I only learned from the report in the paper, stayed dead.

Nothing of what I'd told her had either shocked her or come as a complete and genuine surprise to her.

'I don't think I've told you anything you haven't already imagined,' I said.

I wondered what she'd thought about the hole in the cabin wall during her own visit to the salvage yard. I wondered what *she* had been searching for.

She picked up the folded sheet and put it into her bag.

'I doubt if your mother expected to hear much more,' I said.

'Don't pretend to know what she did or didn't expect,' she said, and again she signalled her immediate apology for the remark.

The bottle on the table between us was empty.

'Is that it, then?' she said. 'Is this where everything ends?'

'I can carry on,' I said. 'But I doubt if there's much more to come to light, and certainly nothing that will cause anyone else to be interested again.'

'And, meanwhile, Fowler and the others sit there laughing at us. And everything he wants, he gets.'

I told her what had happened at the reception at Lister Court, what I'd hoped to provoke either Fowler or Webster into doing or revealing.

'And so far?' she said.

'Nothing,' I admitted. I asked her how soon she would see her mother and repeat everything I'd just told her.

'She'll want to hear it from you,' she said. 'I'll tell her, but she'll still want to hear it from you. I'll let you know when she's up to it. She was talking again about John Maxwell last night. Four in the morning, and she started talking about him, having hardly been able to breathe unaided for the previous twelve hours.'

'At least you can tell her it's over,' I said, realizing immediately how glib and insensitive this sounded.

'Why – because you say it's over?' she said. 'It'll be over for her when she dies.' She stopped abruptly. 'Listen to us,' she said.

I wanted her to tell me that she accepted all I'd told her, that, above all else, she would consider only her mother's needs in all of this, and that she would now turn her attention to the dying woman and not attempt to act on anything I'd just revealed to her.

She asked me when she could see me again, but when I suggested a day she made excuses and said everything now depended on what happened to her mother.

She called a cab and I walked with her to the dual carriageway, waiting with her mostly in awkward silence until it came.

36

I called John Maxwell that same night, after ten, when the heat of the hottest day had finally died, and when the returning tide filled the river with water and brought with it its own cooling breeze.

In the street below, the warehousemen again worked late unloading a succession of waiting lorries.

John Maxwell answered after the first ring. Since the death of his wife, he had suffered from insomnia and rarely slept before two in the morning, awake and up again by seven.

I told him everything I'd discovered concerning Alison Brooks's missing daughter.

When I'd finished, he said that most of what I'd just told him was conjecture.

'I know,' I said. 'But everything fits.'

'Meaning you hope it's what she'll want to hear and that she'll be grateful to you for putting her mind at rest and letting her die in peace.'

It struck me as another unnecessarily harsh judgement on all I'd achieved over the previous three weeks.

'What would you have done?' I said.

'Probably exactly the same. It's what she wants and it's what you're giving her.'

'But?'

'But that's exactly where I'd leave it. Write up your report, file everything away and start on something new.'

'I might have no alternative,' I said.

'You wouldn't have aggravated Fowler and Webster like you did if that was your intention,' he said.

'If I'd heard all Steven Rix had to tell me a couple of days sooner, there would have been no need for that.'

'What did you think either Fowler or Webster was going to do?'

'I don't know. *Something*. Perhaps they've already done it.'

'You're not thinking straight,' he said. 'Just because *you* think you've discovered what happened on the day Helen Brooks was killed, you think everyone should fall into line behind you, and that thanks to your perseverance, justice should finally run its course. It's not going to happen. Not without anything more substantial. What did you expect – that Alison Brooks was going to prosecute Fowler for the death of her daughter through the Civil Courts?'

'Louise still might,' I said.

'Louise Brooks is about to lose her mother and find herself all alone in the world. Don't you think her priorities might change? Don't you think *yours* might change when she comes back to you after Alison's death?'

It was the first time I'd heard him call her by her Christian name alone, and I heard his distant affection for her in the name.

There was little chance that he didn't already know of or suspect my involvement with Louise, and that he was avoiding mentioning this directly. Despite all my denials and assurances, he knew as well as I did that I had compromised my work for her mother by becoming involved with her. I wanted to tell him that he had done that with his phone call on the eve of Alison Brooks's appearance, and by allowing her to come to me with his name, knowing that I would not refuse her. And that Louise had mentioned him just often enough since then – and spoken of her mother's distant attachment to him – to let me know that he remained a constant presence in all I had done for the two women.

If I'd confronted him with any of this now, he would have agreed with everything I said.

'Do you think I should let the police know everything I've uncovered?' I said.

'Everything you *think* you've uncovered. I doubt they'd thank you for it. Perhaps you should send everything you've got directly to the coroner who brought in the open verdict in the first place. I doubt he'd be able to act on it, but at least everything would then remain on *his* files if the bodies ever did turn up. Or if your showdown with Fowler and Webster does lead to something. Or if either Marco or Nicholson begins to feel Fowler creeping up on them and decides to make a full confession.' As intended, each of his suggestions sounded increasingly unlikely.

'They've all got too much to lose,' I said. 'There's no

way now any of them can put any distance between himself and the others. If one falls, they all fall.'

'That's the real reason Nicholson's wife was killed,' he said. 'My guess — if everything *you've* already guessed turns out to be true — is that Marco also promised to get rid of the body and that Nicholson has no idea now where it is.'

'And Marco might lead the police to it if ever it profited him to do so?'

'To it, and, presumably, to the gun or knife covered in Nicholson's fingerprints. I'm not necessarily saying that Nicholson killed her, just that it was an option Marco couldn't afford to ignore.'

'And something neither Nicholson nor Fowler knew about?'

'What *you* need to decide,' he said, 'is whether or not Fowler knew about Marco's little side-arrangement with Nicholson before it happened.'

I told him I'd already considered this.

'Because if Fowler *still* doesn't know about it, then you know something Marco knows, but Fowler doesn't. My guess is that Fowler would have considered the killing of Nicholson's wife an unnecessary and dangerous complication to his own otherwise meticulously calculated arrangements. Just because Fowler sanctioned the killing of Helen Brooks and the trafficker doesn't mean he was going to make a habit of doing it.' He paused. 'You should think, too, about what Marco might know that Nicholson doesn't.'

'Because it would be a way to Nicholson?'

'Perhaps.' He fell silent again. 'I read about the man at the salvage yard. It was the man you spoke to.'

'I think he called Fowler after my visit. I think he

knew something – something about the salvaged yacht, or something he'd found there and sold to Fowler fifteen months ago – and which he didn't tell me about. Something Fowler had already paid him once to keep quiet about. He'd lost his job. I think he tried to squeeze some more money out of Fowler. Either that, or he just called Fowler at the wrong time, when he was feeling particularly vulnerable, and Fowler sent Marco to the yard.'

'To put himself back in control of events until whatever he's planning with Webster is under way?' He sounded sceptical.

'Something like that.'

'Any ideas *what* Fowler might have been looking for?'

I told him about the damage to the cabin, about the photographs Helen Brooks had taken there, and about the chart the man at the yard had given me. I had searched every inch of the chart and it had revealed nothing other than the simple pattern of Helen Brooks's careless scribble.

He asked me where the assault on the woman in Walmsley Street fitted into my theorizing, and rather than explain to him how I believed that Sunny, Yvonne, Irina Kapec and myself had all been decoyed by the attack, I said I didn't know. Sunny still had no idea what, if anything, had been taken from the agency, though I now knew, having seen Yvonne's photos of Nikki, Fowler and Webster together, that his file on Fowler had not been as complete as he believed it to have been.

Then John Maxwell asked me why Irina Kapec had received her own threatening photos. I told him I was still working on it, by which we both understood that I didn't know. It still seemed too simple an explanation to me to regard the photos purely as another of Fowler's intimidations or distractions.

He asked me how Sunny intended using the pictures he'd taken of Fowler and Webster at Lister Court.

'They were only taken to aggravate the pair of them,' I said.

'Exactly,' he said, meaning I ought to think again about the true purpose of the photos sent to Irina Kapec.

I'd called him that night because, after everything that had happened over the past few days, I'd hoped this might be another ending of sorts. But all he'd done was to point out to me the questions I'd left unanswered. And if I'd denied this he would tell me even more forcibly that I was only looking at those connections and events that I wanted to see – those which fitted my story of Helen Brooks's death, and which I would feel confident enough to repeat to Alison Brooks in the near-certain knowledge that it was all she wanted to hear from me.

'She was talking about you last night,' I said, remembering what Louise had told me earlier at the Baltic Wharf.

He remained silent for a moment, and then said, 'It was almost forty years ago.'

And the instant he said it I knew precisely what he was telling me. And I knew, too, that with the possible exception of his wife, I was the only other person to whom he had ever made this confession.

We faced each other in our silence, both of us

searching for the means of taking a single step backwards, away from the possibility that Louise Brooks was *his* daughter.

I wondered if this was what Louise, too, had guessed or calculated, or if it was what her dying mother had finally confessed to her in her own forced and accelerated laying bare of the past and all its secrets.

'You'd have come to a similar conclusion eventually,' he said.

I imagined him in the night's coolness, in the half-light of the room, opposite me, sitting upright, both his feet on the floor, his hands in his lap, his head tilted slightly forward.

'No one's judging you,' I told him.

'No?' he said. Meaning he'd judged himself for all of those forty years, and that this judgement was the harshest that might ever be passed on him.

'Will you try and see her?' I asked him, meaning Alison Brooks. I offered to fetch him and then to drive him home.

'I don't think so,' he said. 'I made a promise to Mary.'

I was about to tell him that he should consider his own feelings now in all of this, and perhaps those of Alison Brooks, but I knew that this too would sound like a judgement, and so I said nothing.

'When you last called, did you intend telling me that Alison Brooks was on her way to see me?'

'I knew you'd put two and two together,' he said. 'I didn't want all this to have a bearing on what she wanted from you.'

'I don't think it would have made any difference,' I said.

'Of course it would,' he said. 'We ought not to deceive ourselves on that particular point.'

And before I could say anything further, the line went dead – a fumbled click and then a dying whirr into the lines and the darkness of that overheated night.

37

The following morning I called Andrew Brownlow at the Tower Grange police station and told him everything I'd told Louise Brooks the previous afternoon.

He listened with few interruptions to what I had to say, and when I'd finished he said that he sincerely hoped I *hadn't* told her half of what I'd just told him.

Neither of us spoke for a moment, and then he said, 'There's still nothing there that's going to persuade anyone here to re-open the case.'

'But it all fits,' I said, knowing as I said it that this wasn't even the beginning of a convincing argument.

'Of course it does,' he said. '*Everything* fits in a murder where there's no body, no reliable witnesses to the killing, and no willing and convincing confession. I might just as well try and pin it all on James Salter and his friend in Immigration. *That* would fit, and in all probability make considerably more sense to considerably more people.'

'All Steven Rix did—' I began.

'All *he* did was confirm everything Salter had already suggested to you. Perhaps the pair of them have been harbouring their grudge against Fowler for all these years just waiting for this opportunity to get even with him. Perhaps it was why Salter chose to come up here in the first place.'

I told him he was being ridiculous.

'Am I? Am I really? If I'd been sent – yes, *sent*, banished, exiled, whatever – from the Met to Howden, I'd be fairly pissed-off. And he only got that particular posting because it was the better of two alternatives. Without his friend in high places and the need all round to save face, he wouldn't even have been offered that – he'd have been out on his arse.'

'And Immigration?'

'A man who has to come a hundred miles from his office and all those others sitting round trying to over-hear what he's telling you before he'll even talk? Get real.'

'Everything they both told me can be corroborated by the Met and Immigration records,' I said.

'Or a version of it. Look, I'm not saying that this is what did or didn't happen. All I'm saying is that every-thing suddenly got a bit convenient for you. All that missing evidence, hearsay and supposition, and then along comes Salter followed by Rix and suddenly it all makes perfect sense. I'm not criticizing you; I'm just saying it puts everything a bit too neatly into place. In fact, if you think about it, you've had a lot of these back-up witnesses and alibi-providers right from the start. Rix backing up Salter, Marco backing up Fowler, Fowler behind Marco, Nicholson behind the pair of them, Fowler behind Nicholson. Christ, even your client – even Alison Brooks – everything she told you, her daughter went on saying over and over. I daresay the same will work in reverse.'

'I know all that,' I said.

'Then you should also know that in his deposition alleging harassment against you, Simon Fowler also dropped some very heavy hints about you and Louise Brooks, about the true nature of your relationship, and about your motivation for doing what you're doing.'

'What sort of hints?'

'You seriously want me to spell it out for you?'

'He's just providing himself with a bit more back-up for when all this finally blows up in his face,' I said.

He laughed. 'I wish I was as convinced as you are that that was going to happen. Listen, I honestly do wish we'd been able to get to the bottom of all this fifteen months ago, and that if Fowler had played any proven part whatsoever in the killing that he'd been arrested and charged then. But that didn't happen. I know you think we were lax, I know everybody sat back for too long waiting for the bodies to show up, and I know we all bought too easily into the tragic-accident-at-sea story, but as far as everybody was concerned then, *those* were the facts that fitted, *that* was all we had to work on. I'm on your side, but it's not up to me. Bring in Nicholson and let him make a full confession and convince a judge that he was making it out of a sense of remorse and that he hadn't been forced into making it, that he wasn't making it in fear of his life, and *then* we might have something to start poking around with again.'

'Nicholson has too much to lose,' I said.

'And from what you've just told me, he stands to lose it a lot sooner than he might have anticipated.'

I asked him what he meant.

'Now who's being disingenuous? You know as well as I do that he's the biggest liability in all of this – Fowler and Marco might have something on him, but he can just as easily return the favour. And they, I imagine, will think they have considerably more to lose than he does.' He paused. 'In fact, I think Nicholson was the real reason for you calling me now that you imagine you've got it all worked out. I think you know better than anyone – or at least as well as Fowler and Marco do – how vulnerable Nicholson has suddenly become in all of this, and I think *you're* the one providing himself with a bit of back-up for when either Fowler or Marco – or Fowler through Marco – decides to do something about him. What do you reckon – another boating accident, a desperate suicide by a lonely man racked by self-loathing and remorse? I sincerely hope you haven't already set anything in motion, Mr Rivers, I really do. Because you hanging Nicholson out to dry like this in full view of Fowler and Marco makes you no better than either of them in my book. *You* might think you have just cause, but, believe me, you don't. Do you know how many people Jane Nicholson's age go missing every year?'

'Surprise me.'

'Twenty thousand. Thirty thousand in total, but twenty thousand like her. I won't tell you what a tiny – tiny as in infinitesimal – fraction of that number actually turns up dead.'

'And the ones who never turn up at all?'

'Like Helen Brooks and her mysterious companion,

you mean? You're grasping, Mr Rivers. Leave it. You've got your own best-option version of events. Stick to it. Tell Alison Brooks what she's half-known and accepted all these months. It's what she wants to hear from you. It's *all* she wants to hear from you. And it's certainly what Louise Brooks wants her to hear. And what I imagine neither of them wants to read about in tomorrow's papers are Fowler's counter-allegations about you and Louise. Again, I'm not blaming you for that, but don't come pointing your finger at us – at me – until you're ready to stand up and be counted yourself.'

He was right in everything he'd suggested about Nicholson. I'd spent most of my time since talking to Louise and then John Maxwell trying to work out how I could use him to provoke some response from Fowler, which would in turn bring him back under suspicion.

'Are you still there?' Brownlow said.

'You think I should leave everything at that?' I said.

'I think you've done what you were asked to do.'

'And Nicholson?'

'What about him?'

'Is there anything *you* can do to persuade him it might be in his own best interest to talk to you?'

'Why – because Fowler will want him as dead as Marco wanted Nicholson's wife once he realizes that Nicholson's starting to get even more scared than he's already been for the past fifteen months, and that he might be about to do something about that?'

'Perhaps if Fowler saw that you lot were more interested in Nicholson, he might think twice about trying to get to him.'

'I don't think there'd be much of an effort involved, do you? If what you say is true, then either or both Fowler and Marco have had Nicholson on the end of a rope for all this time and all either of them has to do now is to jerk that rope occasionally to remind Nicholson precisely where he stands. The plus side of that little scenario for Marco and Fowler, of course, is that, unlike Helen Brooks, Jane Nicholson's body is likely to be somewhere retrievable – somewhere we could get to it and find all that lovely DNA instantly identifiable as Nicholson's.'

'What if *I* came to you officially with my allegations of the murder of his wife – wouldn't that give you legitimate grounds for a visit to him?'

He considered this. 'Not once his lawyer learned about this conversation. Besides, Fowler knows what's happening, where *he* stands. Why go on knocking at the door? He knows you're there, he knows what you know.' Someone spoke to him and he called across the room in which he was sitting for someone else to wait for him. 'Time to go,' he said to me. 'Please, consider all I've just said. Consider where you stand now in relation to all you've just told me about Nicholson. I'd hate to see you being the only one arrested for his own dirty little part in all of this.' He hung up before I could ask him what he meant.

But, in truth, I knew exactly what he was telling me. And perhaps he was right: perhaps I had come closer to the end without realizing it; perhaps I had spent too much time looking backwards through those months of loss and anger and uncertainty, and the time had finally come to start looking forward again.

413

38

Yvonne arrived unexpectedly an hour later. She knocked as she opened the door, came into the room and sat opposite me, looking at me without speaking.

'This is a pleasant surprise,' I said.

'Half right.'

'Pleasant?'

'Getting colder.'

It was the first time I'd seen her since our meeting in the bar on the eve of Fowler and Webster's celebration.

'Sunny told me what happened,' she said. 'I wanted to see the bruises before they faded completely.'

'You should see the other guy,' I said, doing my best to sound like George Raft, or Edward G. Robinson, or James Cagney.

'The one walking away laughing and wiping your blood from his hands while you and Sunny tried to control your shaking?'

'It wasn't quite like that,' I said.

'He also told me your entertaining little story of how and why you think Helen Brooks died. You must be very pleased with yourself.'

'Not really.'

I'd called him with everything I thought I'd worked out an hour before talking to Andrew Brownlow.

'But you've got to consider Alison Brooks's feelings above your own? And certainly above any notion you might still harbour about bringing Fowler to justice?'

'Her doctor wants her to go into hospital.'

'And? Is the saintly Louise still insisting on self-lessly caring for her at home?' She held up a hand as though to stop herself from saying any more. 'I know — I'll regret that remark later.'

'You regret it already,' I said.

She acknowledged this with a shrug.

'I know it's not perfect, but it was never going to be,' I said. 'It was fifteen months ago.'

'How many times have you said that? It's not perfect because it's *wrong*. And even if it's not *completely* wrong — because even you wouldn't allow yourself to become that self-deluded — then it's still too wrong in too many places. It makes sense to you only because most of the facts fit, and because you think you know as well as Alison Brooks does what she really wants to hear from you.'

'And the bits that I haven't got right, the bits that don't fit?' I said.

She was talking about Irina Kapec and the injustice being done to the asylum-seeker tenants who were about to exchange a bad landlord for an even worse one.

'You don't need me to tell you about that,' she said.

415

'No, but it's why you came. I was employed by Alison Brooks to find out to the best of my ability what happened to her daughter. I know there are inconsistencies and gaps, but at least there are now enough solid pieces for those gaps and inconsistencies to exist.'

'And the moments of stolen happiness with Louise – what was that? Some kind of bonus?' She paused. 'Yes, I'll probably regret having said that, too. But probably not until long after all this is over.'

'It might already be over,' I said.

'What?' she said. 'Everything or just the you-and-Louise bit?'

'Both.'

'The you-and-Louise bit was over before it began,' she said. 'How do you refer to it in your report to her mother? A moment of weakness? Two people clinging to each other in adversity, finding solace and comfort in an uncaring world?'

'It wasn't like that,' I said uselessly.

'I know it wasn't. But even now you can't convince yourself that it wasn't part of the same thing.'

'Perhaps,' I said. I had told neither Sunny nor Brownlow what John Maxwell had revealed to me the previous night. 'So tell me – what do you think I should do?' I said.

'That wasn't why I came.'

'I know. But since you're here . . .'

'To begin with, I think you should tell Alison Brooks face to face everything you've already told Louise, make sure *she* left nothing out. And then I think you should tell Louise everything you're still not admitting to yourself.'

'Such as?'

She closed her eyes and shook her head. 'Even you must have thought it was all a bit iffy. Alison Brooks switches on the engine, and ever since then her daughter's been the one in the driving seat, forever telling you where all this is supposed to be going, and making sure you – you, specifically – know exactly where you've been.'

'They never made any secret of the fact that they were sharing everything I told either of them,' I said.

'Perhaps. But you still regard Alison Brooks as your client – *she's* the one you've been focused on all the time you were looking.'

'Meaning what? That Louise was only there to keep me on course?'

'Two sob stories for the price of one. They probably genuinely expected you to turn something up that the police could use to re-open the case.'

'And if I had turned up something which even half-implicated Fowler?'

' "Half-implicated". Good to see you still know how to dodge those speeding bullets.'

I told her of the near-identical conversation I'd just had with Andrew Brownlow.

'He's a real cop,' she said. 'He hates you. You get all the intrigue and glamour, and all he gets is the foot-work and the paperwork and the good honest citizenry avoiding him like the plague.'

'Do *you* think it's all over?' I asked her.

She rose from her seat, went to the filing cabinet and took out the whisky. She blew into two glasses and poured us both a drink. 'You know what *I* think,' she said.

'You think I should have gone for Fowler via the exploitation-of-the-asylum-seekers angle.'

'It would have made a lot more sense to a lot more people.'

'It wasn't what I was being paid to do.'

'I'm not saying it was. Just that if you'd given it a bit more time and thought while all this was happening, then you might still have had a stick in your hand to rattle through the bars of his cage.'

'Because all he cares about now is his money and his reputation?'

'It's all he *ever* cared about. All you did was catch him at a tricky time when the two things were in the balance.' She emptied and refilled her own glass. She looked slowly around the room, as though sensing something of Louise's recent presence and what had happened there six days earlier.

I knew then that she had another reason for being there.

'You don't need to read me chapter and verse on how Louise and her mother got me over the barrel,' I said.

'I know. And whatever you and Edith Cavell got up to, I doubt it would have changed anything, or that we wouldn't all have ended up precisely where we have done.'

'Edith Cavell,' I said. 'I'm impressed. And by "we", I assume you're referring equally to Irina, the woman in Walmsley Street and all the others as much as you are to you, me, Sunny, Alison or Louise Brooks.'

'Can you even remember the name of the woman in Walmsley Street?' she said.

'I never knew it.'

'Exactly.' She pulled a face at the taste of the whisky. 'Yesterday, Irina had some kind of official confirmation from someone.'

'That she's finally about to be called as a witness?'

'You make that sound like a very grand and noble thing. No – that someone somewhere has finally been able to identify her husband's body, or what remains of it after all these years. Apparently, he was excavated along with a few hundred others from a mass grave outside Srebrenica. See how easily that "few hundred others" trips off the tongue?'

'What will she do?'

'She's talking about going home. Well, not home exactly . . .'

'You'll miss her,' I said.

'Of course I'll miss her. She wants to go home and bury him. She wants her ending just as much as you want yours.'

It would have been crass of me to make any reference to the body Alison Brooks was still hoping to have found and identified. And I think she understood this, and that this was also why she was there – pointing out to me how all the lines in this tangled skein of an investigation were all slowly untwisting and moving in roughly the same direction, in wavering parallels, touching and parting in unfelt collisions, and all aimed at the same uncertain goal of a hopeful conclusion.

I held out my cup for more drink.

'You could go with her for a while,' I said.

'I suggested that to her.'

And Irina Kapec had told her not to even think about it – that it was a world Yvonne knew nothing about, and one she would be wiser never to even begin to know about – a world where every single member of your family, or everyone you had ever loved and who had ever loved you, could be killed on a whim or in hatred or ignorance, and all the rest of the civilized world would ever do was talk about Humanitarian Disasters and stand back wringing its hands.

I wanted to hold her.

'Sunny still thinks you're going to try something,' she said.

'Until two hours ago, I probably was.'

'He thinks you want to get to Nicholson.'

'So, it's not just great minds that think alike, then.'

'Meaning Brownlow warned you against it as well.'

'I always imagined I was a lot less transparent,' I said.

'Louise Brooks certainly saw right through you. Sorry.'

'What do *you* intend doing now?' I asked her.

'I'm not sure.'

'Is that "not sure" as in attend Fowler's Guildhall Second Coming in two days' time and make sure you let the whole world know what you think of him, and Webster, and what all their plans will involve?'

'I was working on it with Irina until the news of her husband arrived.'

'And now her priorities have changed?'

'Something like that. Besides—' She stopped talking.

'Besides what?'

'I was going to say that you'd be better off asking Louise what *she* intended doing now with regard to Fowler in light of all you've just revealed to her.'

'Do you honestly think she'll try and do something about it?'

'Imagine it was *your* sister who'd been killed. Suppose it was *your* mother who was dying and who was still all twisted up with not knowing and wanting to know. Suppose all that, and suppose you knew everything that had just come to light concerning the man you always believed had killed your sister and had then deprived your mother of her reason for living.'

'It's the cancer that's killing her.'

'Don't fool yourself. And don't pretend that her dying hasn't always played a part in all of this.'

'As much as was played by her coming to me at John Maxwell's recommendation?'

'You said it.' She put her empty cup on the table and told me she had to go.

I offered to walk back to the agency with her, but she said she'd prefer to be alone.

'*Will* you go to the Guildhall?' I asked her.

'Why are you asking? So you'll know to stand well clear of me when the baton charges start?'

'I'd never get the blood out of this shirt,' I said.

She looked at me, smiled and closed her eyes. 'You just worry about yourself,' she said.

'If it's over, then it's over,' I said.

'I know. But just because someone says something is over, it doesn't necessarily mean it is. Write that down.'

'You've lost me,' I said.

She stopped smiling. 'I lost you weeks ago.' She put a finger to her lips to stop me from answering her.

39

Louise called me at home the following morning and told me that her mother had been taken into hospital the previous evening. She asked me if I could visit her there as soon as possible.

It was not yet six. I had been awake since four, unable to sleep, and uncertain why, knowing only that this uncertainty was fed in part by my growing sense of failure.

I had tried to read in the rising light, but had been unable to concentrate.

I asked Louise where she was.

'At the hospital. I've been here since she was brought in. I practically live here, anyway, these days. Her being here means I can keep a closer eye on her.' It was both an excuse and an admission of defeat and she did nothing to disguise the fact.

'How is she?'

'She's been sedated since she arrived. Sleeping. One

of the last things she was able to say was to ask to see you today.'

I heard the traffic behind her, the slowly rising note of a siren, and then silence.

'I came outside for a smoke,' she said. 'Can you come?'

'I spoke to Andrew Brownlow,' I told her.

'Don't tell me – nothing's changed. Let the old woman die, let everything go away again and let him get on with doing whatever it is he does that doesn't involve stepping on other people's toes.'

'Something like that. He certainly left me in no doubt as to what I *hadn't* achieved over the past fortnight.'

'You did what she asked you to do.'

And everyone kept telling me that, too.

'Is that why she wants to see me – to hear me say it all to her?'

'She wouldn't be up to reading one of your reports,' she said. I could sense her anxiety and her exhaustion in everything she said.

'What have the doctors said?'

'Guess,' she said, meaning that whatever they might have told her, she, at least, knew how close her mother had now come to dying. And if Louise knew it, then Alison Brooks certainly knew it.

She told me where her mother was and I arranged to meet her there.

I arrived half an hour later.

Louise was sitting beside her mother's bed, holding one of her hands in both her own and talking to her. I thought at first that Alison Brooks was awake, but saw as I approached closer that she was asleep.

Screens had been drawn along each side of the bed, leaving only the bottom open to the ward. A line with a valve had been taped to one of Alison Brooks's arms. An oxygen mask lay to the side of her mouth. I could hear the occasional gentle hiss of its flow. Her breathing was shallow and even.

At my arrival, Louise motioned for me to go with her to the end of the ward, to the window where we could look down over the city.

For the first time in almost two months, rain had been forecast, though this and the summer thunderstorms which were expected to bring it remained stubbornly south of the river. There had been reports of rain elsewhere in the country on the early-morning news.

The sky over the city was pale and cloudless. A haze lay along the estuary, and in the distance where the Wolds began their gentle rise.

'She'll be awake soon,' Louise said. 'She'll be reasonably clear-headed and lucid for an hour or so. It's why she wanted you to come now.'

'How much do you want me to tell her?' I said.

'Whatever you need to. I told her everything you'd already told me, but I imagine there are things you didn't tell me that you might want to say directly to her.'

'What do you think I'm keeping from you?' I said.

She shrugged, unconcerned by all the question implied. 'I don't know. And to be honest, if there was anything, I doubt if it would matter much now.' She looked back towards the screened bed. 'I think all she really wants to hear from you is that what we've both known right from the very start was the truth –

that Fowler, for whatever reason, was responsible for Helen's death, and that it wasn't the stupid and perfectly understandable accident everybody else wanted it to be.'

She was about to say more when her pager bleeped.

She looked at it and switched it off. 'Environmental Health want to carry out their tests on the new air-conditioning ducts.' She pointed upwards to the roof five floors above us. 'I have to be there.' She straightened her jacket and tugged at her sleeves. 'Go and sit with her,' she said. 'She'll wake soon.'

She walked with me back to her mother's screened bed and then left me.

I pulled a chair closer to where Alison Brooks lay, wondering what she really wanted to hear from me, what kind of unconvincing blessing I was there to confer on her.

She woke a few minutes later, took several deep breaths and then looked around her without moving her head. She raised her hand and beckoned for mine.

She thanked me for coming. Her voice was no more than a whisper, but in the quiet of the ward I could hear her clearly.

I told her it might be easier for her if she let me tell her everything I'd already told Louise, and for her to let me finish before either questioning me or asking me for further details.

She nodded at this and closed her eyes as I began to speak.

My story lasted twenty minutes. Her grip tightened and slackened as I spoke, and was her way of encouraging me to continue.

When I'd finished, she released my hand and tried

to put the oxygen mask over her mouth. I did this for her, stroking her fringe out of her eyes. She slowly regained her breath and became calm.

When, after a further five minutes, she was able to speak again, she asked me where Louise was.

I told her that she'd been called away.

She hesitated before continuing. 'Will you go on seeing her?' she asked me.

'I'm not sure,' I said.

'Because you think she – because you think we both – used you?'

'I would have uncovered what I uncovered either way,' I said.

'I know. She didn't *use* you,' she said. 'And if that *is* what she thought she was doing, then I know hers will be the greater regret. Don't think badly of her, of either of us.'

'I don't,' I said.

There was something I had wanted to ask her ever since Louise had first spoken of the likelihood of her mother coming into hospital. 'Are you worried she'll try to do something to try and get the police interested in Fowler again?' I said.

'When I'm dead, you mean?'

It occurred to me only then that it now hardly mattered to make the distinction, so close was she to dying, so convinced of what lay ahead of her.

'I've already told her how much I regret everything we've lost between us,' she said, avoiding my question. 'I *do* regret it. You never see these things happening at the time, and afterwards you can see nothing else.'

She stopped talking and held the mask back to her

426

mouth. I watched her breath cloud in shifting patterns inside the clear plastic.

'I spoke to John Maxwell,' I said. 'His wife died in here.'

'In this same ward,' she said.

I wondered if knowing this had played any part in her own last concession to her daughter.

'By the window on the far side,' she said.

'Did you visit her?'

'I came. Once.'

'With him?'

'No. He would never have countenanced that. I came because even then, even after all those years, I knew I owed her something, even if it was only my respect, my final nod to a dying woman.'

My father had died six years earlier in the ward above us and I was lost for a moment in my own thoughts.

'I know what you're thinking, Mr Rivers,' she said. 'And you're wrong.'

I thought at first that she was lying to me.

'It's what John Maxwell believes,' I said.

'Half-believes. It's something he convinced himself of because I wasn't strong enough at the time to *stop* him from believing it. And before you ask me why, or accuse me of something, I was as confused as he was about what had happened between us. He loved his wife, I loved my husband, but for that one short spell we loved each other more than we loved either of those other people. When I discovered I was pregnant with Louise, we both knew it might have been his child, but we also both knew that whatever we might have done about that would have been the wrong thing to do.'

'Because too many other people would have been hurt?'

She nodded. 'It would have destroyed my marriage. It would certainly have destroyed his. His wife might have forgiven him, but he would never have forgiven himself, and it would have eaten away at him, no matter how long it took.'

'And after Louise was born you never did anything to establish her paternity for certain?'

She shook her head. 'It was what we both wanted. He'd known for a few years that his wife couldn't have children. We agreed to live our separate lives.'

'With the uncertain idea that Louise might or might not have been his daughter to keep the two of you attached in some way?'

'I never said it was a good idea. But that was how things started out. We kept apart from each other. And eventually things got easier.'

'He told me to tell you he was thinking of you,' I said.

'There's hardly a day goes by when I don't think of him,' she said.

'And Louise never suspected?'

'Never. I did once consider telling her, but by then I'd remarried, Helen had been born, and things had already changed between us. Sleeping dogs, Mr Rivers.' She had exhausted herself and she signalled to me that she was unable to go on until she had rested.

I remained sitting beside her, holding her hand, knowing that *this*, and not my story of her daughter's death, was the true purpose of my visit. I had come to hear her confession, and now she had made it.

Beyond the screens, others began to wake and to

move around the ward. Nurses came and went. A radio was switched on, its channels scanned. A woman by the doorway woke and started singing.

Alison Brooks opened her eyes and listened to all this. She smiled at the sound of the singing woman.

'Tell him you saw me,' she said.

'Anything else?'

'He knows everything else there is to know,' she said. 'It was never a question of confirmation or denial.'

'Just of knowing?'

'Just of knowing,' she said.

We were interrupted by a nurse, who drew back one of the screens and stood at the other side of the bed. She checked the drip and the tube and the valve. She asked me how long I'd been there and how long Alison Brooks had been awake.

'Five minutes,' Alison Brooks told her.

We'd been together for almost an hour.

'Any pain?' the nurse said.

Alison Brooks let out her breath and shook her head.

Then the nurse straightened the sheets on the bed and the pillows beneath Alison Brooks's head. This caused her some further pain, but she said nothing.

When the nurse had gone, she said, 'I may not see you again, Mr Rivers. *You* may consider your investigation not to have been wholly successful, but I don't. I want to thank you. I see John Maxwell in you. You may not want to hear that, or thank me for saying it, but I do. I don't have time for lies or evasions.' Her grip on my hand tightened for a moment and then she released me.

'I'll give everything to Louise,' I said. 'Things might

come to light in the future which . . .' I stopped speaking, she was still looking up at me, but she was no longer listening.

'Do whatever you feel you have to,' she said, and closed her eyes.

40

I went from the hospital to Humber Street to find
Fowler waiting for me there. He was alone and sitting
in a chair he'd pulled close to the window. It was the
first time I'd seen him since Sunny and I had gate-
crashed Lister Court.

'Get out,' I said to him.

He remained where he sat. 'Is that it – "Get out"?'

'We both know why you're here,' I said. 'You've
come to gloat and to—'

'I came—'

'You came to gloat. Whatever it is you're about to
say, you came to gloat. And judging by the fact that the
boy Marco is nowhere in sight, I'd say you suddenly
felt either brave enough or safe enough to do it all by
yourself for once.'

'See,' he said. 'You're doing it again. You're only seeing the man you want to see. The man you wanted me to
be right from the start of this pathetic little charade.'

'And what – you're not that arrogant, greedy, self-serving little empire-builder everyone else knows you to be?'

He smiled. 'Not everyone, Mr Rivers, not everyone.'

'I asked you to leave.'

'You told me to get out. Just like I told you and the Incredible Hulk to leave Lister Court last week.'

'I seem to remember that Webster did most of the talking on that occasion, and that he also seemed to be the one most concerned about what was happening, at what he stood to lose.'

'You embarrassed us. We could have done without the upset. It was a little lunchtime freebie for all those tame councillors, that's all. You haven't changed anything, Mr Rivers. Whatever you might like to think.'

'I'm still going to prove you killed Helen Brooks,' I said. Under the circumstances, it seemed a reckless thing to say, more another confession of my failure than a credible statement of intent.

He shook his head. 'No, you're not. She was a greedy, drug-taking little whore with ideas above her station who was never going to be anything else. A photographer? Yeah, right. A hundred quid bought her for whoever I wanted to give her to for the night.' He stuck an invisible syringe into his arm. 'If you know what I mean. And I'm certain you do, Mr Rivers. I'm certain you do. She died, that's all. So let's just leave it at that, shall we? Who really gives a fuck apart from her own dear old dying mother? You think that half-sister of hers gives a toss?'

'You killed her,' I repeated. 'You killed one of those three traffickers who followed you here, and you killed her.'

'Him?' He laughed. 'And who the fuck ever missed him? They should have given us a fucking medal for letting those three cavemen walk into their net. Immigration? Don't make me fucking laugh.'

'If you're going to suggest that you did what you did as part of some kind of arrangement or trade-off with Immigration, then you're lying again,' I said.

'Suit yourself,' he said. 'But they were never going to prosecute any of us – not the men who mattered – not with anything that counted, whatever they believed then or might be saying now. So what – so we hired a few hundred wogs for a few quid a day – fuck 'em, they were happy to get it. Who do you think Immigration would rather have got their hands on – the poor stupid fuckers we were employing, or the greedy bastards who were flooding them in here a hundred at a time? Work it out, Rivers. Look at the big picture for once in your shitty little life.'

'You still killed Helen Brooks,' I said.

'Helen fucking Brooks. How many times do I have to tell you? She was a worthless little fuck-up who got above herself, that's all. So she died, so what?'

'No – you killed her,' I said.

'You're beginning to sound even more tedious,' he said. 'In fact, you're beginning to sound as though you've got nothing else to say.'

'Perhaps. But you wouldn't have come here, not so close to getting everything you ever wanted, if you didn't want to hear me say it and to find out what else I knew about the cosy little arrangement you had with Marco and Nicholson.'

' "Had"? *Have*, Mr Rivers. Have. Or, to put it another way – What cosy little arrangement? I've absolutely no idea what you're talking about or why you insist on making these crazy and unfounded allegations against me.'

Everything he said continued to sound rehearsed.

'And from that I take it you had no idea about Marco and Nicholson's private arrangement concerning Nicholson's wife,' I said. 'Or at least not until after the event. And now that you *do* know about it, you don't feel quite so confident about Nicholson's silence. Or, come to think of it, about Marco's, either. Who's to say that Marco isn't going to say that you knew about it from the very start, perhaps that it was even your idea to kill Nicholson's wife to ensure either his perfect story or his silence afterwards? Anybody who's ever seen Marco following you around will assume that he was acting on your orders.'

'Nobody's telling anybody anything,' he said.

'Perhaps. Or perhaps not. Or perhaps not yet. But that *is* why you're here. Perhaps you even think I already know where Marco put the body once he'd driven it all the way back from Leeds. I assume, of course, that that's why you left him in his kennel today – because you wanted to get everything clear in your own mind before you decided what to do about the pair of them to ensure there was never going to be any connection made back to you, and from there to Nicholson's part in your killing of the trafficker and Helen Brooks.'

I knew by the way he avoided looking at me that I was right in most of my guessing.

He turned to face me. 'Sadly for you, and as with everything else in this pointless little crusade of yours, you have no actual proof of any of this,' he said.

'No,' I said. 'But Marco does. And that's another reason why you couldn't resist coming here, and why you came alone – because you want me to confirm for you that Marco was doing all this behind your back, creating his own little insurance policy for if ever you two boys had a falling out, or for when the time came for someone else's head to be put on the block.'

'You've lost me,' he said, feigning disinterest.

'No, I haven't. Marco knew better than anyone that one day someone like me might come looking through all that had happened, and that *he* was the one most likely to get the finger pointed at him.'

'My word against his, you mean?'

'Your word as what – local dignitary, councillor, mayor, saviour of a dying city?'

'And Nicholson?'

'I don't imagine Marco's long-term plans allowed for Nicholson being around for too much longer, especially after tomorrow. Except, of course, all that might have changed now.'

'Meaning?'

'Meaning that before you knew all this, it made sense to get rid of Nicholson. Whereas now, Marco might be able to persuade Nicholson to point another accusing finger at you and keep the two of *them* off the hook. I daresay Nicholson's altered testimony about what really happened to Helen Brooks and then to his own wife would make fairly compelling reading in some quarters.'

'Nicholson's a—'

'Nicholson's a what? Another one of those little people you use and then throw away? Perhaps that's even how Marco thinks you treat *him*. I can't see him being too happy to go on playing your little lapdog for much longer – not now he knows something you don't, but wish you did. And especially not when you consider all the risks he's taken on your behalf, and how you seem to be the only one benefiting from those risks.'

He considered all this without speaking. He looked out at the street and the men below.

'It's still not going to happen,' he said eventually.

'What's not going to happen?'

'Any of it.'

'Why? Because you say so? Wake up, Fowler – it's all started to move just that little bit beyond your control.'

'Is that what you honestly believe? You don't know the half of it, Rivers.' He seemed more confident again, as though I had come to the end of my accusations and none of them had pierced him fatally. 'And any day now, the mother is going to die – it might even be any hour now from what I hear – and then that even bigger whore of a daughter is going to come to you begging you to forget that any of this ever happened. Who knows – there might even be another cheap wet night at the Holiday Inn for you if you play your cards right.'

I wasn't certain what he meant by the first of these remarks, but I said nothing.

'Run out of accusations?' he said.

'I was about to turn to the man in the salvage yard,' I said. 'That second tragic accident.' I'd hoped the remark might keep him off-balance, but he seemed almost reassured by what I'd said.

'Like I said,' he said. 'You don't know the fucking half of it.'

'And you had *him* killed because either he knew something about what had happened on the yacht or because, after my visit fifteen months later, he'd become greedy again.'

'I haven't got the faintest idea what you're talking about.'

'No – what you have no idea about is how I managed to connect his death with the destruction of the yacht and what had happened on it a few weeks earlier.' It seemed a pointless accusation to make knowing how completely the yacht had been destroyed.

'You haven't connected anything to anything,' he said. He laughed. It was forced laughter, but I was unable to ignore the relief it masked.

I had been about to mention the assault on the woman on Walmsley Street, but I knew by his response to this last accusation, that this would not now serve any purpose other than to bolster his growing confidence, and so I said nothing.

He rose to leave, looking at the buildings opposite and at the Humber beyond. I wondered what he saw there.

'They've forecast rain,' he said.

'I heard,' I said. 'Perhaps it'll come and wash all the dirt off the streets.'

He looked at me warily. 'By the time me and Webster and all those others have finished, there won't *be* any dirt left to wash off the streets.'

'There's always dirt,' I said. 'It's always there. Sometimes you just have to know where to look for it. Give my regards to Marco when you see him. Tell him I've already told the police everything I know. It might help him sleep a little easier.'

'It might,' he said. 'But I wouldn't bet on it.'

'See you tomorrow,' I said.

'You still intend coming?'

'To hear your wonderful announcement and watch you and all the other worthies sign on the dotted? I wouldn't miss it for the world.'

'They won't let you try and fuck this one up,' he said.

'Who said I'd want to?'

'Not you. Not the fucking ape you had with you last time. And certainly not his sidekick and all *her* friends.'

'The wogs?'

'It's what they are, Mr Rivers.'

'If you say so.'

'I do.'

He went, pausing to look at the scorch mark on the wall where Marco had burned the map. He touched his finger to it and then studied the mark this left there. Then he made a show of taking out a white handkerchief, shaking it open and wiping his finger clean.

41

I called Louise the following morning to ask about her mother, and to reassure myself that she had no intention of attending the announcement at the Guildhall later in the day. I was still concerned that she might try to disrupt the proceedings there in a final attempt to discredit Fowler.

'Don't worry,' she told me. 'I'm not going. I thought it best. Not after everything else.' There was neither anger nor frustration in her voice, only a disappointed realization that events had finally moved beyond her control, and that Fowler himself was similarly beyond her reach. 'Besides, I need to be with my mother now. She's having a bad day.'

'Tell me,' I said.

'She's only just woken up, and the doctor's concerned about her breathing. I've been home for a couple of hours' rest. I'm on my way back there now.' It was almost eleven.

Then she asked me why I was insisting on watching Fowler on his big day.

'Because this is what it's all been about,' I said. And because I didn't want to give Fowler the satisfaction of thinking that anything he'd said to me the previous day had kept me away. 'I could let you know what happens,' I suggested.

'We know what's going to happen,' she said. 'Perhaps you should just let me have your final bill.'

'If that's what you want.'

'Why, what did you expect?'

'That we might at least see each other again?'

'Why – because I'll soon be reeling from the death of my mother and I'll need a shoulder to cry on?' She paused. 'I'm sorry, Leo, but it wouldn't be yours. We're both grateful for everything you've done, but for me to go on seeing you would feel wrong. It would tie me to this thing for ever. I thought you'd understand that better than anyone.'

'I do,' I said. I didn't.

'Don't make this too easy for me,' she said. 'I know how badly I've behaved. Perhaps it's *you* who should start putting a bit of distance between us. The dominoes are falling, can't you hear them?'

I wanted to tell her to let it end with the death of her mother, but I knew how callous this would sound. I heard the noise of the traffic around her.

I asked her where she was.

'Near the hospital. Look, I have to go, OK? Let me know later how it all went.'

'I could come to the hospital,' I suggested.

'No, I'll come to you. My mother was drugged and asleep for twenty-four hours after you left her yesterday. You saw her at her sparkling best. There's only so much counting breaths per minute I can take. I'll call you.' She hung up.

I left Humber Street and walked to the Guildhall.

I met Sunny at the corner of Hanover Square, smoking another cigar and talking into a recorder. He already held a press pack under his arm. There was ash on his shirt front. I was surprised to see him there.

'Leo Rivers, Ace Investigator, approaching,' he said into the machine as I arrived beside him, and then clicked it off.

He studied the last of my fading bruises.

I guessed then that he was there because he expected Yvonne to appear, and just as I had fooled myself into believing I might have tempered any of Louise Brooks's outbursts against Fowler, so he was there to do the same for her.

'Yvonne?' I said.

'They're planning a protest. "Asylum-Seekers Have Rights Too".'

'Not that you'd notice,' I said.

'"New Tenancy Arrangement Leaves Asylum-Seekers Even More Vulnerable"?' he said.

'Catchy,' I said.

'She thinks so.'

'Do you think there might be trouble?'

'I've just been in there. Security coming out of the woodwork. Real security. None of the shaved-headed, tried-hard-to-get-into-the-police-force or own-my-own-Alsatian variety.'

We watched as a succession of chauffeur-driven cars and taxis arrived at the main entrance, as drivers held doors open, and as all the local dignitaries arrived.

'Fowler's already in there,' he said. 'And Webster and all the others.'

'Did they expect a reception committee?'

'Probably.'

We waited where we stood in the shade of a wall until several minutes before the reception was scheduled to begin.

I asked him what time Yvonne was coming.

'She wouldn't tell me. It's a them-and-us thing.'

'And we're still a "them" as far as she's concerned?'

'Look at the score-sheet,' he said, and then dropped the last inch of his cigar to the ground and trod it out.

I followed him to the doors.

Inside, the Banqueting Hall was filled with chairs.

There was a stage, upon which more chairs had been arranged.

The room was lined with the plans and architects' models I had seen there earlier. Giant posters and designs filled the walls above the models. The words Hull City Initiative filled the space above the stage in ten-foot-high lettering.

The room was full of people. Sunny pointed out the other journalists and photographers to me. He was surprised and disappointed that so many had come. The more who wrote their own stories, the fewer who would buy those stories from the agency. I searched for either Fowler or Webster. I recognized several of the men I'd seen at Lister Court.

Sunny left me, telling me he'd be back soon.

'Don't start anything until I'm there to protect you,' he said. He flicked his eyes to where one of the councillors was talking to two security guards, pointing us out to them. Then he pointed over my shoulder and I turned to see Fowler climbing the steps to the stage.

When I turned back, Sunny had gone. I saw him at the rear of the room talking to a group of photographers unpacking and setting up their equipment.

A microphone was switched on and someone called for our attention. We were asked to take our seats. I sat at the end of a row towards the rear of the room. Each chair held another press pack. I pretended to read through this while looking around me. Two guards stood at each door, and when the first announcement was made they began closing and securing these.

Music began to play as the developers, planners, councillors and other dignitaries continued to mount the stage. There was a round of applause at the appearance of the mayor and his wife. His chains of office reflected the spotlights which were switched on above him as the room's other lights grew dimmer.

I searched again for Sunny and saw him at the end of the back row, sitting alone. He nodded to let me know he'd seen me, and that he, too, was aware of how secure the room now was.

The music grew briefly louder and then faded.

The city planning officer came to the microphone and made a speech lasting twenty minutes, during which there were a dozen further orchestrated bursts of applause. The man held up his hands to quieten these and looked surprised and gratified by every one.

After the speech, he announced that there had been a slight change to the day's proceedings, and that he hoped we would all understand why this change had been considered necessary.

We had all gone there expecting to witness the historic signing of the documents that would set in motion the transformation of a great city into an even greater one, he said. We were participants in History. This day would be remembered for decades to come.

The reporters sitting ahead of me began to talk among themselves.

The planning officer said he'd kept us in suspense for long enough. The agreements, he said, all the documents which would pave the way for this exciting new process of renewal and rebirth, had been signed an hour earlier. The process, he announced, was under way. History was already being made, and we were all now a part of it.

There was a moment of silence, and then several of the men sitting on the stage – Fowler and Webster included – began to applaud. The room followed. The music returned. The lights changed.

Few of the men sitting in front of me applauded. I turned again to Sunny, who held up his own un-clapping palms to me.

The mayor came to the microphone and, without explaining why it had happened, thanked us all for understanding why this change to the day's proceedings had been considered necessary. There would be no more formalities, he announced, but everyone involved would remain available for questions. He appealed for the members of the national press to ask as many questions as they liked, and to tell their readers how Hull was once again Looking To The

Future. He motioned to the words behind him as he said this, and then he returned to his seat.

Fowler sat beside him. He leaned close to the mayor and whispered to him as he sat down. The mayor held out his hand and Fowler shook it. They held the pose long enough for several photos to be taken.

Sunny came and sat in the seat immediately behind me.

'Any sign of Yvonne?'

'They've locked the front doors,' he said. 'They'll keep them outside, wait for them to start obstructing the traffic and then get the law to move them on. I doubt if anything's going to be allowed to rain on this particular little parade.'

He left me and went to join the men sitting in the rows ahead. Their own disappointment was now a palpable presence in the room. The city's press officers tried to encourage them to visit the models and ask questions of the people involved, but the journalists felt cheated at not having been able to witness the contract-signings and were now reluctant to do this.

I continued searching the doors, still not convinced that Louise wouldn't show up and attempt to reach Fowler.

I went to one of the tables between the models and took a glass of wine.

There was a tap on my shoulder and I turned to face Fowler.

'Smart idea,' I said, meaning the pre-emptive signing.

'We have you to thank for that,' he said. He took a glass of water from the table.

'Because of what happened at Lister Court?'

445

'You don't think any of the little vote-counters over there were going to want a repeat performance of that particular — what shall we call it?'

'Protest?' I said.

'OK, protest. Whatever it was, they weren't going to put themselves through anything like that again, particularly not on their home ground, not here, and certainly not in front of all these cameras.'

'Is that why you let Sunny and me into Lister Court?'

'Do you really think I'm that smart, Mr Rivers?'

'Is that why one of your informants let Yvonne and Irina Kapec know that something was happening there in the first place? Presumably someone via whom you've been feeding information to Irina Kapec, and who has then been selling information back to you regarding her and all her delaying tactics.'

He feigned a look of hurt surprise. 'Smart *and* devious. I'm flattered.' He pretended to look around us. 'No Louise Brooks?' he said.

'She's got better things to do,' I said.

'Says who? Oh, her?' He laughed and touched his glass to mine.

I tipped my wine on to the floor, splashing our shoes and staining the bottom of his trousers. He was unprepared for the gesture and stepped backwards, colliding with the people standing behind him.

'Clumsy me,' I said, holding up my empty glass. I put it on the table beside us.

Turning back to Fowler, I said, 'Is that why you let Webster do all your dirty work for you at Lister Court — just in case things *did* go wrong and some of the councillors started having second thoughts about some of the people they were about to start working with?'

'The phrase is "Getting into bed with". Surely you, of all people, have heard of that one.' He looked to where Sunny still stood with the other reporters. 'They're not even going to get into the building,' he said, meaning Yvonne, Irina and the other protestors.

'Perhaps not, but I imagine they'll get their faces and some of their banners onto some of the front pages.'

'What banners? That would take organization.'

I looked around us. 'Still no Marco? Two days in a row. You *must* be feeling confident.'

He pretended to consider this. 'He's otherwise engaged. He's been overdoing it recently – we all have – so I gave him a few days off. Probably gone on a short holiday somewhere. I'll tell him you were asking after him, shall I?'

'Tell him I—'

'Tell him yourself, Rivers,' he said abruptly. 'Tell him yourself what you told me and then tell him exactly where he stopped being an asset to me and everything I'm doing here and started becoming a liability.'

Before I could answer him, we were interrupted by a man who shook Fowler's hand, told him he was leaving and asked Fowler to call him to arrange a round of golf. He made no acknowledgement whatsoever of my presence.

Outside, several cars sounded their horns.

'Sounds as though their little protest's started,' Fowler said. 'Perhaps you could go out and tell them that they're wasting their time, that it's all over, and they lost.'

We were again interrupted, this time by the mayor and his wife. The woman made a comment to Fowler about what was happening outside. The mayor said something to me about there always being people opposed to change, people standing in the way of progress. He was delighted to have met me and shook my hand. Fowler kissed the man's wife and the two of them left us.

We were then distracted by a loud rapping on one of the side doors and a commotion there as it was unlocked and held closed by two of the guards. Four more went to their assistance.

I thought at first that the protestors had managed to force their way into the building, but as I watched, the guards stood back, and I saw Andrew Brownlow come into the room, his warrant card held into the face of the nearest man.

Fowler looked briefly anxious, but quickly regained his composure.

Sunny came to join us. 'Looks like they've finally come for you,' he said to Fowler.

At the door, Brownlow was followed into the room by two constables in uniform. Several of the councillors went to them. Brownlow searched the room, and seeing me where I stood with Sunny and Fowler, he called my name and came quickly towards me.

At his arrival, Sunny grabbed Fowler's arm and said, 'Officer, arrest this man.'

Brownlow looked at them both. 'Highly amusing,' he said. He pulled me to one side. 'You're coming with me. No arguments. Now.' And lowering his voice, added, 'I don't want to hear a single word.'

Beside us, Sunny released his grip on Fowler and watched as Brownlow and I walked to the door and the two waiting constables. I knew he would do his best to follow us.

Reaching the door, I turned to face him to let him know that I still had no idea what was happening.

He signalled back to me that he understood and that he knew what to do.

Beside him, Fowler smiled and raised his glass of water to me.

42

Outside, I saw Yvonne and Irina Kapec held behind a barrier that had been erected at the Guildhall entrance. Alongside them stood only a dozen or so other protestors. Seeing me, my arm still held by Brownlow, Yvonne stopped chanting and called my name. Brownlow told me to ignore her.

I pulled free of him and went to her.

'Fowler, Webster and the rest signed hours ago,' I said. 'This is all just an after-the-event round of backslapping.'

'What's Brownlow doing here?'

Brownlow came to stand alongside me.

'What I'm doing here is asking for Mr Rivers's co-operation regarding the developments of events elsewhere,' he said. 'I need him to answer a few questions for me.' He was about to hold my arm again, but thought better of the gesture in front of all those others. 'As soon as possible, if that's convenient,' he said to me.

'I imagine you expected a bigger turn-out,' I said to Yvonne, who looked around her and said nothing.

By then, Sunny had come out of the Guildhall and was standing on the steps. He hailed a cab.

Brownlow saw this. 'Happy now?' he said.

'Talk to Sunny,' I said to Yvonne.

I went with Brownlow to a waiting car. The two constables were already sitting in the front.

'There's a cab following us,' Brownlow said to the driver. 'Let it.'

We moved away from the Guildhall, along Lowgate to the junction with Garrison Road, where we waited to turn left.

'Where?' I asked Brownlow.

'Would it come as a great surprise to hear me say "Paull Holme"?' He gave me a cigarette and lit it, winding both our windows down.

'Nicholson?'

'Unless you know anyone else who lives there.'

'Has he decided to talk?'

'Talk?' he said.

'Which suggests that Fowler's probably already tried to get to him. Anything Nicholson tells you now, he's telling you because he's trying to squeeze himself out from between Fowler and Marco. He knows they'll corroborate each other's stories, and that he's going to be the one left holding the smoking gun. If you'd been to see him earlier, knowing what I'd already told you, you might have got something out of him worth having, before Fowler started turning the screws.'

'Finished?' he said.

We left the Mount Pleasant roundabout and turned on to Hedon Road, where we were held up in the traffic. We passed the entrance to the King George Dock, where I'd watched Nicholson meet Marco.

Ten minutes later, we were at Salt End and on the road to Paull.

'What has he said about the night of the alleged drowning?' I said.

Brownlow asked the driver if the cab was still behind us. It was.

We turned through the village and on to the lane leading to Nicholson's home overlooking the river.

Another constable stood on the road ahead of us, held up his hand and came to us. Seeing Brownlow, he waved us on.

Ahead of us I saw where a cloud of pale smoke hung above the shoreline.

'Nicholson's?' I said. 'Is that what Fowler did? Is that why he's talking?'

'Questions, questions,' Brownlow said.

We approached closer. Two fire engines were parked between the lane and the smouldering remains of Nicholson's wooden home. There was little left but wreckage. A small fire still burned at its centre. Men moved around the smouldering timbers and furniture, directing their hoses and scattering the mounds of ash and charred timber.

Brownlow told the driver where to park. He opened his door and told me to follow him.

'When did this happen?'

'Guess.'

'While Fowler was sitting on the stage in full view of all those other worthy and reliable witnesses?'

'You and Summers were in there somewhere.'

I turned and saw the cab draw up behind our parked

car. Sunny emerged and paid the driver. He was prevented from coming any closer by one of the constables.

'It's as far as he's coming,' Brownlow told me, leading me closer to the wreckage.

'Where's Nicholson now?' I asked him.

He called one of the fire officers over and spoke to him, leaving me alone beside a chair which had been untouched by the blaze.

He came back to me.

'Nicholson', he said, 'is over there.' He pointed into the centre of the charred and smoking timbers.

'He was inside?'

'When it burned, yes.'

'Killed by the fire?'

'We'll have to wait for the autopsy. After listening to you the other day, I looked again at the report on the dead guy at the salvage yard.'

'And Nicholson has similar injuries?'

'Something heavy and blunt to the back of the skull. Don't get too excited. It might have been a falling rafter. The body, as you can imagine, isn't a particularly pretty sight.'

'The man at the salvage yard could have been burned after he was killed to destroy evidence,' I said.

'Is that the best you can do?' he said. 'You're suggesting this is a copy?'

He walked ahead of me in a circle around the smoking debris.

'Does it matter?' I said.

'It probably did to Nicholson,' he said.

'No – what matters now is that you lot can no longer ignore the connection between Fowler and Nicholson and what happened that night and then afterwards in the salvage yard.'

'Perhaps,' he said.

'I'll come back to Tower Grange and make a full statement,' I said.

An ambulance arrived and negotiated the parked cars and fire engines to come close to the ruined house. One of the fire crew directed the two men carrying a stretcher to where Nicholson's corpse lay.

'Are you sure it's him?' I said.

'Meaning could it be Marco? It's Nicholson,' he said. 'I imagine even Fowler could see the disadvantages of leaving his right-hand man in the middle of Nicholson's burned home with his skull looking like a dropped egg.'

'Marco wasn't at the Guildhall,' I said. 'Fowler made a point of letting me know.'

'Meaning he wants us to start squeezing him? Where's the sense in that? Marco's a smart boy. His little insurance policy as far as Nicholson was concerned might just have become useless, but he's not stupid or desperate enough to leave himself exposed to whatever Fowler might now want to throw at him.'

'At least not yet,' I said.

He shook his head. 'With Nicholson out of the way, and nothing so far to point to whoever stuck him in the toaster, Fowler and Marco are going to come to some new arrangement between themselves. Find Marco's solicitor, find out what's supposed to happen in the event of his sudden or unexpected death. Forget it. Fowler and Marco are going to be the best of friends for a long time to come.'

'Arrest Marco,' I said. 'Get his clothes. Swab him.'

'Great idea. I was hoping *you* might know where he was. I assume you know how many properties Fowler owns.'

'Owned,' I said.

'Besides, Marco will have scrubbed away two layers of skin by now,' he said.

We were approached by the fire officer to whom he had spoken on our arrival. Nicholson's body was waiting to be removed. The police photographer moved around the corpse. He signalled to Brownlow that he had finished his work.

Nicholson's head, chest and arms were completely blackened. His arms were twisted by the heat, his fingers gone. None of his hair or his features remained. Only his legs from the knees down were not burned. Water pooled around the corpse as it was pulled clear of the debris which had fallen on to it. Even in that condition, I could see that the skull had been crushed.

Brownlow called for all the remaining pieces of clothing to be gathered up and bagged.

'The skull's practically empty,' he told me. 'Blackened inside and out.'

I watched as the ambulance men covered the corpse and other remains and carried these back to the ambulance. Even in that condition, there was no doubt in my own mind that it was Nicholson and not Marco who had died in the fire.

'Do they know yet how it was done?' I asked Brownlow, who was walking towards the river.

'No one's certain yet. It even looks as though Nicholson might have started the fire himself. They've found the remains of a much smaller fire a few yards from the back door. He appears to have been burning some clothes.'

'As you do.'

'We'll see.' He pointed to a small mound ahead of us. 'That's where he lit it. It's separate from the bulk of the main wreckage. Everything, the house, the garden, the surrounding land is bone dry.'

'And what – a spark flew from the fire to the house and Nicholson never noticed? He set fire to the last of his wife's clothes and then went inside for a quick nap after his morning's exertions?'

'It might be useful to find out from her sister what she was wearing on the day she disappeared,' he said.

'The day she was abducted and killed by Nicholson and Marco, you mean? Besides, you can't seriously believe that this was Nicholson's fire, or that it *accidentally* burned his house down with him in it.' I did nothing to hide my disbelief at the line he was taking.

'So, let me get this straight – Marco, waiting until Fowler was in full view of the nation's press, came out here, persuaded Nicholson to get rid of everything still belonging to his wife, waited until the blaze was well alight and then coshed Nicholson, dragged him indoors and helped those wayward sparks towards him?'

'It makes more sense than anything else you've suggested,' I said.

'They found traces of accelerant,' he said. 'Not petrol. We'll know soon enough. Probably something that Nicholson already kept in the house.'

Pieces of scorched clothing lay around the remains of the smaller blaze where they had been pulled clear of the flames. Brownlow told someone to gather these up.

Then the fire officer called to him and he left me.

I crouched down and pushed a stick into the sodden ash and tatters of material.

Being persuaded by Marco to get rid of the last of his wife's clothing, and then leaving the remains of this smaller fire alongside the larger one, made perfect sense, made just enough connections – especially if Fowler and Marco were about to start telling identical stories – to tie Nicholson, and Nicholson alone, to his murdered wife. I could imagine Fowler's puzzled, aggrieved tone as the details of Nicholson's death were put to him.

Something in the scattered remains of the smaller fire caught my eye – a piece of brightly coloured material. I fished it out and held it, squeezing it dry and feeling the water drip through my fingers. I sniffed at it, catching the last of whatever faint smell it still possessed. I regretted not having asked Jane Nicholson's sister what she'd been wearing on the day she had disappeared.

Brownlow called me over and I put the material in my pocket.

'Any sign of Marco yet?' I asked him.

He shook his head. 'And Fowler, apparently, is still at the Guildhall.'

'Of course he is. What if he used someone else to do this?'

'Then Marco had better be doubly sure of whatever insurance he's holding. You don't honestly think we're going to find something here tying the fire to Marco, do you? A favourite signet ring or an inscribed watch, perhaps?'

Two men in white suits passed us, each carrying a bag to gather up what remained of Nicholson's wife's clothes.

Beyond where the house had stood, the ambulance negotiated the uneven ground towards the lane.

'By the time you get any forensic – for what it'll be worth – Fowler and Marco are going to be home and dry,' I said.

'Thank you for pointing that out to me. What do you suggest I do – go back to the Guildhall and arrest Fowler in front of all his new friends while the ink's still wet on their precious contracts?'

'It'd be a start,' I said.

'No, it wouldn't.' There was a black mark on his brow where he'd wiped a hand across his face.

I was about to leave him and go to Sunny when my phone rang.

'Who?' Brownlow mouthed to me.

I didn't recognize the number. I answered. It was Laura Lei calling to tell me that she'd just had a visit from Louise Brooks, who had been kept out of the house by several of Laura's friends, and who had then become angry and abusive. The exhibition was over, she said, and her model of Helen Brooks was in the house.

I told her I'd get to her as soon as possible.

'I take it that wasn't Marco with his confession and with smoke in his lungs,' Brownlow said.

I told him who Laura was, but in his eyes, the investigation had long since left Helen Brooks and everything that had happened to her far behind.

I asked him for a lift back into Hull for me and Sunny, and he called the driver of our car to me. He would have to remain at the site for at least another hour. We made arrangements for me to give him my full statement later in the day.

'Will you let me know if Marco shows up?' I asked him.

'Only if it turns out to be any of your business,' he said. 'Get in the car.'

I went to Sunny.

'"Local Hero Dies In Tragic Blaze"?' he said as we walked to the waiting car.

'Try "Clothes Of Murdered Wife Lead To Richly Deserved Fifth Killing",' I said.

I climbed into the car with him, indicating for him to say nothing that might be overheard by either of the two men in the front and reported back to Brownlow.

43

We arrived at Park Grove an hour later. Sunny had been reluctant to accompany me, preferring instead to return to the agency and work on the story of the fire. He gave the film from his camera to a developer on Spring Bank. The prints would be ready in an hour. When he asked me why I wanted him to go with me to Laura Lei's, I showed him the piece of material I'd retrieved from the fire.

I told him what I thought it was, and where I thought I'd seen it before.

What I told him alarmed him.

'And you never thought to mention this to Brownlow?' he said.

'I didn't want him to take his eyes off Fowler,' I said.

He tried calling Yvonne, but her phone was switched off. We both hoped she might have returned to the agency by then, but she hadn't.

We reached Park Grove. Laura Lei looked out of the

window at the front of the house as we approached the door.

She let us in. Her encounter with Louise Brooks had clearly shaken her. Four boys her own age sat around a television in the front room. Laura introduced them to us. They had all been there earlier when Louise had arrived, and had prevented her from entering.

She led us through to the room at the rear of the house.

The model of Helen Brooks stood beside the window, a fourth presence among us.

It was the first time Sunny had seen the sculpture and he went to examine it while Laura made us a drink.

'What did Louise say she wanted?'

She nodded at the life-size figure. 'She knew the exhibition ended yesterday.'

'And that you'd bring the model of Helen back here?'

'Where else? She offered to buy it from me. She told me that her mother was more ill than anyone realized, that she might soon die.'

'You think she wanted to buy it so that she could destroy it?'

'When I refused to sell it to her, she offered to pay *me* to destroy it.'

I looked to Sunny to ensure he'd heard everything she'd said. He examined various parts of the model. He asked Laura how it all held together, how long it had taken her to accumulate the various pieces.

'We collected them together,' she said. 'Helen and me.'

'What *do* you intend doing with it now?' I asked her.

She said she didn't know. There was a permanent display at the university, she said. She'd offered the piece to them, but someone – she didn't know who – had declined.

'Louise became abusive the instant I told her I had no intention of letting her in,' she said. 'She said the piece was rightfully hers, and that everything I'd done, from making it, to exhibiting it, to bringing it here now had been done deliberately to hurt and embarrass her, and to make her mother's last few days even more unbearable than they already were. Is she really that ill?'

I nodded.

'I never met her. Helen hardly mentioned her. I don't think they ever spoke or saw each other for the few months before Helen died. Once Louise came back, it was just easier for Helen to stay away.' She gave Sunny his drink.

He sipped at it, grimaced, and said, 'Delicious.'

'Gunpowder tea,' she said. 'It's refreshing.'

'You're Chinese,' he said. He took another sip and pulled the same face. He asked her if he could take pictures of the sculpture and she told him to go ahead.

She said she would leave the city soon. She had already applied for several jobs in London.

'Where's that?' Sunny said. He had lived there for seven years. It was where his estranged wife and their thirteen-year-old daughter had died.

Laura went to stand beside him. She held her cup to the model's lips.

'I talk to her,' she said. 'I sometimes dress her up.'

I told her that Louise had sorted through Helen's

462

photos long before bringing them to me and then going through the motions of searching them again.

'What does it matter?' she said.

I explained to Sunny about the triptych of collages. I admitted that even though I knew a great many pictures had been taken from Helen's files, I had never been able to establish which ones, or why. I told them of my blackmail theory – either Helen blackmailing Fowler with something she'd captured on film; or Louise attempting to do the same to him with something she'd come across amid her sister's possessions after her death.

Sunny was sceptical. 'It would have come out by now,' he said. 'One way or another, Fowler would have told you all about it.' He continued to move around the model, taking pictures. Just like the police photographer had moved around Nicholson's corpse. He continued asking Laura about its constituent parts and how these had been put together.

'*Will* you destroy it?' I asked her, guessing that this was what she was now going to do to the figure.

'That was another reason I wanted you to come,' she said.

'To watch it happen?'

'You could at least tell Helen's mother what I'd done. So that if she genuinely was upset by it, then she could stop worrying.'

'Why not take Louise Brooks's money and *then* destroy it,' I suggested, knowing that Helen's own exhibit had been the cause of considerably greater concern and regret to Alison Brooks.

'If I did that, it would look as though I was doing it because it was what she wanted me to do. I loved Helen.

I really loved her. To Louise, all this is just an uncomfortable reminder of something she'll be happy to put behind her. To me it's – it's—' She started to cry.

'You don't have to explain,' I said.

'Yes I do. Because there was something I never told you.' She held her hands over her eyes.

Sunny looked up at the remark.

'It's something I should have made clear to you right from the start,' Laura said.

She rose from where she sat beside me and went across the room to the model at the window. She caressed Helen Brooks's upper arm, held a finger to the lipstick pieces of her lips. She ran her hand down over the papier-mâché and material of Helen's stomach and rested it on the clippings of pubic hair and used sanitary towels at her crotch. She hesitated, withdrew and then replaced her hand. She seemed momentarily uncertain of herself, half lost in her reverie of remembering.

I started to say something, and Sunny told me to shut up.

Laura Lei started to pull at the glued-on hair and the stained towels, letting them fall to the floor as they came loose. Her tears continued to run unchecked over her cheeks. She pulled harder at the thicker layers beneath the hair and scraps of material – the old tights and knickers – until she had torn a hole in the model. She held her other hand against Helen's chest to keep her steady and upright. Eventually, the hole she was tearing was large enough for her to reach inside the figure, where she groped around for a moment, and then withdrew holding a collection of white sticks.

She held these out to me.

'Pregnancy testing kits,' she said.

She laid them along the arm of the chair in which I sat, rearranging them, placing them in a specific order.

'It was Helen's idea.'

Sunny came closer.

Laura Lei started holding the sticks up for me so that I might see them more clearly. There were ten of the indicators, and she counted as she performed the simple ritual.

She paused at number eight.

The previous seven indicators had shown a single, vague blue line at their tips. The final three showed double, darker lines.

'Spot the difference,' she said.

'Helen Brooks was pregnant,' I said, the words and the thought and the realization and all they implied forming simultaneously, and all three of them far ahead of any true understanding of what I was being shown and told.

'Three months,' Laura said. 'The final fuck-up. The fuck-up to set the seal on all the other fuck-ups. Fuck-up: The Musical.'

Sunny photographed the indicators on the arm of the chair, and then the three Laura still held.

'Who knew?' I asked her.

'Who do you think?'

'Her mother?'

She shook her head.

'Louise? Fowler?'

She raised her eyebrows and shrugged. 'Helen told me she'd told her sister – something to do with Louise working at a hospital – Birmingham, she said – and being able to get her a scan without anyone here ever finding out.'

'And Fowler?'

'She didn't want him to know. I thought Louise would have told you all this by now.'

Sunny took the three indicators from her and laid them with the others.

Laura Lei's sobbing became convulsive.

Sunny put his arm around her and pulled her to sit beside him on the sofa. He was three times her size and she was lost in his embrace. His hand rested on her head and he stroked her short black hair.

I looked from them to the hole in Helen Brooks's groin, at its frayed edges and at the darkness inside. I heard the boys in the other room through the thin wall, cheering something on the television. The sun coming through the window beside the punctured model showed every collapsed web, dead fly and desiccated spider of that long dry summer, and I looked up into it and was momentarily blinded by it.

44

'I think your priority now is working out what it all means,' Sunny said.

We sat together on a bench in Pearson Park, the glasshouses behind us. Ahead of us the grass was covered with sunbathers and playing children.

'It *means* Louise lied to me from the very beginning,' I said. I tried to remember what she'd told me about her own unwanted pregnancy and termination ten years earlier.

We'd come into the park from Park Grove before returning to the agency. Sunny called Yvonne every ten minutes, but her phone remained switched off. He didn't share my concerns regarding the implications of Helen Brooks's pregnancy, and he in turn was angry that I didn't share his concern over Yvonne, who he was convinced had been arrested. There was nothing from her on his voicemail.

'It means that not only did Fowler kill Alison

Brooks's daughter, but her grandchild, too,' I said. It was only the beginning of my understanding.

'About which she was totally unaware,' he said. 'What are you going to do – tell her? Don't you think one unresolved and unpunished murder might be enough for her to have to cope with at the moment?' He'd been reluctant to leave Laura Lei, and had followed me out of the house only at her promise to call him if Louise returned.

'Are you saying that Louise kept it from me for the same reason – because her mother never knew and she wanted her never to find out?'

'It's more than a possibility. What would you want if you were the woman's only surviving child?'

'I'd probably do the same,' I admitted.

'Precisely.' He called Yvonne again, but there was still no answer.

I offered to go with him to the Queen's Gardens police station.

'Too early,' he said.

'It's why Louise made such a big thing of the photographs she'd taken from Helen's files,' I said. 'She wanted me thinking more about *them* than about Laura's model because she knew what I might find there.'

He shook his head. 'You were never going to find anything without Laura Lei showing you. Talk to Louise. Tell her you know. I don't see what more you can do, or what real difference it's likely to make to anything, not now. You've got Brownlow sufficiently interested again. Leave things to him. Fowler or Marco will fuck up eventually.'

'What – and this time Brownlow will be waiting and all will be revealed?'

'No. But enough might come to light to secure convictions concerning Nicholson and his wife.'

'Nothing's ever going to do that for Helen Brooks,' I said.

He took out a handkerchief and wiped the sweat from his face. 'I imagine Fowler's been giving all this considerably more thought than you have,' he said.

'Meaning he's got his own clean, well-lighted path out of all of this and that nothing's going to stop him from walking?'

'In all likelihood, yes. I think it's something you ought to get used to.'

I shook my head.

'Suit yourself. But suppose Alison Brooks *did* know right from the start about Helen's pregnancy – how would you feel about things then? If I were you, I'd be thinking long and hard about how you've been used in all of this.'

'Meaning if I hadn't gone to Fowler with my theory about Marco, Nicholson and Nicholson's wife, Nicholson would still be alive now? And if I hadn't gone back to the salvage yard, the old guy there might still be alive?'

'I'm just saying it's something you should think about, that's all. No one made Fowler – or whoever – do what he did.'

'But I pushed him into jumping sooner rather than later?'

'That would be one interpretation. Another would be that it was what Louise Brooks wanted you to do all along because she knew what was likely to happen.'

'And you think she might have gone to Fowler with everything I discovered about Nicholson before I did?'

'It makes sense in light of what just happened to him,' he said.

'And if Marco killed Nicholson without Fowler knowing about it?'

'Same thing. Marco still knows what he knows about the night Helen Brooks died, and about what happened to Nicholson's wife as a consequence of that. Now it's just his word against Fowler's. Like I said, leave them to Brownlow and start thinking about what you're going to tell Alison Brooks. Fowler's only let you go on pushing him this far because he needed to see how it was all going to play out; because he wanted his deal with Webster to be completed; and because he needed to know as much as you did about what was going on between Marco and Nicholson. You might think you've been worrying him by bringing all this back out into the light again, but you've also done him one or two favours along the way.'

'Meaning Marco's going to turn up dead soon, and all Fowler's going to do is point out the connection between Marco and the Nicholsons and finally wash his hands of the whole affair?'

'Or perhaps Marco will go the same way Helen Brooks and the trafficker went. Perhaps he'll sleep with the shellfish for a very long time to come. Either way, there would be nothing left to tie Fowler – via either Marco or Nicholson – to what happened to Helen Brooks out on the sea. If it makes you feel any better about your own part in it all, go to Louise and tell her that you know she's been lying to you all along.'

'And then what? Listen to her say, "So what?"?'

I regretted the remark immediately.

I regretted even more the fact that everything he'd just suggested, every speculation, guess and connection he'd made had been wrong, and that I'd known before sitting with him on the bench that the truth of everything lay in another direction completely. The piece of cloth in my pocket told me that much. All I'd been doing was using him as a sounding board for the version of the truth I most wanted now to fit the changing facts.

Finally exasperated by my remark, he rose from the bench to leave me, and as he did so, his phone rang. He answered immediately. 'Yvonne.' He closed his eyes. 'Arrested?' He said nothing for a minute. 'I never even gave you a second thought,' he said. 'Plus, there have been one or two developments out here in the real world.' He asked her where she was and told her how long it would take him to get to her with his solicitor.

He repeated everything she'd told him, unable to hide his relief.

'You'd better go to her,' I said.

He started walking away from me, then paused and turned. 'Think about what I said,' he called to me. 'It's always wise to know when your part in something's over.'

'Tell Yvonne I said, "Hello, jailbird."'

'She'll appreciate it. It'll help with her Woman Of The People image.' He turned away and continued walking.

Waiting until he was out of sight beyond the glasshouses, I took out the piece of material

I'd picked from the edge of Nicholson's small fire.

I laid it in my palm, smoothing out its creases. I looked at it closely and sniffed it again. And then I closed my hand around it and put it back in my pocket.

I left the park in the opposite direction to that taken by Sunny.

On Beverley Road I caught a bus back into the city centre.

I walked from Victoria Square along the marina back to Humber Street, where I sat for the rest of the afternoon clearing my mind and trying to decide what to do next.

At six, I went to the Minerva, sat outside for an hour with a drink, walked to the empty pier and then to the footbridge over the river. The aquarium rose starkly above me, its tinted glass in shadow, no longer reflecting the sun which heliographed the building's presence like the coming future over the old and empty harbour and the silted dock basin.

At dusk, I returned briefly to Humber Street.

I called Louise Brooks and left her a message, asking her to call me.

The rain which had held off for the previous six weeks was again promised for either later that same night or early the next morning. It had already rained in Wales and the south-west, and summer storms were gathering on the far side of the Pennines. The forecaster on the radio sounded desperate to be believed, as though his need for this had some bearing on what now happened, on whether the rain finally came or if it continued to stay away. He told those of us who were the most desperate for the downpour – those of

472

us who felt as though *we* had dried out over the summer — to pray for it. Just put your hands together, lift your faces to the sky and pray for it, he said, near-evangelical now in his own uncertain desire.

45

I called Andrew Brownlow the next morning. Everything I asked him about the fire made him more evasive. It was almost midday; I'd been trying to contact him since nine.

Finally, he started to answer me.

'To begin with,' he said, 'all this is preliminary. Nicholson died of *both* smoke inhalation and the blow to his skull. The fumes meant he was probably unconscious when the timber fell and finished the job.'

'And that's the all-inclusive official line, is it?'

'Just listen. There was a two-inch bolt in the timber. The skull fracture was just as likely to have been caused by that as by anything else.'

'You can't even convince yourself of that,' I said.

'Excuse me? Man found lying in burned-out wreckage of his home, lungs full of soot, beam with bolt lying over his skull. It sort of adds up. If you know differently, then tell me. Now.' He waited for me to say something.

'And the small fire of burned clothes?' I said.

'You were the one who told me why Nicholson might want to get rid of the last of his wife's possessions. There were patches of burned grass between that fire and the house. Nicholson had tins of turps, white spirit, boat varnish *and* diesel in the lean-to. He was covering the last of his tracks and it all went wrong.'

'And, presumably, you've spoken to Fowler between then and now.'

'He was at the Guildhall at eleven in the morning. He left at two. The fire officer puts the fire as starting somewhere between twelve and one.'

'Good margin of error calculation on Fowler's part.'

'Believe what you want. Whoever started the fire, it wasn't Fowler.'

'And he, of course, has no idea who might have done it, or who else might have wanted Nicholson dead.'

'Accidents happen, Mr Rivers.'

'They do in the cases *you're* supposed to be investigating.' I expected him to hang up, but he knew as well as I did that however Nicholson had died, he had been killed, and that the fire had been started in an attempt to cover this up.

'You're not telling me something,' he said eventually. 'Why is that, I wonder. Because you think it gives you the edge? Because you know that, whatever else happens, nothing bad is now going to find its way back to Fowler, and you plan on doing something about that yourself? Or, as Fowler again suggested to me yesterday, is it because you're not seeing things as clearly as you once did and you now have a wholly personal motive in all of this, in trying to pin everything on

Fowler and get yourself even deeper into Louise Brooks's good books?'

'That's—'

'What? A malicious and unfounded allegation? Of course it is. But nine times out of ten, they're the ones that make the most sense. That's why people make them. You need to look more closely at the cards you think *you're* still holding, Mr Rivers, before you start pointing out everyone else's deficiencies.'

'Meaning?' The word was a reflex; I knew exactly what he meant. Everything he was telling me, Sunny had already told me in the park the previous day.

'Meaning that until Helen Brooks's evidence-covered body shows up, nothing is going to connect her death to Fowler — not in the way you and her sister want it to be connected. Meaning that without Nicholson, and without his wife — who might or might not have known about what *you* allege he alleges he saw — then ditto. Meaning that no one, Fowler included, knows where Marco might now be. Meaning we can all make our guesses, Mr Rivers, but that's all they are. And even though you might think your guesses carry more weight than mine, they don't. Meaning that Louise Brooks herself never once came to us after the coroner's verdict with any of this. Why do you think that was? Why do you think she came to you with it all with her cleavage showing and her legs opening and closing until you properly understood all she was asking you to do? I daresay you've asked yourself the same question, but I don't imagine for one minute that you've looked too hard for an answer. You're very quiet now, for instance.'

I hadn't spoken to Louise since seeing her at the hospital.

'What's wrong, Mr Rivers?' he said. 'Some of those benefits been withdrawn a little sooner than you'd anticipated?'

'Where do *you* think Marco is?' I asked him.

'I think he's somewhere where he hopes Fowler will never be able to find him. At least not until he makes Fowler fully aware of the benefits of the pair of them living together into a ripe and peaceful old age. And when that happens, then the last of *your* tiny cracks closes shut and stays shut.'

'What does the fire officer think?' I said.

The question exasperated him further. 'I've already told you – he's got his source, an accelerant, and a probable cause of death. And, like me, he's got better things to do than waste his time getting your love life back on course. Besides, he's got other things on his mind right now.'

'Such as?'

'Not that it's any of your business, but there was a fire at a house on Mayfield Street early this morning. Multi-occupancy.'

'Asylum-seekers?'

'There you go again.'

'Owned by' – I almost said Fowler – 'Webster?' Mayfield Street was a minute's walk to the west of the agency, just as Walmsley Street had been a minute to the east.

'You're grasping,' he said. 'No one was killed or even badly injured.'

'Just terrified out of their wits? What happened?

Webster start his brownfield site clearances earlier than expected?'

'The trouble with you, Rivers, is that you want all this to fit too neatly into *your* version of events. And when something doesn't fit, you start twisting things and seeing things where they don't exist. Stop looking. You got what you wanted. Stop pretending you're some kind of champion of the underdog, because you're not.'

'Like Yvonne, you mean?'

'Is that what she is? She's ridiculous. She'll get a fifty-quid fine and be bound over to keep the peace for a year. It's hardly the Bandit Queen, is it? I'm going now. I hope this is our last conversation. Either that, or I hope that the next time we talk you've got something to give me that makes some sense from where *I'm* standing.'

He hung up.

46

I waited until the early evening before finally returning to the hospital.

Alison Brooks still lay unconscious, her arm fed by the drip, her face half-covered by the oxygen mask. She looked pale, the skin of her forehead and cheeks tight. Her eyes fluttered occasionally, but never opened.

I was there to do a terrible thing, and perhaps because I was the coward both Sunny and Brownlow had accused me of being, I wanted to reassure myself that Alison Brooks, in these last hours of her life, was finally beyond all true understanding of what I was there to do. She was dying, and I was there to take away from her the last of everything she had once loved and held dear to her.

I sat with her for ten minutes. I held her hand, but nothing registered with her — nothing to suggest that she was even remotely aware of my presence.

The liquid painkiller continued to drip in its slowly deflating bag. I followed its course through the slender pipe and the same steady dripping in the valve at her wrist.

The ward was peaceful at the end of the day. There were a few other late visitors, but most of these sat in the same uncomfortable silences around the other beds.

Louise came to me at eight. Her hair was wet. She looked tired.

'I went home for a shower and a change of clothes,' she said. She showed no surprise at seeing me there. She looked at her mother. 'She's been like that since you were last here.'

'Is she dying?' I asked her.

'The doctor thinks so.'

'Did he say how long?'

'Nothing too specific. You got to talk to her just in time.'

'To tell her everything she wanted to hear?' I said.

She looked at me for a moment. 'Everything *I* wanted her to hear, you mean? You can say it. I know you've been trying to get in touch. I know you've probably worked everything out by now. I know why you're here. I've taken a few days' leave so that I can be with her until . . .'

'Can she hear us?' I asked her.

She shook her head.

'Is this why you didn't come to the Guildhall yesterday?' I said.

'Fowler's big day? I never had any intention of giving him the satisfaction of seeing me there.'

I rose from the chair beside her mother and she took

my place. She held and caressed her mother's fingers.

'I found this,' I said. I put the piece of material on the bed beside their two hands.

'Her yellow scarf,' she said. 'That was careless of me.'

'I recognized it from her first visit to me.'

'I hoped Nicholson might still have some of his wife's clothes around the place – you know, as proof that he was still expecting her to return to him.'

'Marco will have talked him into getting rid of everything long ago.'

'I took some of my own stuff along, and some of the things my mother would never wear again, just in case.'

'Because you not only wanted to kill Nicholson, but also to point to his lost wife. Why?'

'Because no one ever pointed to my lost sister – at least no one who ever counted. And because after all you'd told me about Nicholson, I knew as well as you did that she'd be the key to Fowler and Marco's involvement in everything else.'

'The police don't believe me,' I said. 'And without her body or a confession from Marco, there's nothing else I can do.'

She leaned forward and kissed her mother's cheek. 'Can we go outside?' she said. 'Anywhere, away from the bed.'

She rose and I followed her out of the ward and to the lifts.

We descended in silence.

As we reached the ground floor, she asked me if she could have the piece of scorched yellow scarf. I gave it to her.

'I'll let you have it back,' she said. 'You'll need it as evidence.'

'Perhaps,' I said.

We walked through the reception area and out of the main entrance.

'I cut the labels out of everything,' she said. 'I made sure that all that was left was enough to be identified as pieces of a woman's clothing. I even sprayed some of Nicholson's wife's cheap and nasty scent onto the remains. He's still got a bottle in the bedroom. Probably sprays it onto his pillow on the few occasions he wants to remember her.'

'I smelled it,' I said.

'*You* were never meant to go there,' she said.

We crossed Argyle Street and sat on the low wall of the hospital car park.

'Did you kill him because of what I uncovered about his lies concerning the night Helen died?'

'Of course I did. But don't blame yourself for any of this. I had a choice. Just as Nicholson and Fowler and Marco had choices. No one forced me to do what I did.'

'Not like you believe Fowler forced Helen?'

'Is that what I believe? How much forcing do you think it took? It was *her* choice to stay with Fowler after everything my mother and I had done to try and warn her, after everything we'd told her about him.'

'Beginning with how he'd cheated your mother over the florist shops?'

'He didn't cheat her. She had the chance to sell early, but she didn't; she held on for reasons which made no good sense. That wasn't his fault.'

'It was still something you made sure *I* knew

about before I heard it all from Fowler himself,' I said.

'We thought it best. Or at least I thought it best, and persuaded her to go along with telling you.'

'The same time you both lied to me about being at the hospital together immediately after she'd been to see me?'

'We thought it might add a sense of urgency to the proceedings – not that we needed it, as it turns out.' She looked across the road to the fourteen floors of the hospital, searching for the block of light within which her dying mother now lay.

'And when *you* first came to see me alone?' I said.

'I waited. I took the morning off work, waited, and then made everything appear casual, unplanned.'

'I was late that morning,' I said. 'You must have waited for two hours. Why?'

She shrugged. 'Because anything else might have seemed too much, too obvious?'

'And because you wanted me properly involved and up to scratch on everything – Fowler in particular – before I started putting two and two together for myself?'

'Something like that.'

'What did you kill Nicholson with?'

'A crowbar. From Maintenance. No one missed it. I've still got it; I'll give it to you.'

'The police think a falling timber crushed his skull.'

'I saw it come down on him.'

'Was he alive before it fell?'

She nodded. 'I watched him burn, scrambling around, barely conscious, choking. I could see that he was still breathing. When the timber fell, everything else started falling.'

'And so you left.'

'And so I left.'

'What if he'd still been alive, even then?'

'And what if Helen had still been alive when he helped Marco drag her off the yacht?'

'You even warned Nicholson that I was going to visit him, didn't you. Why?'

'Just to get him jumpy again. I had no idea about his wife. I pretended to be calling from the coroner's court, told him there had been some new developments, that someone might need to talk to him again.'

'Making sure he went straight to either Fowler or Marco.'

'I thought Fowler. I was wrong.'

'And then *I* showed up asking questions.'

'You did what we asked of you,' she said. 'It was the only way to get things moving.'

'It seems a little callous to have waited fifteen months before—'

'What – because I waited until my mother's cancer had returned and knew that this time she would refuse all their treatment? Because I used her illness to convince *you* of our sincerity, of our *need* to see all this resolved once and for all?'

I nodded. 'I also assume that *you* believed that Helen's death had something to do with your mother's decision not to accept any more treatment, that she'd lost the will to persist, to endure.'

' "Endure"?' she said disbelievingly. 'Of course she'd lost the will to *endure*. This was the third time it had come back. And how exactly do you think that made *me* feel? How long would she have *persisted*, how long would she have *endured* if it had been *me* who had been killed, and if Helen had still been alive?' She covered her mouth with her hand. Her exhaustion showed in her every word and gesture. Her feet were off the ground and she swung them gently from side to side.

'I understand what you thought you'd lost with the arrival of Helen,' I said.

'I didn't *think* I'd lost it: I lost it.'

'And the fact that she was pregnant?' I asked her.

She stopped swaying her feet and bowed her head.

Ahead of us, an ambulance, its siren blaring, negotiated the Anlaby Road roundabout and went into the hospital driveway. We both stopped talking to watch it.

'Would it have given too much away to have told me?' I asked her.

'My mother never knew.'

'And you were never certain whether Fowler knew or not, and you couldn't risk him throwing it back at her?' I knew that this could not have been the full story.

'It was more complicated,' she said, unwilling to explain further.

'Did it have something to do with your own termination?'

'My mother always wanted grandchildren. After my termination, I was never able to do that for her.'

'And the next-best option, ten years later, was Fowler's baby to your drug-addicted sister.'

'Fowler's baby to my drug-addicted sister who didn't give a toss one way or the other about whether she had the baby or not, and who, in all likelihood, would have held either the decision or the kid itself over my mother like a sword.'

'How hard did your mother try and persuade you to leave the circumstances of Helen's death behind the two of you?' I said.

'Hard enough.'

'And then the cancer returned and she finally relented? Is that why she called John Maxwell after all those years – just to help set everything in motion?'

'It's probably no consolation,' she said, 'but if we'd gone to anyone less interested, less involved than you, then everything might have taken too long.'

'And you still weren't sure how long she had left. Is that why she pretended to be much better than she felt when she came to see me?'

She held up the piece of yellow material. 'Wearing this. Yes. She was laid up for three days afterwards. I was waiting round the corner for her. That's why I made the follow-up visit and not her. We were both worried in case we'd left it too late.'

'Was it you who told Fowler she was ill?'

'Fowler?'

'When he first broke into my office with Marco, he knew then that your mother was going to die. Just like he knew from the very start that Helen's body was never going to reappear. All that mattered to him then was that everything would end with the death of your mother.'

'Perhaps Helen told him.' She was lying.

'Fifteen months earlier? No – you'd already seen him. Why? To plead with him?'

'Plead? Plead?'

'To threaten him, then. To tell him that you knew something about him that Helen had told you before she was killed. To threaten him with the non-existent photograph of her proof of whatever that might have been. It was why you let me believe that Helen herself might have been blackmailing him.'

'Think what you like,' she said. 'What does any of it matter now?'

'Of course it matters.'

She pointed to the hospital. '*That's* what matters to me now, none of this.'

'You still killed Nicholson,' I said.

'Why don't you crow a bit louder and tell me I've probably saved Fowler a job?' She turned to face me. 'Yes, I killed Nicholson. What now — you run back to the police with the news, they arrest me and my mother gets to die all alone up there?'

I shook my head.

She calmed down and put her hand on my arm.

I struggled hard for the words to say what I next wanted to say to her.

She sensed this, and said, 'What?' But even as the question died between us, I knew that she knew what I was about to say.

'You killed the man in the salvage yard,' I said. 'Why? What did *he* know about what had happened on the yacht?'

'Nothing. He called me. After your visit.'

'Because he knew I'd gone there looking for something that both you and Fowler had gone there looking for fifteen months earlier? What was it? Something Helen had hidden? Evidence of how she'd been killed, who she'd been with? What?'

She shrugged. 'He told me he'd called Fowler and told him about your visit,' she said.

'Did he tell you he'd found something you might both be interested in?'

'No, but he said it would be worth my while going to see him and taking along my cheque book.'

'And you think he'd already said the same to Fowler?'

'It seemed more than likely. The man had just lost his job.'

'What do you think Fowler did?' I asked her.

'When I got there he confessed that he hadn't yet called Fowler.'

'Because he knew that Fowler's approach to the situation might not lead to the outcome he'd hoped for? And when you knew for certain that you were the only one he'd spoken to . . .'

'He was welding something. There was a stack of empty canisters nearby. He told me he was there illegally, made a joke about me promising not to tell anyone.'

'Which you promised him.'

'Which I promised him.'

'*Had* he found anything?' I said.

She shook her head.

'He told me he had, but I knew he was lying.'

'Neither you nor your mother told me you'd been to the yard.'

'We knew you'd find your way there eventually.'

'But you still didn't want me to know that you'd already been there or to start thinking too soon about what you'd gone looking for.'

'We'd just lost everything we'd hoped for in the coroner's court,' she said. 'We went because we knew that if we could find some evidence of who'd been on the yacht with Helen, and which implicated Fowler, which *proved* he'd been lying when he said he didn't know who'd been with her – who *he'd* killed – then we could have had the case re-opened immediately, while the police were still interested. You know as well as I do that everything fell apart and Helen was denied justice because everyone just sat back and waited and then lost interest. Why go looking for the absolute truth when all those convenient little suppositions and guesses amount to something that might be ninety-nine per cent true anyway?'

'You still killed him knowing I'd assume Fowler had been back there, knowing I'd assume my visit to him might have alerted him to the possibility of making some money now that he was unemployed.'

'Fowler wouldn't have tolerated his demands for long,' she said.

'And you did? After which you still let me go on believing that Fowler had killed him, and that I'd led him back to the man.'

'I had no choice.'

'No – you had a choice, and you made it.'

'And *you* saw the hole in the cabin wall where someone had done their best to hide something else.'

It had grown dark by then, and the streetlights flickered into life, darkening further the sky above us.

'How long do you think Helen had been on the yacht?' I asked her.

'What does it matter?'

'It's what alerted me to Fowler's lies about the day she died,' I said. 'He told me when I first saw him that he hadn't seen her for four days beforehand. On the day she died, he told me he'd called her at home to ensure she hadn't forgotten their lunch appointment.'

'And?'

'When I saw Laura Lei, she told me Helen hadn't been at Park Grove for that same length of time. She certainly wasn't there on the day Fowler went to so much trouble to place himself with witnesses every minute of the day. He was lying. The trafficker had turned up and he had nowhere else to keep him out of sight.'

'Using Helen to make sure the man didn't get bored.'

'It would account for all the provisions she took on board, her coming and going.'

'Then perhaps Fowler had her killed because she was the only piece of his plan that didn't fit neatly into place.' But even as she said it, she knew this was unlikely, that it weakened all our reasoning, even if neither of us yet fully understood why.

'You burned the man's face in the salvage yard to draw attention to the fact that he'd been working there illegally,' I said. 'I thought at first that Fowler had tortured him to find out what he might have known.'

'He fell close to where his torch was still burning,' she said. 'I just nudged it towards him.'

'Was that another choice you didn't have?'

'He was already dead,' she said.

'Unlike Nicholson, when you watched him crawling through the burning wreckage,' I said. 'And the fire of clothes – what exactly was that – another diversion – another pointer just in case no one was ready to believe my story about Nicholson?'

'I wanted his death to *count* for something, to prod someone into action.'

'And to make me believe that I'd been right in all I'd assumed. You watched a man *burn*.'

'And Fowler and Marco, and perhaps even

Nicholson, had known for days beforehand that Helen was going to be used and then killed.'

'Is that what all this has really been about – revenge?'

'Perhaps.'

'And to keep your mother from ever finding out that Helen was pregnant?'

'It would have—'

'She wanted the *truth*,' I said, my raised voice attracting the attention of a group of visitors returning to their cars.

Neither of us spoke for a minute.

'I know what she *said* she wanted,' she said eventually.

'But you'd already convinced yourself that you knew better than everyone else how that so-called "truth" might be made more presentable, more acceptable. Nothing to do with the fact that you – *and you alone* – couldn't accept that Helen was pregnant and all that implied.'

'She wouldn't have kept it,' she said.

'You don't know that.'

'The only reason she told *me* was to rub my face in it. I arranged for her to have the scan in Birmingham. She came to stay with me for a few days. I knew then that she was using heroin regularly. It was all Simon-this and Simon-that. Wait until *Simon* heard. What *he* wouldn't do for her, for the pair of them, what a hold she'd have over him.'

'Fowler himself wouldn't necessarily have seen it like that.'

'There's nothing so certain.' She asked me for a cigarette. I gave her one. The night air had grown suddenly cooler. Clouds had been building since the middle of the afternoon, but there was still no sign of the coming rain.

'You told Fowler that I was somehow connected to Irina Kapec and all she was trying to do for the asylum-seekers. Why?'

'Because I knew that he didn't really give a toss about all this renewed interest in Helen's death. All he ever cared about was the bad publicity it attracted to him. Why should he? The bodies were never going to reappear; his own alibi had stood the test of the court; Marco and Nicholson were both still implicated and their stories or silence guaranteed.'

'And so you thought you'd keep Fowler unsettled by pointing him towards me, and then by pointing me towards what concerned him the most.'

'His deal with Webster. The tenants he was about to offload and the wonderful new existence he was about to create for himself with everyone else's blessing and with their praises ringing in his ears, yes.' She raised her head to blow smoke above us.

'You led him to where I was seeing Yvonne and Irina in the bar on Prince's Avenue.'

'Anonymously. He has a hundred informants. I let him know you'd been asking his tenants awkward questions.'

'And he believed you?'

'Of course he did.'

'And you also did it because you knew I'd find it hard to refuse to help Yvonne once she knew who I was investigating and she'd told me everything concerning her own knowledge of Fowler via Irina Kapec. You deliberately confused things to keep both me and Fowler uncertain of what was really happening.'

'I kept *you* pointed in the right direction,' she said. 'That's all.'

'By paying someone to attack the woman in Walmsley Street, knowing that I was close by, and that you could then break into the agency without being disturbed?'

'You'd already told me about how easily Fowler came and went as he pleased. I knew you'd think he was the one who'd broken in.'

'And who'd instigated the attack on the woman. What were you looking for?'

'Nothing in particular. I just wanted to make sure there was nothing in any of Summers's files that might have led *you* to think that I might have had any motive other than avenging Helen's death in any of this.'

'And once again the break-in acted as a pointer. You knew that both Sunny and I would point our fingers at Fowler for that and for the attack on the woman. It never really mattered for us to make any more sense of what had happened.'

'I didn't mean for the men I paid to hurt the woman. I just wanted to keep Fowler uncertain concerning what was happening.'

'And perhaps to believe that the men who carried out the attack were somehow connected to the trafficker?'

'Not much I could do about that, either way.'

'They broke her wrist and her fingers,' I said. 'They fractured her ribs and left her face covered in bruises. She was there illegally. She was terrified she was going to be taken to the hospital, found out, and then separated from her children.'

'I honestly didn't—'

'I don't care what you say you *honestly* did or didn't intend to happen. You paid them to do it because it suited you to have it happen. Just as later, when you knew I was no longer as convinced as I might have been regarding all I'd learned from Yvonne about Fowler's deal with Webster, you decided to do something about that, too – again to keep me pointing in the right direction – by sending those pictures to Irina Kapec.'

'I would never have taken it any further.'

'Am I supposed to believe that?'

She bowed and shook her head. 'I did it because I saw how much Yvonne meant to you, and how involved she and Irina Kapec were.'

Another ambulance negotiated the roundabout and the hospital entrance.

'Did you think that the man in the salvage yard had already sold whatever he might have found to Fowler, and that Fowler had destroyed it – either recently or fifteen months ago?'

She nodded. 'I thought he'd been as guilty as Nicholson in keeping Fowler clean and giving everyone else no option but to believe his story and to feel sorry for him.'

'And Laura Lei?' I said.

She looked up at me. 'What about her?'

'*She* knew Helen was pregnant. She might have told your mother.'

'She'd promised Helen she wouldn't.'

'And you believed her? Why?'

'I knew what she and Helen had meant to each other. She told me Helen had asked her to tell no one

494

until she was clear in her own mind what she was going to do about it all.'

'Then why, having already taken away the photographs for Helen's own exhibit, did you try to prevent Laura from showing her model? Because she might have unwittingly revealed Helen's pregnancy to the world?'

She shook her head. 'She would never have done that. She only showed you afterwards because *I* wasn't seeing things clearly and didn't have the sense to back off from her. I pushed her too far, that's all. I was angry that, having agreed not to show the model immediately after Helen's death, she was doing it now, in the middle of all this.'

'And that was why you turned up at the exhibition,' I said. 'Because you knew I'd be there, and because you wanted to make sure she stuck to her word. That was why you wanted to know what she and I had talked about – to reassure yourself that she hadn't revealed anything to me – not necessarily about the pregnancy, but anything that might have diverted me from the course you'd already got mapped out for me.'

'Fowler killed Helen. *He* was the one you needed to keep your eye on.'

'And just as you thought Laura might be about to reveal something to me at the exhibition, you stepped in like a wounded bird and drew me away from her. You even waited until the mayor and the reporters and photographers were approaching her – because you knew I'd think you were there to make trouble for her, and that I'd go to you and persuade you to leave with me before you got the chance to do anything.'

'I didn't hear you complaining at the time.' She turned away from me as she said this.

'You can tell me that *that* was all part of your plan, too,' I said.

'It wasn't.'

'And the run-in with Marco and Nikki outside the restaurant? Did you think *she* might have been about to reveal something she knew about Fowler and Helen – about Helen's pregnancy – before it suited your purpose for me to learn it?'

'I don't care what she knew or thought. She was waiting in the wings to take Helen's place, that's all.'

'You're wrong,' I said. 'She had nothing to do with Helen's death, and you know that. Just as you know that Fowler and Helen were never the all-inclusive item Helen might have wanted to believe they were. It's why any attempt to blackmail Fowler was bound to end badly.'

'I know,' she said. 'I tried to warn her of that, too. She was with me for almost a week in Birmingham. I could see exactly what she was up to. We probably spoke more to each other in that time than we had in the past ten years.'

I told her about the chart the man at the salvage yard had given me. 'She wrote your name, "Lulu", all along one border,' I said.

This small revelation made her gasp. 'Can I see it?' she asked me.

I told her I'd bring the chart to the hospital.

'What now?' she said. She looked beyond me to the hospital as she spoke.

'You have to take care of your mother,' I told her.

'But then you think I should go to Brownlow and tell him everything?'

I nodded. 'Afterwards. Your mother's more important right now.'

She continued looking at the hospital. 'I don't really want to go back in there. They think another day or two at the most.' She turned back to me. 'How did *you* think all this would turn out?' she said.

'It's never something I like to speculate on,' I said.

'Because it invariably points to more of your failures and mistakes than your successes?'

'Something like that. I think I'd have been able to get to Nicholson eventually and that he'd have told the police what really happened the night Helen died.'

'Because he was scared of Fowler again?'

'Perhaps. Or because he would have worked out by then how Fowler and Marco had used him, just as they'd used Helen. And perhaps because he was starting to feel some genuine remorse about what had happened to his wife.'

'And now?' she said.

'And now Marco's disappeared because he thinks Fowler had Nicholson killed and that he'll have left something behind to implicate Marco in the killing. And short of Marco giving himself up and confessing his part in everything, I don't think there's any chance whatsoever of Fowler even coming close to being charged with Helen's death.'

'Something else I have to blame myself for,' she said.

I neither denied nor confirmed this unhappy realization. It was something she'd known all the time we'd been sitting together. She'd known it with every other self-deluding lie she'd told me.

I slid from the wall and stood beside her.

'Go in,' I told her. 'Let me know.'

'Will you come back in the morning?'

'I'll come with you to see Brownlow,' I told her. 'In the morning, whenever.'

'I posted you a cheque earlier,' she said. 'Along with a note saying that as of midday yesterday your services were no longer required, that, effectively, you were no longer employed by me or my mother.'

'Something for me to wave at Brownlow in case he wanted to tie me in with what happened to Nicholson at a minute past noon?'

'If you like.'

'How did you think it would all turn out?' I asked her.

She held out her hands and I helped her down from the wall. 'What's the saying? "Let Justice Prevail or the Heavens Fall."'

'Something like that,' I said.

'Well, they don't, Leo. They don't.' She kissed my cheek and walked back across the road to the hospital.

I watched her go, waiting until she went through the doors and was lost amid the people inside.

It was almost ten. We'd been sitting together for two hours.

I called Sunny, but his phone was switched off.

I called Yvonne, and then listened twenty times to her dial tone before hanging up. I imagined her looking at my number and knowing that I had nothing to say to her that she wanted to hear.

47

I returned to the hospital early the following morning.

It had finally rained during the night, and though not the long-awaited downpour we had been promised, this was now being confidently predicted for later in the day.

I called Yvonne as I walked.

I told her everything Louise Brooks had confessed to me the previous night.

'Has she been arrested?' she asked me.

'Her mother's about to die,' I said.

'And so, once again, what Louise Brooks wants, Louise Brooks gets?' she said. 'She probably even gave you her word that she'd be sat waiting by her mother's bed when you got there.'

'Where would she go?' I said.

'You should listen to yourself sometimes,' she said. 'And I hope you're not holding off taking her to Brownlow because then your own less than noble part in all of this might seem somewhat less than justifiable.'

'Fowler already saw to that,' I said. I told her about the attack on the woman in Walmsley Street and the threats made to Irina Kapec.

She was angry and relieved in equal measure that Louise, and not Fowler, had been responsible. I expected more from her, but she said nothing, perhaps because she knew that there was nothing she might say to me that I hadn't already imagined her saying to me a hundred times over through the previous sleepless night.

'How's Irina?' I asked her.

'Like you care? How's her mother?' she said.

Like you care? The words hung unspoken between us and she hung up.

I rose in the lift to the seventh floor and went to Alison Brooks's screened bed.

Louise sat holding her mother's hand.

A sheet had been drawn up to cover Alison Brooks's face.

The drips and tubes and masks had been removed from beside the bed and stood on their stands like spectators a short distance away, silent and inert.

Louise looked up at my arrival.

I drew the screen behind me.

'I thought you were the doctor,' she said.

'When?' I asked her.

'Two hours ago. They're sorting everything out.'

'Were you with her?'

She nodded. 'She waited for me.'

'Did she ever regain consciousness?'

'It was never likely to happen. Her breathing

deteriorated, that's all. She trembled a little, and then she just died. I told them I'd stay here with her until they could get everything arranged. The morgue will only just have opened. There are procedures.'

'I imagine you know all about them,' I said.

She smiled. 'I suppose I do.'

'I'm sorry.'

'For this?'

'For everything. No one should have had to go through what you and she have been through these past fifteen months.'

'Perhaps,' she said. She rose and stretched her arms, arching her back one way and then the other.

'Have you slept at all?' I asked her.

She shook her head. She came closer to me, opened her arms to me, and I held her, pressing my palms into her back. She pressed her face into the hollow of my shoulder.

'Being here with her meant a lot to me,' she said.

'And to her,' I said.

She half-turned to look down at the bed. 'I hope so,' she said. She gripped my arms and stood back from me. 'I need five minutes to freshen up,' she said. 'Will you stay with her and tell anyone who might come to see to her to wait until I get back?'

'Of course,' I told her.

'The hospital chaplain was here earlier,' she said. 'He might return. We prayed for her. I said a quick one for myself while his hand was still on mine.'

'It can't hurt,' I said.

'That's what I thought.' She picked up her handbag from the bedside cabinet and went to the bottom of the bed. 'They wanted me to leave while they

501

disconnected her from everything,' she said, looking back at her mother. 'I insisted on staying. I asked them if I had a choice, and they said I did. I could hear you telling me the same thing.' She ran a hand over her face. 'Five minutes.'

She left me, drawing aside and then closing the screen behind her. I heard her explaining to a nurse who I was. The woman looked in at me and told me the doctor was on his way. Then she, too, withdrew and closed the screen.

I sat alone with Alison Brooks's body.

Later, when I left the hospital, I would call John Maxwell and tell him she was dead, and that he and I alone were now the only possessors of the secret he had shared with her for forty years.

The sheet lay over her hand and I laid my own beside it.

'I'll call him,' I said to her. 'He'd want to know.' I felt less uncomfortable being there, whispering to her like this.

I moved closer to the bed. My foot caught something beneath it and I saw a rolled umbrella there. I pushed it to one side and saw the damp mark this left. Louise's cigarettes and lighter lay on the cabinet where her bag had been. A small bunch of freesias stood in a glass.

I waited, calculating how best to approach Andrew Brownlow with Louise, uncertain whether or not I would be allowed to stay with her as she told him everything that had happened. I would insist on her calling her solicitor and talking to him before anything was said to Brownlow.

Several more minutes passed.

I rose from beside Alison Brooks and went to the

end of the bed. The women in the beds opposite looked back at me, all of them already aware of what had happened in the night, and we exchanged nods and knowing glances.

I went to the nurses' station at the ward entrance. The nurse I had seen earlier sat alone there. I asked her where Louise had gone. She told me that the toilets were being cleaned and that Louise had probably been delayed by the cleaners.

'She said you'd be coming,' she said.

I sat by the door. People came and went from the lifts and along the corridor.

A further five minutes passed.

I finally asked the nurse if she could go and find Louise for me.

'She's been awake all night,' she said. 'Ever since she got back.'

I continued looking along the corridor as she spoke. 'Got back?' I said.

Her phone rang before she could answer me. She looked puzzled for a moment and then held the receiver to me. 'It's a detective. Brownlow. He wants to talk to you. Please be as brief as you can.'

I took the phone from her and she left the office and went out into the ward. I continued searching along the corridor as I held the phone to my ear.

'Rivers,' I said.

'I know who you are,' Brownlow said.

'Alison Brooks died,' I told him.

'And there was me thinking all this had finally come to an end somewhere else completely,' he said.

I asked him what he meant.

He let out a long breath. And then he told me he was

at Simon Fowler's apartment in Robinson Court, where, twenty minutes earlier, Fowler's cleaner had found his body, his skull crushed and both his arms broken.

'Dead?' I said absently.

'That would be my guess, he said. 'Judging by the one eye looking up at me. First Nicholson and now Fowler. We're still trying to work out where Marco might be. Any ideas?'

But by then I'd stopped listening to him.

I ran out into the corridor.

The women's toilets were opposite the lift doors. I called for Louise.

An orderly stood at one of the sinks scooping water onto her face.

'There's only me,' she said.

48

I ran the full length of the corridor. At the far end, a porter said he'd passed Louise on the stairs five minutes earlier and pointed to the door behind him.

I ran to them and started down them three at a time, searching over the rail for any sign of her beneath me. Almost fifteen minutes had passed since she'd left her mother's bed. She could easily have been at the ground floor and clear of the hospital by then.

I paused to call Brownlow, but there was no signal in the stairwell.

Above me, a door opened and the same porter leaned over the rails and called down to me.

'Not down,' he shouted. '*Up*. I was coming down; she was going *up*.'

I told him to wait where he was and ran back up to him.

'What floor?' I asked him, breathless, my head down, my hands on my knees.

'Between eleven and twelve,' he said.

There were fourteen floors.

'What's at the very top?' I asked him.

He shrugged. 'The roof?'

'With access to it?'

'Never been all the way up, but I suppose so. There's nothing much up there except some radio stuff and the heating and air-conditioning vents.'

From where Louise had called me twelve days earlier.

I gave him my phone, told him to go where the phone was safe to use and to keep pressing the redial button until Brownlow answered.

'What shall I say?' he asked me.

'Tell him what's just happened. He'll understand.'

I left him and continued running up the stairs.

Nearing the top, approaching the open doorway there, I was surprised to see Louise standing immediately outside, her face raised to the morning sky. I stopped running, going more quietly up the final flights of stairs in the hope that she wouldn't hear me and slam and bolt the door on me. But my breathing was still laboured and loud and she turned and looked down at me as I reached the last flight. She made no effort to close the door or to bar my progress.

I stood in the doorway and held my palms against its sides.

She moved away ahead of me.

'I almost wasn't there,' she said, her face still raised, her eyes closed.

'When your mother died?'

'Imagine the irony and injustice of that – me off at Fowler's and her dying without me.'

506

'Perhaps she sensed your absence and held on,' I said.

She shook her head. 'She's been aware of nothing since you spoke to her.' She opened her eyes, lowered her gaze and looked directly at me. 'Come out and close the door,' she said.

I wanted the door to remain open.

'Brownlow knows what's happening,' I said.

'Of course he does.' She looked at her watch. 'Fowler's cleaner arrives every day at seven sharp, thirty minutes after he's usually left. She spends two hours – though Christ knows what she finds to do in that immaculate little palace – and then departs just as promptly and predictably at nine. Fowler leaves her money in an envelope in a drawer. Every day a new envelope. And guess what – she's an Iraqi, working illegally, working cheap. The caretaker lets her in and then he lets her out.' She paused and looked behind me. 'I asked you to close the door.'

'He'll be on his way here,' I said.

'Of course he will. Close the door. I could easily have shut it on you myself. I could hear you coming from three floors down.'

I turned and pulled the two doors shut. They were metal security doors with heavy, welded handles.

'You can't lock them from outside,' I said.

She indicated the crowbar on the ground beside me. 'Use that. Careful, though – you might not want to add your own prints to mine, and to the bits and pieces of Nicholson and Fowler already on it.' She took out a handkerchief and threw it to me. I left it where it lay and picked up the crowbar, wedging its curve into the handles and securing the doors.

She walked away ahead of me, to the rim of the roof in front of the hospital. A ladder stood propped against the concrete parapet there. The air-conditioning ducts rose to one side of us. Steam hissed and clouded from a succession of smaller pipes.

'What else did Brownlow tell you?' she said, her back to me. She stopped a few feet from the edge.

'Not much. Just that Fowler was dead. I'd already told him everything I thought I'd worked out a few days ago,' I said.

'And now everybody will have to think again?'

'We should wait for him to get here,' I said.

'That isn't going to happen, Leo.' She smiled at me. 'Desperate women like me don't come up onto high roofs like this to pep up their tans before being carted off to prison for the rest of their lives.'

'The court will—'

'The court will what? You think I'm going to throw myself on the mercy of the court – is that still the expression? – after Nicholson and Fowler, after the man in the salvage yard, after everything else I've done?' She fell silent for a moment. When she next spoke, her voice was low and calm. 'Imagine – all that just to avenge the death of a woman I probably hated more than anyone in the world.'

'You did it as much for your mother as to avenge Helen's death,' I said.

Her face fell. 'Is that supposed to be funny? I did it all for my mother and then ten minutes after I've finished, she herself is dead? What would you call that – natural justice? God's own revenge?'

'You both knew the cancer was killing her.'

'Oh, well, that's all right, then.'

'Brownlow knows all about Nicholson and his wife,' I said.

'So what? The only proof he has of *anything* is the proof *I've* left him. When you finally get to talk to him, ask him about the hairs in Fowler's fingers, about the saliva on his face.'

'Your mother's.' I remembered Alison Brooks spitting into the bowl to clear her throat, the hair Louise had carefully saved from the previous treatments.

'We had a plan, once,' she said. 'A proper plan. We were going to wait until we knew for certain that Fowler had killed Helen – that was where you or someone like you came in – and then we were going to find a way to kill him which looked to all intents and purposes like she alone had done it.'

'Because by then the cancer had returned and she'd already refused treatment?'

'Because by then the cancer had returned, and now her precious daughter was dead she had nothing left to live for and so she refused their treatment.'

'It wouldn't have been how she saw it,' I said.

'No, but it was how *I* saw it.'

She walked closer to the parapet and the ladder and I followed her. I stopped at an aluminium cowling and sat on it. Her paces grew shorter as she reached the edge.

'I won't come any closer,' I told her.

'Thank you.' She climbed the ladder on to the parapet and then kicked it away behind her. She looked in a broad arc over the city beneath us. She pointed. 'That's where I was born.'

'Coltman Street,' I said.

'They used to say it was the longest street in Hull. Until they knocked most of it down.'

'You're wrong about your mother's reasons for not accepting their treatment,' I said.

She refused to answer me, lost briefly in her memories of the past.

'Caretakers,' she said. 'I suppose in Fowler's brave new world they'll all be called concierges.'

'Probably,' I said. 'And there'll be a lot more gyms around to make people like me feel even worse about themselves.' It made no sense to point out to her that Fowler's brave new world had just ended with the first or the second or the third of her blows with the crowbar. Just as it had made no sense the previous evening to tell her of Nicholson's own lost child, or of the unrevealed loss of the man in the salvage yard who told me he knew what Alison Brooks was going through because he himself had endured something similar. Wherever you looked, it was a world of echoes which never faded, and which seemed at times to grow even louder the further they receded.

She carefully lowered herself until she was sitting on the parapet, facing me, her back to the city below. It was possible to see for almost fifty miles in every direction from that height. I could trace the Humber to Spurn, see the opposite coastline, the North and South Wolds already rising through the haze.

'Back at home,' she said, 'there are envelopes – just like Fowler's little envelope – letters to various people, arrangements, that kind of thing. Will you see they get delivered for me?' She reached into her pocket and threw me a bunch of keys, which landed at my feet.

Then she took something else out, a photograph, and looked at it. She turned it to face me, but it was difficult to make out what the black and white picture showed.

'It's Helen's scan photo,' she said. 'Her baby. She got one, I got one.'

The final, missing photograph from the centre of Helen Brooks's triptych.

'That was why you searched through all those hundreds of photographs,' I said. 'Looking for hers.'

'And the yacht,' she said. She turned the photograph back to her and stared at it intently.

'Do you think that Fowler had already made sure it wasn't there to be found, or that the man at the yard had already found it and sold it to him?'

'Either that or he was still negotiating, or pretending to negotiate, because no one had ever found the picture in the first place; or because all he was ever selling to Fowler was his silence. You might even say it served my purpose as much as it served Fowler's not to have Helen's body turn up.'

'Because then your mother would have known and her loss and grief would have been doubled?'

'You live in a world of neat and reassuring answers and judgements,' she said. 'I wish I could make everything fit from where I'm standing.' She stopped speaking as a siren sounded beneath us. She half-turned and looked down from the parapet. 'Police,' she said. 'That'll be your friend Brownlow.'

'He's not my friend. If he'd done his job properly in the first place, none of this would have happened.'

'You're wrong. Whatever neat and reassuring conclusion of their own they came to in that court fifteen months ago, all this would still have run its course one way or another.'

A further two police cars followed the first into the hospital entrance. She looked back down, watching them.

'No one even knows we're up here,' she said.

She was wrong, but I said nothing.

'I think Fowler knew all along that Helen was pregnant,' I said. 'I think that was why, knowing her body was never going to turn up, he knew it would all end with the death of your mother. What did he try and offer you – his silence about the pregnancy so that your mother could die without ever knowing? In return for what – a promise from you to let everything drop when she finally died?'

She shook her head. 'There was never any offer. He never cared enough about anyone or anything except himself and his own ambitions to trust anyone else.'

'I still think he knew,' I said.

She rose from where she sat, the photo still in her hand.

'*Stop saying that*,' she shouted. '*Of course he knew. I told him*.' She stopped abruptly, as though surprised by what she'd just revealed. She kissed the photograph and slid it carefully back into her pocket.

'*You* told him?'

She looked around her before answering me. She slid one of her feet to the edge of the parapet and then drew it back again.

'When we discovered Helen was pregnant, I tried to persuade her to have nothing more to do with him. You can imagine her response to that. So then I tried to persuade her to stop using all that shit he was endlessly giving to her to keep her exactly where he wanted her. I tried to tell her what it would do to the foetus, the baby, her baby, our baby. She laughed in my face. She called me hypocritical and sanctimonious. She knew about my own termination. She laughed at me and said that perhaps it was her turn to play at being the "good daughter" for a change. She started talking about what a good mother she'd make, what it would mean to my mother to have her first grandchild. Taunting me, rubbing my face in it.'

'And all the time you knew it would be Fowler's child.'

She shook her head. 'I wasn't convinced then that she'd go ahead with it. Like I told you – she talked about her pregnancy like it was a sword she could hold over Fowler: if he wanted it, she'd threaten to get rid of it; if he wanted rid of it, she'd go ahead and have it. She started talking about the child as though it was her key to that same wonderful future in which the two of them would live together for ever, and where she'd get everything she ever wanted. I knew how misguided she was, how deluded. I don't think she ever saw anything clearly the last year of her life – it's what made all that official concern and regret so fucking unbearable.'

'What happened?'

'I made her promise not to say anything to my mother until everything was sorted out one way or another. I told her that if she had a termination, then the best thing would be to say nothing at all.'

'And that if she went ahead with the pregnancy, you'd do all you could for her, and then continue trying to get her away from Fowler?'

'I was never certain how I'd achieve that, but, yes, something like that. I thought perhaps I could make him turn on her, kick her out, show himself to her for what he really was.'

'And if he did kick her out, then she might come home to you and your mother? To where the three of you would bring up the baby together?'

'Like I said, it was never a perfect plan.'

'No – but it might be a reason for your mother to want to go on fighting her illness if it returned.'

'It all made a kind of sense to me at the time.'

'What happened?'

'Simple. I called Fowler and told him she was pregnant. I told him the child was his and so it was in his own best interest to stop stuffing her full of whatever he'd been giving her.'

'For the baby's sake, if not for hers?'

'He never cared about her. I did it because I thought it might shock or scare at least one of them into doing the right thing. The way things were, she was either going to get rid of it or harm the foetus, and neither of them were going to give a toss about that, one way or the other.'

'And now you think he killed her *because* he knew?'

'Because I'd told him, yes. He was going to use her anyway, and me telling him was the clincher which convinced him to go ahead and do it. Two birds, one stone – the trafficker who tied him to the past he was doing his best to erase or reinvent, and the stupid girl who was about to tie him to a future which featured in none of his own wonderful plans. Great timing, eh?'

I was about to say something when we were both

514

distracted by someone hammering on the doors behind us. Brownlow called out to us.

Neither Louise nor I answered him.

'You'd better talk to him,' she said eventually. She motioned for me to go back to the doors.

'Why?' I said. 'It's not going to change anything, is it?'

'This, you mean? No, it isn't going to change anything.' She again slid her feet closer to the edge, this time staying there. She leaned forward slightly so that she could look directly down.

I remained where I sat, knowing that any attempt to try and reach her or restrain her would be futile.

'I think Fowler would have killed her whether he'd known about the pregnancy or not,' I said.

'You don't have to keep on trying,' she said. 'Not now. I knew what I was doing. I'm sorry you feel used by me, by us, but I'm not sorry about any of the rest of it.' She paused, thinking. 'I wish I could have stayed by her bed, with her, a little longer, especially now, but that's all. It might sound ridiculous to you, but I honestly think she was the only person who I ever truly loved, and who ever truly loved me in return. Listen to me. I'm thirty-nine, for Christ's sake.'

'It doesn't sound ridiculous at all,' I told her.

'No?' She looked at me hard.

'No,' I said.

'Helen once told me that part of the resentment she bore against me was because she believed that neither my mother nor I had ever properly loved her – especially me – and that my mother had loved only me.'

'Exactly what you felt about your mother and Helen after your mother remarried and Helen was born.'

'I know.'

'It was your name she wrote around the edge of the chart,' I said.

She laughed. 'No, it wasn't. She told me that if the baby was a girl, then she'd call it Lulu. I could never decide whether it was her first attempt at some kind of reconciliation, or if it was just another of her sick jokes, something to go on mocking me for another thirty years into the future.'

'I'd guess at the first,' I said.

'Thanks,' she said.

We were interrupted again by Brownlow banging on the doors and by his shouting. After a moment of silence, a spray of sparks appeared between the handles as someone began using an oxyacetylene cutter. We both watched this for a moment, both of us reminded of the salvage yard and the man who had died there. Little of the heat remained concentrated on the crowbar holding the doors shut, and the flame rose and fell in a fountain of sparks with each small movement of the torch.

We both continued watching this, mesmerized by the cascade of dying lights and by the way they bounced and scattered on the roof.

Last night's rain had fallen for less than an hour, and there were shallow puddles where it had not yet evaporated in the rising heat. The sky was again clear and cloudless, and in the short time we had been up there the haze had lifted completely from the Humber. Vessels waiting to enter the docks manoeuvred into position in the Hull Roads and in the deeper channels on the far side. The traffic on the Humber Bridge glinted and flashed as it crossed the narrow span.

I finally rose from where I sat.

She looked down at me. 'I'm glad it's just you,' she said.

'Come back down,' I said. 'Please.'

She shook her head. She shuffled forward until her toes were an inch beyond the edge. She closed her eyes.

'I know what you think,' she said, surprising me. 'About my mother and John Maxwell. About me.'

'What did she tell you?'

'Nothing. Neither of us ever mentioned it. We both lived with our imperfect understanding for all those years.'

Just as Alison Brooks and John Maxwell had lived with theirs.

'She loved him and he loved her,' I said.

'I know.'

She raised her arms slightly — either to steady herself against whatever up-draught rose against the building, or simply because it was what people about to throw themselves off high places to their deaths below did.

Behind us, some part of the door was finally severed, and fell to the ground.

We both turned to look at this.

When I turned back to her she was again facing me.

At the doors, someone cheered. A gap appeared and was pushed wider.

I wanted to call to Brownlow and tell him to stay where he was, but I remained silent, my eyes fixed on hers.

'It looks as though they're through,' she said.

I said nothing.

She nodded once, looked quickly around her, took a single deep breath and said, 'Goodbye.'

And because I still couldn't answer her, I simply raised my hand to her.

She saw this and raised her own in reply.

And then she stepped forward and was gone.

There might have been a small involuntary cry as she fell, a final reaching out or pointing of her hands as though she were a diver on a board, but I could swear to neither of those things — just that one instant she was there, her hand raised briefly in farewell to me, and the next she was gone and there was only silence.

I waited where I stood, and seconds later, fourteen floors beneath me, someone screamed, and a few seconds after that the men at the door behind me stopped cutting and shouting and they too fell silent.

49

I called John Maxwell an hour later and told him what had happened. The first thing he said to me was that Louise Brooks was not his daughter. Despite what her mother might have told me, or what I might want to believe, she was not his.

After that, he wanted me to leave him alone so that he might go somewhere else in his empty house and grieve for Alison Brooks properly. I promised to let him know when the funeral was arranged. He thanked me and hung up.

I wondered who there was left in the world who might now console him, or if he would even thank anyone for trying. His affair with Alison Brooks had been his one shameful secret, and the guilt he felt at this had not diminished in the slightest by the loss of his own wife, whom he had loved for forty years until her own death in the same hospital.

* * *

Further enquiries were made in both Hull and Leeds concerning the disappearance of Jane Nicholson.

I called her sister in Leeds, but the woman had heard nothing. She knew of Nicholson's death and the destruction of his home, and there was something close to both relief and satisfaction in her voice as she spoke to me. She asked me to tell her honestly if I thought her sister was still alive, and I told her I believed Jane Nicholson had been killed on the day Nicholson had arrived in Leeds pretending he wanted to take her home with him. Despite what she'd said, she was not prepared for what I told her, and she began to cry uncontrollably. She fumbled with the phone she held and then the line went dead.

I gave Brownlow my statement, starting with Alison Brooks's first appearance at Humber Street and ending with Louise stepping silently off the hospital roof. He had tried to detain me at the hospital, but I had easily avoided him. He was suddenly out of his depth and struggling to stay afloat. I told him I hoped the oxyacetylene torch he'd used hadn't burned all the incriminating evidence from the crowbar.

Afterwards, I went to Alison Brooks's home and let myself in. I found the envelopes Louise had told me about and I posted them. One of them was addressed to John Maxwell, written by Alison Brooks. I'd hoped Louise might have left something for me, but there was nothing.

The bodies of Helen Brooks and the Albanian trafficker were never found. No one ever expected they would be. Fowler had seen to that all those months earlier.

In one of Louise's letters – the one addressed to a local funeral director – she asked for a Service of Remembrance to be held for her dead sister at Victoria Pier, close to Humber Street and the marina. The funeral director called to tell me of this and I told him I'd attend.

Fowler's death did little to delay the rebuilding and renovations he had planned. Webster offered to buy what remained of his empire and then guaranteed to the city council that everything they had planned together, he would now see to completion.

It was suggested at one of the council's hastily arranged meetings to confirm these arrangements that one of the new courts or apartment blocks might be named in memory of Fowler. The motion was voted through unanimously.

Three days after the death of Louise Brooks, I went with Sunny, Yvonne and Irina Kapec to the airport to see off Irina and her daughter on the first part of their journey home.

I had seen Yvonne on each of the previous three days.

She had arrived at my home with a bottle of brandy less than two hours after Louise stepped off the hospital roof. We divided up and cancelled out our regrets and our apologies, and then we drank them into the past. When she told me about Irina's imminent departure, she too cried uncontrollably. The next morning she asked me if she'd cried, and I told her she hadn't. Good, she said, because she wasn't one of those women who cried over things like this.

At the airport, the two women held each other and Yvonne cried again. Irina Kapec's eight-year-old daughter stood with her arms around them both. From Humberside Airport they would fly to Amsterdam, and from there to Zagreb.

And at some point after that, Irina would be shown the bagged remains of her murdered husband and she would then be able to bury him, and for the first time in many years she would be able to think about her own life ahead.

I stood with Sunny and watched them. Irina shook my hand and kissed both my cheeks. Her daughter did the same. And as the girl stepped away from me, I hoped that they might both go back to being the people they themselves had once hoped to be.

Yvonne cried as the plane took off, and then again as she drove with Sunny and me back across the river and into the city.

Fowler and Nicholson lay in the Spring Street morgue, the inquiry into their deaths still in progress.

Another of Louise Brooks's letters had been addressed to the Hull police. It was a thick envelope, containing a detailed account of everything she'd done, and why. At the end of it she asked that her own body be released and buried alongside that of her mother. The same funeral director had already been sent instructions.

Alison and Louise Brooks were buried together at the end of August in the Western Cemetery. Their graves lay side by side, their headstones simple and identical. I laid flowers on each grave.

As promised, I told John Maxwell about the ceremony, but he didn't attend.

Brownlow was there, still angry that Louise had evaded him. He asked me where I thought Marco might now have gone to ground, and I told him that I thought Marco was already dead, that he'd been killed and disposed of shortly after Nicholson had been killed. Marco believed Fowler had killed Nicholson, and Fowler thought Marco had done it, and couldn't afford to have him reappear in the future pointing his finger. Brownlow told me I was wrong. I told him to believe what he wanted.

Four days after the joint burial, Laura Lei called and told me she'd destroyed the model of Helen Brooks. She was leaving Hull and going to live in London. She'd been offered a job at an advertising agency, and she sounded excited and happy.

I told her about the memorial service being held for Helen a week later.

'I'll be gone by then,' she said.

She told me that when she'd been a baby, her family's name for her had been 'Li-Li', and that Helen Brooks had known this and had sometimes called her by the name when they were drunk or stoned together. I asked her if she thought this was why Helen had decided to call her own child Lulu.

'It's what she once told me,' she said, hesitating.

'But?' I said.

'But she lied a lot,' she said.

We both laughed.

She told me the ashes of the model, including the pregnancy-testing kits, lay in a mound in the small rear garden at Park Grove. They'd had a party around the fire in celebration of Helen, she said.

I told her it sounded more appropriate than the memorial service her sister had planned.

'It was,' she said, and hung up.

THE END

SWAN SONG
By Robert Edric

Hull, autumn 2005 and private investigator Leo Rivers
finds himself at the overheated heart of an inquiry into the
savage killing of several young women. Approached by
the mother of the chief suspect, he soon discovers not only
that this suspect is not involved in the killings, but that
several hitherto unconsidered and scarcely credible
connections link the murders to a single perpetrator.

In pursuing his case, Rivers has to contend with an
ambitious, career-minded Chief of Police, who will stop at
nothing to make a name for himself, sacrificing not only
Rivers but also his own colleagues along the way.

Set against a backdrop of the Humber and the long and
violent destruction of Hull's once-cherished fishing
industry, Robert Edric reveals a world of exploitation and
ambition; a world of old men who burnish their festering
grievances and vanities; and a world of long-suppressed
but finally uncontainable brutality, in this final volume of
a trilogy of outstanding and acclaimed contemporary *noir*.

NOW AVAILABLE FROM DOUBLEDAY

0 385 60578 1

Doubleday

CRADLE SONG
Robert Edric

'A REWARDING EXPERIENCE . . . THIS IS MURDER AT ITS
MOST FOUL, CRIME AT THE DEEP END'
Spectator

An imprisoned child murderer unexpectedly appeals his
conviction. In return for a reduced sentence, he offers to
implicate those involved in the crimes who were never caught;
providing evidence of Police corruption and, most importantly
revealing where the corpses of several long-sought, but never
found teenage girls are buried.

Distressed at what may come to light, yet desperate to locate the
body of his own missing daughter, the father of one of these girls
approaches Private Investigator Leo Rivers with a plea for help.

Rivers' enquiries stir cold and bitter memories. Long-dead
enmities flare suddenly into violence and a succession of new
killings. Everyone involved, then and now, and on both sides of
the law, is unprepared for the suddenness and ferocity with which
these old embers are fanned back into life. As the investigation
progresses, it gathers momentum, and now must speed inexorably
to the even greater violence and sadness of its conclusion.

'*CRADLE SONG* IS A SUPERBLY PACED BOOK . . . THIS IS
CLASSIC CRIME NOIR . . . EDRIC CAN ALSO PRODUCE
BEAUTIFUL PROSE AND ARRESTING IMAGES AS WELL AS
INCISIVE SOCIAL SATIRE . . . MAGNIFICENTLY ACHIEVED'
Giles Foden

'HIS NOVEL IS SOMETHING SUBSTANTIAL AND DISTINCTIVE
. . . EDRIC HAS A CLEAR, ALMOST RAIN-WASHED STYLE,
EMINENTLY SUITABLE FOR HIS HULL SETTING . . . CRADLE
SONG IS A STRONG AND SERIOUS NOVEL, SOBERLY
ENTERTAINING AND WELL WORTH YOUR WHILE'
Literary Review

'HIGHLY ACCOMPLISHED... FANS CAN LOOK FORWARD TO
HIS USUAL SHARPLY REALISED CHARACTERS OPERATING
IN A TENSE, PRESSURED ENVIRONMENT' *Independent*

0 552 77142 2

BLACK SWAN

PEACETIME
Robert Edric

'HAS A SERIOUSNESS AND A PSYCHOLOGICAL EDGE THAT NINE OUT OF TEN NOVELISTS WOULD GIVE THEIR EYE TEETH TO POSSESS'   D. J. Taylor, *Sunday Times*

Late summer 1946: the Wash on the Fenland coast. Into a suspicious and isolated community comes James Mercer, employed in the demolition of gun platforms. He befriends the wife and daughter of Lynch, a soldier soon to be released from military gaol. He also finds himself drawn to Mathias, a German prisoner with no desire to return home, and Jacob, a Jewish concentration camp survivor.

Lynch's return threatens violence; and in a place where nothing has changed for decades, where peacetime feels no different to wartime, Mercer finds himself powerless to prevent events quickening to their violent and unexpected conclusion.

'A MARVEL OF PSYCHOLOGICAL INSIGHT AND SUBTLY OBSERVED RELATIONS. ITS SPARE, UNADORNED PROSE HAS POETIC RESONANCE'   Ian Thomson, *Guardian*

'EDRIC'S LANGUAGE HAS A MYTHIC, ALMOST BIBLICAL QUALITY, WHERE EVERY WORD CARRIES DUE WEIGHT AND YOU HAVE THE EERIE SENSE OF THINGS BEING LEFT OUT . . . WHAT MAKES EDRIC'S WRITING PROFOUND IS HIS REFUSAL TO BE TIDY OR DOGMATIC . . . HE IS A GREAT NOVELIST'   John de Falbe, *Spectator*

'*PEACETIME* GRADUALLY UNRAVELS THE CONTRADICTORY HUMAN IMPULSES THAT BIND LIVES . . . A MORAL DISSECTION OF LOYALTY, FORGIVENESS AND HATRED' James Urquhart, *The Times*

'A NOVEL OF AMBITION AND SKILL, AT ONCE A HISTORICAL MEDITATION, AN EVOCATION OF A DISINTEGRATING SOCIETY AND, PERHAPS MOST STRIKINGLY, A FAMILY MELODRAMA' Francis Gilbert, *New Statesman*

0 552 99971 7

BLACK SWAN

THE BOOK OF THE HEATHEN
Robert Edric

'MORE DISTURBING EVEN THAN CONRAD IN HIS DEPICTION OF THE HEART OF DARKNESS'
Peter Kemp, *Sunday Times*

'RELENTLESS . . . AN IMPRESSIVE AND DISTURBING WORK OF ART'   Robert Nye, *Literary Review*

1897. In an isolated station in the Belgian Congo, an Englishman awaits trial for the murder of a native child, while his friend attempts to discover the circumstances surrounding the charge. The world around them is rapidly changing: the horrors of colonial Africa are becoming known and the flow of its once-fabulous wealth is drying up.

But there is even more than the death of a child at the heart of this conflict. There is a secret so dark, so unimaginable, that one man must be willingly destroyed by his possession of it, and the other must participate in that destruction.

'MANY RESPECTABLE JUDGES WOULD PUT EDRIC IN THE TOP TEN OF BRITISH NOVELISTS CURRENTLY AT WORK . . . AS A WRITER, HE SPECIALISES IN THE DELICATE HINT AND THE GAME NOT GIVEN AWAY'   D. J. Taylor, *Spectator*

'STUNNING...EVOCATIVELY BRINGS TO LIFE THE STIFLING HUMIDITY AND CONSTANT RAINFALL OF THE CONGO'
John Cooper, *The Times*

'A VERY GRIPPING STORY . . . THE READER IS DRAWN IN INEXORABLY TO DISCOVER WHAT HORROR LIES AT THE HEART OF IT . . . AN APOCALYPTIC FABLE FOR TODAY'
John Spurling, *The Times Literary Supplement*

'RENDERED IN PROSE WHOSE STEADINESS AND TRANSPARENCY THROW THE DARK TURBULENCE OF WHAT IS HAPPENING INTO DAMNING RELIEF. IT WILL BE SURPRISING IF THIS YEAR SEES A MORE DISTURBING OR HAUNTING NOVEL'   Peter Kemp, *Sunday Times*

0 552 99925 3

BLACK SWAN